I0745926

Wild Union

by A. M. Ladd

Paperclip Publishing, LLC
Tempe, Arizona

WILD UNION

Published by: Paperclip Publishing LLC

Editor: Noelle S. LeBlanc
Cover Illustration: Shaun Cochran
Cover Design and Interior Typography: Hannah Thigpen

Library of Congress Control Number: 2021945552

ISBN: 978-1-7346207-7-1 (paperback)

ISBN: 978-1-7346207-5-7 (hardcover)

ISBN: 978-1-7346207-6-4 (eBook)

Printed in Rephen Printing, Co. LTD in Guangzhou and the United States of America

First Printing: 2022

Paperclip Publishing LLC
1840 E Baseline Road Suite A-1
Tempe, AZ 85283

www.paperclippublishing.com

In dedication to my sons, Brandon and Jeremy. Thank you for your endless supply of patience listening to all my book ideas and spinning back twists and turns of your own. You never fail to amaze me with your depths of creativity.

You Both Inspire Me.

Contents

Contents (continued)

Prologue

Deep inside the Coconino Forest far from humans, Willow sprinted through the trees. How long did she have before they found her? Hazel eyes scanned her surroundings. There. That's the one. An old Rocky Mountain juniper. A long-time favorite. It took effort, but she stuffed her body into the hollow. Well, for the most part. The fit wasn't quite like she remembered. Her height at five-foot-two wasn't the problem, but rather her curves. She adjusted the needle-like leaves for cover and tried to ignore the yank of her long platinum hair as the locks tangled among the branches. Her heart pounded, anticipation building as she waited. Seconds later, small feet pounded the earth, spraying dirt as they ran past her tree. She held her breath. Three little girls called out her name in their excitement running back and forth. Squeals of laughter echoed across the lake. Willow rustled the branches and gave an animalistic huff.

Mae stopped in her tracks, wide amber eyes darted between smooth brunette braids, "Did you hear that?" Her voice quavered. Of Willow's three younger sisters, Mae was the most cautious. At only three years old, her senses were already hyper-aware of her surroundings. Well, most of the time.

Red slammed into her back and they tumbled to the ground.

Mae shoved her sister and sprang to her feet. "Hey!" She shook her fist.

Red rolled on her side propping a hand under her chin as she stared at her sister. Twigs and leaves protruded from her copper curls at odd angles. She blew a lock revealing twinkling emerald eyes. "It wasn't on purpose. You just stopped."

Mae sighed and held out her hands. She hefted her much larger sister to her feet. Red was unusually large for a four-year-old. She had sprouted this past year and was nearly double Mae's size. The growth spurt had caused her to be a little clumsy at times, but what she lacked in grace, she more than made up with confidence. Rumor had it that her father was a giant, but no one knew for certain.

Willow peered between the branches, leaning forward for a better view. It must have been just enough movement because a petite blonde whirlwind tackled her from the side, popping her body from the hollow and out into the open.

Little Ellie shrieked in her high-pitched two-year-old voice, "O'ma! Found you!"

She clutched Willow, hanging like a monkey from her neck with her golden locks floating around her head like a feathery halo.

Willow hugged her youngest sister. "You're brilliant, little one."

Ellie slapped tiny palms on Willow's cheeks and planted a big wet kiss smack on the lips. Her youngest sister was by far the most adorable toddler Willow had ever seen. She also had the biggest heart, always giving away food to stray animals. Her only vice, if a two-year-old could have one, was her sweet tooth.

Willow set her down gently. She scrubbed her chin, noticing Ellie's red fingers. "How many berries did you steal from the basket?"

Ellie counted on her fingers. "Twelfty-twee."

"That's not a real number, squirt." Willow gave her a stern look. "And how many did you leave for your sisters?"

Ellie gulped. Her huge blue eyes blinked several times. "They so yummy." Her lip quivered. "Forgot share."

"Well… In that case, I'll just have to teach you a lesson by… eating your fingers." Willow shoved her sister's berry-stained fingers in her mouth, softly nibbling. Ellie giggled.

"Give fingers back, O'ma. You silly."

Willow smacked Ellie's behind and told her to go play. The sisters started their own rendition of hide and seek, which morphed into a game of chase and tackle with loads of giggles. Willow took a deep breath. The crisp bite to the air was exhilarating. Between the shafts of light streaming through the forest canopy, she could make out a beautiful clear blue sky. It was a perfect day. Or would have been if their mother was here. She had been gone for days and Willow had no idea when she would return. In the meantime, she was stuck looking after her sisters. She marveled at the toddlers' ceaseless energy as they ran and played. She sighed. Maybe not such a burden after all. When they weren't asking a million questions or getting into mischief, they were pretty darn cute. After the girls had spent a good deal of energy and were winding down, Willow decided it was time for lunch.

"Who wants a picnic?"

Her sisters all jumped up and down screaming 'me.' Willow shook her head at their excitement and settled them into a line from oldest to youngest. She had implemented this rule recently to prevent wandering. They had a better chance of sticking together if they all held hands. Mae, the middle child of the three toddlers, took this task very seriously. As the girls skipped and jumped over logs and around trees, Willow started singing one of her mother's favorite songs. It was an old tune in a language few understood. Willow only knew a few hundred words in Dryish. Her mother had taught what she remembered, but sadly it had been forbidden to speak the language for so long that most of their kind had forgotten it. Thinking of her mother, she wondered what she was doing right now. Nearly a week ago her mother had left on an important mission. Willow tried to get details, but her mother had refused, reciting official laws on forest security. Blah, blah, blah. Typical forest politics. Her mother, Ilana Ashbrook, held a position of great power. She was the Guardian of the Coconino Forest.

For most of Willow's life, Ilana had been a free spirit, the life of every party. But just after Willow's sixteenth birthday, two months ago, her mother's behavior had changed. Drastically. Ilana had sunk into a deep depression and would sob uncontrollably for no reason. Her exuberance for life hadn't just dwindled; it had died, and no one seemed to know why. There were no more weekly parties with the Satyrs and Centaurs. No dancing. No drinking. The only songs her mother sang were somber melodies. Since her mother was Guardian, she was connected to everything within the forest. When she felt sorrow, the forest responded trying to soothe and comfort. Branches from trees would fold over her body while she wept. Leaves would brush away the tears. The wind would take flower petals to dance all around her to lift her spirits. Her mother seemed to walk in a daze. Even her daughters' demands for attention couldn't break the spell. Willow had always looked out for her sisters as a sort of surrogate mother figure being so much older, but over the last two months she had taken over the role full time. The youngest, Ellie, had started calling her O'ma instead of Willow. She made up her mind to confront her mother when she returned. Screw forest security. She was due some answers.

Once the girls got to the clearing, Willow pointed to a low rock table at the center. She gave each sister a task. Red set out dishes, strips of wood for plates and tightly weaved baskets for bowls. Mae selected sticks to use for utensils, and Ellie gathered wildflowers for decoration. Willow went over to a pine at the edge of the clearing where she had stored their feast. The basket had a secret compartment with extra berries. This wasn't the first time Ellie had wiped out their stash of sweets. After their lunch of salad, nuts, and berries, the girls decided to play on their own. Mae collected and sorted leaves into neat piles by color and shape. Ellie played peek-a-boo with a wolf cub that had wandered into the clearing. Red found a radio someone had abandoned by an old campsite. She played with the dials until she found a rock station. Her little red curls bobbed up and down as she danced to the music. They were so vastly different from one another in personality and appearance. Not a single eye or hair color was the same. You would never think they were related let alone all shared the same mother. Willow wondered not for the first time who her sisters' fathers were. She had asked her mother once why she had not settled down with a single mate. Her mother's eyes lit up as she pointed to a midnight sky filled with glittering stars, "How would you pick just one from the vast assortment? And why should you? The sky would be boring with just a single star." She patted her head and twirled away dancing to some song in her head. Willow had stared into the sky for hours trying to determine which star she would choose. At the end of the night, she realized her mother made a valid point; all the stars pretty much looked the same.

Strange vibrations from deep in the ground shook her from her reverie. The trees trembled violently. Leaves fell from branches as if blown by an invisible wind. Clouds covered the clearing casting gloomy shadows across the glade. She reached out to the earth searching for seismic activity. The mystical connection that was second nature was simply gone. It felt like someone had severed a limb from her body. She didn't feel pain, just a numbness that crawled up her spine. In all her sixteen years, she had never felt anything like it. Red screamed. Ellie cried. Mae lay passed out in a pile of leaves. Before Willow could get to the girls, her body was pushed back like she had been punched in the chest. A loud whump sounded, and the earth shuddered. The dirt beneath her feet rolled like a wave in the ocean. Then, complete silence, as if the world held its breath. Seconds ticked by. Finally, noises slowly started coming back.

A daring bird tweeted. A cricket gave a tentative chirp. The clouds gradually cleared. Willow scanned the glade. The wolf cub Ellie had been playing with now licked away her tears. Mae blinked up into the sunlight with confusion. Red leaned down to help her from the leaves. A squirrel scurried from the trees and stopped in front of Willow. It was Sammy, one of the forest's best messengers. He bowed before her and spoke a series of quick squeaks relaying a message from Council demanding her immediate presence. She vaguely heard him say his brethren would watch over her sisters until she returned. The knot in her stomach tightened as she walked to the nearest pine. Her feet felt like lead. Every step seemed to take an eternity. There was but one reason to be summoned like this. Something had happened to her mother. She took a deep breath allowing her body to meld into the tree and thought of her destination. Willow traveled in seconds exhaling and exiting from another pine many miles away. She was close to Sedona, but in a pocket of space only magical creatures could enter.

Willow looked around the clearing and felt small and insignificant surrounded by the towering ponderosa pines. Power pulsed within the Sacred Circle of Trees. The crescent-shaped red rock bench seemed to grow taller as she stared. Council was already seated. Their expressions were all grave. She didn't want to be here. A gray hawk swooped down offering her a white cotton robe. Willow put it on feeling like a sacrifice.

The TreeAnt, Abraham, cleared his throat. All eyes were riveted on him. It was rare for him to speak. His brittle weathered bark crunched and cracked as his body twisted to face her, "Willow Ashbrook, you have been called forth to fulfill your destiny. Present yourself before Council."

Her eyes started to tear up. She knew what would come next. She had felt it in her bones but didn't want to believe. Her mother had died. There were so many questions going through her mind. How had it happened? What mission had she been on? How was she going to manage all her new responsibilities? Willow wasn't ready. Knowing it was forbidden to speak of the dead until the ceremony of passing was complete, she held her tongue and stepped onto the red sandstone dais at the center of the clearing. Ancient symbols had been etched into the stone, and she could feel the magical energy vibrating through her body. She thought her knees would buckle at any moment. Willow bolstered her nerve and forced her chin high, shoulders back, blinking back tears as she met the gaze of every member of Council. There were nine in total. Each represented a faction of the forest creatures. Her mother gave vital information on each member's political agenda. Willow had once asked why Council was necessary if her mother was supposed to rule. Her mother had laughed saying it was a damn good question and one she had no answer for. Council's existence was tradition, and one did not argue with that. Just a few months ago, her mother admitted to being unprepared to be Guardian and didn't want Willow to struggle like she had. They had increased training after that, but there had been no time. She felt stupid for not recognizing the signs. Her mother must have known how dangerous her mission was. The Council members would have known as well. She studied them carefully.

On top of the bench at the far left was Roz the raven. She represented the lower creatures. She was only two feet tall, but with her piercing gaze and ruffled feathers, she appeared much larger. Willow knew her wingspan was close to four feet, but she rarely flew these days, relying on her underlings to do her bidding. Her mother had warned Willow never to use her full name, Rozlustit, or she would attack. Roz's vanity was legendary, so her vote could be influenced by flattery. She was also a bit of a kleptomaniac and notorious for stealing shiny objects. You needed to hide your gold and silver around her. Willow glanced down at her chest. Her mother had given her a special gold necklace before leaving on her mission; luckily, the robe covered it.

Next to her sat the Pixie leader, Torikki or Tori for short. She wore a hot pink frilly dress with matching slippers. Her hair and chair cushion were the same soft pale pink, both the texture and color of cotton candy. She would often change her hair to match the décor. Tori's tribe was a highly creative bunch and had become the official party planners for the forest. Her iridescent wings fluttered for a moment as their gazes met. That was interesting. Did she feel guilty, or did she just not like being sized up? At full height, Pixies were between twenty-four and thirty inches tall. Willow couldn't tell for sure but guessed Tori was on the short side. Her appearance was all child-like innocence with chubby cheeks and big hazel eyes, but Willow knew better. Pixies would often use that charm to trap humans. They were notorious pranksters and being magical didn't protect you from their practical jokes. Pixies were equal opportunity mischief-makers.

Willow frowned at the giant gray rock sitting next to Tori. She tilted her head wondering why it had been placed on the bench. The gray rock blinked. Willow's eyes went wide. It was another Council member. His gray skin and gray camouflage robe had blended perfectly with his rock throne. Goron, the Gnome's leader, was all drab to Tori's bright. He was only a foot taller, but four times as wide. He had pointy ears, black beady eyes, and a long matted gray beard. Willow remembered her mother commenting he had an odd trait for a Council member. Goron didn't like attention. She could relate. Willow wished she too could blend into the background. His tribe hailed from the mountains to the north. Not only did he represent the Gnomes, but all the mountain creatures living in the Coconino Forest. There were small communities of Giants and Demons that didn't have the numbers to warrant their own seat on Council. Her mother labeled Goron a rare politician, one who was both noble and fair.

Next to him standing militant straight at three-and-a-half feet tall was Rabuwa, the Goblin leader. Her dark reddish body was covered in black ink tribal tattoos and black studded leather armor. Her muscular physique, sloped forehead, and protruding lower fangs gave you the impression she was just dumb muscle, but there was a sharp mind behind those piercing red eyes. She was unlike most Goblins who were notorious for their short tempers. Rabuwa would think before acting. It made her not only exceptional but downright dangerous. More than one Goblin assassin had underestimated her at their own peril. She was also General of the Goblin army and even though there hadn't been a war in seven years, her soldiers trained relentlessly. They remained vigilant of a pending attack. Grandma Ashbrook had shared stories of her training with Rabuwa and had been greatly impressed by her fighting skills and strategy. Willow put a fist to her chest in respect. Rabuwa's lip curled in a fierce toothy grin, and she returned the respect with a loud fist pound to the chest. Most of Council jumped. Willow had to stifle a laugh.

Cyrus, the leader of the Centaurs, nodded to Willow. He was one of the few who stood behind the tall bench. The male had so much charisma, it was hard to be in his presence without sighing. He was over nine feet tall and had been appointed Council leader when her mother took office. Most of his wavy auburn hair hung loose, framing his face. Only the top was pulled back into a high ponytail. It made his high cheekbones more prominent and gave his dark brown eyes a slightly slanted look. He looked regal with his Roman nose and square jaw. His massive chiseled chest sprouted from a stout horse's body with a beautiful chestnut coat. His long thick tail swished. The color was a perfect match for the hair on his head. With not a single gray, Willow couldn't begin to guess his age, a secret he kept well-hidden by magic. He had to be quite old by the number of offspring he had sired. Many of his clan had left for other forests to keep the population down. Having too many Centaurs in one location was risky. He was one of the few Council members she had spent time at length with. He would often be found playing games with the young animals in the forest. Cyrus had a large ego, but a good heart and a great sense of humor. He had been a faithful ally to the Ashbrooks for as long as she could remember.

On the other side of him stood Terra, the Elven leader. She was tall for a Fey at six feet but looked like a dwarf next to Cyrus. She too had a regal stance, but for her, it wasn't merely posturing or self-confidence. Her family descended from royalty. Her ancestors immigrated from the Black Forest in Germany centuries ago. She wore her long gray hair loose except for two thin braids that framed her face. Terra was one of the few on Council who could easily pass for human, no magic required. She only needed to hide her pointy ears. Of course, you would never see her do that. She was far too proud of her heritage. Terra had a long lanky body with tan skin and pale hazel eyes. She wore a light green tunic with brown leather pants and a vest. Intricately braided leather bracers covered her forearms. Terra carried her bow and quiver of arrows at all times. Soft leather boots allowed her to sneak up on prey. The Fey were a race of hunters and warriors that were bound to the earth. Out of all the species on Council, the Fey were the closest relation to the Dryads. It was said Dryads were once Fey that had become so attuned to the magic of trees that the two species had merged. Regardless of their shared ancestry, Terra wasn't an ally. But she wasn't an enemy either. The Fey remained mostly neutral, except when it came to their own interests.

Next to her was Donna Bacchus, leader of the Satyrs. Smoky kohl outlined her large sapphire eyes. Soft curls of thick brown hair framed an angelic face. Her ample bosom looked ready to burst from her scarlet bustier. She enjoyed flaunting her curves, teasing males that lusted after her body. Even her hairy goat legs, tail, and horns couldn't detract from her beauty—at least, on the outside. Inside she was a mean, vindictive bitch. She pursed her pouty red lips. Donna looked at Willow like she was something nasty that had gotten stuck in her hoof. Donna and Willow's mother, Ilana, had been rivals since before she was born. Just like Donna, Ilana had plenty of male appreciation, but unlike her, Ilana had never settled down. Years ago, Donna married the Satyr leader Ben Bacchus. He had been on Council since before Willow was born.

During their marriage, she and Ben had eight kids, seven boys and one girl. Donna took over Ben's position on Council after he had died mysteriously about a year ago. It had been well known throughout the forest that Ben had cheated on his mate numerous times with humans. In jealous rages, Donna threatened to kill him on multiple occasions. Ben's three brothers suspected foul play in their brother's death, but nothing could be proven. Willow's mother gathered evidence, but it disappeared before it could be presented to Council. The case had been dropped, but the rumors spread, and Donna's hatred for Ilana had grown.

To Donna's left was Fuath, the Sprite's leader. He was the smallest of the Council members at twelve inches tall. He had a wispy thin body and translucent green wings. He wore armor made from leather and devil's ivy. The Sprites were skilled potion makers. There was a very old law preventing the sale of unauthorized potions, but in the seven years Fuath held office, the law had been loosely observed. He was also Donna's lapdog. Whatever way she voted, he would follow. Willow's mother hadn't been certain how the alliance had come about. He could have been smitten like many of the other males, or they may have come to a financial arrangement. Either way, her mother cautioned her that both Donna and Fuath should be treated as adversaries.

At the far right of the bench was Liska, the Shapeshifters' leader. She was humming a tune and braiding her long auburn hair. She was a Fox Shifter, but not only could she change into an animal, she could alter her human form as well. Liska would often change forms in the middle of a meeting when she was bored. Her mother had referred to her as 'not quite right in the head'. Willow watched as Liska tried to shoo away some imaginary bug flying in front of her nose. Fuath eyed her nervously. He had been swatted in the past. He edged closer to Donna. Liska's claim to fame was her skill at finding plants. Her nickname was The Herbalist. She had a shop in Sedona for the Magicals. Her storefront was a cave. She was by far the most mysterious of all the Council members. Her mother said she was the only one on Council that didn't seem to have an agenda. Although it could have been more due to her lack of focus.

Cyrus began pawing the ground impatiently as the crowd grew around the circle. Willow noticed the woods were now jam-packed with creatures here to bear witness. She had never seen so many magical creatures gathered in one place. He finally gave a nod of satisfaction and clopped over to a petrified tree trunk. It had been removed from Sunset Crater after a lava flow over 800 years ago to be used as a podium. The clip-clop sounds of his hooves striking the stone walkway echoed in the clearing. The crowd quieted. He nodded to Willow somberly, then faced Council. "I nominate Willow Ashbrook to the role of Guardian. It is her right by blood and tradition. The Ashbrook clan have watched over the Coconino Forest for three generations."

Willow knew what to expect. She had been trained for this but still couldn't believe it. She vaguely heard the words as he expounded on the accomplishments of the Ashbrook Dryads and how their spirits would guide her to greatness. Her grandmother and great-grandmother had both lived long lives and had saved the forest many times in epic battles against numerous evil invasions. They had been great warriors and healers. The Ashbrook clan had been huge at one time, but the wars had been brutal. Her grandmother, her aunts, and all her cousins had perished in that final battle. Only her mother and Willow had survived. Both sides had wanted peace, so a truce had been drawn and signed as her mother's first official act as Guardian. During the seven years she held office, the forest had flourished in love and laughter and, well, a lot of parties. Her mother had been adored by her people, but it had nothing to do with battle skills, not that Cyrus could expound on that. He was restricted from speaking of the recently dead as well. Ilana had not been a fighter, but she had been the perfect leader during a time of peace.

Donna Bacchus, leader of the Satyrs, cleared her throat interrupting Cyrus's rant. "I understand your need for tradition, but Willow is so young, only sixteen. Is it right to put that kind of pressure on such slender shoulders?"

The Sprites' leader, Fuath, nodded his head in agreement. "The young ones are impetuous. Willow would make frivolous decisions as teenagers often do."

Willow blinked slowly. She pulled back from the fog realizing she had just been insulted by two members of Council. Her temper started simmering while Council debated her future as if she wasn't standing there listening, waiting for them to decide her family's fate. Willow knew it wasn't her place to speak, only adults on Council could debate unless you were at the podium stating your case, but her eyes bulged at their insensitive comments. She had to literally bite her tongue to keep from screaming. Willow couldn't believe some of the things they were saying. Could Council really stop her from becoming Guardian? She had always accepted the role as her destiny. Being the eldest of Ilana's daughters, it was her title by right. Willow might have doubts about her ability, but she had Ashbrook blood in her veins, and her family had ruled for as long as this forest had been named. They weren't just disrespecting Willow; they were disparaging her entire family.

She was close to interrupting when Donna's ten-year-old daughter, Bella, pulled on her mother's sleeve whining that they should make her older brother Faustino the Guardian.

Donna shushed her daughter but gave her a pat on the head. "My daughter spoke out of turn, but she has a point. Faustino would make a formidable Guardian. He is several years older than Willow and has fought in several battles, earning much respect. He would be a fearsome warrior and would protect the Coconino Forest from evil influences. I nominate my son, Faustino Bacchus."

Willow snorted. Donna gave her an evil glare. She shrugged. Her mother had trained her on Mother Bacchus's tactics. She would try to take advantage of any situation to get more political power. But her strategy was flawed. The eldest Bacchus brother was a complete playboy. He spent more time flirting and drinking than fighting. Yes, he had 'attended' a few battles in other forests because he had grown bored. And yes, he had somehow managed to come out of those battles unscathed, but she would hardly consider him fearsome. He was a fun-loving flirt, usually the life of the party. It reminded her a little of how her mother used to be. But at least her mother had gone out of her way to care for the forest. She spent time healing in between festivities. Would Faustino do the same? Did he even have the ability? Willow seriously doubted it. He always seemed more concerned about his own needs than those of others. Did we really need a battle-hungry egomaniac leading us? Wouldn't it be better to have someone compassionate and kind? Surely Council would see through Donna's ploy.

After all the debating had ceased, the Guardian nominee names were called, and their votes were cast. Faustino received two votes from the Satyrs and Sprites. The other seven Council members voted for Willow. She breathed a sigh of relief. At least one thing in her life was certain.

Before the laurel wreath was presented, Donna protested the election once more.

"I beseech Council. Willow should not be allowed major decisions until she is eighteen. The potential for corruption is far too great for one so young."

Willow let out a huff of frustration. She couldn't believe Donna Bacchus was lecturing her on corruption. The woman had devious down to an art form. She wore a cloak of deception like a second skin. After a few minutes of whispering from Council, they sided with Donna. Willow would be granted limited Guardian duties until her eighteenth birthday. Donna gave her an evil grin. Willow desperately wanted to wipe that look off her face. A quick elbow to the nose ought to do it. She smiled sweetly back at Mother B, a nickname Ilana had given her years ago. The B stood for Bitch not Bacchus.

The wreath ceremony was relatively simple. She walked the short distance from the Council bench along a rocky path to a neighboring meadow with a giant Alligator Juniper at the center. It was a sacred tree, one of three to exist in the forest. One was the heart, one the body, and the Alligator Juniper was the mind. Creatures from the forest lined the path to witness the crowning of a new Guardian. As Willow approached, the tree's limbs twisted to reshape the throne, shortening for Willow's height. Just before the throne, she turned to face those that had gathered. The oldest citizen had been given the honor of bestowing the wreath. A wrinkly old female Elf came forward. She smiled warmly at Willow. The Elf closed her eyes and whispered words in an ancient language Willow didn't recognize. Once the wreath was placed on her head, she comprehended the words of the ancients calling on her ties to the earth, linking her forever to the forest. She felt the connection building until she could clearly see the edge of the forest for the first time. It was like a glowing map had been burned into her brain. The forest was larger than she imagined, over 1.8 million acres. She hadn't traveled to all of it. The overwhelming energy pulsed through her veins. It felt incredible. She now understood why Council had been concerned. It wouldn't take much to become drunk with power. The old Elf gestured for Willow to take a seat. She leaned back into the branches.

They reshaped to adjust to her body as she moved. Willow's gaze scanned the crowd surrounding her, intrigued by their expressions. Most gave smiles of encouragement, but a few seemed downright hostile. She raised her eyebrows as a group of woodland creatures shifted restlessly and parted. Bella emerged from the gap. She must have shoved and kicked her way to the front for a better view. She stuck her tongue out at Willow. Well, well. No surprise there. The daughter was just like her mother. Bella the Bitch. *Tough luck, BB. No Brother as Guardian. So sad. Ashbrook rules! Bacchus drools!*

Chapter 1

Sixteen years later

ICE-COLD FEAR THRUMMED through Willow's veins as she jolted awake. She listened for movement, but only heard rustling as a rodent scavenged for a snack in the dry leaves. She stretched her limbs and the branches above her swayed and shivered when she yawned. She wiggled her toes in the cool dirt. The tree roots massaged her feet in response. It took effort to blink open her eyelids. Dark. Way too dark. She sighed long and loud. Willow startled when the echo bounced off the rock caverns across the lake. It reminded her of the sound Abraham made when frustrated by her lack of patience. Great. She could do an impression of an ancient TreeAnt. What a talent! Suddenly Willow felt way older than her thirty-two years.

Protect. The source of danger flickered like a beacon in her mind. Willow sent her spirit flying through the trees seeking the flare of panic that had triggered her instinct. She floated above for a moment with an aerial view but couldn't locate the threat. She needed a different angle. The creature hiding in the bushes was the point of origin; her reason for being here so early this morning. Despite her frustration from being woken up for the tenth night in a row, her heart filled with compassion as the deer peeked from the sage bush. Willow's spirit floated down until she could see through its eyes. The fear had frozen it in place. The two hunters stalked closer. They both wore similar clothing; jeans and flannels and caps with ear flaps to keep them warm on this chilly autumn morning. They didn't look particularly threatening. Actually, one looked ready to fall over. Her attention concentrated on the more stable of the two. The deer stared unblinking at the rifle in his hands. That weapon had made the loud cracking sound that had caused such immobilizing terror. The hunter adjusted the weapon up to his shoulder, searching for movement. The rifle swooped to point directly at Willow.

She tried to pull back, separating herself from the deer, but it was too late. She was stuck. Just like the deer, she was unable to move or blink. The deer's spirit clung to her like a drowning victim does its rescuer. The fear itself was pulling them both under. Willow threw an imaginary buoy line out to her birth tree and it grounded them both.

It was such a rookie mistake to link oneself so closely to another. She should know better at her age. Willow took a deep breath and focused her energy on a tree close to the hunters. As she exhaled, her body re-formed beneath the bark of that tree. She sensed her location was about twenty miles northeast of her birth tree. Travel in this manner was a natural Dryad ability. She could journey for hundreds of miles in a forest she was tied to. Willow had never ventured further than the boundaries of the Coconino Forest even though she had once dreamed of traveling to exotic locations all over the world. But fate had other plans. At such a young age, her mother died and her role and life had been set. During those first few years, she had rebelled as most teen-agers would, but ultimately her sense of duty had won out. Now she was older, wiser, and more disciplined. She accepted her responsibilities and would bear the burden of her role until the day she died.

Focusing back on the threat, she watched the hunters as they staggered from tree to tree. Their boots crunched heavily through dry leaves. Neither had stealth or seemed very observant for that matter, otherwise, they may have noticed the unusual sway of the branches or the bark eyelids opening to spy on them. The deer was still frightened, but the panic began to subside, easing away with Willow's presence. She knew her body gave off a calming scent of lavender when those around her were nervous. She wondered if the ability was genetic or if it had been given to her when she became Guardian. Willow thought back to her early childhood. She didn't remember it ever happening when she was young, but then her life had been pretty stress-free growing up. Even the loss of her father hadn't been all that devastating when she was fourteen. Of course, he hadn't been around much. Most days with her mother had been a celebration of life with singing, dancing, and revelry. Life had been so sweet without any worries. When her mother had passed, she had been completely overwhelmed. Not only had Willow been tasked with caring for an entire forest at sixteen, but she had become the primary caretaker of her three younger sisters. Willow had embraced the challenges but knew she had made a lot of mistakes. The lower forest creatures would say it was her unshakable courage that held her fast and true those first few years. Abraham would say it was the streak of stubbornness flowing through all the Ashbrooks. Willow would admit, although only to herself, it was the fear of failure that had pushed her the hardest. She still couldn't believe she had been doing this half her life. Even with the prestige of her Guardian position, she was growing more annoyed each year by the monotonous tasks and the politics of Council. There was never a reprieve from the forest creatures' demands. Willow had loved her job at one point, but lately, it was wearing her down.

One of the men leaned against the tree trunk Willow currently occupied. His breathing was labored. The acrid scent of beer made Willow nauseous. He had a loose grip on his rifle. His brows furrowed in concentration trying to keep his balance. *This'll be too easy.* Willow focused her energy on the tree roots beneath his feet. The roots twitched, pitching him face-first into the bark. He slid to the dirt. His buddy gave an abrupt chuckle as he heard his friend groan. *Oh, that's funny, huh? You're next.* No, she wouldn't kill them no matter how badly they needed it. It would draw too much attention. It was a simple equation. Death equaled investigation bringing in more humans, which equaled forest destruction and possible exposure.

By the time the hunters retreated, bloody and bruised, there was a soft pink and orange glow to the sky. Her body emerged from the tree with a yawn. A few leaves fell into her hair and she shook them loose. The deer butted its head against Willow's hand and gave a long, drawn-out squeak. It was Clover, one of her favorites. She was expressing her gratitude and apologizing for waking her. Willow had known her mother. She had been called when Clover had been born. Her mother hadn't survived the birth, but Willow had found another mother doe to take care of the newborn.

"Getting rid of the hunters was my pleasure," Willow replied.

She watched Clover take off at a run, wondering what mischief the deer had in store for today. The deer was notorious for getting into trouble.

With a smile on her face, she merged back into the tree and traveled home. Sunrise usually marked the start of her day, but Willow had earned some extra sleep. She had to be rested for her afternoon visit to town. It was an important event held once a month. The security of the forest relied on the information collected, or at least that's what she told Council. While town visits could garner helpful insight about things happening in the forest, she mostly just enjoyed getting a break from her duties. As Willow snuggled into her tree and drifted off, she dreamed what the afternoon would hold. The females from town were a source of great entertainment and a steady supply of the juiciest gossip. She could hardly wait.

Chapter 2

B RAY STARED AT the words displayed on his laptop screen. *Connection Lost*. It was the third time in twenty minutes. He glanced around the small room looking for help. There was no admin waving for a technician to resolve the issue. It was nothing like his office in San Francisco. After a thorough appraisal of the peeling paisley wallpaper and worn carpet, Bray concluded the hotel spent little on décor and even less on guest amenities. Their internet service sucked. He shook his head. Maybe this was a sign he should take the break he'd promised himself. Unfortunately, Bray wasn't the type of person to leave someone hanging. He dialed back into the conference call, this time without video.

"Listen, I know you think I should be involved in every decision, but really I trust you can handle this without me."

"I know," Pam sighed, "But we don't want to make any mistakes. You've always been the go-to person for these things.

"Come on guys." Bray groaned. "This isn't rocket science."

"Except for the app we did for NASA," George replied.

"Are they having issues?" Bray asked. That was a huge project worth millions.

"No." George said, "But you see our point. Some of these contracts are your babies. You were the main designer. If questions come up, we need your help."

"I give," Bray said with exasperation. "Assign values to the issues. If they are critical, you can contact me, and I'll see what I can do. But if they aren't, then they need to be assigned to my backups. I need this vacation. I've earned it."

"Sorry, Bray." Pam said, "You know we wouldn't disturb you unless it was important."

He felt guilty. Pam had been his executive assistant for years and was a super sweet gal. But she didn't know how to react. It was his own fault. He had never taken a vacation. In the past, she had reached out to him night or day with any questions because that's how he wanted it. Bray had stayed involved in every aspect of the business, from designing applications to sales calls with clients to executive board meetings. Now everyone was scrambling trying to figure out their role. He wanted to help but needed to draw clear boundaries.

"I understand there will be a learning curve, and we might not be able to respond as quickly as we have in the past. But you guys can do this. I believe in you. If there are bugs in an app or a hack to a program, set the customer's expectations. Let them know there is a new engineer going through the code and it might take additional time for resolution. We've had programmers leave for positions at other companies. We can't always reach the original designers. I'm giving you guys permission to re-write my code if you need to."

There was silence on the call. The seconds ticked by.

"Did I lose you?" Bray asked.

Nick laughed. "I think you stunned everyone in the conference room. You've never wanted anyone to mess with your code. I believe I've even heard the actual phrase, 'touch my code and die.'"

He could just picture the room and their expressions. Bray would have paid to see that. Nick was probably the only one in the room who had the balls to call him out like that. That's why they were such good friends.

"Well, I have to be practical. My new cabin is in a remote part of the forest. I very much doubt it has internet, and that's the point of this vacation to get away from everything. You'll have to muddle through without me. I'm not going to be available twenty-four/seven. You have my official blessing to change programs as you see fit."

Bray thought he heard a gasp. He could tell Nick was chuckling. He knew that hearty laugh. It made him smile. He was glad to amuse. They needed a little shake-up over there, and he definitely needed the time off.

After that, they went through high-priority issues needing his attention. He set up another call with the executive board to go over last-minute instructions in the morning. Bray thought it had all been handled before he left, but apparently, he had to do a little more hand-holding for them to feel comfortable. He was anxious to see his new cabin, but one more day wasn't going to kill him. The anticipation had been building for weeks. In the back of his mind, Bray wondered if he was setting himself up for disappointment. His expectations were sky-high. Was there even a remote chance reality could live up to his vivid imagination? Bray decided to be optimistic. Even if the cabin was a complete bust, at least it was a break from work. Two months of peace and quiet, that's all he wanted.

Chapter 3

AT THE EDGE of the woods, Willow stood in the shadows. Excitement thrummed through her veins. Even after all these years of visiting with humans, she still felt a nervous thrill when she left the safety of the forest. She eyed the concrete road that would lead to her destination. It always felt strange to walk on the surface, like it contained some numbing agent to the earth's energy. Before she was able to take a step, a grey and red squirrel with tasseled ears and a long white tail bounded down from the trees and slid to a stop at her feet.

It was Sammy, one of the Abert's squirrels that worked for the Magical Delivery Service. The company was a worldwide organization dedicated to delivering mail and packages to those within the magical community. Several years ago, Sammy, along with his brother Dave, led a squirrel strike in the Coconino Forest demanding better wages and working conditions. There had been a month where little communication had flowed into or out of the forest before Council was forced to agree to their terms. A special reserve fund was established to import gourmet nuts for payment, and senior-level messenger squirrels like Sammy received special magical backpacks to conceal and carry packages.

"I missed you at home." Sammy squeaked. "You put in a request this morning."

"I did?"

She didn't remember asking for a delivery.

Sammy pulled out two wallets from his backpack and handed them to Willow.

She flipped them open. They held the hunters' IDs and credit cards.

"Clover asked us to send a retrieval team. Since you're the recipient, I figured you instigated the request."

Willow grinned. That devious little deer.

"Do you need payment?"

"No need. This delivery is no charge. Clover told us all about the hunters. I'm sure there will be plenty of others that want a piece of the action."

Willow shook her head. She could just imagine. Most of the creatures of the forest lived in fear of hunting season, but there were others that used the time to their advantage. For them, it was an opportunity to get back at the humans. Hunting accidents ran rampant around this time.

"Is Red involved?" Willow asked.

"Isn't she always?"

She shook her head. If there was trouble, then Red was usually in the thick of it. But in this case, Willow had an idea of her own. Even if the humans stayed clear of the forest, she had another way to punish them. They had it coming. Not only were they hunting outside of deer season, but it had been before dawn and they had been drinking. All violations. With their wallets, she had enough information to hand over to the Wildlife Manager Keith. He was one of the few human males she was willing to socialize with.

"Thanks again, Sammy."

He bowed, and with a twitch of his ears and a swish of his tail, he left. She watched as he scrambled along the forest floor and jumped into a large pine tree.

She stuck the wallets into one of the bundles and adjusted her bodypack. Humans would often frown when she used that word, but the term backpack just didn't fit. A small child in town had once said it looked like Willow was giving a lumpy scarecrow a piggyback ride. It had made Willow laugh so hard because it was such an accurate description of the contraption she had created out of necessity for these trips into town. The bodypack was made of scraps of natural hemp wrapped around misshapen baskets filled with supplies. They were all tied to a rack of branches strapped to her back. It would have been nice to have one of those magical backpacks with unlimited storage capacity like Sammy had. Although since she was visiting humans, it might raise too many questions. Her thin dress of pale green organic cotton hugged her curves as she leaned to one side and plucked off a pair of dangling flip-flops. As she set them down and slid her toes into the ratty old sandals, you would think she had just donned ruby slippers. Well, they did sparkle—a little. A few iridescent beads sewn into the leather straps glittered in the sun. Willow admired the shoes for a moment before she continued walking. She was practically skipping by the time she got to the rec center. The women from town never failed to entertain. She wondered what new and interesting bit of gossip they would share this afternoon.

Willow stopped at the edge of the parking lot behind a tall honeysuckle bush and waited. It wasn't long before a white Ford pickup pulled in. It was Susan. She was typically the first to arrive. Susan had barely stopped the truck before hopping out with several shopping bags. Her curly brown hair bounced as she jogged to unlock the rec center's front door. Willow didn't understand the concept of locking doors, especially in this town. It wasn't like Bellemont, Arizona, was a hotbed for crime. The town's population was in the hundreds. Susan moved here last fall from Chicago after a nasty divorce. She wanted to get as far from her family as possible. Apparently, her family didn't allow that sort of thing. She was seen as a pariah. Willow had no idea what that meant but had nodded politely and given her a hug. It must have been the correct response because after that they became close friends. Susan and Willow were both in their early thirties, but that was nearly all they had in common. For some reason, it hadn't mattered. The only other townsperson Willow halfway trusted was Bobby. Her mother had known her for years and said she was a kindred spirit. Bobby was brash and bold like her sister Red, but with a heart as big as Ellie's and as down to earth as they came.

Willow walked to the door. The loud thump to the doorframe announced her arrival. That made her grin. She often forgot how wide the branches on her bodypack were.

"Why don't you unload on the porch? I'll come help in a minute." Susan yelled as she set out supplies on the crafting tables.

Willow shook her head. "No need. You finish what you're doing."

She slid the pack off her shoulders and started untying the baskets. Leaving the majority on the porch bench, she carried in a few at a time filling the tables as Susan organized. The first she brought were several baskets with autumn leaves in red, gold, and orange. Mae had been in charge of sorting them by color, size, and shape. Mae and Susan shared the same orderly trait that few in Willow's family possessed. The next batch had baskets of dried flowers tied into neat little bundles. Ellie had gathered most of the flowers with help from the forest creatures. Next, she retrieved several heavy baskets filled to the brim with smooth river stones. Red had been unavailable most of the month but had delivered the rocks just yesterday. She had overheard one of the daughters from town wanting to make pet rocks for the Christmas fair. Red had played it off like it was nothing, but Willow had been touched by her sister's gesture. Balancing several baskets of twigs, acorns, and pinecones, she placed those on another table. The basket of herb leaves and berries was set on the snack table. The final basket contained feathers that had been collected mostly by the squirrels. They had really outdone themselves.

"Wow. This is amazing." Susan picked up a colorful feather. "You must have been searching the forest every day this month."

Willow shrugged. She felt a little guilty taking all the credit. The majority of the actual gathering had been done by the lower forest creatures, not that she could share that with Susan. Willow had only given the order and organized the supplies. There were a few perks to being Guardian after all.

"My sisters helped a little. But it's hard to organize that bunch."

Susan laughed, "I don't know how you manage. Those girls are wild to the core."

Willow smiled. *You have no idea.*

It didn't take long for the rest of the ladies to join them. Most of the women dressed for comfort, in jeans and t-shirts, with a few in sweatpants. There was a frenzy of activity as they all arrived. The volume in the group increased until their chatter sounded like cicadas in summer. Bobby was the last to arrive. The laugh lines crinkled on her weathered face when she saw Willow. She pulled her into a bear hug that lifted Willow right off her feet. Bobby was built tall and sturdy, but her age hadn't diminished her strength one bit. She was in her sixties but acted much younger. That's probably why Bobby, Susan, and Willow all got along. Well, that and they were all single. Bobby was a widow, Susan a divorcee and Willow had never even married, or mated as most of the magical world would call it. As a matter of fact, she hadn't dated for over a decade, although not exactly by choice. After putting her cowboy hat on a hook, Bobby took a seat across from Willow and Susan.

When Susan stood, the group quieted.

"This month's meeting of the Frugal Girl's Craft Club will now come to order. Thank you all for coming today and bringing such a wide array of supplies." She winked at Willow. "It's with everyone's combined efforts that make this club so successful. I'd like to welcome a new club member to our group, Gail Hamond." She gestured to a woman in a stylish black suit and high heels. The woman smiled as the group politely clapped. Many of the women from the group stared at the newcomer. Willow felt pity for her. She could sympathize, being an outsider herself. She often felt out of place. Willow heard a few women whispering about Gail's clothing. Fancy clothes, especially at a craft club, were odd, but the woman oozed confidence. Either she didn't notice or just didn't care.

"A few announcements; We only have a few months until the holidays, so we need to finish up any projects before the Christmas fair. I have a sign-up sheet for booths over on the supply table. Also, if anyone wants to volunteer for the church bake sale, there's another sign-up sheet on the snack table. The floor is now open for new business." Susan looked around expectantly. No one responded.

"Wonderful! Then, commence crafting."

Everyone got up at once. There was a little chaos as bodies clamored around the tables, selecting various items before getting back to their seats. Willow grabbed a paper plate, pinecone, and glitter. She loved anything that sparkled. Willow was normally covered in glitter by the time she got back to the forest. It was one of the many things her sisters ribbed her about. But the gossip was worth it. She squirted her pinecone with glue as Bobby started off the conversation.

"So, most everyone here knows that Jim Miller, rest his soul, passed last spring."

Several nods from around the room.

"Well, his family just sold the old Miller cabin. Ya know, the one that's been vacant for twelve years."

Willow was very aware of that cabin. In fact, it was on her land and had been built around a very special tree. She sprinkled glitter on her pinecone as she listened intently.

"Well, I heard from one of my contacts down at the post office that a new P.O. Box was opened. Some hot-shot computer geek from California. A Mr. Brayden Graham."

"Did your contact have a date when he's moving?" Willow asked.

Bobby glanced at her plate and grinned. "Honey, you got enough glitter on that?"

Willow looked down and scowled. The pinecone was half-buried. The lid must have come off mid-shake and she hadn't noticed.

"The computer guy's already here." Bobby handed her a paper towel. "My contact said he checked into the hotel yesterday." She tilted her head at Willow. "Are your sisters camped close to the cabin?" Bobby slapped her hands on the table with excitement. "I've got it! I'll set up a recon. Ya know. Gather intel." She gestured to her cell phone. It was in a holster next to her gun. "I've got another contact in housekeeping at the hotel. Just say the word." She looked expectantly at Willow.

Abby rolled her eyes, "Geez Bobby, we aren't all Green Berets like your late husband. Not everything is some covert op. You need to get a hobby."

"What? Like crafting?" Bobby waved her arms dramatically. "What exactly are we doin' here people? And besides, being prepared and aware is just smart." She turned to Willow, "So about your sisters?"

"Well," She looked around the room. Most everyone was listening. Bobby's conversations tended to do that. Giving away information about her family was a risk, but Bobby was different. She genuinely cared. "We usually migrate over to the Miller's cabin around this time of year. The lake by the house is pretty nice and it has some rock over-hangs that offer shelter from the rain."

The new gal edged closer, "You camp there often?"

"Yeah. I guess you could say that."

A few of the women snickered. Willow threw a handful of glitter at them. As reluctant as she was sharing with the stranger, she had no choice but to provide the basics. With this group of gossips, she would find out anyway.

"My family lives in the Coconino Forest. We have for generations."

"Like survivalists? Do you live in tents?" Gail scrunched up her face. She looked downright horrified by the idea.

"Tents?" She shook her head. "Absolutely not. Nothing factory-made. Nature provides everything we need."

"Wait, does that mean you stay in the woods all winter long?"

"Yeah. All year. We've been doing that since I was born, and my mom and grandma before me." She shrugged. "The forest is our home."

Willow felt antsy. This woman was asking too many questions. She got up and grabbed a plate from the snack table on the other side of the room hoping to end the conversation.

When she sat back down, Gail started in again. "You know, the closest thing to camping I've ever done is staying at a Motel 6." She flashed the room her blindingly white teeth. "I lasted five whole minutes."

No one laughed at the woman's attempt at humor.

Susan patted Willow's shoulder. She must have realized her discomfort. "The Ashbrooks have been here long before most of us. They're naturists."

"Don't get me wrong, there's nothing wrong with that. Lots of my friends are tree huggers too."

Willow tilted her head. She had never been called such a thing. The description was sort of accurate. She did hug trees while she merged with them as part of her way of travel. "Are you also vegan?" She pointed to the plate of herbs in front of Willow.

Susan laughed, "Yeah sure. Let's call it vegan."

That got a few chuckles from the group.

Gail frowned. "Isn't that what a naturist is?"

Willow shook her head. It always came back to this and she never understood. "It means, we usually don't wear clothes. This dress," she pointed at what she wore, "is an exception."

Gail's jaw dropped. "You aren't serious. You run around the forest," she lowered her voice to a whisper, "in the nude?"

Willow nodded.

She gasped, "Wait a minute. Even in winter?"

Willow shrugged.

Her eyes went wide. "Are you nuts?"

Bobby raised her nose at the woman, "People here are built from sterner stuff. We aren't all soft from California living."

Gail leaned back, scrutinizing Bobby carefully. "How do you know where I'm from?"

Bobby gave her an evil smile, "I've got friends everywhere, girl."

Gail tipped an invisible hat. "Very well. Don't divulge your source." She turned back to Willow. "I'm sorry. I didn't mean to be rude. I've just never met a nudist before. You'd think being from California I'd be more liberal, but my family's conservative. I meant no offense."

"No worries."

The conversation shifted to kids, and Willow was grateful she was no longer the center of attention. The mothers either bragged or complained about how their little ones were doing in school. It made her yearn for her own kids. Not that it would happen anytime soon. For that, she needed a male, and Council was picky on who they deemed worthy as a mate for a Guardian.

"My daughter Hope wants to try and make something different to sell at the Christmas fair. Does anyone have a suggestion?" Penny asked.

"I completely forgot." Willow pointed to several baskets on one of the tables. "Red collected all those river rocks over there for Hope's project. She mentioned your daughter wanted to make pet rocks."

"You'll have to thank her. Your sister is such a sweetheart. Red is Hope's favorite teacher."

"Teacher?" Red hadn't mentioned working at the school.

"Well, I know she's just temping while the science teacher is out on medical leave, but the kids all love her. Hope can't stop talking about the field trips, the nature walks, and the scavenger hunts."

Laughter bubbled up before Willow could stop it. Red, a teacher? That was too hilarious for words.

Penny frowned.

"Sorry. My sister didn't mention she was working at the school."

"Really? That's weird. Anyhow, Hope loves school this year. She's never been excited before. Miss Ashbrook is all she can talk about when she gets home, and everything she's learned. And it's not just Hope. I've heard from other mothers as well. Red has made a huge impression on her students."

Willow could just bet. She wondered why her sister would have kept something like this from her. She must have realized Willow would find out. It's not like she would have stood in her way. She was an adult. At twenty, she could do her own thing.

After several hours of gossip and crafting, the group winded down and packed up their projects. Willow helped Susan gather the remaining items and put them into bins to store until next month.

"Do you want a ride to the creek?"

Willow sighed, "Why do you always ask?"

Susan shrugged. "It seems a shame to walk when we have cars."

"Sorry. I just don't feel comfortable in them. Although, I did sit in a parked truck this summer. My sisters dared me. Well, we all dared each other. Red lasted the longest, but the driver came back too soon. She had to slip out the back." Willow grinned. "Or I should say she squeezed out the back window, got stuck, landed into the truck bed, and rolled off the tailgate."

"Oh my." Susan laughed, "I can just picture it. Did the driver catch her?"

"No, but it was close."

Mae had tripped him with vines, and Ellie's friends, a group of rattlesnakes, had distracted him long enough for Red to escape. Not that she could share those details with Susan.

"I wish I had sisters.' Susan sighed, "You have such fun together." She gave Willow a hug. "I guess I'm starting to miss my family, even if they are a pain. My Nana always said, 'family is everything.' Most don't appreciate 'til it's too late."

Willow said her goodbyes and hurried to the edge of the woods going over all the things she had learned. She would have to postpone her meeting with Keith, the wilderness manager. As much as she wanted the hunters to pay, this outsider moving into the cabin posed a larger threat. As Guardian, protection fell to her. She had evaded Bobby's question asking her to snoop. As much as she would have loved to get the intel Bobby offered, there were too many witnesses listening to their conversation. If something unfortunate happened to Mr. Graham, and the authorities came around asking questions, they could suspect her family. She would never allow that to happen. This situation required a delicate touch. But it also required speed, which meant she needed help. She sighed knowing just who to recruit. Unfortunately, delicate wasn't their style.

Chapter 4

WILLOW LET OUT a deep sigh as she stepped into the shadows of trees. Safe. Willow slipped off her dress and sandals wrapping them in a spare piece of hemp. Her toes wiggled in the dirt and she reconnected to the forest. As much as she enjoyed spending time with the women from town, she could never completely relax. There were too many threats, with too few places to hide. She spied the special oak tree with the hidden knothole and carefully stowed her supplies. The hole was deeper than it appeared courtesy of a little magic. She had these hidey-holes all over the forest to stash supplies. It saved time, since her preferred mode of transport didn't allow for anything other than the body to travel unless the items were magical. No weapons. No materials of any kind, and certainly no clothes. Not that it mattered to her. She walked over to the closest pine and rubbed her hands together calling the power within. She laid her palm on the bark of the closest tree and took a deep breath. On her exhale, she melded into the bark. On her next breath, her body reformed about forty miles to the south and emerged from another pine. She strode the hundred yards to her final destination; Grandfather Pine.

This part of the forest was cloaked from humans. She wasn't entirely sure how the magic worked, only that it did, and it had never failed. The border consisted of a circle of sacred trees. Within the circle was where Council would convene every month, or in rare cases they would meet for an emergency. This evening the stone bench was vacant. Behind the bench to one side stood Grandfather Pine. He was the oldest ponderosa pine in the forest and had links with every tree within it. As long as her sisters were in the forest, she could contact them. Willow rubbed her hands together once again summoning the power within and knocked on the tree calling her youngest sister. "Ellie Ashbrook. I call you forth."

She stepped back and a few moments later, a tall slender female of stunning beauty stepped from the tree. Her streaked golden hair had pink wildflowers weaved throughout. "O'ma," the girl smiled. Her blue eyes twinkled in the fading light. "It's so good to see you."

She took two steps and jumped into Willow's arms, wrapping her long legs around her. It might have been awkward, but Ellie had been doing that since she was little. Willow had grown used to bracing for impact when her youngest sister was around. Pouncing is just what the girl did, especially when excited and happy, which was pretty much always.

Willow set her down. Ellie towered over her.

"I think you've grown another inch."

Her cheeks flushed green, a common Dryad trait when embarrassed. "I'm still five-ten and couldn't have grown that much since yesterday." She frowned. "And besides, I'm eighteen now. I've decided. I'm all done growing."

"Just like that?" Willow muffled her chuckle. "We'll see about that." Willow knocked on the tree again. "Mae Ashbrook. I call you forth."

Within seconds a dark brunette with amber eyes emerged from the tree cautiously. Her eyes darted back and forth, peeking between smooth braids until she saw Willow and let out a breath.

"Oh, thank the gods it's just you, sister. I thought something wicked summoned me."

Willow pulled her into a big hug. "Why on earth would you think such a crazy thing? You and your imagination. No one can summon you but one of us."

"So naïve." Mae patted her sister's head, "I used to be like that."

Willow rolled her eyes thinking Mae and the town gossip Bobby could swap conspiracy theories. She turned and knocked on Grandfather Pine a third time. "Red Ashbrook. I call you forth."

Several minutes passed. The sisters stared at one another, then glanced back at the tree. Could she have been outside the forest? Red had always been independent, ever since she was a toddler. She probably spent more time in the human world than Willow did. The seconds ticked by and her nervousness evolved into panic. Had Willow not warned the girls enough about the risks of humans? Had Willow's own fascination with humans passed onto Red? Was her sister in danger? She lifted her hand to knock again, and a tuft of red hair emerged from the tree, followed by a pale face with bright emerald eyes.

"What's up buttercup?"

Willow let out a sigh of relief. "Get your butt over here. It's important."

"Uh, how long's it gonna take?"

"As protector of this forest, I order you to come here now."

"Whatever," Red smirked, "Hang on, sis."

She disappeared into the tree. Willow stood tapping her foot. Several minutes later, Red burst from the tree in an explosion of leaves and dirt that sprayed everything in the vicinity. Red's body was scratched and smeared with mud.

Mae gasped, "Were you in battle?"

"Not unless you call getting Satyr tail a fight."

Ellie brushed dirt from her shoulder. "Faustino again?"

"What again? I haven't had him. He's too fast for me." Red fluffed her copper curls, "And besides, last time I saw him he made fun of my rear." She pointed to her very large rounded backside. "He said it looked like the perfect landing pad for Pixies."

Mae snorted, "Sounds like his version of a compliment."

Red leaned her six-foot frame back against Grandfather Pine and studied Mae, "Does he say stuff like that to you?"

"Don't be absurd." Mae smoothed her already perfectly neat braids and mumbled, "He doesn't notice me."

Red grinned wide. "Ah-ha. Now I get it. Our sweet little Mae's got the hots for Faust."

Mae blushed a deep green.

Red chucked her on the shoulder, "Finally you show some interest. I thought we'd have to recruit an incubus to seduce you. So, tell us, Mae, you gonna give it up?"

Mae looked ready to faint.

Red seemed oblivious to her sister's distress. "I overheard a bunch of Nymphs saying they had witnessed your utter indifference to the opposite sex. Drop-dead gorgeous Satyrs and Centaurs parading in front of you, and you barely blinked. They've given you a nickname. Want to know what it is?"

"No."

"I'll tell you anyway. They nicknamed you Mental Mae."

"I'm not mental just because I have standards," She shoved Red, "How could you let them trash me like that?"

"You don't give me enough credit." Red chewed a nail, "No one says shit about my sisters and gets away with it. Those Nymphs I mentioned met with an accident."

Mae gulped. "You killed them?"

"My. My. You're bloodthirsty today."

"No, I'm not."

Red laughed. "No need to concern yourself over the death of innocents. The Nymphs were involved with an incident involving a beehive, a disgruntled bobcat and... what else... Oh, yeah, a woodpecker. They didn't die, but they might have wished for it. I believe they learned their lesson. They won't be making fun of you again."

Mae's mouth twitched, "Well thanks. I guess."

"And don't worry about Faust." Red rubbed her hands together with glee, "He's officially off the market. I'll make it my personal mission to crimp his extra-curricular activities, well at least until you grow tired of him." She grinned at Mae. "But the way the Nymphs brag about his stamina, I think you'll enjoy him for a good long while." She turned to Willow and gave a fake sniffle. "Our little sis is finally gonna be a woman."

Mae shoved Red's shoulder. "Shut up. You're only a year older than I am."

"Does that make me a woman too?" Ellie squirmed in between her sisters hopping up and down. "I'm only a year younger than Mae."

Red ruffled Ellie's hair, "Honey, you bagged a sexy Werewolf at sixteen." She kissed her cheek. "The way you made that wolf howl." She sighed, "You put us all to shame."

"Well, Almighty O'ma", Red bowed to Willow, "The ho-gang's all here. So, what's the dealio?"

Willow grew gravely serious. Enough of the jokes. This was important. "The Miller cabin was sold." She solemnly looked from sister to sister, "The man who bought it is already here in town. You know what that means?"

Red kicked the tree root and unearthed a flask. She raised it to the sky and in a menacing voice said, "Blood will spill."

"Geez. You talk about me being bloodthirsty." Mae said.

Willow shook her head. "We don't have to kill him. Just scare him off."

"You're no fun." Red took a swig from the flask and passed it to Mae.

Mae scrutinized the flask's engraving, "Did you steal this from Faustino?"

Red gave a look of outrage, "Moi, steal? Never. I borrow. Now, drink up, Mae. The Bacchus brothers like a woman who can hold their liquor. Consider yourself in training."

Mae took a small sip and grimaced. Red glared, so she chugged. With watering eyes, she wheezed and handed it to the youngest.

Ellie sniffed the contents, "I don't think the Bacchus brothers are all that picky. Maggie doesn't drink a drop of this stuff and she's always hooked up with one of them." Without taking a drink she passed it to Willow.

"Well, there's certainly enough of them." Willow took a healthy swig enjoying the fermented moon wine the seven Bacchus brothers were famous for. She had grown up drinking it like juice. She passed the flask back to Red.

"Come on, girls, you know Mae needs all the help she can get. I mean really," Red gestured to all of her, "she's gotta loosen up."

The sisters all turned as one to stare at Mae. Willow could admit Red had a point. Mae had never been a wild child. When she was little, Mae would cry if she stepped in a mud puddle or if her hair got wet during a rainstorm. Even at a young age, she was always neat and clean. Her hairstyle had never changed. She still wore it parted in the middle with two smooth braids. Mae twirled them now. It was a nervous habit. She hated being the center of attention.

Willow felt pity and changed the subject. "Well, girls. We have a long night ahead of us. Our enemy arrives tomorrow." She started sketching out a rudimentary plan on the forest floor with a stick. Ellie pulled out parchment and a pen from a knothole in a nearby tree, and the sisters plotted their strategy. War had been declared. Lines had been drawn. The stranger would never see it coming. He was about to find out just how territorial his new neighbors could be.

Chapter 5

BRAY FELT LIKE a kid at Christmas. He couldn't believe he was finally going to see his new property. As he set up his laptop for this morning's conference call, his mind wandered back to the party from months ago and the overheard conversation between Gene and Claire Miller. The one that had started this whole adventure.

"Grandad loved that cabin. It seems a shame to sell the place." Claire said.

"Are you going to use it?" Gene asked. "I don't know about you, but I'd rather get cash. Who wants to go to bu-fu Arizona?"

Claire pulled a picture from her purse.

"This photo must be twenty years old. Who knows what kind of shape the cabin is in? No one has been out to the property in over ten years."

Bray had been on the sofa next to the two of them, counting down the minutes before he could politely leave the boring fundraiser his mother had organized. He glanced at the picture and did a double-take. He had never seen anything like it. It was a cabin treehouse, but instead of putting the house in a tree, they had built the house around a tree. If that wasn't bizarre enough, the tree itself looked unreal, with strips of random colors splashed across the bark.

"Excuse me, but did you mention selling?" Bray asked.

Gene's eyebrows raised and he grinned wide. "Yes. We were. Prime property on a secluded lake in Arizona close to Flagstaff. It's on two acres of land nestled in the Coconino National Forest. Perfect place to get away from everything."

He snatched the photo from his sister and thrust it in Bray's hand for a better look.

Bray chuckled to himself at how Gene turned on the salesman charm. Just a minute ago, while discussing with his sister, the property had seemed like a dilapidated eyesore. Now suddenly it was a hot vacation paradise. He knew the home's value would continue to climb in price the more interest he showed, but he couldn't help himself. The architecture was a mixture of odd angles and smooth edges. The outer shell of the structure looked like the bark of a tree. But it was the giant tree growing out of the roof that seemed to call to him. He didn't understand exactly what the appeal was. The rainbow colors of green, orange, blue, and red on a tree were unique, but there was something more. Something he couldn't quite identify. He needed to see this tree in person. Bray blamed his designer clothes and the venue filled with wealthy socialites for the outrageous price tag Gene proposed.

"Is this image photoshopped?"

"How dare you accuse us of such a thing." Claire plucked the photo from his fingertips and slipped it back in her purse. She turned and walked away, clutching the Coach bag to her chest. Her heels made loud clip-clop sounds as she walked across the room to the bar.

"Don't mind my sister. She'll come around."

Over the next hour, Gene went into detail about the property. His grandfather had been a student of Frank Lloyd Wright and had designed the treehouse cabin to be a part of nature. The tree was already growing on the property and it was an unusual species for this part of the world. The Rainbow Eucalyptus tree was indigenous to wet climates like the Philippines, but somehow this species had been planted and had thrived for years. The cabin was on the outskirts of a small town called Bellemont, Arizona. Within a week, Gene had supplied him with the original blueprints, and Bray paid for the property in cash, sight unseen. It was impulsive and reckless. Normally he was careful how he invested, but the design and that tree had captivated his imagination. It was all he could think about. When Gene suggested putting it on the market, that had clinched it for him. Bray refused the chance of being outbid. He doubled the asking price, much to the delight of the Millers. It had been a long time since he felt this level of excitement over anything.

The other executives at his company were astounded when he announced he was taking a two-month leave of absence. Bray was a workaholic. He never took time off. Several people asked if he had been diagnosed with some terminal illness. That made him laugh. For those, he explained he wanted to focus on a new acquisition. That seemed to appease their curiosity. He wouldn't reveal the real reason to anyone, not even to his closest friends. It was simple. He had to get away. The job was wearing him down. He had amassed enough wealth to live comfortably for several lifetimes. Now Bray needed a new challenge desperately. This wasn't just a vacation. He needed a lifeline.

Claire called this morning to remind him that the cabin had been abandoned for years and might need some work. She seemed worried he'd be upset if it didn't look exactly like the picture. He wondered if she feared him backing out of the deal or if his mother had called her. Juliet Graham was a fierce woman and had a knack for spreading guilt. She didn't understand Bray's need for such a small property in some remote location. She had given him all the reasons it was unsuitable and had been trying to convince him to get rid of the ridiculous purchase for the past month. She called this morning right after Claire.

"I want to protest one more time."

"Mother, please. We've been through this."

"If it's the money, then donate it. It can be a tax write-off. I'm sure someone local would be glad to take it off your hands. You said it came with some land, right?"

"Yes, but I'm not selling. And I'm already here."

"Quite clever of you to sneak out when I was busy with an event."

He admitted it was a chicken move, but his mother had a way of convincing people to do what she wanted. He was no exception, usually, but in this, he wouldn't budge.

"I thought you would have come to your senses by now. You're book-smart, Brayden. That's not going to help you in the wilderness. The woods can be dangerous."

"I'll be fine."

"I've seen a picture of that so-called cabin. That thing is going to need a lot of work."

"That's why I've got two months to get it in shape."

"What? You're going to attempt the repairs yourself? You don't have the skills."

It grated that his mother hit a nerve. She was right, but that was the very reason he wanted to do this. Bray was thirty-five years old. He had spent his whole life in front of a computer, creating programs and growing his business. It was time he experienced all the things he had missed out on.

"You've never even been camping. What if you get hurt?"

"I'm sure they have doctors out here if I happen to hack off my arm with a hammer."

She sighed. "You should be back here helping me with my fundraisers. I could introduce you to some friends. Some gorgeous single friends. Hmm? You don't need to go mope out in the wilderness all alone."

"I'm not moping."

"Uh-huh. Well, whatever you call it, you haven't been happy."

Bray didn't realize his mother had noticed, but he shouldn't have been surprised. His mother had a way of seeing through his bullshit.

"Gotta go, Mom. I love you. I'll call when I can."

"Love you too. Be careful."

He blew out a breath, glad to get that over with. He knew the real reason for her increased efforts for him to stay in the city. His favorite aunt had informed him of his mother's plans to marry him off. She had been plotting to play matchmaker. His mother really wanted grand-children. It was just one more reason to get out of town. He hoped his mother would move on to some charity project by the time he returned.

After his calls, he settled his hotel bill, drove to the hardware store, and then to Tent World. The sales associate helping him had been friends with the previous cabin owner, Jim Miller.

"It was over a decade ago, mind you, but I used to own a bait and tackle shop and Jim would come by for supplies from time to time. He was a good man but more of the solitary sort. He liked his privacy. When he moved back to California, the place stayed empty. It's a shame the kids wanted to sell. But then you wouldn't be here, and you seem like a nice fellow."

The elderly gentlemen had a wealth of information about the town and its inhabitants.

"Now that you've officially moved to our little town, I can fill you in on some of its secrets." He whispered.

Bray hadn't bothered to correct the man about only being there for two months. The tales had been tall, but he enjoyed the man's company. After a few hours, he finally grew impatient.

"I really should get going. I wanted to be at the cabin before dark."

"Right you are. Very wise. You don't want to be traveling into the woods at night. Too many stories of strange occurrences after dark."

The man helped him load the purchases into his pickup.

"You be careful, son."

Bray waved and set his GPS to the coordinates.

The man said it should take him no more than half an hour to get from the store to his cabin.

Before long, his GPS chimed.

"Turn left," the voice instructed.

He turned onto an unpaved road from the highway, and within a few minutes lost the signal. The man from Tent World had warned him this might happen. Bray pulled to the side of the road and unfolded the map the man had drawn. It had several twists and turns, most of them with unnamed roads. He had been extremely detailed giving landmarks along the way and markers that may or may not still be up. He explained that no one had been out to the property in years, so some of the signs could have fallen or been covered by foliage. Luckily, at least one sign had survived. It said 'Miller Cabin' and had a hand-drawn arrow. It directed him down a path barely wide enough for his truck. Bray put it in gear and slowly edged down the path. He was grateful for the four-wheel drive when the road became even rockier. The bumps in the road managed to spill most of his cold coffee on the map making the chicken scratch even more illegible. He was praying for another signpost when the road abruptly dead-ended. He slammed on the brakes. Even though sunset was hours away, the dense woods made it difficult to see far. He got a flashlight from the glovebox and climbed out to investigate. He walked up and down the dirt road trying to find the turn he had missed. He had driven slowly the whole way and was sure he had followed the directions precisely, or at least what he could read. Bray tried to wipe coffee from the map, but all it did was smear the images further. He gave up and popped down the tailgate. He hooked the ramp to the back and climbed into the truck bed. Bray wondered just how difficult it would be to back the quad down the ramp. He remembered snickers from some kids who had watched him load it onto the truck bed at Tent World. He had been worried about smashing the quad into the back of his truck. It had taken him five attempts to figure out the right amount of gas to get it up the ramp without rolling back down. The elderly man had offered to drive it up on the truck bed, but Bray had wanted to do it himself. He put his helmet on, whispered a few prayers, did the sign of the cross, and revved the engine. He slowly reversed his way down the ramp.

He let out a loud whoop when he reached the bottom and punched the sky. Bray was glad there was no one there to witness his pathetic excitement at not wiping out. He decided to pack up a few supplies before driving out to the cabin, just in case he got lost. He really had no idea what direction to go, but after all, he was a genius. Or at least that's what his mother told him. He had graduated at the top of his class. He could figure anything out with logic. After a few minutes of thought, he popped open one of the sealed containers in his glove box. He unpeeled the backing on a small one-by-one chip and slapped it to the dash inside his truck. He threw the rest of the containers into his backpack along with some water and protein bars. When he was a few feet from the truck, he closed his eyes and spun in a circle with his arm straight out in front of him. When he stopped, he climbed on the quad, set his watch timer for fifteen minutes, turned on an app on his phone, and started off in the direction he had pointed. He revved the engine to the quad and peeled off into the woods with a roar of laughter. Bray thought about his plan as he drove. With simple logic, if the trip was supposed to take thirty minutes, and he had already driven fifteen minutes, then he would have to drive no more than fifteen more minutes to get to the cabin. He had designed an app to find lost items. With the chip active in his truck, he could use that as a reference point. Using a spiral grid pattern, he could tighten the search circle until he came across the cabin. The logic was sound. He refused to go back to town admitting to anyone he had gotten lost.

After searching for several hours, he found the cabin. Since it was close to sunset, he figured he should get his truck first before exploring inside. He placed another sticky tile on the front porch and followed the original signal back to his truck. When the path dead-ended at a patch of vines, he discovered the reason for missing the turn. His cell app indicated the *Lost Truck* was five yards in front of him. He found it odd that the vines had grown so heavily in this one section of forest. He circled the trees and started digging around in the truck cab for the chainsaw. He had been anxious to use all his new power tools, but this one had looked particularly badass. Bray had gone on a shopping frenzy at the hardware store early this morning. The clerk had practically drooled when he pulled out his black AMEX card and said he needed top-of-the-line tools to fill a very large toolshed. The owner, the clerk's father, had shown up minutes later and had been more than happy to unbox any tool and demo the equipment. The guy had blinked slowly a few times when Bray asked very basic handyman questions, but then would grin and offer more 'must have' items. Bray pushed several buttons and pulled the crank start on his new chainsaw. It was heavy and loud, and he felt very manly as he cut through the vines. He was proud of his first success with one of the new tools. It took him a few times to get the quad back up the ramp and into the truck bed. But even that didn't dim his good mood. Ten minutes later, he was at his new cabin. He automatically clicked the remote lock for the truck and had to shake his head. Who would steal his stuff all the way out here?

He walked to the front porch noticing an old swing and a few rockers that had seen better days. The wood was weathered but both pieces looked sturdy. The cushions were shot, but those were easy to replace. He had plenty of sandpaper and stain from the hardware store. Bray decided those would be his first project to tackle.

He stood with keys in hand, trembling with excitement. This was the moment he had been waiting for since he had first laid eyes on those blueprints. He unlocked the door and flipped on the light switch. The sight that greeted him was not what he expected. First, the lights shouldn't have worked. The packet with the blueprints had come with instructions for turning on the power. It included which breaker to flip and what box controlled the load center and inverters. It was a very detailed list of how to turn on, maintain, and monitor the sophisticated solar system that had been installed in the cabin. He had completely forgotten about it. Bray didn't dwell on that mystery for long. He was more distracted by the destruction. It looked like a tornado had hit inside the cabin.

To his left, the cabinets and drawers in the kitchen were all open. Leftover boxes of food were ripped and the contents strewn across the counters. Cracked glass and broken dishes created a collage of chaos on the floor. It looked like an animal with tiny paws had finger-painted jelly on the walls. Mud prints, dirt, and leaves were everywhere. The antique bronze chandelier in the foyer, the only item that looked untouched, cast a soft amber glow over the debris. To his right, a large couch in the living room had been torn to shreds by wild animals. The torn fabric looked like a green plaid print, but it was tough to tell. A slight wind blew in from the open front door and stirred the stuffing from the floor. They floated like clouds over to the large tree in the center. Bray stared in wonder. The architect had made it the focal point of the room. Large tree branches melded into several sections of the roof. He wondered how the architect accounted for the tree's growth over time. Bray couldn't detect any signs of foundation shifts or gaps in the roof. His boots crunched as he walked closer and examined the rubber seal rings. Bray assumed the rubber must expand as the tree grew and the trunk or branches got thicker over time. It was fascinating. The architect had obviously loved this tree.

He stared at the beautiful multicolored trunk. It revealed even more colors than what the picture had shown. Fluorescent strips of purple and pink as well as blue, red, yellow, green, and brown decorated the tree. Bray pulled out the photo he had been shown at that party months ago. It had arrived with the keys to the property after the sale closed. At the time, the tree seemed like some impressionist work of art mixed with modern architecture. Seeing the tree in person, Bray was blown away. He didn't think it was possible, but the tree was even more amazing. He had researched the Rainbow Eucalyptus tree online. As part of the growing process, the bark would shed thin layered strips revealing the inner bark beneath. It would start out as neon green and, after exposure to the air, would change to other colors before turning back to the original brown. Since it shedded in pieces and not all at once, the bark looked more like a patchwork quilt than a tree. Bray laid a palm on the trunk and felt such incredible peace. He let out a deep sigh. He moved some of the trash and discovered there were accent lights in several colors casting shadows around the room. There were also hidden alcoves along the walls. Bray was anxious to see what other interesting things he would find under the debris. This was more than he had hoped for.

Grinning ear to ear, he went back to the truck for bags. His boots crunched on broken glass, smashed cereal bits, and uncooked rice as he waded through the rubbish. He whistled as he swept and cleaned. Bray uncovered sections of walnut hardwood flooring and artificial grass. The floor plan started off normal with a kitchen, bath, and bedroom to the left and a large living room to the right as you walked in the front door. But after that, it got a little odd. Green grass pathways led from every section of the cabin to the tree including alcoves along the outer wall. They were at least a dozen all randomly spaced and each offering something different. One provided a bench and window to view a special feature outdoors, while others provided a space for a plant that was still thriving after being abandoned for over a decade. Bray wondered if there was an irrigation system still pumping water to those sections. Many of the alcoves displayed pieces of art; everything from paintings to sculptures to unusual rocks. It was all beautiful, from the textures and colors to the lighting used for accent. But after several hours of scrubbing walls and floors, he was exhausted. He opened the bedroom window to let in the cool evening air before collapsing onto the unmade bed.

Bray awoke the next morning sore and itchy. He looked down at his body. It was covered in mosquito bites. He stretched and lumbered over to the window he opened last night.

"Huh."

There was a large hole in the screen that had been clawed out by some animal. He didn't remember seeing it, but then again, he had been exhausted. After a quick shower and a healthy application of calamine lotion, he headed outside to the front porch with a hot cup of coffee. The sight that greeted him was not what he expected. All the bags he had used to clean up the garbage inside were now littered across his front lawn and most of his front porch. He picked up a worn cushion from one of the rockers, shook off the debris, and turned it upside down. He sat with a sigh. Bray didn't blame the animals. He knew it was his own damn fault. If animals had easily gotten into the cabin, logic served that the thin plastic garbage bags wouldn't have offered any better protection. Bray knew there would be a learning curve. What little knowledge he had regarding being an outdoorsman had been learned from books over the past three weeks. He drank his cup of coffee taking in the beauty of his new property. Off to his left, the sun glistened off ripples in the lake. A slight wind rustled the leaves of the forest trees surrounding the cabin. He inhaled the crisp clean air. This place made him feel alive. Even the mess couldn't take away from the splendor.

After the last sip of coffee, he stood and stretched. Studying the debris decorating his lawn, an idea popped into his mind. He grinned as he opened the truck cab and dug through the boxes until he found the one; a leaf blower. The hardware store owner had demonstrated a setting for suck. Bray had thought the man was joking at first. Anxious for a chance to try another tool, he unboxed it and plugged in the long extension cord. Bray made a game seeing how quickly he could suck up the garbage. Once finished, he unloaded all the tools into the shed by the lake, then refilled the truck bed with the newly filled trash bags and headed into town. Bray couldn't wait to discover all the hidden treasures in his new backyard, but first, he needed a few more supplies.

Chapter 6

THE NEWCOMER'S BEHAVIOR was puzzling. He wasn't anything like she expected. She was reluctantly impressed with how he used technology to find the cabin. Even when he cut through the vines, she found herself more fascinated than afraid. Ellie had shivered with fear and Mae's jaw had dropped at the effortless swipe of the chainsaw cutting through vines that took them hours to grow. Yes, he was a threat, but he didn't appear to be an overly destructive sort. Not that intent mattered. He still had to go. She thought he would have gotten lost and headed back into town before nightfall. Willow was glad she had the foresight to have the animals trash his place as a backup plan, but his attitude toward all the trouble was odd. How could he maintain such a positive attitude after everything that happened? They covered his mattress with mosquito attractant and the animals had done another number on the garbage outside during the night. She expected frustration and anger, but instead, he seemed determined to conquer any difficulty thrown his way. When he drove to town this morning, she thought they had gotten the better of him. The sisters celebrated together with a picnic by the lake. Her squirrel surveillance team interrupted their party in the late afternoon, announcing his arrival. She gaped at the new locking trash cans, screens for the windows, and a bug zapper. He was clever. She'd give him that. The sisters watched as he installed everything and worked around the cabin. It was obvious he was from the city. His lack of skill with the most basic tools amazed them all. Even Red, dubbed the Ashbrook clutz, thought he was clumsy.

"The man is going to kill himself." Red gestured to a pile of jagged wood chunks. "Did you see how he swings an ax?"

Ellie nodded. "I overheard him talking to that flat black rock he carries around asking it how to chop wood. He said something about not being able to enter the net."

Red chuckled. "He was talking to his cell phone and he can't get internet this far into the woods."

The girls watched as he came around the house carrying an old ladder. He got it settled just so and climbed up with a nail and hammer. Before he got more than a few steps up, the ladder fell to the side and he landed squarely in a thorn bush.

"What an idiot." Mae shook her head. "We hardly need to sabotage him. He does that all by himself."

"Well, to be fair, I think the beavers damaged the ladder." Red giggled. "And wait 'til you see what they did to the dock by the lake."

They watched as he got up, dusted off his backside, and picked a few thorns from his jeans. After scrutinizing the ladder for a few minutes, he flipped it over. He grabbed the hammer and a new nail and climbed up again. This time he made it to the top. He pulled something from his jacket pocket and hung it. He got down from the ladder and grinned at the cracked plaque: Home Sweet Home.

Red nudged Willow, "Uh sis. That's not a good sign."

She gritted her teeth, "He'll crack soon. Just you wait." She turned to her youngest sister when the stranger started walking toward the dock. "Ellie, to the other side of the lake. Signal for Daisy."

Ellie took a deep breath and let it out as she merged with the closest pine.

A few minutes later, the stranger walked the length of the dock. He realized the instability too late as the dock collapsed beneath him. After trying valiantly to leap for a stable section, the whole dock crumbled. Bray yelped just before the splash. His whole body submerged, and he came to the surface sputtering water.

Willow gave a silent golf clap and grinned at Red and Mae. "See."

He trudged through the water and stomped to the shore, shaking out his hair like a wolf. His clothing stuck to his body like a second skin, but he grinned like a madman. He yelled at the water, "Is that all you got?"

Willow knocked on the pine, "Ellie," she whispered. "It's time."

Ellie's face appeared in the bark of the tree. "Daisy doesn't want to. She feels sorry for him."

"Ugh." Willow looked to the sky for guidance. "Remind Daisy of her duty to her cubs. She doesn't have to hurt him, just scare him."

"Ok. I'll tell her." Ellie's face disappeared.

The stranger climbed back into the water and started pulling out planks of wood. He was making a pile on the shore when he saw a black bear enter the water from the other side of the lake.

"Holy shit."

The stranger stood frozen in place, up to his knees in the water, and stared as the black bear swam towards him. It let out a series of teeth clacking and grunting. The man stood unmoving except for the flash of his camera phone as the bear got closer. The bear stopped ten feet from the stranger standing on its hind legs and moaned long and loud. They stood staring at each other in silence. The seconds ticked by. Willow wondered if the stranger had gone into shock and couldn't move. The flash from the phone went off again. The bear blinked and slowly backed away, crossing to the other side of the lake and back into the tree cover.

"Woah." The man's knees buckled when he went to take a step, almost wiping out on the rocks. He caught himself and turned to the shore.

"That was fucking awesome!" He exclaimed as he made his way back to the cabin.

When the front door closed, Mae cleared her throat, "And they call me Mental?" She gestured to the cabin, "That one should get an award. He's obviously got something wrong up here." She gave a knock to her head.

Willow bit her lip. He didn't respond the way he was supposed to. Everything they threw at him backfired.

"I can't believe how positive he's stayed. Most humans would be pissed with all the trouble we've thrown his way." Red shook her head. "It doesn't make sense."

Ellie reappeared from the pine. "Daisy likes him. She thought he was very brave."

Their chatter died when the front door sprang open. He walked directly toward them with purpose. The stranger had taken off his glasses. Had they fallen in the lake? Or maybe he left them inside? Could he see that well without them? They were mostly hidden in the shadows, but she ducked behind a tall bush and gestured for her sisters to do the same. Willow peeked through the branches and watched as he unbuttoned his shirt. The wet fabric clung to his skin. He peeled it off and she barely glimpsed his wide chest before he turned his back and pinned the soaked shirt to the clothesline. She followed a drop of water as it rolled over his broad shoulders, down his toned back, and into the waist of his jeans. When he unzipped those, he had the sisters' undivided attention. Willow wasn't sure she liked how her sisters ogled the stranger as he wiggled from his pants. He pinned the jeans to the line and ran his thumbs back and forth across the elastic band of his boxers. He looked left and then right. Was the man shy?

Willow frowned as Red mouthed the words go go go, giving silent encouragement for him to lose the shorts.

He shucked the boxers and pinned those to the line as well.

Red's eyebrows bobbed as she looked back at her sisters with a wink. Mae rolled her eyes.

He leaned over and buckled his sandals as Willow admired his backside. She hadn't really noticed before, but he was sort of sexy. Well, for a human. He wasn't overly bulky with muscles. His body was tall and lean.

"He's got a great ass," Ellie whispered. "But he's awful pale."

Then he turned, and they got the full frontal. Mae's mouth hung open. Ellie covered her eyes and stifled a giggle.

Red mouthed 'nice' and nodded her approval.

Willow felt her whole body tighten. His clothes had hidden just how fine the man was built. Unbelievably, his front was better than the back. She couldn't conceal her appreciation. Her skin flushed a deep green and she shivered. Red noticed. She was sure of it. But Willow couldn't tear her gaze from the man in front of her. His deep brown hair was slicked back from his face revealing dark intelligent eyes with long thick lashes. Her eyes danced over the sparse hair dusting his hard chest and flat abs, down his goody trail like an arrow. Her mouth went dry as she took in his sex. It hung heavy between sculpted thighs. If this was what he looked like soft, what would he be like when hard as steel and thrusting inside her? She closed her eyes and stifled a moan. Where had that thought come from? humans weren't allowed she recited to herself over and over. She blinked and watched as he grabbed a towel. It seemed a tease, watching as bits of flesh appeared and disappeared beneath the towel as he roughly scrubbed the fabric over his skin. He wrapped the towel around his waist and she could suddenly breathe again. Willow hadn't realized how unfocused she had become. She needed to get a hold of herself and rein in her sisters. Ellie and Red were pushing each other trying to get a better peek around the tree they were hiding behind. Red was chanting softly to lose the towel. Even Mae who whispered something about him being the enemy seemed distracted by his body.

Willow shoved them all back with a burst of power and in a loud whisper said, "Mae's right. Plus, he's twice your age." She was suddenly brimming with jealousy.

Red smirked, "I was waiting for you to call dibs. So, you're using age? How very antiquated."

Willow blushed a dark green and turned to watch the stranger walk back to the cabin. He hadn't heard the outburst. Luckily some birds had drowned the sound with their chirps.

When the door finally closed, Red's eyes glittered with mischief. She turned to her younger sisters, "Come along, girls. Show's over. Our sis needs some alone time with her sexy human." She sashayed further into the woods. Ellie and Mae gave Willow a nod and followed Red.

Willow didn't know how to respond. She was puzzled by her reaction. She had never felt possessive of a male. Not even for her ex-lover Lucian. She hadn't cared if females ogled his massive chest rippled with muscles or fawned over his handsome face. Her total carefree attitude about whether he took another lover should have been a red flag. But she had stayed with him for years because she thought they were good together. Their relationship was comfortable. Their families had a shared history and they were friends. She remembered giving all the reasons to Council. Lucian was a great defender. A powerful warrior. Any threats were squashed immediately by his mere presence. He was an imposing male that others would follow. Maybe she had been a bit rebellious in her youth, and it had been a rash decision to choose him for a mate. Not that it mattered. Council had decided her application for life mate was denied. She remembered their words like it was yesterday, 'A Demon is not appropriate for a Dryad, especially a Guardian.' In recent years, Council had encouraged her to seek a life mate, but she was done dating. Nope. Not interested. They had crushed that dream long ago. She refused to get her hopes up again.

Even a sexual fling hadn't appealed in years. Apparently, her libido had not died completely. She felt a rather large spark for this stranger. It wasn't just his kicking bod that made her react. It was his intelligence, quiet demeanor, and the unbreakable spirit she reluctantly respected.

She found herself conflicted with her need to break down his resolve and her silent hope that he would overcome all the obstacles they were forced to throw his way. He had easily won over Daisy the black bear, a fierce mother of two feisty young cubs. She sighed. He needed to leave. The forest creatures all depended on her for their protection. So, her body craved his? It didn't matter. He had to go. He was from the city and obviously had no idea the dangers out here in the woods. She would put the fear into this man if it was the last thing she did. Mind made up, she turned from the cabin and headed back to her tree for some well-deserved rest. He would be gone by the end of the week. She was sure of it.

A week later, Willow was beyond frustrated. She spent all her spare time watching the stranger. Her sisters had grown bored after the third day. But Willow wouldn't give up. She couldn't fail on her mission. He managed to smile or laugh at every misfortune that happened to him. The man had no sense of self-preservation. His determination to love the woods and the cabin was starting to wear on her. She decided to see if there was something keeping him preoccupied inside his cabin. But for that she needed clothing. Humans tended to get all weirded out if they spied her naked. She had no idea why. Willow merged into a pine and exited from another close to town. She grabbed her dress from her hidden pack. Since she couldn't meld into the tree with clothes, she hiked the ten miles by foot. Worry about her sisters seeing the stranger naked again made her pick-up speed. She sprinted the last few miles and was panting by the time she arrived at the edge of the clearing. He was out on his front porch, whittling. His attempt at cutting the chunk of wood was so inept she was concerned he would lose a finger. She leaned forward to get a better look. She seriously doubted he had ever used a knife in his life. He looked to be in his mid-thirties. How had he survived this long? She wondered what his life had been like back in San Francisco. She knew a few things about him from the women at the crafting club. They had said he was wealthy. Did he hire servants to cook for him, or perhaps cut his food? He seemed to lack basic survival skills. What was this magical land of San Francisco like?

"Son of a—" The man shook his hand.

She gasped and stared at the blood as it dripped from the wound. "Who's out there?"

Willow put a hand over her mouth. She hadn't meant to be so loud. She backed up quickly and tripped. Her dress snagged on the thorn bush behind her. This was why she hated clothes. She yanked herself free as the stranger ran toward her. She slipped deeper into the woods. Willow doubled back to watch from another section at the edge of the clearing. What was he holding? A scrap of cloth. She looked down at the hem of her dress. He had the missing piece. She sighed. Good riddance. He could keep it. She found a nearby tree and stashed her dress, so she could travel home by tree. The current plan wasn't working at all. Instead of growing tired of all the pranks and misfortunes, the stranger was growing more and more in love with the cabin. She needed a new strategy. It was time for drastic measures.

Chapter 7

SUNLIGHT TOUCHED THE tips of her leaves. Willow yawned. Her tree shook. She hadn't slept well at all staying up half the night coming up with a new strategy. Willow decided to make herself known. She didn't like the idea of hiding from him. She wasn't afraid of anything. He was on her land, period. It was simple. He had to go. She continued to convince herself why this was the proper course of action as she went through her chores for the day. Willow ran out of meaningless tasks by sunset. She couldn't delay any longer. She walked from her tree to his cabin. It was strange how close they lived to one another. It was only a half-mile from her birth tree. Not that it usually mattered. She could travel hundreds of miles in seconds via tree. Willow located the hole where she had stored her dress and slipped it on. She spent a few minutes ripping the edge trying to even out the hemline. She sighed. Her once knee-length dress was now a mini. The few hours of sleep she had managed last night had been filled with erotic dreams of the stranger. Willow shook her head trying to focus. She ran hands through her hair, getting rid of the tangles, fluffing up the slight curl. She scowled. Why was she primping for a human? Her mission was simple. Meet with the man, learn if he was a security risk, then ask him politely to leave by way of a kick in the ass. She didn't like this fluttering feeling in her stomach. How could she be nervous? She approached the cabin slowly eyeing several dishes set out on his front porch. It smelled wonderful. A variety of fruit and nuts. Her mouth watered. He must have put them out recently, no animals had gotten into them yet. She noticed a few critters on the other side of the clearing eyeing the bounty. Willow made several squeaks and chirps telling the animals to stay clear. She took a deep breath and walked into the clearing with her head held high. She hesitated at the porch steps for a moment. Willow sensed she was being watched. She eyed some rare nuts in one bowl that looked especially tasty. Willow snagged a few and hopped off the front steps.

"Are you trying to lure me into a trap like some wild animal?"

The screen door opened slowly. She noticed as the door swung wide, the glass was tinted dark on one side but clear on the other. He had been watching her all along. Her enemy was clever. She reluctantly acknowledged the man had a few skills. Willow chomped on a nut in bliss. It was macadamia; a rare delicacy for her. "Mmm. These are good."

The man watched her in silence. He was wearing his glasses again, but that didn't distract from his sex appeal. He seemed mesmerized by every movement she made. No magical enchantment needed. She shrugged letting herself fall back into a rocker. The small table next to it held several bowls. She leaned over gathering up more goodies. She crossed her legs and heard a loud intake of breath. She paused with raised eyebrows and studied him carefully. He stood rigid straight with arms crossed. Her perusal of his body was slow. Her gaze slid down his body and she stared at the bulge in his jeans. It twitched. She sucked on a date and refocused on his face. "You ought to sit before you fall."

"I don't think I can."

His deep voice was sexy. She hadn't heard him say much except for the occasional yell. It was a welcome surprise. He mumbled a curse under his breath. Willow smiled, enjoying the rumbling sound as she sifted through the nut bowl digging for her favorites. She put a few in her pocket for later. Eyeing another fruit bowl, Willow walked over and snagged a juicy red apple. She took a huge bite and moaned. Delicious. The perfect amount of sweet and tart. The man stared at her from a foot away. Willow was only five-two and the man stood at six feet. She had to lean back to look him in the eye. It was ironic he was the one that seemed nervous. The man gulped loudly as some apple juice slid down her chin. He followed the drop as it rolled down her neck and into her cleavage. She swiped the juice with her thumb and sucked.

He made some kind of strangled growl.

She stared at him waiting for him to say something. The seconds ticked by.

"So, what's your name, stranger?"

He licked his lips as she took another bite from the apple. Was she making him hungry?

"My name's Bray." He held out his hand.

She dropped the half-eaten apple in his open palm. "Thanks for the snack."

He tried to grab her arm, but she twisted out of his grasp and glared.

"Sorry." He ran a hand through his hair. "I don't want you to go. Will you stay for a bit and talk?" He set down the apple on a table and handed her a nut bowl.

She made no move to take it. He shrugged and set it on the table closest to the patio swing. It was a three-seater. Willow sat at the opposite end, farthest from him and closest to the nut bowl. She grabbed a few and popped them into her mouth, munching in bliss. She leaned back trying to get comfortable.

"What do you want to talk about?"

"I don't know. Tell me about yourself? I'm guessing you're a neighbor, right?"

She studied him for a few moments. "Yeah. What's to tell? You're in my woods."

He gestured to the trees. "You own everything here, huh?" He grinned. "Apparently this is prime real estate. You must be rich."

That smile did funny things to her insides. She shrugged and squinted into the trees.

"Are you alone?"

"Why do you ask?" *Did that sound suspicious?* This human was throwing off her game. She was here on a fact-finding mission. *Time to turn the tables.*

"Well, it's a little unusual, you know. A girl out here. By herself. In the wilderness."

She rolled her eyes. "I can take care of myself." She started rocking the bench back and forth. "Maybe you should worry about yourself. I heard you've been having some trouble."

His eyebrows rose, "How do you know about that?"

She plucked at the frayed hem of her dress. The fabric shifted higher as she faced him. He sucked in a deep breath. For some reason, the reaction pleased her.

"It's a small town. News travels fast."

She continued to rock back and forth. They remained quiet for several minutes. It was peaceful. He must have oiled the swing because it didn't squeak; just made a soft whooshing sound. He edged his way to the middle of the swing slowly, getting closer inch by inch, like he would a skittish animal. Which, let's face it, she was. Her body tensed. If he touched her, she would bolt. She got ready to spring, but he stopped moving. Bray stared off into the trees. She took a deep breath ready to blast him with questions when he started humming. The tune was beautiful. Something in the melody called to her. She lost her train of thought. What had she been wanting to do? Oh yeah. The interrogation. The reason she stopped by. She stared at his profile and followed his line of sight out into the trees. It was nothing special. The same old forest she had lived in her whole life, but to this stranger it was new. She could sense his excitement when a critter came into the clearing, scurrying through the tall grass. He grinned when a bird swooped down to grab a worm. Slowly she started to relax, leaning back into the swing. After a few minutes, his long leg stretched out and their knees bumped. Surprisingly, it felt nice. In fact, she scooted a little closer, not minding at all when their thighs touched. His body was so warm. She rested her head back against the arm he stretched out behind her and let out a long sigh. He smelled so good. She snuggled into his side to catch more of that delicious scent from his skin. "Your porch swing is really comfy."

He rested his large hand on her shoulder. "Yeah. The swing."

Safe. Why did it feel so natural to trust him? This wasn't like her. She never let her guard down. She was the protector, not the other way around, but his humming was like a homecoming, his scent like a drug. She couldn't remember her mission. His warmth enveloped her. She felt herself falling into a dream world. And for the first time since she was a little girl, there was someone there to catch her.

Willow jerked awake. She glanced around trying to get her bearings. She was alone on the swing. A super-soft down comforter was tucked around her legs. It was hard to remember a time when she felt more relaxed. Glancing at the moon, she calculated the time. It was very late in the evening. She must have been out for hours. Willow couldn't believe she fell asleep on some stranger. Stupid. Reckless. What had she been thinking? Maybe he used a spell or drugged the food. She sniffed the fruit and nut bowls. They smelled fine, but what did she really know about this stranger? Although, the man had kept her safe and warm while she was defenseless. He hadn't taken advantage of her. Not that she'd give him a second chance. The cabin looked dark. Where had he gone? Peering through the front window she noticed a beam of light reflecting off the walls. She sprinted toward the trees. His flashlight lit up the swing as she reached cover at the edge of the clearing. Breath heaving, she smiled relishing her small victory of escape. Willow started to walk away but turned at the last minute, glancing back at the cabin. She was intrigued by the way he clutched the comforter to his chest. She felt a pang of regret for leaving without saying goodbye. He whispered into the night; something about a dream woman. Willow paused thinking back on their conversation. She'd never mentioned her name. She could still fix her mistake. Realizing what must be done, her stomach knotted in pain.

Chapter 8

BRAY'S TRUCK RUMBLED through the forest slowly. Streams of sunlight filtered through the canopy directing him down the dirt path. In such a short time, he had become accustomed to the twists and turns. Driving by rote, he went through a mental list of errands to do while in town. Bray was especially anxious to see if the security cameras had arrived. When would that beautiful neighbor visit again? Was she always so trusting with strangers, or had she just been exhausted? He recalled how she fell asleep on the swing. It was amusing how suspicious she was one minute and out cold the next. Bray never met anyone who could sleep so soundly. When her head fell to his lap, he thought for sure she was faking, but then he heard a soft snore. It took every bit of willpower he possessed to remain still, his erection throbbing under her cheek as she snuggled. He watched her sleep for what felt like hours, memorizing all those luscious curves in that skimpy little dress. His fingers tingled with want. Bray debated smoothing a hand down her back, cupping that sexy ass, but didn't want to chance it. At one point he decided to get the comforter from his bed. She hadn't budged. When he resettled himself on the swing covering her more for his own sanity than from the cold, she curled against him again, clutching him close, as if afraid he'd slip away. Not likely. It was strange. Normally Bray didn't care for clingy women. Sex was one thing, but he didn't remember ever holding a woman like that. It felt tender. The second time he rose to use the facilities, he must have made a noise searching for the flashlight. When he returned to the porch, she was gone. He stayed outside waiting, wondering if she would return, hoping his imagination hadn't played tricks on him. But after inhaling the lavender fragrance from the comforter he knew she was real. He went to bed wrapped in her heavenly scent. He woke this morning thrusting into his hand, coming so hard he thought the cabin shook. That was a definite plus to living in the woods. Privacy. No need for embarrassment from neighbors overhearing a yell to the rafters at four a.m.

In addition to privacy, he felt a complete lack of stress. He hadn't realized how much pressure his life had been under until he got away from everything. No constant text messages. No emails. No worries. Being a technology junkie, he thought for sure he would be suffering from electronic withdrawals. He was surprised at how easy it was to go without those gadgets he took for granted. Although it would be nice to have a few amenities when visitors stopped by, he didn't feel the need. There was so much stimulation in the natural setting around him. So much to investigate. Every day he discovered some new critter scurrying about his property or down by the lake. Even though he made a ton of mistakes, he loved it here. Bray felt like each day he awoke with new purpose. Having a scantily clad neighbor took his cabin in the woods from great to glorious. He longed to see her again, but first, he needed to stop at the hotel. The CEO at one of his accounts had demanded the software designer be on the call for the project launch. The hotel was the only business in the area that had high-speed internet. Bray grinned coming up with another item to add to his list. He needed info on this mystery woman and figured someone from town would have details. Who was she? Where did she live? And, more importantly, was she single?

At the hotel, Bray signaled to the gal at the front desk and gestured to the conference room. She nodded and waved. He had already made a deal with the hotel manager to let him use the room for calls whenever he needed. Luckily, the launch went smoothly and didn't take up too much time. He had been thinking about his mysterious neighbor almost non-stop, wondering if she had stopped by his cabin while he'd been in town. It made him want to rush back even with his list of errands. He looked down at his erection. Obviously not thinking with the right head. If he wanted to be more available, he had to get the cabin set up with internet, that way he didn't waste whole afternoons in town for work. Cable wasn't available that far into the woods, so the next best option was satellite. He called a programmer friend who had boasted about getting one installed at his summer home. After a few minutes, his friend recommended a pro installer at HughesNet. He called the tech's personal cell and set up an appointment for the following week. Bray grinned thinking if he could set up his cabin with satellite, he could work remotely whenever he wanted. His two-month vacation could be extended indefinitely. The possibilities with that sexy neighbor had him so distracted he didn't notice the young woman walking toward him in the lobby until they collided.

"Geez. Didn't see you there." He bent down to pick up the notebook she dropped.

Her expression of annoyance transformed into a wide smile once she saw his face.

He noticed her Louboutin pumps, Versace business suit, and Gucci handbag. This polished woman with a perfect chignon and flawless makeup didn't belong. She looked like a mix between a movie star and corporate mogul. He wondered if she had made a wrong turn on the highway. Although, if he were totally honest, he was just as out of place as she was. He wore ripped jeans, a printed tee, and flannel, all designer and probably just as expensive as the outfit she wore.

"Dolce & Gabbana?"

"What?"

"Your jeans."

"Uh. Yeah."

"I thought so." She grinned. "Instead of an apology, how about you buy me a drink?"

"Oh." Bray flushed. Where were his manners? "Sorry for bumping into you. I wasn't paying attention. Sure. A drink is the least I can do."

He glanced at the front desk hoping to get a recommendation, but the gal was busy with another guest.

Bray shrugged, "I'm new here. You have any suggestions?"

"Oh, I've got all kinds of suggestions." She gave a devilish grin, "But how about we go to the Roadhouse Bar and Grill down the street."

She gently touched his chest, sliding manicured nails down. He caught her hand before it drifted below his navel. He gave her a brief handshake and let go. She smiled.

"My name's Gail."

"Good to meet you. I'm Bray."

"Well, Bray, do you mind driving?"

She turned and walked out the front door before he could reply. He got the impression she didn't experience rejection very often. He followed behind her, admiring her ass in that form-fitting skirt and high heels. She was exactly the type of woman his mother would set him up with. It wouldn't surprise him to find Gail involved in some marriage plot devised by his mother. She stood next to his truck. He glanced around the parking lot wondering how she had known which was his. He scanned the other vehicles. His was the newest on the lot, but low-end by his standards. Maybe she noticed the temporary plate. He had mentioned he was new to town. Bray opened the passenger door and helped her into the cab. The drive took all of two minutes. They could have easily walked to the restaurant, although Gail's high heels might have presented a challenge over the gravel lot. Once they entered the bar, he felt instantly at home. It was warm and inviting. He loved the '50s style with neon signs casting a soft red glow across the room. Along one side was a long oak bar with plenty of barstools. At the far back, past the pool tables, was more '50s paraphernalia. The delicious aroma of burgers and fries made his mouth water. It reminded him he hadn't eaten yet today.

"I know you said drink, but how about I buy you lunch as well? I'm suddenly starved."

She shrugged, "I could eat. And the burgers are really good." She pointed to the grill. "You want to do the honors?"

He realized that people were grilling their own burgers and steaks. *How bizarre, but fun.* He wasn't the best cook, but grilling was one of the few things he could manage.

Over lunch, he discovered Gail just moved from San Francisco. She was still deciding if she wanted to live here permanently. It seemed he wasn't the only one wanting to get away from the big city. She hadn't made any attempt to seduce him, so he figured his paranoia was misplaced. If his mother had sent her, she would have been trying to seal the deal. He relaxed, enjoying her company, finding her dry wit refreshing. She was cultured and wealthy but was also down to earth. What few defenses he had seemed to melt away. Bray felt like he could trust her.

"This seems like a stretch since you just got here," Bray scratched his head, "but I'm curious if you've run into this one woman I met in the forest. Maybe you've seen her around town. She's pretty unique."

She paused in mid-bite of a fry. "I'm intrigued. Tell me more."

"Well, she's on the petite side, maybe five-two, with long white-blonde hair and hazel eyes."

Gail grinned. "Oh yeah. I met her. That's Willow. She's a nudist."

Bray choked on his beer.

She pounded hard on his back.

Wheezing, he replied, "You don't say."

She smiled. "Yeah. Her whole family lives in the forest. They're naturists."

"Does that mean survivalists?" Bray started sweating. He pictured a family filled with shotgun happy hillbillies that would misunderstand his intentions. Well, if he were honest, his intentions weren't all that pure.

Gail laughed. "Survivalists? No. Think more hippie, free love kind of thing. She's lived in the woods her whole life. It's just her and her three younger sisters. Their mother died sixteen years ago, and their dad passed before that."

Bray pondered this new information. "Do you know how old she was when her mother died?"

"Not sure, but from what Bobby told me, it sounds like she'd been a teenager when it happened. She raised her sisters all by herself."

He was outraged thinking of Willow as a young girl with both parents gone, fighting for survival in the woods. "Why didn't family services get involved? They could have died out there all by themselves, especially in the winter."

She nodded. "I'm right with you on that one. I was outraged as well. But look where we are. They have one hardware store, one hotel, and one gas station. They don't have the population for a foster care system." She sighed, "Bobby said the townsfolk did what they could to help. They donated food and clothing even though most times their offers were refused. Her family constantly moves camps in the forest. It's difficult to find them. Apparently, Willow pleaded with the townsfolk to stop searching and leave them alone. She was determined to keep her family together."

"It's surprising they had no relatives to take them in. Don't they have any extended family?"

Gail shrugged. "Not that Bobby knew of. Willow's mother had talked of distant relations up North at one point but never gave any details. The Ashbrook family stayed pretty much to themselves." Gail grinned. "Willow must have made quite an impression. Most of our conversation has been about her."

"Sorry." He said sheepishly. Bray realized how rude he'd been. He hadn't asked Gail anything about herself. Again, his manners had left him. If his mother were here, she'd have his hide.

"Don't worry about it." Gail winked. "So, what's your story?"

Bray was usually a very private person, but Gail was easy to talk to. He found himself revealing things he normally wouldn't have shared with a stranger.

After lunch, Bray dropped Gail back at the hotel. He finished his errands including a quick stop at the post office to pick up a few packages. On the way back to his cabin, he thought of all the things he had learned about Willow and her family. He was even more fascinated than before. She was still a mystery, but after hearing about her strength of character and pride, he wanted to discover everything about her. It wasn't just because she turned him on, although that didn't hurt. She was nothing like the women he had dated in the past. Willow hadn't grown up pampered and entitled. Her life had been hard. But she had survived and kept her family together all those years. Someone that dedicated was rare. Bray made it a point to seek out unique individuals his whole life. His mother said he had an eclectic taste in friends; a politically correct way of saying his friends were strange. He didn't care. Bray liked who he liked and was fiercely loyal. Trust wasn't just a fluffy word that looked good on a corporate chart, it was who he was and what he expected. He'd been disappointed with past girlfriends who didn't get it. But with Willow, something clicked. She was so trusting and down-to-earth. Even with his cynical view of women, he couldn't help but hope this one might be different.

Chapter 9

WILLOW WATCHED FROM the woods as Bray pulled up. She had followed him along the dirt road, going from tree to tree, following his progress back to the cabin. He seemed preoccupied. She wondered if he was thinking about her. He had certainly been on her mind. Her stomach was still in knots about what she had to do. The dread mixed with anticipation confused her even more. Willow had decided to enchant him and make him forget they had ever met. If he was susceptible, she could convince him to do anything, including selling the cabin and moving back to California. Enchantment was an innate ability for her kind. It took effort and training to keep it bottled up. Her mother had warned her about using it on humans, especially the 'men-folk' as she called them. There were stories of men becoming so infatuated, they would stalk a Dryad to her death. Each rejection increased the insane obsession. Willow enjoyed her freedom far too much to be tied to a human. She planned to be extra careful when casting the enchantment tonight. He finished putting up little cameras all around the perimeter of his cabin just as the sun started to set. The blue sky was streaked with pinks and oranges when she walked into the clearing. The colors matched the Rainbow Eucalyptus tree she was there to protect. She felt a pang of disappointment that he would soon be gone. It had been fun spying on him. For this short amount of time, she had enjoyed her job as Guardian. She was not looking forward to going back to her boring routine. Willow wished she had more time to get to know him. But her duty was clear. He was a major security risk. He had to go. At least she would have this one night to remember him by.

Before she had a chance to knock, the door opened. Bray stood holding a shoe.

"I was hoping you would stop by. Come in... Willow Ashbrook."

She stutter-stepped her way into the cabin. He knew her name. She let out a deep breath. *So, what?* People in town talked. No big deal. It would only make it slightly more difficult to wipe his memory.

"Thank you, Brayden Graham." *Yeah, I got your number.* "I thought it would be neighborly of me to come check on you." She watched him take off his other shoe, followed by his socks. She stared at his bare feet. No hooves. No hair. *How exotic.* Why did she find that incredibly sexy? Oh yeah. Maybe because most of the males in the Coconino magical community were Satyrs, Centaurs, or Shifters. Willow forced her gaze from his feet to look around the cabin. "I see you've made changes."

Bray nodded. "Did you know the previous owner well?"

"Jim Miller? Not really. He and my mother were good friends for several years. I used to play on the front lawn when they socialized. It hit him hard when she passed. He visited the cabin a few times after she died, but it wasn't long before he just stopped coming altogether."

Willow gestured to the front of the cabin. "She used to sing on the front porch in one of the rockers while he sketched portraits of her. I never got to see them, but I remember asking. You didn't happen to come across any drawings?"

"No. Sorry. I didn't find anything like that. Although the place was a mess when I first got here, garbage everywhere." He shrugged. "It's possible there could have been drawings in the debris. I wasn't paying all that close attention. I tossed everything."

"It wouldn't have been in the mess."

Bray studied her. He must be curious how she could know that.

"I have a premonition about the two of us."

She quirked an eyebrow.

"I'll bet we'll be as close as Mr. Miller and your mother. Very. Good. Neighbors."

Willow's cheeks turned green. The man was perceptive. She'd give him that.

Bray gestured to the couch in the living room. He must have thought she felt sick. People often made that mistake when she blushed. Her Dryad skin would turn green instead of pink.

She cleared her throat. "Yes, good neighbors would be nice."

Bray came a little closer, invading her space. His body was so much bigger than hers. "I think it would be more than nice."

Willow felt flustered. This human had smooth moves and that deep voice of his kept her completely off guard. She walked to the couch. All the rips had been duct-taped. She started to feel guilty about the level of destruction. Willow played with the hem of her dress when she sat down.

That seemed to distract him. He coughed. "Where are my manners, do you want something to drink? I've got soda, beer. Maybe some wine, or tea?"

"Nothing. Thanks. I'm good."

She looked around at the walls, the floor, the ceiling, where the branches of the tree escaped from the cabin. This was a mistake coming here. Bray's eyes were wide and expectant. They looked like the eyes of a mule deer she had loved as a child. She couldn't do it.

"I should go." She stood.

Bray put his hand on her arm easing her back to the couch. "How about you don't act so skittish around me? I'm not going to bite."

She let out a nervous giggle. He wouldn't bite, but she might. His lips looked delicious.

He rubbed his thumb in gentle circles on her arm as she looked into his deep brown eyes and felt herself falling. Willow tore her gaze away, glancing around the room looking for an exit. When she glanced back, all she could concentrate on were his lips. He was there. Willing. Why couldn't she indulge a little? No one would know. She could have her way with the sexy human. Suddenly, it seemed like a grand idea. She let out a breath and launched herself into his arms. The kiss seemed to take him by surprise, but only for a moment. He responded, licking his tongue along her lower lip, tilting his head for a better fit, and deepening the kiss. When their tongues touched for the first time it was electric, tearing a moan from her lips. She pushed enchantment power into him over and over, making his mind pliable, open to suggestion. His hands were everywhere, rubbing her back, massaging her butt. He couldn't seem to touch her enough. She climbed onto his lap, straddling him, making eager sounds as she rubbed against his length. They were both panting. Willow knew she was stalling, but he tasted so good. With one more roll of her hips, she forced herself to lean back.

"Bray, will you suck my toes?"

His lids were at half-mast, "What?" He shook his head like he was clearing it. He rubbed his thumb over her swollen lips and leaned in for another kiss. She dodged it and licked his throat. He shivered.

"You got some sort of foot fetish?" Bray glanced at her dirty feet and raised his eyebrows. "How about we wash them, first honey, then see how it goes."

She frowned. He should do anything she commanded without question. Maybe her enchantment skills were rusty. They went back to kissing and she pushed even more power into him. This was for her family's protection, even if he kissed like a god. Several minutes later she pried herself away from the kiss.

"Bray." She didn't recognize her own voice, all deep and throaty. "You must forget me. Forget I was ever here."

He laughed. "Not a chance. Those little sounds you make when you rub against me are un-fucking-forgettable." Bray grabbed her hips and started rubbing her back and forth on his length until she moaned. They went back to kissing. She continued to pulse power into him until she grew weak with the effort. Willow was tapped out.

She pulled herself away and glanced around the room while she relearned how to breathe. There. On a side table. She handed him a paring knife.

"Bray. Cut yourself."

Bray's eyes went wide. "Whoa! Is this some sort of test?"

She shuddered in his arms. What was she doing wrong? The confusion must have shown on her face.

"Look," he scratched his head, "I'm sorry but I'm not into that kinky shit. You're a weird chick, but I like you anyway."

She gave his shoulder a shove and stood up. "You think I'm weird?" *No, the enchantment had definitely not worked.* So much for being infatuated.

Bray ran a hand over his face. "I take it we're done kissing?"

She smoothed her hands down the front of her dress. "You got that right." She tilted her head to scrutinize him and frowned. *Why hadn't it worked?* "I have to leave."

His head dropped. "Yeah, I kind of figured."

Bray got up with a sigh and walked her to the door. "Will you come back? Maybe visit again soon?"

She smirked as he half turned, trying to adjust himself discreetly. After what they had been doing, she found it adorable that he was trying to be polite about something like that. Well, at least she had gotten one reaction from him. "We'll see."

Willow sauntered off the front porch. She glanced back over her shoulder when she reached the edge of the clearing. His gaze was glued to her ass. She may not have magically enchanted him, but her assets certainly had him charmed. Willow gave a hip shake. His eyes slid up to her face and he grinned. She blew him a kiss. He caught it in mid-air and put it to his heart. She laughed at the silly gesture and continued her way into the forest.

She needed to find the old TreeAnt, Abraham. Her mother and grandmother used to seek him for counsel. A natural ability for a Dryad had failed on a human. It was unheard of. Did he possess a charm of protection, or was there something more to this human? Willow rarely used enchantment as an offensive weapon. She felt guilty giving commands and essentially taking over someone's will. But maybe with so little use, her skills had faded. That was a scary thought. She went to the nearest pine seeking the quickest path to a creature that had lived for a millennium. He possessed more wisdom than she could ever imagine. Now, if she could only wake him up.

Chapter 10

WHAT THE HELL just happened? Bray had been so excited to get a visit from his backwoods bombshell. She had been ready to leave one minute, then climbing all over him the next. And that kiss. It had leveled him. His whole body felt like an electric conduit the moment her tongue touched his. And by God, that woman could move. He knew lap dancers from San Francisco clubs that could take lessons from her. It had taken everything he had not to rip off her clothes and mindlessly fuck her senseless. The thought was so completely out of character, it had pulled him back from the brink. Bray was a big guy at six feet, not overly muscled, but certainly stronger than this petite woman that drove him mad with lust. If he had let that animalistic need take him over, he was afraid of what would have happened. It wasn't just their physical differences and the threat of hurting her body, but he was used to being in control, and she tore that away from him with ease.

Bray decided to refill the bowls he set out for the animals. As the weather got cooler, he figured they needed extra food, as their normal resources became limited. With the help of some wilderness guides, he had identified several animals that would visit and researched their preferred diet. The last thing he wanted to do was give the little critters tummy aches by giving them the wrong foods. His favorites were the squirrels. Bray had read that the Abert's squirrels usually ate bark and cones from the ponderosa pines, but the ones that hung around his cabin only enjoyed the finest nuts. He found himself once again sitting on an old log having a conversation with the two squirrels that usually showed up as a pair. One had a larger red patch on his back and was a little more outgoing than the other.

"You know, back in San Francisco, women considered me a catch."

The squirrel tilted his head.

"What? You don't see it, huh?" Bray laughed. "I'm a pretty nice guy. Not that I came here looking for a woman. That was the last thing on my mind. But a fling wouldn't hurt. I'm sure you like getting some tail now and again."

The squirrel turned back to him with a nut in his mouth and squeaked a reply.

"Yes. You are a very handsome guy. I'm sure all the female squirrels throw themselves at your feet."

Bray cracked up when the squirrel spun around, puffed out his chest, fluffed his tail, and twitched his ears. The fella obviously liked the compliments. More likely though, he was just responding to Bray's deep voice. Regardless of the reason for the squirrels' continued visits, he enjoyed their company. Whenever he felt lonely or discouraged after failing at a seemingly simple task, he would come out here and commune with nature. All his problems would disappear as he inhaled the fresh pine, felt the soft breeze in his hair, and watched the animals. Today was no different. Apparently, he had done something wrong with Willow but couldn't figure out what. He replayed their interaction, not sure what to make of her odd requests. Suck my toes. Forget I was here. Cut yourself. His logical brain tried to puzzle out her behavior by coming up with all sorts of theories. One idea, she made a bet with someone to see how gullible he was. Or maybe it was a prank for being new to the neighborhood, a sort of hazing. At one point it seemed like a test. Or maybe she had trust issues. He definitely didn't mind strange and was willing to cut her some slack if it was all in fun, but he wouldn't tolerate someone playing mind games.

As he filled the birdseed, he talked to a few birds sitting on branches waiting for him to finish.

"What do you guys think? Is she worth it?"

The birds chirped back and forth. It didn't help answer his question. He imagined they were telling him to just finish already so they could eat. He found a spot in the grass to lie down and observe. One beautiful blue Steller's Jay flew down to the feeder. It watched Bray carefully for several moments, then made a chip-chip-chip calling noise. It was the equivalent of ringing a dinner bell. Several more birds descended from the trees and they fed in a frenzy.

He thought back to his encounter with Willow. In the end, she had seemed genuinely disappointed and frustrated that he didn't do as she asked. He could normally figure things out with logic, but women's motives had always eluded him. Could it be a simple misunderstanding? Maybe these were common phrases in the woods that meant something different than what he thought. In any case, Bray needed to research her further, which meant digging deeper to uncover more about her. His only source of information so far had been from Gail, and she was new herself. The locals would offer a much better resource and hopefully provide some insight.

He continued to go through more theories throughout the day. One of his far-fetched ideas was that she could be a spy and her phrases were codes. He knew how ridiculous it sounded and chalked the whole idea up to his love of James Bond movies. Bray also wondered more about Mr. Miller. He hadn't done much research on the man prior to the purchase. The only information he knew for certain was he had worked with Frank Lloyd Wright as an architect and had designed the cabin. More research on the owner might provide clues on his association with the Ashbrook family. Jim Miller had obviously known Willow's mother quite well. Bray couldn't remember being so energized in a long time. His work hadn't elicited this level of passion in years. This woman and this puzzle had awakened a part of him he thought was long dead. Bray didn't know quite what it was about this particular woman that intrigued him so, but he was eager for their next encounter.

Chapter 11

Finding Abraham was simple. He was in the deepest, darkest section of the forest. He enjoyed his solitude. Waking him, however, would not be easy. She asked him politely to wake. No response. She sang a song of his praises. He hummed along in his sleep. She begged and pleaded for his counsel. Nothing. She scratched his bark and he purred. Willow went down to the river and got a bucket of water and doused his leaves and bark. He shook like a dog after a bath and she stood there soaked to the skin. Grumbling, cold, and wet, Willow sat on the tree's weathered roots and tried to recall her mother's lessons from long ago. She had mentioned something about a knot on his back. She crawled around the base of the TreeAnt and found a small hole. She stuck her hand inside and wiggled her fingers. Abraham let out a roar of laughter.

After his twitching and laughing died out, he turned to face her. "You, my dear, have no patience. Just like your mother."

Willow stood and curtsied before him. "I'm sorry, but I have little time and I need your help."

He sighed. "To endure you must learn, my dear."

"I appreciate your counsel, Oh Wise Abraham. May I ask your forgiveness and humbly ask for guidance?"

His bark eyebrows rose. "Perhaps I was hasty. Your mother may have taught you a few things. And here I thought those lessons were lost on her." He gazed off into the forest absorbed by some memory from the past.

Willow took a seat in front of him. Her mother had told of his penchant for getting distracted. That's probably why she hadn't visited all that often in her sixteen years as Guardian. Luckily, she had donned her mother's necklace before today's visit. The necklace was one of the few treasures she kept in a secure safe under her favorite pine. The necklace contained several gold charms, one of which had a tiny tree with a bell. She shook the charm gently and it pulled his attention back to her.

"So, what is this most important reason for waking my slumber?"

Willow took a deep breath, "My enchantment skills have failed."

It was embarrassing to admit, but if there were an issue, it was her duty to bring it to someone's attention. Especially one that wouldn't judge or make fun of her. She respected Abraham's ability to evaluate a problem without assigning blame.

"Hmm. That is very interesting." He paused in thought. "Tell me more."

She relayed the encounter, breezing over some of the more intimate details.

"Have you tried to enchant anyone else since yesterday?"

"Yes. I caught a Satyr and a Nymph in flagrante delicto and told them to go meditate by the stream." Willow chuckled.

"And they followed your instructions?"

"To the letter. I believe they're still there."

"Perhaps they found the error of their ways?"

"It was Faustino and Maggie."

"Oh well, that is another matter." He pondered again. The silence stretched as she waited.

"Have you thought of the possibility that Mr. Graham could be your eternal soulmate?"

Willow sucked in a deep breath. She had never considered that. "But he's human." She chewed her lip. "How could something like that happen?"

"I have lived a long, long time. In my lifetime, stranger things have happened."

That gave Willow something to think about. "Are you leaning toward that theory?"

Abraham was silent for a long while. "I will think on it."

Willow sighed. Because of a TreeAnt's life span, they did everything very slowly. She would have grandkids before he made a decision on the subject.

"I am glad you stopped by, Willow. There is another related matter we should discuss."

"And what's that?"

"Council is scheduling a meeting to discuss the living arrangements of Mr. Graham."

Willow's jaw dropped. "I hadn't heard about that."

His lips curled into a smile, "You are not listening to the trees, my dear."

She laughed. He was right. "I guess I've been distracted by the stranger."

"Hmm. Yes, I see that." The trees around him vibrated as the wind blew through their branches. He watched them for several minutes before she shook the charm and brought his focus back to her.

"The forest is divided. Most want him gone, they think the risk is too great for an unknown. That group is led by the Satyrs and your sister, Miss Maple."

"She hates that name."

He shrugged his branches. "It is her given name."

"And what about the rest of the forest?"

"The Black Bears and most of the lower creatures stand with Miss Elm. They think the human should stay if he wants to. Her stance is for tolerance. She feels we should not discriminate against the human when he has given us no reason."

"Ellie always roots for the underdog. And I think most of the smaller critters in the forest are being fed by his constant supply of nuts, seeds, and berries." Willow blushed thinking of how they met. She had been no better than the other animals stealing from his snack bowl. Everything about him was tempting.

"And Red?"

"Ah Miss Redwood. I think her exact words were, you should bang him like breakfast, then kick him to the curb."

Willow laughed. "Yeah, that sounds like her."

"I am completely bewildered by your sister's language."

"You and me both."

"Mr. Graham's residence status will be one of the discussion points at this month's Council meeting."

"Where do the TreeAnts stand?" Willow asked.

Abe's eyebrows rose, "You know better than to ask that, Miss Willow." His leaves ruffled, and his roots shifted beneath the soil with unease. "We do not take sides."

She shrugged, "It would make things a lot easier. Everyone looks up to the TreeAnts. You are very wise, and your counsel is much appreciated."

He smiled. "But this new bit of information about a potential eternal soulmate. Hmm. That is very interesting. It could change things."

"Is there a way to know for sure if he is?"

"Yes, but you will not like the answer."

"Why? What do I need?"

"Time."

She groaned. "That's your answer for everything."

"Have you never heard the phrase; time will tell?"

"But I'm the Guardian. I can't wait to make decisions and hope for the best. The security of the forest is my responsibility. Protecting those within it rests on my shoulders."

Willow stood. She felt agitated and didn't wish to be rude to Abraham. But there were things he didn't understand. Her world felt off balance. She needed a clear direction or she was going to lose her shit. He was great at looking at the big picture and offering multiple perspectives. But this was her life. She needed answers, not more questions. Maybe Red had the best idea. Get him out of her system and move on.

As was common with these meetings, they ended with a ritual exchange of power. She took a deep breath and let her hand slide into his bark. Her hand remained merged inside his tree trunk as he chanted in an old language. It always left her fingertips tingling for hours. She never asked what Abraham felt. It seemed impolite to ask. But afterward, he would be completely out of it, like it gave him a buzz. His branches would sway like he was dancing to a song only he could hear, then he would slowly settle into his coma-like state.

When the TreeAnt was sleeping soundly, she left debating what to tell her sisters. By the time she got back to her tree, she decided to keep Abraham's hunch to herself. No reason to pass on mere speculation at this point. She would give it time as he suggested. Willow wondered if wisdom could be catching.

Chapter 12

EARLY THE NEXT morning, Willow came across Bray filling several bowls of nuts close to the forest's edge. The sunlight lit up the cabin and most of the clearing but he had strategically placed the bowls low to the ground and in the shadows. Two squirrels peeked from behind tree trunks staring at the bounty. He started talking to them in that deep voice of his, encouraging them to come closer. She wanted to melt on the spot. Something about his voice was so soothing. She made a few squirrel squeaks to tell them it was safe. He was so excited when the critters came out to steal nuts from the largest bowl. He was wildly taking pictures with his cell phone. She laughed watching his antics. He didn't realize but he was way funnier than the squirrels.

"Who's there?"

Willow walked into the clearing. "Just watching the show."

"I know. Isn't it awesome?" Bray said staring at the squirrels as they danced around the bowl. Willow understood the small squeaks. They had decided to race to see how many nuts each of them could pack away. They had always been super competitive.

"I see you've met Sammy and Dave."

"You named them?"

Willow closed her eyes and thought back to their births. "Actually. Yeah, I did. The two are brothers, littermates. Sammy has the larger patch of red on his back."

"You were there when they were born?"

She nodded.

"That would have been so cool."

They watched in silence for a few minutes. Bray slipped the phone into his pocket. "I'm glad you came back. I was hoping I didn't insult you the other day. It wasn't my intent."

Willow sighed. "I'm the one who should apologize. You're right. I was being weird. That's not how I usually am." She looked up into those dark brown eyes. "I'm not myself around you."

"How about we start again?" Bray held out his hand. "Would you join me for breakfast, neighbor?"

She grinned. "Do you feed everyone you meet?" She slipped her hand into his and they walked to the cabin.

"It does seem to be a pattern lately," Bray laughed, "Although none are as pretty as you."

"Will the food be as sweet as your words?"

He concentrated on her lips, "I'll let you be the judge of that."

He was even more charming today. Willow was pulled into his side as he opened the door. When they got to the kitchen table, it seemed like he didn't want to let her go. She stared up at him, unsure what she wanted. After several moments, he released her and pulled out a chair. Bray brought her a scone and a jar of raspberry preserves.

"Tea?" He asked.

"Why not?"

She selected one of the bags and he poured the hot water into her mug. They sat eating scones and sipping tea in companionable silence. She liked that he didn't feel the need to talk. Most people from town seemed to detest silence, filling any pause with mindless chatter. But this with him felt natural. Willow felt the same level of tranquility the first time they met. It still amazed her she had fallen asleep on the man. She was a good judge of character, and luckily nothing had happened, but having no defense against a stranger. *Scary*. If her powers were failing somehow, she needed to know before it became a security issue. Allowing a human to take advantage of her could be devastating. Willow's mind seized on that thought. He could take all kinds of advantage of her body. His heated gaze promised all kinds of wicked delights. Humans were taboo, but if by some magical chance Bray was her eternal soulmate, well that was another matter.

"So, what are your plans today?" Willow asked.

"I'm not sure. I thought I'd run to town this afternoon. Maybe after a swim in the lake."

"Will you be wanting company?" She asked.

"Which part are you offering?"

She had to ponder that. Going to town other than the monthly craft meeting was highly unusual, but she did want to spend time with him and explore the whole eternal soulmate possibility. "Both."

"Do you have a swimsuit?"

She grinned. "Nope."

"Oh boy." He cleared his throat. "Let's clean up first."

Willow helped wash the dishes, setting them on the rack to dry. He held her hand as they walked down to the shore. Her mouth went dry when he pulled off his shirt. Then came the pants. He kicked them off and stood facing her in snug cotton boxers. They did nothing to hide his erection. She licked her lips.

"You need to catch up."

Forcing her gaze away, she pulled off her dress in one swoop and tossed it to the pile of clothes.

A sharp intake of breath whipped her head back towards him. Her lips curled at his expression. His eyes glittered with hunger.

"Damn."

Her nipples tightened. She could feel his gaze almost like a hot stroke over her skin. Willow suddenly needed to cool off. She ran down the dock and dove in. Bray had rebuilt the thing. It wasn't exactly level, but it was functional. Maybe she could ask the beavers to help fix it. They had been the ones to destroy the original. Willow surfaced to him swearing. He charged down the dock after her. She squealed when he jumped next to her with a splash. Swimming around each other, she stayed purposely just out of reach, evading his grasp. Eventually, she let him catch her and pull her close. Willow stared at his lips, hypnotized. She licked hers. With a groan, he took her lips like a man possessed. She moaned against his, letting her tongue dart out until his lips parted. Willow was just as desperate to touch and taste him. She couldn't seem to get close enough, wrapping her legs around him, rubbing up against him.

He pulled away with a groan. "Would you be doing that if I didn't have my boxers on?"

"Probably not." She ground against him again, throwing her head back. Panting. Loving the friction.

"So, I'm an idiot for trying to stay decent?"

"Actually, you get more points for that. I like that you don't take things for granted. You're safe."

"Safe, huh? Should I be insulted?"

"Don't be. It's an aphrodisiac out here in the woods." She gave him a long, lingering kiss.

"Then call me the Safety god." He roared to the sky with his arms wide.

She giggled amused by his strange outburst. She briefly wondered how many gods he worshipped. Willow was a pagan herself. But safety? Only a human would come up with such a bizarre god. The kiss continued to escalate as they drove each other more and more wild, until she knew they had to stop. An involuntary whimper slipped from her lips as she forced them apart. They panted, sharing breaths. She blinked at him, trying to focus past the lust.

"Come on," Willow gulped in a large breath, "Let's head in."

He kissed her one last time and she wrapped her legs around his waist tighter. Bray grabbed her ass, walking them both out of the water. He lost his footing on a slippery rock and they almost wiped out. At the last second, she released a leg in time to catch them both before falling. She held their combined weight on one leg until Bray got his footing.

"Damn. Your reflexes are fast. And you're a strong little thing, aren't you?"

"You have no idea." She mumbled.

"What was that?"

"It's the wilderness. It toughens up everyone."

"Well, thanks for saving us. I would have been mortified if I'd been the cause of a single scratch to that beautiful body of yours."

"No problem." Willow grinned. "It's only fair. Since you were so distracted by my chest."

Bray looked down at her breasts. They felt heavy under his concentrated gaze. Her rosy pink nipples stiffened.

"Well, there is plenty to distract." He licked his lips like he wanted to taste them. Willow knew she could never allow that, no matter how desperately she wanted it. When aroused, her skin would flush green. There was no way to hide it. The risk was just too great.

They walked back to the cabin hand in hand. Grabbing two towels, he gave one to her and wrapped the other around his waist.

"I'll be right back."

She watched from the window as Bray ran back to the shore and picked up their clothes. He stood still for a few moments staring at her dress and the lake. She wondered what he was contemplating. Was he looking for an excuse to stay naked? She had the same thought as well, but she knew better. Bray was already too tempting. She closed her eyes and imagined if she had slipped down his boxers in the lake. Willow was certain he wouldn't have protested. She shivered thinking of him inside her. Hot. Thick. Pumping.

"What's pumping?"

Willow turned in shock. Had she spoken that aloud? "Uh, nothing."

He handed her the green dress.

"I saw you down by the river. What were you doing?"

"I'm not sure I want to admit it. But I was thinking about accidentally dropping your dress in the water."

"Accidentally or on purpose? And why would you want to do that?" She smirked.

His face heated. "Then maybe you'd stay that way a little longer."

Yes. They had been thinking the exact same thing. "Turn around you perv."

She quickly slipped on her dress, hoping that slight barrier might somehow tame her hormones.

He laughed as he turned his back. "Hey, you're the one who dropped dress and drawers. And by the way, I couldn't find them."

"What?"

"Your drawers."

Willow frowned. Sometimes humans used odd words to describe things. The townsfolk called those words or phrases slang. But she didn't want to seem stupid. "Oh, I'll get them in a bit."

"Please get them now. I can only stay noble so long."

She had no idea what that meant but decided to walk down to the lake. After waiting a few minutes, which she hoped was sufficient time to find 'drawers,' she came back to the cabin.

He invited her out on his front porch to sit and swing for a while. Bray started humming, and just like before she was out like a light.

A few hours later, he woke her. It was a strange sensation not feeling the smooth inner bark of her birth tree. Instead of smelling the damp earth and pine, the only fragrance she could detect was warm, musky male.

"Mmm. You smell delicious." She nuzzled his neck.

He laughed. "I smell of lake water and sweat. I should have showered."

Wash away that heavenly scent that was all Bray? No. She'd much rather he stay just as he was.

"Do you want to head to town? There's a bar and grill if you're hungry."

Feeling more relaxed than she had in ages, she agreed.

They walked into the Roadhouse and were greeted by the bar-keeper who introduced himself as Max. He was a large burly fellow with beefy arms and a scruffy beard. He set them up with a few beers. When they went to order, Bray found out Willow was a vegan. She ended up getting a salad and he settled for nachos after the face she made when he tried to order a burger. Ten minutes into their meal, a regular stopped in and asked the bartender about the new folks. Most of the town knew of Willow and her family by name but few had met her in person.

"So, it took a Cali man to get her out of the woods." The man grinned. "That deserves a beer." He hollered for Max to get them another round. "My name's Chuck by the way."

They both greeted the man and thanked him for the beers. Willow kept the conversation light, careful not to reveal too much. The man seemed nice, but she rarely socialized with men from town. They usually made her nervous. Although, being with Bray seemed to give her a boost of confidence.

"Hunting season just started, so you two need to be extra careful," Chuck said.

Willow thought the warning was ironic since the hunters had more to fear from her. She made a mental reminder to set out more traps for the humans.

After another beer, they decided to leave. Bray pulled Willow close and covered her ass with his large hand, pulling her dress a little lower in the process. Willow watched him intrigued by this show of domi-nance. She didn't know why, but she found that downright adorable.

He got her settled in the truck's cab. The hem of her dress lifted a few inches when he buckled her in. Bray's face turned bright red. Humans really had the most peculiar way of blushing.

"You're not," he took a deep breath, "wearing any."

"Any what?"

"Any underwear."

"Oh that," She shrugged. "Nope. Don't own any."

Bray wiped a hand down his face. He muttered, "You're killing me."

He shut the truck door and walked to the driver's side while Willow puzzled over the expression.

When he opened his door she asked, "Is that what drawers are?"

Bray nodded as he climbed into his seat. He stared at her bare thighs. It made her feel warm all over.

"So, most people wear underwear?" Willow asked.

Bray hesitated and then buckled his seatbelt. "Yeah. Well, I guess. I mean I think so." He looked out the window. "This is a strange conversation." He sighed. "Women usually wear short dresses and no underwear if they want to get laid. It broadcasts they're easy."

"Do you think I'm easy?"

Bray chuckled. "Honey, nothing about you is easy." He gave her a quick kiss. "But I know you're worth the wait."

His words gave her tingles.

"Well, this is my only dress for when I go into town. I hadn't really mentioned it before, but my family and I are nudists."

"Yeah, I heard."

She wanted to do more kissing, but Bray seemed to be lost in thought.

"I have an idea, and I don't want you to take it the wrong way. I know of a small boutique not far from here if you'd like to get a few things. It would be my treat."

She stared at the tattered hem of her well-worn dress. Willow figured if she was going to spend more time in town, she needed to expand her wardrobe.

"What's wrong with this dress?"

"Is this one of those questions where anything I say will be wrong?"

"Probably."

"I just don't want you to be hassled." Bray's gaze seemed to penetrate the thin cotton fabric. "And that dress is way too revealing."

The nerve of this guy. She opened her mouth to blast him and felt pulled into those deep brown depths. His eyes were so sincere. She was compelled to do whatever he wanted. It was as if *he* had the power to enchant *her. How utterly ridiculous.*

She shook her head trying to clear the fog from her brain.

Willow sighed. "Fine. Buy me a few things if you must."

He grinned. "You know, most women are more eager to let a man buy them stuff. But you're not like most, are you?"

"I guess not."

She didn't like being different. It made it difficult to blend in. That's how she stayed safe all these years. Infiltrating town as a human was done to gain information that was essential for their survival.

"Hey," Bray cupped her chin. "The last thing I wanted was to make you feel bad."

"I know."

He gave her a gentle kiss and put the truck in gear.

She looked out the window as the forest passed her by. Bray drove slowly and carefully. Willow hadn't told him about her phobia of vehicles but he seemed to sense her apprehension on the drive into town. The fear was still there but it lessened considerably. On some level, she trusted this man would keep her safe. It didn't make sense but her instincts had never been wrong. Willow wondered exactly what it was about him that made her so relaxed. Did his skin emit a soothing scent? She inhaled deeply. He smelled nice, but she couldn't detect any drug that would cause this reaction. Maybe it was the few beers back at the bar? She tried to recall how she felt before the alcohol and quickly dismissed that theory. Perhaps it was the way he held her hand as he softly rubbed his thumb in circles on her wrist. She focused back on their conversation about clothes. It had always been an issue with the women from town. Willow didn't realize it would be an even greater problem with human men. She decided Bray's expertise in city camouflage could be useful.

The boutique was in a small pink house on the outskirts of Flagstaff.

"How did you come across this shop?"

"I had to make a pit stop on my original drive out from Flagstaff to Bellemont. The gal running the shop is an absolute doll. You'll just love her."

When they strolled into the shop, the woman seemed to recognize Bray immediately and waved. She popped out from behind the counter and rushed to greet him. The woman had bright red frizzy hair and caked on makeup. She wore a billowing skirt of pink and purple scarves and a low-cut black silk blouse showcasing generous cleavage. Willow despised her at once. She scowled as the woman pressed those large breasts against Bray in a tight embrace, leaving him with a red lipstick stain on the cheek.

"I knew you'd be back, sugar." The shopkeeper purred, rubbing his chest with long painted nails.

Bray stepped to the side and the woman's eyes bulged with excitement as she stared at Willow. "And you brought me a customer."

Willow frowned. She didn't understand. Why would this woman be glad to see her? Didn't she want Bray for herself? *Over my dead body, human.* She blinked. Where had that thought come from? Bray put his large hand on the small of Willow's back. She gave him a goofy grin. It didn't look like Bray reciprocated the shop keeper's desire. *Perhaps the human can live.*

"Yes. This is Willow, and she needs a whole new wardrobe. She was recently robbed."

"Oh my god," The shopkeeper exclaimed. "You poor dear."

Willow gave him a puzzled look.

The shopkeeper pulled Willow into an embrace showing genuine concern. This human baffled her. "So, you have nothing, my dear?"

"Um, no, just this." Willow gestured to her tattered dress.

The woman's eyes teared up and she sniffed. "Such a shame. I thought we didn't have that sort of thing out here." She took out a tissue from one of her sleeves and dabbed her cheeks. "Well, I guess there are bad sorts no matter where you go." She twirled Willow around and stared at her figure.

"These should be your size, my dear." She gestured to a rack of clothes. "Why don't you look through some of these and see what grabs you."

Bray relaxed back into the loveseat and watched Willow intently. The shopkeeper stared back and forth between the two, then nodded her head. She approached Bray and whispered in his ear. It made Willow want to scratch her eyes out. *How dare she get close to my man? He's mine, bitch!* Willow took a deep breath, confused by her emotions. She didn't understand where all this jealousy was coming from. It wasn't like her at all. It was as if another personality inside herself was coming alive.

Bray handed the woman a black credit card and her eyes sparkled.

"I've got a few new things that just came in." She pointed to an empty rack in front of a curtained room, "Go ahead and put anything you like over there. I'll be back in a jiffy." Her bracelets jangled as she ran into the back room.

They spent the next few hours trying on outfit after outfit. Willow had originally liked more loose-fitting dresses like the green cotton gown she already owned, but Gigi, the shopkeeper, convinced her to try some form-fitting dresses that had Bray sweating. He sat stiffly on the antique loveseat with a frilly cat pillow in his lap. He seemed determined to say yes to almost everything. Willow even got a few pairs of jeans. She especially liked how they hugged her legs and bottom. Bray seemed quite impressed with the fit as well. It left him speechless. She now had shoes, hats, and jewelry to match every piece of clothing. He had also insisted on a winter jacket she didn't need.

The only thing Bray hadn't gotten to see was the lingerie Gigi recommended.

"Girl, the way that man looks at you. I swear. It could start a forest fire." Gigi fanned herself.

Willow grinned as Gigi showed her another complicated piece of lingerie from Paris.

"Wearing lingerie is not just for men. The anticipation can be a form of foreplay, my dear."

Willow shrugged. "Um, what's foreplay?"

The shopkeeper gasped. Apparently, it was something essential.

"That boy needs a lesson in manners." Gigi left the changing room in a huff.

A few moments later, Willow heard a thwack and a male groan. She peeked from the curtain.

"What was that for?" Bray rubbed the back of his head.

"I expected better of you." Gigi crossed her arms and scowled at him.

"I don't understand."

"I'll let Willow discuss it with you later."

He cleared his throat. "Are you almost finished?"

"Yeah. I'm done." She had no idea how exhausting shopping would be.

After Bray paid for the purchases, they put all the bags in his truck. It took several trips and filled the back cab completely. Willow wondered where she would put all her new clothes. Bray obviously had no clue how she lived. But he was so excited about each new item. How could she refuse? He seemed to love the idea of buying her things. She assumed this was the custom where he was from. Gigi pulled her aside right before they left and reminded her to demand foreplay. She gave Willow a tight hug then turned to Bray and glared.

"If I don't get a glowing report from Willow next time you visit, you'll get more of the same from me, young man." Gigi wielded her antique fan like a weapon.

Bray nodded his head but was clearly confused. "Yes, ma'am."

She pulled him into a big hug. "You're a good boy."

This time, when she pressed her voluptuous body against his, Willow didn't see red. She had gotten to know the woman better and realized it was just her personality. She was overly affectionate with everyone. Gigi smiled wide and waved from the front porch as they drove off.

On the way back to the cabin, they stopped at the local grocery store. Bray decided to make dinner on the grill. Willow was in heaven in the produce section. There were so many exotic fruits and veggies she had never tried. After discovering that, he started grabbing a little of everything, saying they should sample the lot to see what her favorites were. She grinned, flattered by how much he wanted to please her.

Her look of horror morphed into disgust in the meat department, when Bray stopped to order steaks. He frowned at her expression when he put them in the cart. He covered them with a bag of salad as if hiding them somehow made it better. She tapped her foot.

"What gives? I need meat."

She crossed her arms and turned her back. He was so different from her; it was a wonder they got along at all.

Bray turned her shoulders to face him. "How about I promise not to cook it in front of you? We'll stick with just veggies tonight."

Oh no. Those eyes again. Innocent, pleading. How did he do that? How could she refuse? He really was trying. He cursed under his breath and pulled her in for a kiss. His lips were firm and tasted of the berries they had sampled from produce. She ran a tongue over his lips. He was so delicious.

"Please?"

Willow groaned. She nodded, reluctantly agreeing. How could she say anything else? Bray rubbed his nose in the crook of her neck and gave her a love bite to her neck. He gave her a hug, lifting her off her feet, and spun her in a circle. Well, if he was this excited to buy meat, maybe it was selfish to deny him. And if he needed it to survive, maybe they could find a way past the issue. Willow felt herself grinning as he set her down. She barely even noticed the stares from the other shoppers.

At the cabin, Bray started the grill. He prepared eggplant burgers with sweet potato fries. Willow chopped up the veggies and fruits, filling platters and bowls with the variety. After dinner, she sat him on the couch.

"Don't you dare budge from that seat."

Willow wanted to show him a few of the pieces he didn't get a chance to see at the shop.

"Gigi said this piece came from Paris. It looks really complicated with all the laces, doesn't it?"

Bray nodded.

"But look." She put her foot on the couch armrest and displayed the snaps at the crotch of her teddy. "Gigi called it easy access."

He gave a strangled grunt.

She frowned. "I'll try on another."

Bray tried to grab her a few times while modeling the outfits, but she didn't trust herself enough to risk it. The last outfit was skinny jeans and a halter that had Bray swearing. She finally gave in and straddled his lap. His kiss was fierce and demanding, but she loved the intensity, moaning into his mouth as their tongues dueled for dominance. They stayed like that for a long time. Finally, she came up panting for air.

"I'm sorry but it's getting late, and I should really be going."

He ran a thumb over her lips. "Is there anything I can do to convince you to stay?"

He rocked his hips. His erection slid over just the right spot and her eyelids fluttered at the sensation.

"No." Her voice trembled. "But I promise to be back in the morning."

Bray blew out a breath, clearly frustrated.

"Can I drop you off?"

"No need. I live close by."

"What about all your clothes? Will you be able to carry them all?

"Um."

"Unless you want to leave them here?"

He said it a little too quickly, like he had already worked out she would have no place to put them. She wondered if that had been his intention all along.

"Yeah? You wouldn't mind?"

By way of answer, he gave her a scorching kiss goodbye. She left on wobbly knees, grinning all the way back to her tree.

The week progressed with her stopping by every morning for breakfast and them going for a swim. In the afternoon, sometimes they would run through the woods chasing each other. Other times, they would hike for hours and Willow would show him a hidden glen, or a valley of wildflowers. Each new place they went, he approached it with the same fascination. He was like a kid seeing the world for the first time. It made Willow want to show him more. Even though it went against security protocols, she took him through magical portals transporting them to special hidden pockets of land at the farthest edges of the forest. Of course, he had no idea they had traveled hundreds of miles in the blink of an eye. To circumvent security, she would push power into the earth while holding his hand through a rift. He would often be disoriented for a few moments, but would shake it off easily and explore. She enjoyed spending time with him no matter what they did. He especially loved meeting the animals. Willow would talk to them in squeaks, barks, or chirps letting them know he meant no harm. Bray was especially good at mimicking sounds, but since he didn't know the words, his conversations would often confuse the creatures, like when he asked a beaver to build a dam on his head. She had desperately tried to correct the situation between bouts of laughter before the beaver followed through with the odd request.

Of course, in between traveling, they did a lot of kissing. Whenever they would do more, something would inevitably go wrong. Once while they were relaxing under a pine, she went down on him. He had come so hard and screamed so loud that the forest seemed to shake. Bray had laid buck naked in the leaves stretching and Willow had sighed wanting to burn that image in her memory forever. *Her sexy man* lying under one of her favorite pines. She wanted to roll around on him like she did the leaves in fall. He was so adamant about reciprocating and so persuasive with his kissing, she agreed. Bray had rolled her over, kissing down her torso, sucking her nipples, giving little love bites to her hips. When he revealed how much he wanted to taste her, Willow's legs had fallen open in surrender. And his kiss, gods she could still remember when he suckled her clit rolling it on his tongue like the sweetest berry.

She cut him off, pushing him back before she came. Willow had been so close. One more flick of his tongue would have brought her. But she had been lying over a place of great power, and her ties as Guardian had stirred the energy in the earth. Tree roots beneath had started to move and vines had sprouted from her head. Luckily, Bray didn't seem to notice anything odd. The last thing she wanted was for him to see things he couldn't comprehend. She couldn't bear to see him frightened by her true nature. Willow didn't mean to continually tease them both, but she had no choice. There was a reason she couldn't allow herself to come. Unfortunately, she couldn't share that with Bray.

Today, they were in a magical pocket of land, one with a waterfall. The setting was incredibly romantic, and she had barely stopped them in time. They were still breathing heavy when two squirrels descended from the trees to give Willow a message. It was Sammy and Dave. A Sasquatch convention was in the forest and they needed her assistance. There had already been two 'sightings' by humans in the area.

"I'm sorry, Bray, but I have to run."

"Don't tell me it's another club appointment you forgot about?"

She cringed. Willow had used that excuse before when called away on an emergency. It had been happening with more frequency, any-thing from campers polluting the lake, dangerous hunters in the area, beetle damage to elder trees, or even disputes between magical citizens.

Bray shook his head, "I don't understand how you can always be so busy. It's not like you have some demanding corporate job. How much time do you need to devote to your little nudist club? Don't put clothes on. Check. What more is there?"

Willow whipped her head around. She wanted to scream at him, but she bit her tongue. He didn't know just how important her job was. She couldn't tell him. Willow wanted to make him eat those words. Yeah, maybe it had been a bad idea to use 'nudist club' whenever she had to run off. But to most humans, that was a deterrent. They got all weirded out about being naked. Initially, it had been the same for Bray, but now he started asking more questions like he might want to join one of these times. She had no idea what she'd do then.

Willow knew their arguments stemmed mostly from sexual frus-tration. Her nerves were just as frayed as his. When would it finally become too much? He seemed on a razor's edge, but then he would pull back, take a deep breath and give her a gentle kiss, smooth a thumb down her cheek and hold her gently in his arms. Those tender moments where he showed his patience seemed to break down what little defense she had left around her heart. Willow was getting attached, damn it, but she wouldn't—no, *couldn't* allow herself to fall in love. Not with a human. They were forbidden. Council would never allow it. Willow remembered how devastating it had been when she had been denied Lucian, and he had only been a friend with benefits. Bray was starting to become her everything. If she lost him, Willow didn't think she would ever recover.

Chapter 13

THE INSTALLER FROM HughesNet was scheduled to be here any minute. Willow and Bray had just sat down for breakfast when he heard a truck roll to a stop on the gravel. Her eyebrows lifted in question.

"Sorry, but we're about to be interrupted."

There was a knock on the door.

"I'll just be a minute."

Bray opened the door and stepped onto the porch, closing it behind him. The satellite was meant to be a surprise. He wouldn't need to travel to town for an internet connection when he had to work. The more time he spent with Willow, the more he wanted. Two months wasn't going to be nearly enough.

"Do you have the parcel map?" The installer asked.

Bray handed him the map he had gotten from the county assessor's office showing his property line.

"I'll need to take measurements and do some readings before I can give you an estimate."

"No problem. I'll be inside if you have questions."

The installer nodded and went to his truck.

Willow was waiting for Bray just inside the door. Had she been listening to their conversation?

He couldn't keep it a secret any longer.

"The man's here to give us internet service."

She tilted her head. "I didn't know that was possible out here."

"Anything's possible with enough money." He handed her a brochure.

She briefly flipped through the pamphlet.

"I'm not sure I understand. Can you explain how it works?"

"He's going to install a dish and a modem. It will bounce the internet signal from a satellite in space. It means we can spend more time together. I won't have to go back to San Francisco."

Bray pressed Willow against the kitchen counter. So many expressions passed over her face. He expected excitement. Did she realize what he was saying? His lips met hers. He tried to explain without words what she meant to him. She moaned into his mouth, her body going lax. They were interrupted before long with another knock on the door.

"Fuck." Bray looked down at his erection.

Willow grinned. "You started it."

Bray led the installer to the kitchen to discuss his findings.

"At least a dozen pines will need to be removed for satellite reception." The installer said, showing Bray the paperwork with his notes.

A teacup rattled in the sink, and Willow turned around. He hadn't thought she was listening.

"What do you mean removed?" Willow asked through gritted teeth.

"Uh. You know. Cut them down." He scratched his head looking to Bray for help.

The man glanced back at Willow and his face paled.

Bray spun around in his chair. Willow was giving the man a death stare that sent shivers down his spine. She didn't look sad or disappointed, Willow looked downright furious as if the man had contemplated murdering her whole family.

Suddenly, she grabbed the man. She hoisted the large man from the chair, twisting his arm and pushing him out the front door. Willow literally tossed him on his ass.

The installer sat on the porch clearly confused about what just happened.

He scrambled to his feet. "Now wait just a minute."

"We aren't interested," she yelled before slamming the door in his face.

Bray watched the scene with bewilderment. He had never seen Willow so fired up about anything. It was sexy as hell. She was breathing heavily. Her hazel eyes turned icy blue right before she pounced. She backed him to the tree in the living room. She kissed him with such ferocious urgency. He hardly noticed the vines from the tree getting wrapped around his wrists. Without warning, she slipped her hand into his jeans and started stroking his cock.

"You will promise me, Bray. Right here, right now. You won't cut down any trees." She punctuated each word with a stroke.

His eyes rolled back in his head. He pulled at the vines. He couldn't move. She had his body pinned. Willow made him repeat the promise. She brought him to the brink over and over, stopping him just shy of climax. She squeezed the tip when he bucked his hips.

"Not yet." She whispered.

"Please." He begged.

He had no idea what had come over her, but this take-charge woman turned him on like nothing else ever had.

"I'll do whatever you ask. Fuck, Willow. Just let me come." Bray pulled at the vines, but they held him secure. He would have vowed anything in that moment.

He watched her eyes change color, blue then green, brown then gold. It was mesmerizing. Maybe it was the accent lights in the cabin. He didn't know and didn't care. She had reduced him down to one giant ball of throbbing, pulsing need, mindless with lust.

Satisfied, she finally brought him. He came harder than ever before. He felt the cabin tremble beneath him. It felt like an earthquake, but that couldn't be right. It was just his imagination and the most powerful orgasm he had ever experienced. When he could breathe again, Bray was anxious to reciprocate. She released the vines from his wrists and pushed him to the couch.

"Stay."

He didn't know if he could move anyway.

Willow stormed from the cabin, and even that turned him on. He sat on the couch, sprawled where she left him. He waited half an hour for her to return before he realized she wasn't coming back.

The next day she showed up, acting as if nothing had happened. Every time he tried to bring it up, she would change the subject. Finally, she warned him to leave it alone if he ever wanted a repeat. That did it. He shut up. They finished the evening back at the tree. He even got permission to touch her as well, not that he was allowed to bring her to climax. But he had learned how to push her buttons over the last few weeks. Bray knew exactly what made her just as mindless. He wanted her to beg. He got her so close.

"Stop."

She grabbed his hand, pulling it from between her legs. They both watched as her juices dripped from his fingertips. Her hips writhed. Bray had her upper body pinned to the tree. Willow buried her face in the crook of his neck and groaned. Leaves had fallen into her hair and her skin gave off a green glow from one of the accent lights in the cabin. Again, he felt the trembling of the earth beneath them. He wondered briefly if the generator line ran under the tree roots.

Another week passed with more of the same. He had quickly learned what drove her crazy, paying attention to the smallest detail. A sharp intake of breath, a squirm, a groan. He made a mental note of everything. He brought her to that edge again and again, but she would always make him stop. He didn't understand. Teasing was fun and all, but with no release? No, thank you. At least when Willow teased him, she would eventually allow him to come. In fact, she usually got him off multiple times a day. He had never been that sexually active before her. There was just something about her that always kept him primed. She had this sensual way of moving. He'd get a whiff of her lavender-scented skin and grow hard.

One time while exploring a new part of the forest, they swam together naked by a waterfall. He had been desperate to taste her and convinced her to lay back on the shore. The romantic locale, her scent, her taste, everything had overwhelmed his senses. He had feasted between her thighs. He stiffened his tongue, going in and out of her pussy. Unconsciously, his hips moved in a rhythm simulating sex. The noises she made were so fucking hot. He wondered if he could come like this, just from her taste, grinding his cock into the earth, spilling his seed on the dirt. Would she be disgusted, or would it turn her on as much as it did him? He could feel her core tightening. This was it.

"No." She pushed on his head.

He growled with frustration.

Willow stared at his face, clearly frightened by what she saw. He must look wild. Bray felt like an animal. His fist hit the dirt. She turned her head to the side, refusing to look at him. Fuck. Was she scared he might hurt her? Each time she denied herself it seemed to deepen the void between them. When would she trust him? Bray wondered how much more he could take before doing something he'd regret.

Chapter 14

ON TIPTOES, WILLOW tried to reach the tall birdhouse feeder. It was one of many Bray had around his property. He built them himself, and it showed. She couldn't decide if the garishly bright paint distracted or enhanced the mistakes. The ramshackle little houses were askew, but the trays for seed were level and the holes were a good size for most small birds in the area. She was trying to refill the seed on the tray without spilling it everywhere. Willow had already chirped she would be done soon to the birds anxiously waiting in nearby trees. Bray was bringing the last bag of seed to finish the trays. His heavy footsteps abruptly stopped halfway across the clearing. She glanced over her shoulder. He was staring at her. She followed his line of sight. Her dress had ridden up. She cleared her throat. He grinned. They finished filling the rest of the trays and headed inside for breakfast. It was always done in silence, a ritual dance of movements that had become routine in such a short time. Bray seemed to understand her need for ceremony in everything she did. He would start the teapot as she cleared off the kitchen table. He would grab cups from the top shelf while she grabbed the teabags. She would get the scones and preserves, and he would be there with the plates and a knife. He would pass her a piece of fruit, and she would cut it into bite-sized pieces. He would hand her the platter, so she could arrange the pieces just so, while he rinsed off the cutting board. Then, they would both sit down and talk about their plans for the day. Bray seemed especially impatient this morning, rushing through the steps.

Willow took a seat at the table. Bray was vibrating with energy. He seemed ready to blow. "Go on already. You're about to explode."

He smiled. "I pick up my friends from the airport on Friday."

Willow looked down at her plate concentrating on her scone. She didn't want him to see the disappointment. It made sense he would want to spend time with friends, especially if they were making a special trip out. She felt guilty about not wanting to share him.

"How long are they staying?" She tried for enthusiasm, but her voice fell flat.

He leaned over and lifted her chin. She was forced to gaze into his warm brown eyes so full of concern. "Why the glum face? I was about to ask if you wouldn't mind inviting your sisters over for a party."

Did that mean he wasn't choosing his friends over her? And meeting them was a big deal. But her sisters? They were wild and certainly distracting. They could easily entertain his friends leaving her with more alone time with Bray. But how would her sisters react? They thought she had been actively sabotaging his stay this whole time. Well. She guessed they would find out the truth sooner or later. Making up her mind to convince them, she gave Bray a tentative smile. "Yes. I'll ask them. I'm sure they'll want to meet your friends."

"I already know you too well. What's wrong?"

She blew out a breath. He did know her, more than she seemed to know herself lately. "Well, you might find my sisters a bit odd. But they love a good party." She patted his chest. "Don't worry. Your friends will love 'em." She gave him a peck on the cheek and stood turning her back on him while reaching for a napkin. "So," she cleared her throat, "when do they leave?"

Bray grinned and stood behind her, sliding his arms around her, hugging her from behind. "You're already thinking of how to get me alone again?" He put his chin on her head. "I like how you think." She felt the growing erection at her back, knowing exactly what was on his mind. "Don't worry. They leave Sunday night."

She sighed. Just a few days. She could manage that. He started nibbling on her ear and she suddenly couldn't remember why she had been worried. Her body always responded to his touch. He turned her around and took her lips, lifting her hips onto the counter. He thrust against her rubbing his erection against her clit in slow hip rolls. She locked her legs around his waist and held on for the ride.

He was nothing like her past lovers, always so aware of everything that turned her on. She didn't have to tell him anything, he just knew. Her previous sexual encounters had consisted of wild ruts behind bushes, barely any words spoken, only grunts and demands. No wonder she had stayed away from males for so long. With Bray, she felt cherished. He would bathe her feet or wash her hair, scrubbing the dirt away and massaging until she groaned. He would tease and tickle. They would play, chasing each other in the woods or around the cabin. She loved when he finally caught her. He would always make it worth her while.

When she was a teenager, she had been fascinated by the moonlight. She would follow it as it danced across the water or hid and then reappeared in between the trees. That's how she now looked at Bray. He was her mysterious moonlight and all wanted to do was to dance beneath him forever.

She closed her eyes and forced herself to push away. Each time took more effort to stop before she climaxed. They were both panting. His erection visibly throbbing between them.

He groaned and rested his chin on her head. "I know, sweets. Not yet."

She felt like a fool to deny them both again and again. He desperately needed release. Willow opened her mouth to offer a blowjob. He put a finger to her lips before she spoke.

"I'm good."

She glanced at his erection and raised her eyebrows. He shook his head.

"Yes, you are good." She gave him a quick peck on the lips and they hugged holding their bodies slightly apart. Willow realized that her willpower was dwindling. It seemed only a matter of time before she gave in and they had sex. When that happened, their relationship was doomed. He would see her for what she truly was, and he would leave. Funny how chasing him away had been her original plan. Now, she would do anything just to keep him.

Willow stood in her mother's favorite glade waiting for her sisters. She had sent messages via squirrel to meet at sunset. She was surprised at how nervous she was to talk to them about Bray. Willow greeted them all with a hug, and they took their places on the ground around a low flat rock table.

Once they all were seated, Willow stood. "Thank you for meeting me here, sisters. It is with great honor that I greet thee."

"Bag it, sis," Red snapped, "Give us the low-down. Why are we here?"

Willow shook her head. "Why must you fight tradition?"

"Maybe I was just born this way," Red replied. She popped something in her mouth.

"Is that gum?"

She blew a bubble. "Yep. You want some?"

Willow looked up to the sky and shook her head.

Ellie giggled. "I'll take a piece."

Willow glared.

"Uh. Never mind." Ellie withdrew her hand from the stick of gum slowly.

"Why did you call us forth, sister?" Mae asked.

At least one of her sisters followed customs. Willow had chosen this glade for a specific reason. It held special meaning. It was steeped in energies from the past. The earth vibrated with her mother's energy. Willow could sense it all around the glade. Obviously, her sisters didn't feel the energy quite like she did. It may have been stronger for her because of her role as Guardian. She had never asked her sisters what they felt here. If she were honest, it probably had more to do with the fear of reliving the memories of that fateful day. This place was where everything had changed. They had all felt their mother die and the disconnect with the forest until it had chosen a new a Guardian.

"Well, girls, the reason I asked you here is to let you know, I've decided to let Bray stay at the cabin."

"What?" Mae hissed. "Why this drastic change?"

"Because she's getting some." Red grinned. "And it's about damn time."

Ellie's eyes went wide. "You and the human are doing the nasty?"

"We are not doing any such thing." Willow met their gazes. She wasn't going to lose the upper hand. She squeezed her temple fighting off a headache. "And even if we were, that wouldn't change a thing." She stood straighter, "I am the Guardian of the Coconino National Forest and I say he is not a threat. I have gotten to the know the human through observation and interaction and have determined him harmless."

Mae immediately started sputtering about security, Ellie grinned, and Red held up her hand for a high-five.

Willow stopped Mae's rants holding up a hand for silence. "This is not up for debate. My decision is final. Bray can stay if he wishes. He will not hurt our sacred tree."

"But he could see things and tell others!" Mae exclaimed. "They could hunt us."

"Your fear of the unknown blinds you, my sweet sister." Willow shook her head. "You see dangers where none exist. The world is not filled with villains ready to destroy us. You need to stop worrying so much. I won't let anything like that happen."

Mae's lips thinned, and she crossed her arms. Her sister didn't like it, but she was done arguing. Mae knew just how stubborn Willow could be when she put her foot down.

"With that settled, I wanted to let you know that Bray is throwing a party. His friends are coming out for the weekend and he wants to meet you all. You don't have to go, but I'd like you to be there. It's important to me."

"How hot are his friends?" Red asked.

Willow shrugged. "I have no idea. Does that matter?"

Red gave her a duh look. "Hotness is the single biggest selling point." She closed her eyes in concentration, "We know that Bray's got the goods. I'm going with statistics that he has at least one hot friend. I call dibs. I'm in."

"Bray is really nice," Ellie said. "Look at all the things he does for the creatures of the forest. He feeds them, and he's careful what food to put out. And he picks up his garbage and he's mindful of fires."

Mae rolled her eyes. "Yeah, a regular hero. He hasn't burned or trashed the place yet. Let's give him a gold leaf."

"You know, Mae, you are what the humans call a Debbie Downer." Red put a finger to her lips, "But I think I'll call you Maple Moaner from now on."

Mae launched herself across the table and started pulling Red's hair. "Don't ever call me that name."

"What, you too good for your given name?" Red put Mae in a headlock and started gave her noogies. "Tell me your name, little sister. Come on. Say it. Ma-ple Moan-er."

"Enough." Willow separated the sisters pushing power into them. She normally didn't discipline, but she wanted peace.

"Mae's just depressed because she hasn't seen Faustino in almost a week," Ellie interjected.

"Oh shit." Willow had forgotten all about her enchantment. It should have worn off by now. She hoped.

"That's not like you to swear." Mae chastised. "That's more a Red thing."

"Fuck off." Red gave Mae the finger.

She gestured. "See."

"I, uh, just forgot to do something. So, do you agree to come to the party?" Willow asked.

They whispered together for a few minutes. They came out of the huddle and Mae replied, "Yes, of course, sister. We'll be there for you."

"Speak for yourself," Red snickered, "I'm there for the hot guys."

Willow shook her head.

"And wear traditional Festivus attire. This is an important celebration to welcome Bray."

Willow could hardly wait to tell Bray the good news. She bid her sisters goodnight and headed to the stream to check on Faustino and Maggie. She had to undo the enchantment before her date with Bray that evening. He planned to show her a special box of X game that his friends back home worshipped.

Chapter 15

Bray left Willow at the cabin decorating for the party. He gave her a quick kiss before heading to the airport promising to be back in a few hours with his friends. It had only been three weeks since he had moved to the cabin, but it felt like a lifetime. The cabin purchase had originally started as a vacation property. A place to come when he needed to get away from it all. Now, he wasn't sure he ever wanted to leave. If things worked out with Willow, he wanted a way to extend his stay. He tried setting up a satellite as a way to work remotely. That had been a disaster. He recalled the installer's fateful visit a week ago and how Willow had responded. His cock grew hard thinking of how she had convinced him to her point of view. He blew out a breath, forcing his thoughts from Willow's luscious body and back to the road. It didn't take long to drive to the tiny airport. He found a parking space and checked the flight status. While waiting for his friends to arrive, he thought about his life in San Francisco. From most people's point of view, it looked like he had it all; a beautiful condo with a stunning view of the bay, a prestigious office, and a position of power within a growing IT firm. He wore designer clothing, drove luxury sports cars, and went to glamorous parties. But none of it mattered. He had given his whole life to his career, and his job was demanding. His social life consisted of work events and his closest friends were from his own company. Bray didn't realize how much he had isolated himself until he took a step back. He hadn't been living. Bray was just going through the motions. Then he imagined his sexy neighbor waiting for him back at the cabin. There was no comparison. His world had been dull. His life was a monotonous rhythm until she had come into it and changed everything. Being with her felt right, like she was the missing puzzle piece he had searched for his entire life.

The flight from San Francisco to Flagstaff was about four hours including a layover in Phoenix, but Bray's friends made it seem like he had moved to another country. They loved giving him shit. It was good to see them again. On the drive back to Bellemont, Bray described Willow's exotic beauty and her odd sexual hang-ups. They were excited to see the cabin he had purchased on a whim, but they were more interested in the woman. The one he couldn't stop talking about.

"You can't make her come?" Nick asked. His lips curling in amusement.

"I'm not the one with a problem. She keeps stopping me."

He raised his hands. "Whatever excuse you want to give man. I'm not judging." Nick chuckled.

"Fuck you." Bray grinned. He missed the banter with the guys.

"Are you sure she's into it? Maybe she's faking?" Michael asked from the backseat.

"Speaking from experience?" Nick asked Michael.

Liam laughed when Michael slapped Nick in the head.

"Hey." Nick rubbed his head making his hair spike up at weird angles.

Nick pursed his lips. "Actually, it was a good question."

Bray thought about her responses. They always seemed genuine. "Trust me, guys. She's all hot and heavy, grinding on me. Willow is totally into it. She tells me when she's close. And then bam, she makes me stop."

"Could she be a virgin?" Liam asked.

"I hadn't thought of that," Bray said. "I guess it's possible."

"What about pregnancy?" Michael asked. "If she lives off the grid, she's probably not on birth control."

"Nah, I don't think it's that. We haven't gotten that far."

"Not wanting to orgasm could be a fear of losing control," Liam said. "Maybe she needs a few therapy sessions."

"What if she thinks if you make her come, then you'll want sex," Michael said. "Have you talked to her about it?"

"No. I'm trying to be patient."

"Fuck patience, dude." Nick slapped him on the shoulder. "You need to up your game. Change your moves. If she's got a hang-up, get her past it. Fuck some pansy-ass therapy and getting into your feelings crap. If you want her, take her. Women respond to that shit."

Nick did have smooth moves with the ladies. Maybe he had been playing it too cool, not wanting to pressure Willow, allowing her to retreat instead of pushing her forward.

"Thanks for your input, guys. Willow..." He sighed. "Well, she's special. I don't want to screw this up."

They continued to give him advice on the drive. Some more useful than others. They enjoyed ribbing each other and poking fun, but he had a few good suggestions by the time they arrived back at the cabin. He parked the truck, heart pounding, desperate to see her. His friends chuckled when he jumped out of the truck calling out her name.

Nick elbowed Michael. "Dude's got it bad."

His friends rounded the cabin and came to an abrupt halt. Willow was setting the table. She wore the same green cotton dress she had worn the first time they met. He thought she had thrown it out after he bought all the new outfits. It must be really comfortable, he mused. She had torn the dress even shorter. There was fringe at the bottom with small wooden beads tied to each piece. It framed her ass perfectly. The clacking of the beads and the sway of her hips was hypnotic. He wasn't the only one staring.

He elbowed Nick hard in the gut. "Stop ogling my girlfriend."

He rubbed his mid-section. "Sorry, dude." Nick laughed. "I can't help it. She's got an ass that defies gravity." He lowered his voice, "My research is purely scientific."

Liam chuckled.

Michael patted Bray's shoulder. "Come on. You know us. Even Nick here isn't going to poach. You've made it clear she's off-limits."

Bray rolled his shoulders. "Yeah, I know." He shook his head. Nick was such a hound dog, but he knew the score. All three of them could be trusted. They wouldn't try to steal her, so why did he have this overwhelming feeling of jealousy? It had happened a few times in town as well. Some local would gaze at her with lust and he would lose it, wanting to level the guy. Willow would hold him back saying how adorable he was when he got all riled. She didn't like confrontations and was quite good at distracting him and redirecting his energies.

He walked over to Willow with a grin. She had braided lavender flowers into her long platinum blonde hair. Bray barely stifled a sigh when she grinned back at him. He held his arms out and she jumped into them giving him a big kiss.

"I missed you." She whispered in his ear. She leaned around him to look up from long lashes at his friends.

"I'd like you to meet Willow."

Liam held out his hand. She ignored it and set a vine wreath on his head. Since he was only a few inches taller than her, it wasn't too difficult. She gave him a kiss on the cheek and said, "Welcome."

Liam's cheeks turned red. She went up to Michael and did the same to him. But when she went to Nick, she looked up and up at his six-foot-five frame.

"Oh my, I'm going to need help."

Nick grinned and took a knee in front of her. He stared at her chest, specifically her erect nipples as she set the wreath on his head. She gave him a kiss and turned back to the buffet table.

Michael whacked him in the back of his head. "Knock it off. Bray's gonna blow."

His face heated. Even though Bray knew Nick would never try anything, he still wanted to kick his ass. He watched as Willow leaned over the table setting out another dish. Her breasts strained against the soft cotton; nipples clearly visible. Why the hell wasn't she wearing a bra? He took a deep breath remembering that until very recently she hadn't owned any. Maybe they were uncomfortable. He never thought to ask.

"Sorry, dude," Nick said. "They were just there. Front and center. Hard to miss." He held up his hands and backed away.

"Well, keep your eyes to yourself," Bray said through gritted teeth. "She's mine."

Bray had never felt so possessive. He wanted to pound his chest and mark his territory. That reaction, so unlike himself, pulled him back to his senses.

"Yoo-hoo, boys."

The guys turned as one to see three women stroll from the woods.

"I assume your sisters?" Bray asked Willow.

She smiled. "I'm so glad they took my advice and dressed for the occasion." She sprinted over to them with a squeal of delight.

His friends all had different looks of shock. He couldn't blame them, the four sisters now all standing together giggling and bouncing in their excitement represented a Charlie's Angels assortment of eye candy. Willow with her platinum blonde hair was the shortest of the bunch at five-foot-two in her pale green mini dress. She hugged a dark brunette a few inches taller than her. The girl's dark brown hair was plaited in braids and she wore a bikini made of fall leaves of red and gold. The amber eyes that flashed in their direction held a wealth of suspicion. Willow didn't seem to notice and hugged another sister. This one was much taller with tiny pink flowers woven into her long golden locks. Her outfit consisted of bright flower pasties and a bikini of ornamental kale. Willow snagged a leaf from her sister's behind and munched happily as the last sister gave her a bear hug. This sister was six feet tall with bright red hair and wore nothing more than muddy handprints covering her essentials. It looked like backwoods body paint. Bray wondered about the family dynamic. Were they all adopted? Or at the very least, all had different fathers? Their appearances were so vastly different from one another. Not just the hair and eye color but their features. Bray wondered if he should broach the subject with Willow or if it was another taboo subject she didn't want to discuss. The woman had a lot of secrets.

"I wonder what they would have worn if Willow hadn't made a suggestion," Michael commented under his breath.

Nick snickered, "You don't see me complaining."

Liam laughed. "Like you ever would."

The redhead looked in their direction and the men took a step back; all except Nick. That woman had man-eater written all over her. She gave Nick a wicked grin and her eyes glittered. He had the body of an athlete even though he was a geek at heart.

She looked back at Willow. "Come on, sis. Give us the intros."

"Of course." She dusted mud from her dress where Red had hugged her. "This is Bray and his friends Michael, Liam, and Nick. These are my sisters Red, Ellie, and Mae."

Red walked up to Nick. "So, you like my outfit?"

"What?" Nick asked, but then he grinned as he watched her spin around showing off the extra-large male handprints painted on her overly endowed chest and ass.

She grabbed his hand and held it up against hers. "You'll do."

"What?"

She smirked. "If I go swimming, my outfit will wash off. I'll need help putting it back on."

"Come on, girls, let's see what's on the menu." Red slid her hand down the front of Nick's chest, her fingertips stopped just above his belt buckle. He held his breath as she held his gaze for a few moments.

"I'm hungry." She licked her lips seductively, then abruptly turned and sauntered over to the buffet table and grabbed a plate. Her sisters followed.

Nick stood there, frozen, staring after her. Bray thought it was comical since Nick was never at a loss for words. Red was so bold and outrageous. He may have finally met his match.

Nick let out his breath on a whistle. "Willow's sisters are smoking. Especially Red. I thought she was going to go for the goods, you know?"

Liam sighed. "You always were a lucky bastard."

"And Ellie. She could be a model." Michael said.

Nick grinned. "I dare you to take a leaf from her kale bikini."

Liam laughed. "I double dare you."

"Come on, guys. These are her sisters," Bray begged. "Don't embarrass me in front of Willow. I live here now, and I like her, a lot."

Michael frowned, "This is your vacation cabin, right?" He gave Bray a shove. "You're not moving here, right?"

Bray shrugged.

Liam and Michael both gave him equal looks of curiosity. He knew this wasn't his normal behavior and their stares made him start feeling guilty about taking the time off. Then his gaze followed Willow and his mind blanked. They all took a seat on the lawn chairs he had set out earlier. Willow looked back at him as she whispered some secret to her sisters. His buddies had stopped talking and they all watched in silence as the girls filled their plates and headed back to the group. The girls looked around but there weren't enough chairs. Bray had forgotten to go back into town to purchase more. It had been on his list, but he had gotten sidetracked making out with Willow earlier in the day and ended up leaving late to pick up his friends from the airport. He felt a twinge of guilt, but then stared at Willow's lips and decided hospitality was overrated.

Red approached Nick's chair. "Do you mind getting dirty?"

"What?" Nick asked with a confused look on his face.

"Can I sit on your lap?" She gestured to their little group. "Get with the program, Nick. We're out of chairs."

He moved his hand to the side and she plopped down on his lap and wiggled around. He cleared his throat. "Are you comfy?" His voice cracked.

She looked at him and lifted his chin. His gaze refocused from her chest up to her deep green eyes. "Well, since you asked. No, I'm not. Lose the jeans."

"What?"

"You say that word a lot, you know. Are. You. Slow?" Red knocked on his head and studied him for a moment.

Nick shook his head. Bray was betting no one in his entire life had ever said those words to him. He was a brilliant engineer, even though he looked more like a line-backer. He frowned. "No. I'm not slow."

Red wiggled a little more on his lap. "Your zipper's digging into my hip. You want to make me more comfortable? Lose. The. Pants."

He looked around at the other guys with a bewildered expression. Liam and Michael were both silently laughing. Bray just shrugged.

Nick got a determined expression and stripped off his jeans avoiding all eye contact as he reseated her on his lap.

She wiggled a little more on his lap and his snug briefs got tighter. She leaned against his chest rubbing the soft cotton of his t-shirt. "Ah. That's so much better."

Nick looked almost in pain. He held her hips still.

Michael cleared his throat. "I think I'll get some salad?"

Ellie stood and stuck her butt in his face. "You want some kale?"

Michael grinned and stole a few leaves from her backside. "I really like your family, Willow."

She smiled back at him. "Thank you." She set out a tray of fruits and dressings on the small patio table in front of him and handed him a plate. "I raised my sister to have impeccable manners."

Nick and Liam got up with Bray to check out the buffet table. Their expressions were equally disappointed. Bray couldn't really blame them. He couldn't tell what half the dishes were, even though he had gone shopping with Willow to pick up all the supplies. Some of the food looked like vegetable patés, or maybe casseroles. A potato-salad-like dish looked somewhat appetizing, except for the tint of green. The other half were bowls filled with fresh fruits, chopped veggies, and nuts. At least those were recognizable, along with a single bag of chips, his only contribution to the meal. Willow had been adamant about one thing. No meat. Her sisters were all vegan. She had persuaded him during a weak moment, and he had agreed to let her plan the menu. Looking at the table before him, he wondered how she had convinced him. He spied her picking up something that had fallen from her plate.

Her dress hiked up to reveal the cleft of her ass. She was wearing a silk thong. One he had bought her, and now wanted to remove. Oh yeah. Now he remembered why he agreed. That body of hers could make him do anything. He reluctantly turned back to his buddies.

"What's with the rabbit food?" Nick griped. "Where's the steak, man?"

"Or even hot dogs?" Liam grated. "You got stuff in a cooler waiting to grill?"

He looked so hopeful Bray was sorry to disappoint. "Look guys, Willow's family is vegan. It would be impolite to eat meat around them."

The guys groaned.

Liam grumbled. "Not cool man, we came all the way out here. No steak, no ribs. This is so wrong."

Bray reached down to the cooler and pulled out a couple of beers. He handed them to his friends, "Would you rather I ask them to leave?"

"No." Nick said quickly. "I can live with this," He gestured to the table and winked, "if it means I get a lap dance from a hot redhead, I can suffer."

Once they filled their plates, Bray plugged his phone into the stereo system and selected his '80s playlist. Maneater started playing on the way back to the chairs.

Liam grinned. "It's your lap dancer's theme song."

Nick chuckled, picking up Red with one arm and reseating her on his lap. You could tell she wasn't used to being tossed around.

She squirmed trying to get comfortable, but Bray figured it had more to do with getting a rise from Nick. His friend's pained expression said he was fighting an erection and failing. She gave him an innocent stare and asked sweetly, "What?"

He pinched her ass and she squealed.

The rest of the group ate their food with random chatter about the weather and what they wanted to do over the weekend.

"I'm up for a dip in the lake." Nick wiggled his eyebrows at Red. She punched him in the shoulder.

"How about you, Michael?" Nick asked. "What do you want to do?"

"I'd like some more salad." Michael looked hopefully at Ellie.

She promptly came over and shook her ass over his plate. His face turned red. "Uh thanks, Ellie. That's plenty." The kale was completely gone and in its place was a string bikini. She only had two flowers and a leaf covering her essentials. He took a big bite of his salad trying not to choke.

Ellie kneeled in front of him and licked her lips. "It looks like you have the last of the raspberry sauce in your bowl, can I have some?"

He rested the salad bowl in his lap. Michael nodded. She kneeled between his legs, searching for the berries at the bottom of the bowl. She swirled the leaf around scooping up the dressing. Ellie munched in bliss then sucked her fingers clean. She moaned. "That is so good."

Michael grinned at Bray. "Best. Party. Ever."

Bray glanced at Liam and Mae. They were both incredibly shy. They sat on opposite sides of the circle avoiding eye contact. Well, at least two of his buddies seemed to have hooked up.

Willow was offering the guests drinks when an overly loud, inebriated group walked from the woods.

One yelled, "Mind if we crash your party?"

"Noooo." Willow moaned. "You didn't invite them." She turned to her sisters.

Mae shrugged. "You said to make it a party to remember."

Bray came over to her, "Is everything ok?"

Willow's smile fell flat. "Of course." Her shoulders were stiff. "It looks like my sisters invited more...people. Yay." She mumbled.

Bray smiled, "The more the merrier, right?"

Mae laughed. "I like your spirit." She chucked him on the shoulder and went back to the buffet table waving the group over. "Come get some grub."

Bray frowned. Mae didn't seem quite so shy anymore. And why would Willow be upset? They seemed nice enough, albeit a little rough around the edges. After going through intros and getting to know everyone, he thought the Bacchus brothers were a riot. They passed around their flask of "moonshine wine" and the party started to really liven up. Most of the women wore see-through dresses that looked more like nightgowns. They also wore leaves, flowers, or twigs in their hair in different styles. The only woman wearing regular clothes was the Bacchus sister, Bella. She wore painted-on jeans, clunky boots, and a low-cut t-shirt. The simple attire did nothing to hide her overly curvaceous body. Bella took an instant liking to Liam much to everyone's surprise. She was flirting with him hard. He stammered responses glancing at his friends for help.

Nick leaned in and whispered, "Just roll with it, dude."

Bray got up to wheel the cooler closer to the group. He overheard confusing conversations as he passed out the beers.

Willow whispered to Red, "How did you get everyone to wear clothes?"

She laughed, not bothering to be quiet, "We raided a GoodWill truck on its way into Flagstaff, but don't worry, sis. No one saw a thing. The driver will only remember getting lucky with a hot redhead at a truck stop."

Bray's eyes went wide. Were these people a part of her nudist club? Just how many were there? Maybe he could finally get some info on what they all did.

"Are you part of a nudist colony?" Bray asked the group in general.

Several Bacchus brothers looked at one another with confusion. They all wore jeans, t-shirts, and clunky work boots just like Bella.

Red guffawed. "We aren't a cult, if that's what you're thinking, Bray." She stretched, wiggling in Nick's lap. "We're just fun-lovin' creatures of the forest. No duds required."

Willow's cheeks turned a shade of green and she looked away. This discussion was obviously making her ill. He changed the subject.

After the fifth round on the flask, everyone had lost their inhibitions. Although to be fair, the naturist gang had pretty much started that way. Red suggested a game of Truth or Dare and no one seemed to mind. They came up with more and more outrageous dares, most everyone avoiding truths. As the evening progressed, Faustino implemented a drinking game penalty for swearing. After no time, people were cursing just to do another shot. Bray noticed Mae was really hung up on Faustino. Her eyes watched him wherever he went. Willow seemed to notice as well. The two of them were probably the oldest in the group. They seemed to take on the role of parents watching kids at an underage party. He wanted her to loosen up and enjoy herself, but wasn't sure how to do that. She'd done shots from the flask like the rest of the group, but still seemed sober. He wondered how much she imbibed regularly if moonwine had no effect. The alcohol was hitting him hard. Faustino asked if he could ride the quad. Bray said yes, even with Willow frantically shaking her head no. Minutes later the quad crashed into a tree at the outskirts of the clearing. Apparently, he'd been trying to do something freaky with one of the women. He noticed Red strolling from that section of the forest minutes later, dusting her hands and winking at Mae.

"Hey, anyone up for a bonfire?" Said a booming voice from the forest edge.

The raucous gang all cheered, "Lucian!" He stood with one hip cocked, running a hand through his blonde-tipped auburn hair as if posing for a camera. He flipped back his shoulder-length mane and strutted into the clearing. Wearing nothing more than a pair of worn blue jeans and a devilish grin, he walked directly toward Willow. His darkly tanned chest looked like it had been chiseled from marble. Bray wasn't sure if it was the stranger's cocky attitude, his muscled physique, or his obvious interest in Willow, but he disliked the guy immediately. Lucian's eyes were locked with Willow's. Her lips parted and her eyes were wide like saucers. She turned to her sisters and scowled.

"Who invited him?" Willow hissed.

Red shrugged. Both Mae and Ellie wouldn't make eye contact.

Willow quickly ran to him before he joined the rest of the group. Bray couldn't overhear the conversation, but he knew the body language. Willow was pissed.

"Hey, Bray." Michael strolled up, "Who's the stud?"

"I have no idea, but Willow doesn't like him."

Liam joined the conversation taking a swig of beer. "You gonna make him leave?" He looked over his shoulder. "Dude looks like he could bench press us all."

Nick patted Bray on the back. "Sorry, but I have to share what I learned. Red just gave me the scoop. That guy's her ex. If that's her type—" He winced, "You ain't it. Tough luck, bro."

Bray's stomach fell. He'd never stood a chance. If overly muscled behemoths were what she wanted, Nick was right. He couldn't compete. Bray's body was toned. He tried to stay in shape, but there was no way he could ever bulk up like that. He didn't have the genes for a six-pack, and he also didn't have the desire to hit the gym that hard. Would Willow choose brain over brawn? He watched their interaction. She shook her fist at the guy. The guy stared at her with amusement. Maybe she wasn't hung up on the guy after all. He watched her ass shake in that little piece of nothing she wore. Fuck it. He wouldn't give up without a fight. He left his huddle of friends and walked toward Willow and her ex. The heated discussion cooled when he slipped his arm around Willow's waist. To his surprise, she didn't step away, but instead wrapped her arm around him as well.

"I was just telling Lucian about you." She smiled up at Bray.

Bray put his right hand out to the man, "Welcome to my home, Lucian."

The man snorted. "This is who you're seeing?" He shook the proffered hand, but Lucian yanked him into a one-armed bro hug. It wrenched Willow loose. The man took a whiff of Bray's neck. What the fuck? *That was odd.* Before he could comment, Lucian pushed him away hard. Bray struggled not to fall on his ass. Willow was there at his back. She wrapped her arm around him again and glared at Lucian.

"You've got an interesting scent, man."

"Uh. Thanks. I guess." Bray rubbed the back of his neck, completely confused. He raised eyebrows at Willow.

"Is this guy gay?" He whispered.

Maybe Nick misunderstood the situation.

Lucian turned to Willow and grinned. "You haven't fucked him."

Bray's jaw dropped. He couldn't believe the guy had just thrown that out there, and how would he know?

"That's none of your business." Willow punched him in the arm. She winced, shaking out her wrist.

"I thought so." Lucian walked past them to greet the other party crashers.

Bray lifted Willow's chin up to him, "Do you want me to ask him to leave?"

She patted Bray's chest and gave him a patronizing smile. "I appreciate the thought, but Lucian does as he pleases. No one *makes* him do anything he doesn't want to. If my sisters invited him, then he believes he has the right to be here."

"But it's my house."

She snickered. "He has a whole different view of property."

They watched as he nuzzled a woman's neck and whispered something in her ear. She squealed with delight and climbed him, wrapping her legs around his waist.

Bray let out a breath of relief. "Looks like he's moved on."

"If only it was that simple." She muttered.

With very little effort, Lucian built a blazing bonfire. Everyone gathered around. He told outrageous stories and kept the group laughing. He was easy-going and fun. Bray may have gotten along with him if it weren't for his tireless hints about his past relationship with Willow.

She didn't seem to refute any of the remarks, which made Bray wonder. Was she still interested in him? Lucian was obviously still hung up on her.

"Anyone up for a swim?" Willow fanned herself, "There's so much hot air around here. I for one need to cool off." She started walking toward the lake, snagging Bray's hand on the way.

Willow took off everything, and Bray left on his boxers. They walked into the water hand in hand. Willow kept peering back at the bonfire. Was she hoping others would follow? Or was she, like Bray, secretly praying for privacy? Bray stood in the water chest-deep. She nuzzled his neck, giving soft kisses. Willow blinked up at him, her eyes luminous in the moonlight. She gave a shy half-smile that stole his breath. She was so fucking beautiful. Willow climbed his body, wrapping her legs around his waist. He knew exactly what she needed. The memory of his friend's advice from this afternoon flooded his brain. Whatever her issue was, he was going to get her past it. The numerous shots of moonwine told him this was a fantastic plan. It definitely had nothing to do with the intense surge of jealousy pulsing through his veins. The bronzed god who was witty and charming and irritatingly handsome may have been intimate with her in the past, but she was with Bray. She chose him. Suddenly, it felt absolutely necessary to show her how right she had been. He rubbed her clit in small circles knowing exactly how much pressure to exert to drive her crazy. She moved her hips undulating, rocking on his hand, begging with her body. She was always so responsive. Before long she was panting, whispering wicked words in his ear, what he was doing to her, what she wanted to do to him. She was so close.

Suddenly, she stopped moving her hips and closed her eyes with a groan. He knew it was now or never. She started pulling away but he held her tight. She was trapped in his arms. He leaned in to take her lips. His kiss was fierce with possession. He slid his fingers inside her slick folds, thrusting while rubbing her clit as fast as he could. She struggled against him for a heartbeat, then came hard, pussy clenching his fingers as she rode them to completion. He ate her whimpers and moans trying to mask the sound until she slumped in his arms. He had finally done it, gotten past her hang-up. He felt like a conqueror. She sighed with contentment as he pulled her into a gentle hug, kissing her closed eyelids, her nose, her cheek. His lusty neighbor had chosen well. They stood in the shadows catching their breath.

Bray smiled. "You're unbelievably sexy when you come." He shifted his weight and the moon cast its light over her features. Her face glowed a soft green. Bray thought it was an interesting illusion, the green reflection from the trees. He figured his skin must appear green to her as well. "You look like you've been dipped in glow-in-the-dark paint."

She frowned. He hugged her tighter. "It's sexy as hell. Apparently, I've got a kink for alien chicks."

"You think I'm an alien?"

"Nah." He grinned. "But just in case, I'm not into probes. Unless it's me doing the probing." He rocked himself against her, grinding his hard length. She threw her head back gasping. Would she allow him to enter her like this in the water? He hadn't thought to grab condoms.

"Willow?"

She shook her head. "We can't have sex, but after what you did to me, I want to," she bit her bottom lip, "You know. Return the favor." She lowered her legs and ducked beneath the water. He was abruptly de-pantsed. Bray grinned. He was more than willing to do whatever she wanted. She lifted his feet one by one and he watched his shorts float to the surface, bobbing like a life preserver.

He couldn't wait to see what she would do next. Willow's head cleared the surface, her long hair slicked back. Her eyes sparkled. She reached for his cock gripping it tight. He braced his legs apart as she began pumping him by hand. His eyes went half-lidded as he watched her stroking him beneath the surface. He leaned over and kissed her, moaning into her mouth. She pulled back from the kiss and with a mischievous grin dropped to her knees with a splash. She drew him into her mouth. It was such a shock that it didn't take him long to come. He was barely able to contemplate how she could hold her breath underwater while sucking him so hard before he yelled his climax into the night.

Of course, his friends heard the yell and came running. Bray realized too late just how loud he'd been, but his biggest concern was Willow. The last thing he wanted was for her to regret what happened. They had just overcome a huge obstacle in their relationship.

"Is everything ok?" Liam asked. "I heard a scream."

"Uh yeah." Bray cleared his throat. "Everything's fine." He made an effort to hide Willow with his body.

Nick elbowed Liam and whispered something that had them both chuckling.

"So glad this is so amusing. But fuck off, guys."

His buddies laughed harder.

Nick pointed to Bray's boxers floating a few feet away.

"It's just your friends." She said peeking around him.

"Come out, Willow. What are you afraid of?" Lucian mocked as he strolled over.

She patted Bray's arm and walked from the shadows with her head held high. "You know better than to ask that. I'm not afraid of anything."

Bray pulled her in against his front, covering her breasts with his forearms. Instead of pulling away, she leaned back against him.

Lucian sucked in a breath and his face turned red with anger. "Maggie. We're leaving."

Willow smirked, "Don't leave on our account, Luce."

He scowled and grabbed Maggie by the waist, yanking her to his side. She didn't seem to mind the rough handling. "Bye, everyone. I guess we're off." She blew kisses. After Lucian and Maggie left, the party winded down quickly. Most everyone had passed out on the front lawn. Bray searched through the cupboards and pulled out several blankets. He and Willow walked around covering their inebriated guests. His friends had sleeping bags and were staying inside the cabin. Bray asked Willow to stay over, but she declined, mumbling something about too much temptation. She promised to be back in the morning. He watched as Willow and her sisters walked into the forest. They seemed to be the only ones still sober.

The next morning, Bray had a wicked hangover. Moonwine packed a helluva punch. He decided to make pancakes for breakfast and whipped up a batch. He had strong coffee brewing when Willow walked in wearing the same outfit she had on the night before. Her hair looked windblown, like she had just rolled out of bed freshly tumbled from a night of debauchery. He tried to remember if she and her sisters mentioned heading home. He had assumed so. Not that he had any idea where they lived. Her family liked their privacy. Had Lucian shown up at her doorstep? He suddenly wanted to hit something. Jealousy sucked. He wasn't used to it. Bray took a deep breath trying to think it through logically. Lucian had been pissed when he caught Willow and Bray together at the lake. Before that, he had acted all pompous. Lucian left with that woman, Maggie. She looked like a handful. He relaxed, realizing his competition had been sufficiently distracted for the evening. Bray needed to up his game if he wanted to keep her. He was tempted to ask about Lucian, but he didn't want to play the cliched role of jealous boyfriend. He glanced at his buddies. They were still snoring loudly from the living room. Bray took her hand pulling her further into the kitchen. She tilted her head at the bowl on the counter. Willow wiped a finger over the edge and sucked the batter from her fingertip. Her eyes slid closed and she groaned. Bray's tented boxers twitched. She blinked. Was she pretending not to notice? Her coy smile and the sharp intake of breath gave her away. Willow rubbed his chest trailing her fingers down, stopping just before the waistband.

"I'm going to take a quick shower and choose a fresh outfit from the closet."

She walked away before he could comment. Willow could tongue-twist him most days, but her eyes had sparkled with mischief and his mind had gone blank. Should he join her? Was she hinting? He swallowed. He looked back at his buddies, noticing Nick stretch and roll over. They would be awake soon. Any privacy would be nil until he could get them away from the cabin. Bray suddenly felt like a jerk. His buddies were only here for the weekend. He thought of the guy who coined the phrase, bros before hoes. He had obviously never met a woman like Willow with silky smooth skin and bedroom eyes.

While he poured batter into the sizzling pan, he imagined her showering, water sluicing down her body, soap suds revealing more than they hid. He suddenly wanted to help, an eager volunteer to rub her back, her front, and everywhere in between. He heard the shower shut off. Damn. He had taken too long. She was probably toweling off, standing in front of the closet debating which outfit to wear. He felt a surge of pride that he had provided her such an assortment and she kept them in *his* closet. In the past, he would have freaked if a girl had suggested leaving a toothbrush at his place, but now with Willow, it felt right.

She walked out wearing jean shorts and a blue halter that had Bray grinning like an idiot. She scrunched up her nose. "What's that awful smell?" She pointed to the pan he had forgotten all about. The pancakes looked like flat pieces of charcoal.

He cleared his throat. "I should probably mention, I'm not much of a cook." He slid the burnt remains into a waste bin and started with fresh batter.

"Maybe your skills reside elsewhere?" Willow winked at him.

Was she flirting with him now knowing he couldn't do a damn thing about it? That was seriously wrong.

Bray kept glancing back at his friends. Nick yawned and stood up. Fuck. The dude was naked.

Willow turned to him, "Hi, Nick. Sleep well?"

His friend blinked into the bright sunlight streaming from the kitchen window. He gave a grunt and half-hearted wave before heading to the bathroom.

Bray suddenly wanted to smash the frying pan over Nick's head. He knew his friend was just being himself, but he couldn't seem to control his temper. He took a deep breath and let it out slowly. *Focus on rational thoughts.* Willow hadn't stared at his junk. She was nonchalant around nudity because she was a naturist. No big deal.

Willow scooted past Bray, pointing at his second batch of pancakes that were starting to burn. He flipped them onto a plate and started another. He watched as she got out various herbs from the refrigerator and started grinding them into a powder. She put a spoonful in four glasses and poured juice in each. She found fancy glass swizzle sticks in a drawer and stirred them all in turn. She handed the first one to Bray and when Nick walked past, handed him one as well.

"It's a hangover cure. You'll be wanting the ingredients on hand if the Bacchus brothers visit again." Willow pointed to a list she had posted to the fridge. She dusted her hands. "My work here is done." Nick nodded to them both and headed back to the living room. She ran her hands up Bray's chest lightly resting on his shoulders. Willow looked up from thick blonde lashes. Her gaze held wicked sinful promises. He suddenly wished his friends had never come out for the weekend. She seemed to understand his dilemma and patted his chest. Willow whispered inches from his lips. "It's less than two days. I'll be here tomorrow night after you drop your friends at the airport." She gave him a peck on the lips and was out the door, leaving him strung tight, and distracted with lust. He tried to breathe past the urge to chase her, pin her down, and make her fulfill all those lusty unspoken promises. The sizzling from the pan and the aroma warned him, he had once again burned the pancakes.

Nick came back into the kitchen scowling, "Dude, what's that smell?"

Chapter 16

WILLOW APPROACHED THE dark cabin with excitement wondering if Bray would guess what she had in store for him. *Aww, he left the front door unlocked. How sweet.* Did this mean he was hoping she'd sneak in? Had he spent the last two nights anticipating her return? It had been only thirty-six hours since they had seen each other, but it felt like forever. Willow thought it had a lot to do with that incredible orgasm in the lake that left her body thrumming. He had pushed her past the point of no return. Just a single orgasm after weeks of denial. But Bray already knew her body so well. He was such a generous lover, paying attention to the smallest detail. Willow knew now, they could never go back to the way things were. She had come up with a plan.

Willow recalled when he climaxed, and their friends came running. Such an uninhibited response. It had been so sweet when he tried to protect her from prying eyes. Did he really think she was shy? Willow was a complete hedonist. She didn't mind others watching in the least. The only thing she was concerned about was appearing non-human. Since her skin flushed green with excitement, Lucian had known exactly what it meant. The humans, on the other hand, didn't seem to have a clue. Turns out she had worried over nothing. It amazed her how often humans would convince themselves that nothing was out of the ordinary. She now knew that if she stayed in the shadows or in a dark room, most of her self-imposed restrictions could be thrown out the window.

She taped a note to the front door giving Bray instructions when he arrived home. Willow lit a single candle on the kitchen table. If she left the bedroom door open, it cast just enough light to be able to walk to the bedroom and climb into bed. After that, the room plunged into darkness. She sprinkled flower petals on the floor, then crawled under the covers and waited.

A short while later, she heard the sound of a key. Had he forgotten he had left it unlocked? The front door creaked open. The crinkle of paper from the note she left meant he was reading it. Willow could see his shadow outlined by the candle. She held her breath waiting for his reaction. She smiled when she heard the thunk as his heavy boots hit the floor. His jeans followed as they dropped with the clink of keys. Buttons popped as he tore off his shirt. Her heart pounded. Bray stepped into the bedroom doorway, bare and beautiful.

"I'm on the bed." She whispered.

He swallowed, walking slowly to the edge reaching his hands out in the darkness. His eyes must still be adjusting. He slid under the covers next to her. She scooted over for him to join her. Bray cupped her face and gave her the gentlest kiss.

"You read the whole note?" Her voice was low. The darkness made it seem like a secret somehow.

"Yes," He chuckled softly. "No sex. Got it, but anything else is up for grabs."

"I thought you might like that part, so what do you want to grab first?" Willow slid his hands down until they rested on her breasts.

He paused for several heartbeats, gently rubbing her nipples back and forth. The touch was so light, she thrust her chest up for more contact. Bray leaned down to capture one of her nipples with his tongue, twirling the tip. He sucked and tugged until she cried out. The man relentlessly played for what seemed like an eternity. She wondered if she could come just like this, without any other touch? Her hips started rocking in a rhythm to his licks. He kept her upper body pinned. She felt an empty ache, her pussy clenching, desperate to be filled.

"Bray please."

"Your note said you wanted to beg before I let you come." Bray continued tormenting her.

"I need more. Touch me. Please." Willow didn't recognize her own voice, so deep and sultry.

Bray slowly slid his hand down her torso over her mons, the fingers barely touching.

"Is this what you want?"

She nodded frantically. "Yes. Yes. Please."

His fingers drew moisture from her core, running it along her folds. "Damn. You are so fucking wet."

"The anticipation's been delicious. I've been here waiting for a while."

"I want to bury myself in you so bad." Bray repeated the words in her letter like a mantra, "No sex. No sex. No sex." It was as if he needed the reminder.

The bed shifted. Willow gasped when his tongue touched her clit. He gave the same thorough exploration, twirling his tongue over her bud, sucking slow then fast, keeping her on the edge. Her hips rocked to his lips. He was really good at teasing. She was frantic, head thrashing.

"Please, Bray. I can't take it anymore."

He gave one more lick and blew on her sensitive clit. That was all it took, spiraling her over the edge. Her body felt like electricity was pumping through her veins as her body clenched, torso rising off the bed in a full body orgasm that went on and on. She collapsed back to the bed gulping for breath.

When she could speak again, Willow whispered, "Now it's my turn." She wanted to give him back everything and more. The orgasm had surpassed her wildest fantasies. Willow wanted Bray just as insatiable as she was for him. This was going to be so much fun.

Bray and Willow lay awake whispering in the darkness. He confessed that the dark room had spooked him at first, but after exchanging multiple orgasms, he reluctantly agreed the lack of sight had intensified every touch. Willow snuggled into his side and told him she was shy and needed the dark to relax and let herself go. Well, it was partly true. She did need the dark, but there wasn't a shy bone in her body. He rubbed her back saying he had already come to that conclusion. Apparently, his logical brain had completely dismissed the fact she was a naturist. Just one more example of how humans rationalized anything they didn't understand. He seemed to empathize with her vulnerability. Willow went on to explain that shadows made her more comfortable. Bray wanted more details. She blurted out that an ex had told her she made weird faces during sex. It was the truth. Although not the reason she wanted to keep the lights off. Lucian had mentioned it once, and they had both laughed. She had recreated an expression he made as well, and they had fought over which made the funniest 'O' face. Bray's body tensed. He vibrated with anger. Willow wondered if she should have come up with a different excuse.

Bray blew out a breath. "So, you aren't a virgin?"

"No. Why would you think that?"

Bray cleared his throat. "How long have you had this hang-up?"

Willow sighed. "For about half my life."

"What?"

She nuzzled his chest licking a nipple. That seemed to distract him.

"So, I know Lucian is your ex. Is he the one who made the comment?"

She sighed. "It doesn't matter who." She stopped touching him and rolled over wrapping herself in the comforter. "If you want to be with me, then you'll have to accept me the way I am."

Bray groaned. He uncoiled her from the covers and cuddled in against her back. "I'm not trying to change you. Just trying to understand."

Willow felt so warm and safe wrapped in his arms. She slid one of his hands to her breast and wiggled back against him. He sucked in a breath. His hard length pressed against her butt cheeks. She sighed, feeling content for the first time in a long while, before she drifted off to sleep. Somehow, they were going to make this work.

For the next few days, Bray managed to work around her issues. He put drapes on all the windows so they could explore other areas of the cabin. He had a supply of candles in the kitchen to offer just enough light. After climaxing, they would whisper secrets as they held each other. Bray shared doubts about his job and the life he had back in San Francisco. He told Willow how the company had been sucking the life out of him for years. Willow revealed more things about her family history, how lost she was when her mother died and why her sisters had trouble accepting him. He was an outsider, and that meant uncertainty. As liberal as they seemed, they craved consistency. Their lives had been chaos growing up. Willow explained she had done the best she could raising them, but she couldn't be everything they needed. Lucian's family and hers had been close. Their relationship had started out as friends. He had helped with the girls when they were little, and things had progressed. Willow made it clear there was nothing left between them.

"Have you told him that?"

"Oh, believe me, I've tried."

"I don't think the girls realized what my reaction would have been when they invited Lucian. In some warped way, they probably thought they were helping."

She kissed him. "But don't worry. I've set them straight."

Bray rubbed her nose with his. "If you say so, sweetheart."

She loved when he used endearments.

Each night they continued pushing each other further, testing their physical boundaries and allowing more emotional vulnerability. There was just one rule she wouldn't allow him to break. No sex. One night she woke with him teasing his cock over her clit. Precum moistened the tip making it slick as it slid back and forth. With no visual, she writhed on the bed, hips pumping up and down. She wanted so badly to see how their bodies touched. At one point the crown had nudged inside her opening. They both held their bodies perfectly still. She could have said the word and he would have thrust home. Instead, she found herself unable to move or breathe. He whispered swear words and pulled away. Bray had come so close to penetration. Heart pounding like it could escape her chest, Willow struggled to recall the reason why he couldn't breach that final barrier. That night when she willed herself to fall back asleep, she dreamed of him taking her completely. She woke the next morning achy and miserable despite all their shared orgasms. Denying them both that final step was adding another brick to the wall between them. Even though she had shared so much of her past, there were still too many secrets.

She watched Bray as he concentrated on the road. He had some errands to run in town and Willow had agreed to join him. She enjoyed spending time with him no matter what they did. Riding in his truck no longer made her nervous. He would hold her hand or rub her knee as he drove. Their first stop today was the hardware store to pick up a few tools he had on order. Willow wandered up and down the aisles while waiting. She wasn't paying any attention until a sickly sulfuric aroma stopped her cold. The shelves around her were lined with pesticides and herbicides. She held her breath and dove into the next aisle. Willow didn't think it was possible, but it was worse. Her eyes bulged at the sight of a chainsaw. She shivered. Next to it was an ax. There was a whole rack dedicated to all manner of tools designed to cut wood. Her body's natural form was bark. Willow's closest friends were trees. What kind of sick shop of horrors had Bray taken her to? She started hyperventilating. *Get out!* Her mind screamed as she ran down the aisle. She closed her eyes and willed her breathing back to normal. How would she explain herself to Bray? Willow glanced around the corner. Bray was still talking to the manager. The other man was amused by whatever he was saying. Good. Neither had witnessed her panic attack. They were walking to the register when the little bell on the shop door rang. Gail strutted into the shop wearing a fitted black and red pantsuit with matching stilettos. *What was she doing here?* Her eyes lit up when she saw Bray. Willow wasn't close enough to hear what she whispered in his ear. He replied, and she threw her head back laughing. Her dark brown hair was stunning. It was more a piece of art with a rainbow of colors; caramel, gold, and copper highlights. She drew her fingertips through the locks carelessly. It looked windblown and sexy. She was so attractive and *tall*, something Willow would never be. She was almost the same height as Bray in those heels. Most of the customers in the store were men. A few leaned out of aisles to catch a glimpse. The knot in her stomach tightened. Heat radiated from her chest to her limbs. *What was this sensation?*

She marched over to Bray and wrapped an arm around his. Willow's smile at Gail was more a baring of teeth.

"Gail, what a… surprise." She didn't want to say pleasant, because it was anything but.

She nodded. "It's good to see you too, Willow." Gail gave a wave as she turned down an aisle. "See you around," she said over her shoulder. Willow gritted her teeth. Gail's pert little ass looked perfect in those fitted black slacks. Bray had been staring as well. She cleared her throat.

"So, you almost done?"

He looked back in the direction Gail had gone and then back to Willow. "Yeah. I'm checking out now."

Checking out. Yeah. She noticed.

The next errand was the post office. He had a slip of paper in his P.O. box, which apparently meant he needed to stand in line. Willow strolled through the little store looking at all the envelopes and stamps while he waited. She especially liked the ones with animals. She knew humans used these stickers to send messages back and forth to one another. The humans had created such an elaborate system of communication. In Willow's world, she would ask a squirrel to deliver a message, or one of the ravens if it was long distance. Even if Willow had to get a message to another continent, she would just contact a witch or troll for access to a portal. Communication in her world was simple. Humans overcomplicated everything. Gail walked in. She stutter-stepped when she saw Willow, then grinned.

"Well, hello again." She shrugged. "Great minds think alike."

Willow said nothing. She just glared at the woman. Gail walked in behind Bray and tapped his shoulder.

"Guess who?"

He turned and laughed. "Small town, huh?"

She chuckled. "Yep. Can't get much smaller."

"What are you here for?"

Gail held up an envelope. "Just a single stamp. My niece's birthday."

He gestured for her to go in front of him. "Why don't you go ahead of me." He held up the slip of paper. "They have to go hunting for my package in the back. Mine might take a while."

She squeezed his arm. "Thanks, Bray. That's real sweet of you." Gail glanced at Willow. Whatever she saw on her face, startled her. The clerk called 'next'. It was Gail's turn at the counter. She was in and out in less than a minute. She waved to them both as she left.

Bray seemed to scrutinize Willow's every expression. His eyes followed her movements as she paced the room. The post office was small, and she didn't like confined spaces.

They went to the hotel next. Bray was going on a conference call, whatever that meant. Willow decided to stop by the grocery store. It was Susan and Bobby's normal shopping day. They would meet at the local grocery store for supplies and gossip. They had both been married, so she assumed they'd have insight on the human male. Willow needed help and was willing to resort to asking humans for it. She shook her head at how low she had sunk. But she didn't know what else to do. She felt like the distance between them was growing. Willow figured Susan and Bobby would be the closest thing to experts she could find.

"I'm going to the store while you do your caller con thing."

He smiled. "It's conference call, sweetheart." Bray gave her a quick kiss and handed her some cash. She studied the twenty-dollar bill. What did he think she needed this for? His behavior often puzzled her. Her dark hunter-green dress didn't have a pocket. She looked around for a place to put it. The only part of the dress that was snug was over her chest. She folded the bill a few times and slid it between her cleavage.

"We'll have lunch after this. You must be hungry." His eyes focused on her breasts. She felt herself flush. The lights in the lobby were bright. She leaned into the potted Ficus concealing her green skin in what little shadow it offered. She hadn't worn a bra. Her nipples tightened under his gaze. He wiped a hand over his mouth and his eyes met Willow's.

"I'm starved," Bray whispered.

Everything tightened in Willow's body. His look was predatory. They stared at each other for several moments. Bray's phone alarm went off. Meeting time. He cursed, pecked her on the cheek, and walked away.

"I'll be back in an hour."

Willow took a deep breath. Human. Advice. That's what she needed.

Susan was divorced, and Bobby was a widow. They would each be able to offer suggestions on relationships. Willow was relieved to find them both at the grocery store in the produce section.

"Willow. It's so wonderful to see you." Susan gave her a hug. "That color on you is simply divine."

Willow grinned. She loved the color as well. It was one of her favorites.

"Bray got it for me. He took me shopping." She spun around, and the skirt twirled. "The shoes too." She pointed at the dainty sandals with green gemstones. The shop owner had told her she needed bling. Willow didn't need convincing. She loved anything that sparkled.

"Just because he buys you stuff, that doesn't entitle him to diddly." Bobby shook her finger. "Make sure he knows that."

Willow tilted her head. "What do you mean?"

"Some men think they can buy affection." Susan sighed. "Especially rich men like Bray."

"But what if I want to give him, uh...affection?"

"Well, if it's freely given, that's just fine." Bobby studied an apple and put it in her basket. "But if he oversteps, you just tell me, and we'll sort out the broken bones later." She gave an evil grin.

That's why Willow liked her so much. Bobby had a warrior's soul. She wouldn't let anyone overstep.

Susan bumped her shoulder, "So if intimacy isn't the issue, what's got you tied up in knots?"

Willow sighed. Susan was incredibly perceptive. If she didn't know better, she would think Susan had Fey blood somewhere in her ancestry. The Fey tended to have highly developed empathic abilities.

Willow rubbed the back of her neck. "Well, I kind of get angry when I see him talking to other women. I mean really, super, scary angry. Then I feel bad afterward, but I can't seem to stop. I want to rip out the other woman's hair, punch her in the face, you know, kick her in the sides 'til she can't breathe."

Susan's eyes went wide. Bobby nodded.

"Honey, we've all been there." Bobby patted her back.

"But I've never felt like this before. I feel so out of control." She shrugged. "I worry about what he's doing when I'm not around."

"Have you made it clear to him?" Bobby asked.

"What do you mean?"

Susan and Bobby shared a look.

"I can speak from experience," Susan sighed, "Men are not mind-readers."

"You need to tell him. Make things exclusive." Susan shrugged. "Put it out there and see how he reacts."

"And if he says the wrong thing," Bobby gave an air-kick, "Then kick his ass to the curb. Pow."

Willow went back to the hotel in a daze. Was it really that simple, just tell Bray she didn't want him to be with other women? The concept of monogamy wasn't one she was familiar with. Most of the forest creatures had a liberal view of bedding others. Over the years, Willow had attended numerous orgies, but usually just as an observer. She was more a voyeur than a participant. Willow had certainly seen enough over the years to know plenty, and to realize that lifestyle wasn't for her. It was no wonder she hadn't found a good match from the selection of single males in the forest. Maybe that's why Bray had appealed to her. He didn't seem to go out of his way to gain women's attention. Bray didn't flirt. He didn't flaunt his body. Willow had been attributing animalistic behaviors to a human. He didn't deserve that. Bray had given her zero reasons to doubt.

Gail walked out of the business center leaning against Bray. They were laughing. Willow shot daggers with her eyes. *What. The. Hell.* Not her, again.

Bray's eyes lit up when he saw Willow. He didn't look guilty. She tried to reassure herself that nothing happened.

"Guess who I ran into, again?" Bray gestured to Gail. "Isn't this crazy?" Bray leaned down to give Willow a kiss. "I hope you don't mind, but I invited Gail to join us for lunch at the Roadhouse."

Willow did mind. She minded very much. Damn it. But his eyes were hopeful, and she didn't want to look like a complete bitch.

She tried to smile through gritted teeth. "Of course. Join us."

Willow started walking to the bar. Bray caught up to her and reached for her hand. Willow paused gazing into his eyes. This man was so sweet. She put her hand in his. Gail was on his other side. Her heels slipped on the gravel and she grabbed his other arm.

"Sorry about that. You would think I would learn by now, but I still haven't found the right shoes."

"No problem. Hang tight. I'll get you there."

Gail grinned and steadied herself on his arm. Willow frowned. She didn't like how the woman clutched him. She wanted to scream, 'He's mine, Bitch', but then he would know how jealous she had become. How would he react? She bit her tongue to keep from cursing. She glanced down at Gail's shoes. They were ridiculous. It was a miracle she had made it this far without falling. Who would wear pointed shoes when not in battle? And even then, the spikes should point up, not down. How many enemies are going to willingly lie down so you can walk on them?

Over lunch, Gail spoke non-stop about Bray and all the wonderful things he did for the IT industry. Gail and Bray had burgers and fries, while Willow had a salad. They laughed together when they discovered they had frequented many of the same clubs and events in San Francisco. Willow felt like a third wheel. Gail dominated the conversation. Every time Bray would try to steer the conversation to something local, Gail would ask a question or talk about San Francisco or IT. Two things Willow knew zero about. She was learning a lot about Bray, unfortunately, over half of it Willow didn't understand. Was Gail trying to show Bray how little the two of them had in common? If so, it was working. The woman was slick. Willow would give her that. Although her words of admiration seemed genuine. On several occasions, Bray would blush with embarrassment and look at Willow for a reaction. Most of the time, she stared blankly not grasping what the big deal was. Willow was thrilled when lunch was finally over and they could head back to the cabin. They walked Gail back to the hotel. She gave both of them a hug which perplexed Willow completely. That wasn't the reaction of a woman out to steal another's man—or was it? She knew so little of human behavior.

Willow had to go run her own errands. She needed to prepare for her monthly retreat. She had wanted to discuss the three-day journey over lunch, but with Gail listening in, it would raise too many questions. She decided to tell him over dinner that evening. Bray said he would do veggie shish kabobs. Willow nodded having no idea what that was.

After a few hours, she returned to the cabin. Bella, in painted-on jeans and a low-cut poet blouse, was just leaving. *Oh hell no.* Willow stopped in her tracks, watching their interaction. Bella smooshed her large breasts against him in a tight embrace. She patted his chest, then walked away. A slow heat boiled in Willow's belly. The jealous rage built and built. This was so unlike her. Dryads didn't feel jealousy. It wasn't in their nature. She had never felt it for her ex, Lucian. But she did feel it now. It was so strong she wanted to break things. Willow couldn't get her feet to move until Bray closed his front door and Bella entered the forest on the opposite side of the clearing. It gave her time to calm down.

She took a few deep breaths, then marched to his cabin. Willow knocked. He opened it with a smile.

"Willow." He said with surprise, glancing over her shoulder.

She pursed her lips. "I saw BB just leave."

"Who?" Bray asked.

Willow tapped her foot. "The brunette with the big boobs."

"Oh, you mean Bella," Bray laughed, "Yeah. She stopped by to visit."

He seemed fascinated by her jealousy. "She was one of the party crashers when my friends came out." Bray shrugged. "I thought you two knew each other." He scratched his head. "She sure is nice."

Willow rolled her eyes. "Yes. That's what she's known for. Being extra nice. Especially to males."

She pulled him into the living room.

"I want to talk to you." Willow was determined to get this out. "It's important."

He sat down on the couch, patting the cushion for her to come sit next to him. It was a gesture one would give an animal. She sighed. Willow felt like one. She sat.

"Tell me." He held her hands, gaze expectant.

She was nervous. Her hands started to sweat. "Well, it's about us."

"And?"

She rolled her neck. "Look. I don't want you seeing other people."

Bray's serious expression turned into a wide grin. Ugh. He was enjoying this.

"I see." He couldn't seem to contain his mirth. His lips curled. "So, you're saying no other women?"

Bray seemed to enjoy her possessiveness. She frowned. Why was he ok with this? She thought he would balk. Other males would have. Didn't they typically like their freedom? Wait. He hadn't really said yes or no.

Willow sighed. "What do you think?"

"Of other women?" Bray asked.

"Yes." Willow gritted.

"No other women for me. Got it. And what about you?" Bray's eyes flashed.

Willow smirked. "No women for me either."

Bray glared. "That's not what I meant."

She chuckled. "No other males for me either." She gave him a quick kiss and straddled his lap. "Ok. Now that's settled, I have to tell you about my monthly pilgrimage." Willow grinned stroking his chest. "I'll be gone for three days. But the fun part will be when I get back. We'll have all this pent-up sexual energy." She lifted the skirt on her dress to reveal matching lace panties. She rubbed herself against him, gasping. They both watched as she stroked up and down his shaft. Her panties and his jeans were the only things separating them. Bray grabbed her hips. Willow hoped it was to rock against him. She loved when he did that, but he stilled her hips. Did he want her to beg for it? Willow loved when they played that game.

She licked her lips. "I can't wait."

Bray frowned. "Who are you going with?"

"All sorts that live in the forest. My sisters will be there for part of it."

"Is it a naturist thing?"

Willow nodded and let out a breath. "Yes, that's it exactly." She kissed him. "I knew you'd understand."

A few minutes passed. She wondered what he was thinking about so seriously.

"Can I join you?" Bray asked.

The question surprised her. She didn't think he'd be interested. Willow couldn't very well take him to Council. It was in the sacred circle of trees where only magical creatures could enter, not to mention that one of the discussion points would be about his living arrangements in the forest. She shook her head. "I don't think so. It's sort of private. You have to be invited."

"Hmm," Bray grunted, "Will Lucian be there?"

She shrugged. "He'll probably be there for part of it. I run the thing, so I have to be there all three days."

"I don't understand. If you run it, then why can't you invite me?"

Willow looked up at the ceiling. She didn't want to argue with him. "Look, maybe I didn't say that right. I run things, but I don't make the rules."

When she spoke the words, it hit her like an epiphany. It was the absolute truth. For years, she had been the Guardian but didn't really rule. Council had been the only ones making big decisions the past sixteen years. In appearance only she was the forest leader. But when you boiled it down, she was just a glorified figurehead. She frowned, not liking the sound of that. Bray seemed deeply disappointed too. He dropped his hands by his sides and leaned back. She would miss him like crazy over the next three days. She wanted to make them both feel better. Willow kissed his neck. She whispered how sexy she found him and licked his ear. Willow rocked her hips. He was so hard. She rode him; up and down grinding on his shaft. They locked lips groaning into the kiss. The friction from their bodies was so hot. Bray gritted his teeth. He was so controlled, trying so hard to last. That wouldn't do. Willow wanted him to remember the pleasure she alone could bring him. She unzipped his jeans slowly over his erection and knelt between his knees. Willow smiled up at him as she took him between her lips. His hips bucked when her tongue licked the crown. A few strokes and sucks later, and he was coming hard, eyes rolling back in his head. She smiled up at him licking the cream from her fingertips. Bray stared at her with awe. She reached out a hand and pulled him up from the couch leading him to the bedroom. They had all night and tomorrow. She planned to make the most of their time. He wouldn't be able to think of another by the time she was through with him.

Chapter 17

Bray wondered not for the first time how he had gotten so lucky. Now that she had gotten past her big hang-up not allowing a climax (thank you, Nick), it seemed their relationship was finally on solid footing. He was surprised she had pushed for an exclusive relationship. Judging by her group of friends and their hedonistic activities at his party, they seemed more into the swinger's lifestyle. He had assumed that of her as well. That was probably the reason he had pushed her so hard to overcome her intimacy issues. He still didn't fully understand the no-sex rule. But there could be a lot of reasons for that. He could be patient while they worked on her trust issues. At first, it had been a blow to his ego to learn she had been with Lucian in the past, yet didn't want to have sex with him. Her declaration went a long way to soothe his fierce jealousy. He alone would enjoy Willow's sexy body and her many skills. The things that woman could do with her mouth. God Almighty. And she was strong. At one time, he had been concerned he would hurt her. Ha. When Willow wanted him to stay put, she would pin him down with her slight body, wrapping her legs in the slats of the bed, or gripping his cock, demanding he repeat the words he was hers alone. A lesser man might have been intimidated by her aggressive demeanor, but it was a huge turn-on. In the past, an overly possessive woman would have pushed him away completely. But with Willow, it spurred on his own need. He would lick her pussy until she moaned, undulating on his tongue. Before letting her come, Bray would demand the same, making her repeat the words, just who she belonged to. She would cry out his name, begging for her release. She seemed to love this new domineering side of him.

They spent their entire last day together in bed. Even though they had yet to take that final step and have sex, they had done nearly everything else. The bond between them had grown so strong it was staggering. At times, it would scare him how much he cared for her. After intense, mind-blowing orgasms, they would hold each other in semi-darkness, bodies wrapped around one another, fingers twined, sharing breaths. Willow would rub her body against him almost like she was trying to scent mark him. It was an odd behavior, but he figured being out in the wilderness her whole life, it would make sense for her to have some animal behaviors. He certainly didn't mind, especially when she would rub his cock. But they discovered how sensitive other parts of his body were. He had no idea how ticklish his ears and feet were. She would speak soft words, sometimes in a language he didn't recognize, but he somehow understood the meaning. Willow was thanking him in between soft caresses, and affectionate kisses. Bray was surprised these quiet moments of gentleness weren't more unsettling. He was used to quick affairs for mutual satisfaction. Bray didn't expect or want more. He was always upfront explaining he didn't do long-term. Going past even a few dates was unusual. Whenever he did, the women seemed to think they could convince him to settle down. Over the years he had grown frustrated with their deceit and scheming ways and had stopped dating altogether. It had been several years since he had dated, until Willow came along. Her no-sex rule was even harder after the long wait. But she was nothing like the women from his past. She wasn't a devious corporate gold-digger. Willow couldn't care less what money he had. Bray didn't have to worry she was faking affection. Willow was real and down-to-earth. Her responses were raw and honest. She didn't seem to care if there was a smudge of dirt on her nose or her dress was in tatters. Willow was gorgeous no matter what. Bray didn't want to admit how hard he was falling for her. His backwoods babe was undermining every defense he had built around his heart without even trying.

A knock on his cabin door interrupted his thoughts. He wondered if Willow had forgotten something, or had she changed her mind and decided her nudist thing could wait.

Bray grinned as he opened the door.

"Bella. This is a surprise. What brings you here? Aren't you supposed to be at the nudist retreat?"

"What?" Bella frowned. "Retreat?"

She didn't know about it? Maybe Willow hadn't invited Bella either. He hadn't gotten many details. Only that he wasn't allowed, which still stung. Not that he wanted to be butt naked around strangers anyhow, but a choice would have been nice.

"Oh, yeah." Bella smiled. "I don't call it a retreat though. It's more of a gathering of those in charge. Did Willow fill you in on what took place during this so-called retreat?" She made hand quotes around the word retreat.

Bray tilted his head. He tried to recall her exact words. Willow had been quite vague about the whole thing.

"It all seems pretty hush-hush."

Bella nodded. "Oh, it is. I'm sure she didn't want *you* to know anything about it."

"What does that mean?"

"Oh, Bray. I hate to be the bearer of bad news, but I think Willow is cheating on you."

"No." He shook his head. "That's not possible."

Bella blinked her kohled eyes. She stood there with her hip cocked and stared at him.

"I thought you were supposed to be this super genius. Boy, did she do a number on you."

Bray didn't like where this conversation was going. He trusted Willow, didn't he? There was no reason to doubt where she was going. Why would she have made their relationship exclusive? It didn't make sense.

"It's too bad you're not invited. If you were, you could see what she was up to." She pinched her lips together. "Of course, *I* have an invite."

"You could get me in?"

"Uh. Sorry, unfortunately no. However, I can spy for you and report back. You're a super nice guy, Bray. I don't want her taking advantage of you."

Bray had this tingling feeling in his spine. He realized it had always been there, needling his brain. The secrecy of Willow's outing, how she avoided discussing any details, making it impossible for him to join. He thought back to how many times she had distracted him as he asked questions. Bray hadn't thought much about it at the time. The distractions had been so pleasurable that he hadn't once thought he was being manipulated, but thinking back now, that's exactly how it seemed. Bray closed his eyes. Did he really want to head down this path? If he couldn't trust her, their relationship was doomed.

Bella was waiting. Would he ignore the evidence in front of him? As much as he wanted to, he couldn't. Ignorance to him could never bring bliss. The facts were what he needed before making any rash decisions. He needed more than hearsay. If he'd been back in California, he would have hired his P.I. to spy on Willow. He'd done it a few times with previous girlfriends and discovered just how un-loyal and conniving women could be. He still had faith Willow wasn't like that, but it would eat at him if he didn't utilize the resource right in front of him.

"I have an idea. Wait here."

Bella tapped her foot. "Sure thing. That's why I'm here. To serve."

Bray did a double-take. Bella's words were friendly but her demeanor was off.

She blinked innocent eyes at him and smiled.

He shook his head. The whole thought of Willow cheating was making him misjudge everything around him. Bella had shown up several times to check on him. She had made him feel welcome when he'd felt so out of place.

Bray dug through his closet and pulled out a box.

He unwrapped the small plane and handed it to Bella.

"You can use this. It has video."

During the rest of the afternoon, Bray showed Bella how to work the controller and by the end of the day, she could fly the drone through the trees better than he could. She was quite proficient but swore she had never touched anything like it.

"Apparently you're gifted."

She scowled.

"It's unnatural to be good at stuff like this. I'm just a simple country girl."

Bray laughed. "I don't believe anything about you is simple."

She pursed her lips, "Maybe you're smart after all."

Chapter 18

WILLOW BLINKED UP into the dark sky scowling. She detested these things. She would have done anything to stay with Bray even playing the box of X game he seemed so infatuated with. Willow took a deep breath and trudged into the hidden glade. The portal was just beyond, in between two large ponderosa pines. Just as she crossed the threshold, Willow heard a buzzing noise behind her. She spun around peering into the darkness but saw nothing. It amplified for a second and then was gone. Maybe it was a new security measure Council had installed without her knowledge. It wouldn't have been the first time. She turned around to gaze at the hundreds of fireflies lighting the pathway. It led to a fringe of vines. Willow checked her leaf bikini making sure her essentials were covered. Her soft gossamer skirt of spiderwebs ruffled in the breeze. She had sprinkled her laurel wreath with glitter borrowed from the town rec center. It was her one bit of defiance to tradition. Peals of laughter could be heard over a strain of soft pipes. Willow moved the vines with her powers and strutted into the clearing. Despite her reservations about being here, the setting was always beautiful. This month the Pixies had outdone themselves. The scene was straight out of a dream. A glowing fairy picture of perfection. More fireflies were in large multi-colored crystals dangling from tree branches. They cast rainbow swirls of colors across the clearing, a disco ball of nature. She wondered what Bray would think of the splendor. What secret details would he have observed? He often found patterns in nature that even she missed. His mind never ceased to amaze her. Phosphorus plants cast a green glow across a low stone bar in front of a large cave. A deep walkway had been carved out for the bartenders, but in front of the bar were squat little stools made from tree stumps. The Pixies were the party designers and apparently had created seats for their size. She shrugged. No one seemed to mind. The bar was huge and every seat was taken. Grove and river Nymphs draped themselves over the stools with goblets held high for the Bacchus brothers to pour their famous moonshine wine. Either they had increased the potency or that group had been pounding drinks for a while. She watched Donna stalk into the glade like she owned the place. She glanced at Willow and scowled. That was the last person she wanted to deal with. Willow walked over to the bar, shoved a river Nymph off a stool, and claimed her seat.

"Why'dya do dat, Willow?" The Nymph slurred.

She stuck a thumb over her shoulder pointing to Donna. The Nymph squinted, then her eyes went wide.

"Nuf said." The Nymph elbowed one of her sisters. Both staggered off into the trees. Apparently, both were on Mother B's very long shit list.

Willow tapped the bar with a knuckle and Faustino gave her a cheeky grin. "What can I do for you, gorgeous?"

"Give me the hard stuff and make it quick. Your mom just arrived."

He squinted behind her and scowled. He whispered something to one of his brothers. A half dozen of them were tending bar. Olie bounded out of the cave with a fancy goblet in hand. He rushed it to his Mother and presented it as an offering. Hopefully, it was something to help loosen the stick up her ass. Donna was normally a pain, but when sober she was downright nasty. There was a direct correlation between the amount of alcohol consumed by Mother B and those around her. Most couldn't stand her bitchy condescending self unless they were numb with alcohol. Willow needed to get there in a hurry.

Faustino filled a goblet with a green liquid and handed it to her. It fizzled and popped, and gave off a puff of green smoke. *This is new.* Willow sniffed the contents and immediately regretted it. She grew dizzy just from inhaling. She glanced back at Donna. She was yelling at some poor creature who had crossed her path, in other words being herself. Willow saluted Faustino with the glass and downed the contents in one swig. She held the goblet out for a refill as she wheezed, "Keep 'em coming."

One of his brothers leaned in to whisper, "You better watch it. That stuff is potent. It's a new recipe from a wizard bar."

She knocked on the bar again. Faustino shoved his brother out of the way. "Willow can handle it." He poured her another. Before long,

Willow felt no pain. She knew even Donna and her scathing commentary couldn't bring her down.

After several rounds, her shoulder leaned to the right until she slumped against a Gray Fox Shifter. Willow blinked. *When did she get here?* She vaguely remembered sitting next to Olea, one of the mountain Nymphs from the North. She and several cousins had come down for Festivus. They had been chatting up a storm until just a few minutes ago. She turned her head quickly right then left. When the clearing stopped spinning, she spotted Olea dozing with several other Nymphs in the dirt. Willow snorted. Those hillbillies couldn't hold their liquor. Well, at least they didn't have far to fall. Maybe the reason for the stools being so short had nothing to do with Pixie height and more to do with liability claims. Willow glanced around the clearing, slowly this time. Several Satyrs had already staked claims with inebriated Nymphs or Shifters and were rutting away against trees. She smirked. Typical Festivus. Willow set her goblet back on the bar for another refill. A gasp from behind spun her too quickly and she had to steady herself. She watched with horror as Bella walked into the clearing. Apparently, Mother Bacchus had left, but now her daughter was here instead. *What the hell? Was there a bitch quota for the clearing?* Bella walked hand in hand with Willow's ex-boyfriend Lucian. She looked smug, snuggling into his side, rubbing a hand over his well-chiseled pecs. She whispered something in his ear and nodded to the bar. They walked directly toward her. Lucian's intense eyes flashed in the flickering light. The last time she'd seen him, he'd been seething with jealousy. Willow knew from that look exactly what he wanted. Maybe Bella could distract him. If Willow could just get her legs to cooperate, she could escape before he reached the bar. She set her goblet down and turned. Lucian's crotch was inches from her face. Fuck. His erection grew larger by the second. Why couldn't she tear her eyes away? She leaned back against the bar trying to move away. He smiled wickedly down at her position and leaned in placing a drink order. She was trapped in this embarrassing position. She peeked around Lucian's waist to glance at Bella. She was pissed. Lucian didn't realize what a vindictive little bitch she could be. Willow wondered if she should warn him. He handed Bella her drink then grabbed Willow yanking her into his chest. "We need to talk."

Willow tried to struggle out of his grasp, but it was no use. Her limbs felt like rubber and he was so much stronger. She watched as

Bella took a seat at the bar and stared laser beams of hatred in her direction. Lucian walked her a short distance away and shoved her against a tree in the shadows. Oh, Gaia. The whirring noise was back. Her head was pounding. That wizard liquor was really doing a number on her. Lucian's body held hers pinned against the bark. It was a good thing because she couldn't feel her legs. She would have collapsed just like the Nymphs decorating the bar floor. Lucian's eyes were glued to her lips. She couldn't seem to focus. The forest continued to spin. He took a deep breath, inhaling her neck.

"I missed you." Lucian leaned in and kissed her mouth hard. She tried to tell him to stop, but his tongue was relentless. The muffled words sounded more like a moan. He slanted his mouth for a deeper kiss, clearly encouraged by her response. She struggled to push him back, but it was no use, physically she was no match. And her limbs just wouldn't cooperate. Wait. The tree at her back. She could use its power. Willow exhaled and sunk her hips into the tree, just enough to connect with its energy. She channeled Dryad powers from the tree to her legs. Bark formed, building from her hips, down her leg, to the tips of her toes. With all the strength she could summon, Willow kneed him in the balls. He broke from the kiss bent over wheezing. Willow couldn't believe she had felt sorry for him. What an ass. She paused at the bar just long enough to address Bella before staggering from the clearing, "Enjoy your Demon tonight, BB."

Early the next morning, Willow arrived at the sacred circle of trees not looking forward to the next three days. It was partly due to the hangover from opening Festivus. She had gotten drunk for a variety of reasons. One, it was easier to deal with the Bacchus bitches, but mostly it was to numb the memory of Bray's expression of utter disappointment when she had told him he wasn't invited. Willow was surprised at how much she missed him. He didn't realize how desperately she wanted him by her side, but there were rules. An outsider couldn't be invited into the sacred circle without special circumstances. Bray's residence status was the most important item of this month's Council session. She would save that for the last day. On the final night of Festivus, everyone would party hard. The last day of Council would be the easiest to persuade Council to her point of view. Most would have hangovers and would agree to almost anything to end session early and head home. Today, she would discuss a less controversial topic, prescribed burn days. The local wilderness manager had given her the scheduled dates and sections of the forest assigned to burn projects in the spring. Willow wanted to implement a new forest-wide policy. Every creature in the forest would have a fire buddy. They would do drills so everyone was prepared in case of an emergency. They had to be done in sections with group captains. She had drawn out maps and recommendations for group leaders.

Willow took her place at the podium waiting for Council to assemble. As Guardian, it was her privilege to state agenda items before anyone else. Cyrus, the Council leader nodded for her to begin.

She took a deep breath, still nervous to speak in front of Council after all these years. "I'd like to discuss next spring's prescribed burn days. I think we need a new policy for safety. Several forest creatures died, when it could have been avoided."

Willow signaled for the squirrels to pass out the nine scrolls, one to each Council member. They unrolled the parchment and went through the document. No one spoke for several minutes while they read the decree.

"I don't understand this concept of fire buddy." Donna Bacchus rolled her eyes. She looked at the rest of Council, "Is anyone else confused? I mean why waste time checking on someone else? Isn't the whole point to get away from the fire as quickly as possible?" She glared at Willow, "I think your plan is flawed. But it doesn't surprise me. You've never been all that bright."

Willow gritted her teeth. "Not every creature is aware when there is a fire. If we set up an alarm system, everyone gets a warning. A buddy will help make sure everyone gets to safety, not just the ones that are most aware."

"I believe the humans call it Darwinism." Donna sneered.

The Raven squawked. Her form of a laugh. Roz had a dark sense of humor.

"No one is better than anyone else." She shook with outrage.

"Still naive as ever," Donna gestured to Willow and addressed Council. "It looks like we need no reminder of her ignorance." She put her elbows on the bench and tilted her head studying Willow carefully, "Although, I'm curious about this new boost of confidence? It's completely unwarranted, and so unlike you."

The Sprite's leader, Fuath, cleared his throat. His cheeks flushed pink.

"Care to comment?" Donna asked.

"No. Excuse me. Just need a drink." He signaled for an attendant to bring over a goblet.

Willow sighed. She should have realized Fuath would know of her relationship with the human. He had spies everywhere. Now that Donna mentioned it, Willow's growing sense of self-worth had been skyrocketing in direct proportion to the amount of time she spent with Bray. Crazy how that worked. So, orgasms with Bray equaled kicking ass with Council, huh?

Donna studied Fuath as he pounded wine, not making eye contact with anyone. Based on his reaction, it seemed he hadn't shared the affair with Donna. Perhaps he could be a potential ally? She'd have to think more on it later. Regardless, she wouldn't let Donna squash the first improvement idea she proposed in years.

"If you will turn the parchment to the back, I have a map drawn, sectioning off the forest. There is also a list of potential group leaders I'm recommending to be assigned to do drills."

Cyrus nodded his head, "This is well thought out, Willow. Great job."

She smiled wide, eyes sparkling. Willow did not get praised often by Council. They frequently lectured and scolded. Each confrontation with Council seemed like dealing with nine older and wiser parents ready to pass blame and find fault wherever they could.

They continued discussions around the idea and other members expressed their interest in the unique program that Willow designed. By the end of session, she was genuinely pleased by the outcome. They would begin implementing the plan in stages. It would mean more time away from Bray, but to save lives, it was well worth it.

This evening's party extended invites to family members of Council and key political forest figures along with their guests. Her sisters would be there. She didn't want a repeat of the previous night's debacle with Lucian. She would recruit her sisters' help if he gave her trouble. Willow felt a pang of regret for hurting him so violently, then she remembered how he had taken advantage. The image of Lucian rolling on the ground flashed in her memory. Had Bella consoled him or kneed him again after she left? Either would have worked, as long as he left her alone. Years ago, he had become her lover out of convenience. Their parents had been friends, and they had grown up together. He was an aggressive sexual partner, but at the time it had been exciting. He never wasted time with foreplay. Although to be fair, they had both been teens at the time. Willow smiled, recalling exactly how Bray had shown her the meaning of that word, over and over again. She sighed. Willow missed him. She could have found a pine and traveled back to his cabin for a few hours. It was tempting. But Council meetings only lasted a few days a month. Her duty compelled her to stay.

Willow walked into the clearing. Tonight, Lucian was the one at the bar throwing back drinks. Several Nymphs tried climbing into his lap. He kept pushing them away. She wondered if he was still damaged from the night before. Turning away an easy lay wasn't really his style. She strolled to the other side of the glade staying out of view. Willow wasn't being cowardly. She was just avoiding a confrontation, or so she tried to convince herself. She walked past Elves throwing knives into targets twenty yards away. One of the large boards had a disgruntled Gnome strapped to it. Her eyebrows rose. One of the Elves watching explained that he was a political prisoner, a spy from another forest. He had infiltrated Fey lands and was plotting to overthrow the government, or at a minimum undermine the Elven clan. Either carried a death sentence. Each faction of magical species had their own justice system. Still, it seemed excessive and cruel to torture him before the killing.

Willow shook her head at their treatment and addressed their leader. "This doesn't seem right."

Terra, one of the Council elders, shrugged her shoulders. "We are within our rights. The Gnome was caught with maps of our entire clan. He had locations of every Fey home in the forest, lists of our weapons and magical abilities. I know you strive for compassion, but even you should realize the security risk."

Willow nodded. "You're right. If everything is as you say. But don't you find it odd. Gnomes aren't known for their skills as spies. How do you know this wasn't a setup? Have you gotten information from him? Did you discuss this with Goron?" The Gnome's leader would be pissed if he saw the treatment. He strolled around the corner. Willow backed up. Goron's eyes glittered with fury. His body pulsed with heavy magic. The glow changed colors as he watched the spectacle. Terra hadn't noticed him coming up behind her. Or if she had, she gave no reaction. As Guardian, Willow could mediate disputes. She wondered if this would be on the agenda tomorrow, or if there'd be a throw-down right here.

"We haven't gotten to the bottom of who sent him, but he'll talk soon enough." Terra flung a knife into the target. It embedded into the Gnome's heart. He rattled out a breath and slumped. Willow tilted her head. How was he going to answer her questions now? Terra gave a curt nod. The Pixies' leader, Torikki, flew over and sprinkled dust on the Gnome's head. He came back to life screaming.

Goron growled low.

Terra turned. "Greetings, Goron. Do you know this creature?"

"You should have notified me, Terra." He swore under his breath, mumbling something about Fey and their bloody secrets. He squinted at the form on the target. Goron held his hand out pointing at the spy. His hand pulsed red. "He is not of our clan. He hails from the Roosevelt National Forest in Colorado."

Terra scrutinized the Gnome leader for a few moments. "You speak the truth. Do you not wish to save a fellow Gnome?"

"Give me the charges."

Terra nodded to an underling who handed Goron a scroll. He scratched his chin as he read the document.

"I do not claim him." He grunted.

The Elven leader threw another knife at the Gnome spy without looking at the target. She watched Goron's expression as the spy took a knife to the gut and cried out in anguish. Willow observed with interest. Terra's accuracy was astounding. But what was more curious was how the two leaders stared at one another. Unblinking, they circled each other for several minutes without speaking a word. Terra blinked first. They stopped moving.

"Very well. We will speak on this tomorrow."

Terra nodded to Torikki again. The Pixie sprinkled more powder on the Gnome's head and he fell unconscious. Willow watched the rise and fall of the spy's chest. Whatever they were giving him kept him alive for now.

The Gnomes and the Elves seemed to have called a truce. Goron walked the path leading back to the bar. Willow went in the other direction toward a stage where a band was performing. Ellie stood in front swaying to the music. She wore an intricate fishnet dress made of vine and pink flowers. There were matching pink flowers in her hair.

"Very elegant, Ellie. I hardly recognized you."

Ellie blushed a deep green and hugged her older sister. "O'ma. It's so good to see you." She glanced down at her gown. "I grew it this morning. The flowers took me the longest. I couldn't quite decide which color to go with."

Willow laughed, "You always end up with pink."

Ellie frowned. "Not always." She looked around. "So, who's all here?"

"The typical. Council members and their cronies. I've seen a handful from the main factions. Centaurs are playing midnight soccer. Most of the Elves are throwing knives at targets. The Satyrs, Demons, and Nymphs are at the bar. I haven't seen any Shifters or Werewolves though. Isn't that strange?"

Ellie's eyes got wide. "Why would I care about them?"

Willow grinned. Ellie was smitten with a certain teen wolf that had taken her virginity at sixteen. But if she wanted to play coy, Willow would play along.

"Oh, I don't know. Just thought you'd be curious."

"Well, I thought there was going to be a Werewolf band tonight." She pointed to the Elves on stage playing flutes and harps. The music was beautiful, but a little boring.

"Don't worry. It's just the opening act." Willow confirmed, "They should be up soon."

As if summoned, a group of werewolves strolled into the clearing. *Speak of the devils.* They wore ripped jeans and nothing else. The trio were sexy as sin. Muscles bulged as they hoisted huge speakers onto the stage. Two of them winked at Ellie who blushed and turned away. She pulled at her dress to straighten the vines and fluffed up her hair.

Willow grinned. She wondered which of the males was Ellie's crush. She had never brought him around to introduce to the family.

Red came out of the forest behind them and slapped one in the ass. She grinned when the wolf turned and snarled.

"I'll translate," Willow said. "Don't mess with the roadies."

Ellie giggled.

Red stuck out a hip and glared at the wolf until he backed off. She was wearing chainmail and arm bracers tonight. It was an odd choice for Festivus, but not completely unheard of. The Ashbrook Dryads were a warrior clan. It was within their rights to wear formal battle dress to these events.

"Just who I wanted to see." Red slapped Willow on the back. "Tell me what happened last night. Gimme all the juicy details. Especially the part where you introduced Ms. Patella to Lucian's family jewels."

Willow groaned. "How did you find out?"

Red threw back her head and guffawed. "Come on, sis. You know how quickly gossip travels. I heard from Olie that Lucian had to beg Liska for an herbal healing potion at two a.m. The Fox Shifter gave him tea to soak his balls." Her eyes glinted, "Oh, what I would have paid to see that shit."

Willow winced. She hadn't meant to hurt him that bad. She sighed and filled her sisters in on what took place the previous night.

Red was enraged. "That bastard. If I'd have been there, he wouldn't be walking for a week."

"I feel kind of bad about the whole thing."

Red rolled her eyes. "Don't you dare feel guilty. The dude is tag-teaming some lake Nymphs right now. He's right as rain."

Willow grinned. That seemed more like the Lucian she knew. She hoped he finally found some peace and stopped this ridiculous obsession. She missed having him as a friend.

Chapter 19

Bella paced in the meadow away from all the noise waiting for her Mother. She wanted to get back to the party, but she'd received instructions via squirrel, and you never refused Mother Bacchus. She stared at the crowning tree wondering what made it so special. The crackled bark of the Alligator Juniper had reformed into a throne when Willow had been crowned sixteen years ago. The chair looked brittle and uncomfortable. It would serve Willow right if it was. She was tempted to take a seat while she waited but had second thoughts. The tree still held magic. She didn't know what would happen if someone other than the Guardian sat on the throne. The temptation just wasn't worth the risk. She hadn't been back here since Willow's crowning. She recalled it like it was yesterday. Bella still thought her brother Faustino would have made a much better Guardian.

Her mother staggered into the clearing. She was clearly drunk. The Bacchus brothers had been plying her with liquor all evening. The other members of Council probably insisted. Since dignitaries were visiting from other forests, they had to make nice with the neighbors, not something her mother excelled at. Trade agreements could be won or destroyed in a single evening. Even Bella understood the importance of building diplomatic relations.

Her mother crossed the field of flowers, veering slightly to the left. She stopped halfway to the tree. Bella sighed wondering if her mother needed help. What was it this time? Had her hoof gotten stuck in the mud, or perhaps something worse? Bella smirked. It would serve her mother right, for making them both walk all the way out here for no good reason. Bella saw movement from above. A small creature fluttered by her mother's ear. She squinted. It was a Sprite. It could be Fuath. Her mother and he were close friends. Bella faced the tree not wanting to appear obvious. She strained to hear what they were saying, but the voices were too low. Damn it.

Several excruciatingly long minutes later, Donna finished her conversation and made it the rest of the way to the tree where Bella stood with hands on her hips.

"About time."

"Excuse me? What did you say?"

Bella gave a nervous laugh. "Nothing, Mother."

"Hmm." Donna leaned heavily on Bella's shoulder for support.

Great. She could barely stand on her own.

"I didn't realize how far it was to walk out here. I'm exhausted."

Bella scrunched up her nose at the smell. The alcohol permeated from her mother's pores like she had bathed in it.

"Well, you did pick this locale."

"Yes. Because it's private with no one listening. You can never be too careful."

"What do you want, Mother?" Bella hissed.

Donna tilted her head and glared at her daughter. She pinched Bella's chin. Hard. Even drunk her mother wasn't going to stand for sass talk.

"Plans have changed. I need you to seduce the human."

Bella scowled. It was bad enough to befriend him, but sex? "Mother, that's disgusting."

"It's necessary."

Why was her Mother even suggesting something so foul? Her mother hated humans. She remembered the fights between her mother and father when she was nine. They hadn't known she'd overheard. Her mother always screaming about the affairs. Her father demanding he had to sleep with the human women. He had no choice. He did it for security, to keep them all safe.

Mother Bacchus patted her shoulder, "I'm sorry, but we all must make sacrifices."

"Just like father?" Bella slapped a hand over her mouth. She hadn't meant for that to slip out.

"Don't you dare speak to me about that male. This is different. Your father made excuses for his philandering."

She bit her lip. It seemed very much the same sort of scenario her father had alluded to all those years ago. But Bella knew better than to push. She knew exactly what her mother was capable of.

"What about my Demon?"

"You did well convincing him to try and get back with Willow."

Bella hadn't liked it at all. She didn't like to share.

"It went over better than expected. Rumors are spreading. The whole forest is abuzz thinking she is jealous of the two of you dating."

"She didn't need to incapacitate him," Bella grumbled.

Her mother laughed, a soft tinkling sound that grated on her nerves.

"Stop complaining. The Demon is repaired."

"But why send the lake Nymphs?" She whined, "I could be enjoying him right now."

"You need to learn that he is not *your* Demon." Her mother growled. She blew out a breath. "Bella, dear, you grow too attached. It's for your own good."

Bella pursed her lips. She wasn't happy about it, but she wasn't about to defy her mother.

"Fine. I'll seduce the human. Piece of cake. Is that all or can I go?"

Donna snatched Bella's wrist. "Mind your manners or I'll make you behave." She smiled sweetly. "Drink before you go?" Her mother shook the flask dangling from her belt.

Bella's face paled and she jerked from her mother's grasp. She knew Mother Bacchus kept a supply of potions hidden inside her jewelry box. Most were obtained illegally from the Sprites. Her mother was the reason Bella didn't drink anything served at parties. It was far too easy for someone to slip something in unnoticed. Most of the time, Bella stayed sober and alert while everyone around her got drunk. It made her feel a bit like an outsider, but then she would remind herself, *better boring than dead.*

Chapter 20

ILLOW WOKE TO sunlight streaming in through a crack in her temporary pine. She blinked into the bright light and groaned. The second day of Council was always the worst. Willow had to listen to complaints from dawn until dusk. She rolled out of her borrowed bed, an old Bristlecone Pine, and walked to the sacred circle. The line of forest creatures was far too long. She couldn't see the end. By the way most were eyeing her, she must look as bad as she felt. She used magic to conjure several cushions of vine in front of the Council bench. There were only two of the nine Council members present. It looked like they would be starting late. No big surprise. All of Council had to be present before she could begin. Her mother had always complained about that. Although, it hadn't always been that way.

As she settled into the vines, Willow recalled a time when she was very young and her Grandmother was Guardian. They were all in the meadow. Her Grandmother was seated on the throne. The Alligator Juniper had seemed so large and scary to her at that age, but her Grandmother convinced her to sit on its roots as she braided flowers into Willow's hair. The woodland community sat on the ground surrounding the tree and would bring up their concerns. Her Grandmother would hear all sides of the argument, share her wisdom, and give her ruling. It was all very informal. She didn't even remember Council being there. She wondered when Council had started hearing grievances in the sacred circle instead of the meadow. It didn't make a whole lot of sense. A larger space would make things a lot more efficient, not that Willow would raise the question. That would add hours of debate. She was already dreading how long it would take to hear all the cases. For the past sixteen years, Council only allowed Willow to make judgments on small cases. On large cases, they would debate and vote before giving their verdict. How had the role of Guardian changed so drastically in just two generations?

Donna was the last to arrive. Her eyes were bloodshot, and she carried a flask. Willow smirked. Hair of the dog. *Ruff night, Mother B?*

"Let's begin," Donna said as she sat down.

Mother Bacchus waved the first one in line forward. "State your name and case," Donna ordered in a cold, clipped tone.

Willow was used to Donna's bitchiness. It ran in the family, or at least the female side. The porcupine let out a series of shrieks and grunts. Donna grabbed her head and groaned. Willow grinned. The porcupine and his family had moved from Kaibab last month. A coyote was harassing them. Although normal enemies, Coconino had an immigration law protecting porcupines. They had been hunted so much in the past that there were few porcupines left in the Coconino Forest to help eat the bark of weak ponderosa pines. The creature's diet made her shiver, but they were necessary for the health of the forest. Willow reprimanded the young coyote and sentenced him to community service helping to rebuild the porcupine's den he had damaged.

The next was a black bear that was preparing for hibernation. A woodpecker had moved in next door. The noise was going to keep him up all winter. Willow consulted Roz, the Council member representing the lower creatures. Her ravens maintained the relocation files. They were able to find a new home for the woodpecker.

Several rowdy Mexican gray wolves pushed each other in line. Willow signaled for the Council Bailiff, Luik, to take care of the disturbance. He was an old rattlesnake and would slither through the crowd, hissing and shaking his tail. Luik separated the wolves with a visceral reminder of their fate if they displeased Council.

Cases flew by in the morning including squirrel neighbors that borrowed-slash-stole nuts from other neighbors. The debate over the distinction lasted quite a while. There was a domestic dispute between a male and female tarantula ending in copulation and the female eating the male. *That's one way to end an argument.*

An equal rights activist for the Bark Beetles handed out flyers and spent several minutes making grotesque noises while she ate her lunch. Donna lasted sixty seconds before she yelled for the next case. A Pixie complained that several Goblins attended the Autumn Equinox celebration violating public decency laws by coming fully dressed. Willow shrugged, not sure how to respond. She asked Rabuwa, the Goblin leader, for assistance. The small woman stood. She wore a brown leather vest, skirt, and boots with bracers on her forearms and knees. Any exposed skin including her face was covered in tribal tattoos. Her hair was tied back in a severe ponytail. Rabuwa's beady red eyes stared at the Pixie as she pounded her chest in a slow cadence. No words were spoken. She had intimidation down to an art form. The Pixie trembled with fear and promptly withdrew her complaint.

A fire Demon and Satyr fought over a Nymph causing destruction to property; a local forest pub called the Watering Hole. The owner was seeking payment for damages. Maggie, a Meadow Nymph, waved to Willow. *That girl was always causing trouble.* After witnesses gave their testimony, Donna sided with the Satyr, who just so happened to be one of her sons. Only the fire Demon was assigned community service to help with repairs to the pub.

By afternoon, Willow felt her eyes glaze over as the grievances grew more mundane with unclear resolutions. A javelina mom droned on about the importance of respecting their property line. She had told the jackrabbits numerous times not to cross into her territory, but they continued coming in and riling up her young. The jackrabbits had very short attention spans and didn't follow much of the conversation. Willow scanned the row of Council members. The only ones still conscious shrugged. Cyrus had his head slumped on the bench and was softly snoring. Donna had her eyes closed and looked to be taking a nap as well. Great. For this, they offer no opinion.

Willow cleared her throat. "While territory is a very important discussion point, unless there is a clear threat, I can do nothing legally. You may defend your territory but will still be subject to penalties if you kill without reason."

The mother turned in a huff, unhappy with the decision, and farted. It was nasty and woke those dozing on the bench.

Cyrus made a face, "Dear gods, what's that smell?" He looked around. "Tori, get your Pixies to clear the air?"

Tori snapped her fingers and a dozen Pixies floated in place beating their wings rapidly stirring up a wind and blowing the foul stench away.

Roz squawked, "What's next?"

The Gnome leader, Goron, stood. "I believe we should call the Roosevelt spy to the stand."

Donna nodded. "And this should be the last case of the day. All in agreement?"

All of Council grunted, squawked, or knocked the bench in approval.

Donna waved for refreshments. Several deer carried trays of drinks to the Council members. Clover stopped next to Willow and butted her head against Willow's thigh. She had a flask with Red's initials on it. God love her sis. Willow took a healthy swig of moonwine.

The Elven leader, Terra, had the prisoner shackled and brought in front of Council. His crimes would be heard. Not that it really mattered. The decision for execution had already been given. The only real debate was who and how they would be extracting information. For the bloodthirsty Council, this was the perfect appetizer for this evening.

The third night of Festivus was always the liveliest. All magical creatures from the forest received an invite. The glade was enchanted to expand, accommodating the number of creatures crossing the threshold. The boundaries would adjust throughout the evening. Although most would be so inebriated, they wouldn't notice the gentle fluctuations in their environment. Creatures leaning against a tree might lose their balance as the tree shifted slightly to the side. Those standing by the lake one minute might find themselves soaking wet the next. Willow wondered at one point if a trickster had created the enchantment. It was always best to find a good spot toward the center early in the evening. Preferably away from any foliage. Although not nearly as exciting, it was inevitably safer. The costumes were always exquisite. Willow had donned a corset made of vibrant green crystals. She had harvested them from caves over the years. Willow had a full skirt of weeping willow leaves imported for this evening. Her laurel wreath crown was accented with malachite crystals to match her corset.

Walking into the party, she witnessed Lucian at the same barstool he had been at the night before. She didn't really want to confront him, but it was going to happen sooner or later. Willow decided to get it over with so she could enjoy the rest of the evening. She sauntered up to the bar.

Faustino saw her first. "Green goddess, help me. What can I get to wet your whistle?"

Willow smirked. "That drink from the other night will do."

Lucian turned to take in Willow's attire. "You look nice."

Wonderful. They were being civil. He must not be drunk. "You as well, Lucian." She nodded at his leather pants and fancy nipple piercings. The gold barbells had red fire crystals that looked like flames. They complimented his deep red skin. She sipped from her goblet. The brew was just as potent as the night before. She reminded herself not to get tanked. Tomorrow was a big day in front of Council. She didn't want to screw it up.

"Are those piercings new?"

He looked down at his chest and shook his head. "Yeah. Apparently, I made a bet last night."

"With who?"

Lucian rubbed the back of his neck. "Your sister. Red."

Willow threw back her head and laughed. "Sorry." She said between giggles. "That's not funny."

"It was a hell of a thing to wake up to." He shrugged. "But it could have been worse."

They seemed to be getting along fine, keeping the conversation light until BB showed up. Bella was wearing fuck me thigh highs and a short mini skirt. Her leather corset hoisted her boobs up to her chin.

"Nice ensemble, Willow." Bella put a hand up to her eyes like she was blinded by the sparkles from Willow's outfit.

Willow moved out of the light into a shadow. "Sorry about that."

Bella sighed. "You always were one for the spotlight."

Lucian frowned. He must have known that wasn't Willow's M.O. at all. She usually didn't raise a fuss and never cared about being the center of attention.

Fuck BB's negativity. She turned away from the bar searching for anyone else. She located Red playing a game of backwoods poker with a few Goblins.

Willow grinned and walked over.

"I can't believe you set up Lucian."

"Easy pickings. Not even a challenge. He was so drunk." Red chuckled. "So, is he up for more piercings tonight?"

"Take it easy with the big guy." Willow sighed. "He doesn't mean to be such a twat. Have some sympathy. Look who he's hanging with."

Red glanced at the bar. "That's not helping his case. His judgment is clearly impaired if he chose that bitch for his date."

Willow shrugged. "I appreciate the prank. He definitely deserved it, but fixate on someone else tonight. Ok?"

Red nodded. "Sure sis, whatever. Have fun." She threw down a royal flush. "Gotcha suckers."

The Goblins grumbled tossing coins on the stone table. Red propped up her feet. "Hey one of you losers, get me a drink. Kicking your ass is thirsty work."

Willow wandered around the party watching all the craziness of the evening. She enjoyed observing in the background. If it hadn't been forbidden, she would have merged with one of the pines and watched from that vantage. At the edge of the party near the lake, Willow spotted Lucian standing in front of a bonfire. He was roaring for the blaze to build and build. Being a Fire Demon, he could easily manipulate fire. She leaned against a tree. A throat cleared. She hadn't noticed someone else standing in the shadows. Willow turned. A tall man with golden brown hair and amber eyes emerged from behind the tree. She frowned at his clothing. He was in cut-off jean shorts and nothing else. Festivus was usually a time to dress up. She didn't recognize him. His body was long and lean and very tan. If she hadn't just been staring at Lucian's overblown physique, she would have been impressed.

"You're Willow, right?"

She nodded. "You're new."

He chuckled. "That I am, ma'am. Name's Gary." He held out his hand.

It was a very human custom to shake hands. She found that intriguing. Not wanting to seem impolite she shook hands and felt a burst of power. He was a Bobcat Shifter. He must have bound himself to the forest already. That would have been the only way to feel his nature so clearly.

"Uh. Sorry 'bout that. Forgot." He wiped his hand on his jean shorts. Power tended to come across like static electricity. "I was curious what the laws are here for datin' humans."

She stared at him. He seemed earnest. Not a plant from Council, though she wouldn't put it past them. Willow took a deep breath and gently touched his chest focusing on his intent. She could often feel emotions unless they put up blocks. The male was completely open to her, as bare as his body. He was so lonely it made her eyes blink tears. Willow didn't want to disappoint him. He had waited so long and Council was pretty strict when it came to humans. She was fighting her own battle on that one.

"If you don't reveal your shifting, you should be ok. But don't get attached. And for Gaia's help, don't advertise. You get my drift." She smiled up at him.

Relief washed over his features. He grinned down at her.

"If things get serious, then you'll have to consult Council. That's where things get messy."

He tilted his head, clearly confused. "You're the Guardian, right?"

"Yes," Willow hissed, feeling suddenly uncomfortable. She adjusted her crown. "Enjoy Festivus."

He bowed low as she walked away. She felt insulted he would ask such a question. He was new, Willow reminded herself. But something about the conversation grated on her nerves. The Shifter didn't follow as she walked closer to the fire and found another tree to lean against. Bella's eyes were riveted on Lucian's chest. She licked one of his piercings and tugged. His nipple would have been tender from the recent piercing, not that BB gave a fuck about anyone else's pain, in fact, she usually reveled in it. Instead of shoving her away, Lucian wrapped his arms around her waist and squeezed her to his chest. She squealed with delight as he carried her a short distance away. Lucian dropped his leather breeches while Bella wiggled out of her skirt. She left the thigh-high boots on.

"Corset on or off?"

Lucian stroked his cock. "Off." He said with a gravelly voice.

She loosened the tie at the back and flung it to the dirt. "How do you want me?"

He wiped a hand over his mouth. "Bent over and screaming my name."

Bella grinned. "I like your style."

She leaned against the tree with her tail in the air.

Lucian got her ready then started pounding her from behind. He noticed Willow watching and winked. "What's up, Willow?"

"Nada, but it's clear what's up on your end."

He sneered. "Nothing new about that."

Was he trying to make her jealous? *What a laugh.*

Bella glared at her. Willow could tell she was pissed at the interruption.

"What the fuck, Lucian? A little focus. I'm bent over but I'm doing all the work." She used her leverage on the tree to thrust her hips back earning a loud grunt.

He slapped her ass. "Hold on a minute, BB."

Willow grinned. Lucian knew the secret of her nickname.

He reached around to her clit, twirling his thumb in circles while finishing the conversation with Willow. Bella was clearly not happy with his split attention, but whatever he was doing had her moaning and grinding against him. Willow tilted her head for a better view. She saw sparks and her eyebrows rose.

Lucian grinned, "BB loves her fire play, don't you honey?"

He pushed more sparks to her clit and she groaned, her body jerking against him. Bella pleaded for more, clearly delighted, as she danced on his hand. His cock continued to thrust, never breaking his rhythm.

"You've obviously learned some new tricks over the years."

"Oh, Willow. I've got an arsenal of experience. Sure, you don't want to give us another go?" Lucian pulled Bella up and placed her arms around his neck. He had one hand playing with a nipple tugging hard and the other sending sparks to her clit. Willow stared at the erotic scene. "I know just how you like to be touched."

He licked the crook of Bella's neck where it met her shoulder.

Willow shifted her stance. Yes, he knew exactly what did it for her. He bit Bella's shoulder while holding Willow's gaze. Bella convulsed with an immediate orgasm. She apparently enjoyed bite play as well. Lucian had fangs that could release a small dose of venom. It contained opioid peptides that caused the recipient an endorphin rush. Lucian pounded into her from behind, teeth still buried in her neck as BB spasmed in his arms. Without breaking the stare, he deposited Bella on the ground to writhe with aftershocks. He was still long and hard. All that, and he hadn't come. She felt herself flush a deep green. It had turned her on and he knew it. This male was still beautiful and sexy, and a few months ago, she may have taken him up on his offer. But now she had Bray. No, he wasn't as muscled or as aggressive in bed, but there was something about him she couldn't quite put her finger on. He was hers in a way Lucian could never be. Bray was kind and sweet and made her feel like his only goal was to make her happy. Who would trade that for a one-night stand?

Willow shook her head and walked away. If Lucian didn't understand they were never getting back together again, she would stop trying to explain. Distance was what they needed. He wasn't getting the hint she no longer wanted him. Lucian roared into the night, but her legs didn't falter. She kept her chin raised and walked out of the clearing. She didn't stop until she came to her temporary lodging for the evening. Willow had made an appearance. No one could say she'd been remiss with her duties. Now she could rest up for her big day tomorrow.

Council was in rare form the next morning. Pixies kept the hangover concoctions flowing while Council members groaned. Their normal straight postures were slumped, eyelids already at half-mast. Rabuwa the Goblin leader and Roz the raven, representatives for the lower creatures, were the only ones still alert. Willow grinned. There wouldn't be a better time to bring up Bray's residence status.

"I'm sure we all want to make this last day of Council go quickly, so I've outlined the agenda with some suggestions." She signaled for the squirrels to drop off the agenda page in front of each Council member.

They squinted at the paper, trying to make out the list of items. She had purposely inked it in small print.

She smiled. If we're all in agreement, we can end this early and everyone can head home.

Donna frowned. "What's this last item? I can't read it."

"That's Brayden Graham's residence status. I've investigated him, and he poses no threat. I vote he's allowed to stay."

"Hmph," Donna grumbled. "Another Ashbrook getting some human on the side? The apple doesn't fall far from the tree, does it?"

Willow frowned. "What does that mean?"

Donna shrugged. "Just what I said." She turned to the other members of Council. "I for one don't trust the human. His home encases a sacred tree. I would think a Dryad would see the danger. She's clearly being influenced by this creature."

Fuath knocked his knuckle to the bench. "Here. Here. I agree. Humans are a menace. He's a security risk. We must force him to leave."

Great. It appeared Fuath must have filled Donna in on her relationship. No matter. She had done her homework and recruited a few witnesses just in case.

"Ah," Willow stated, "but if he moves, it means he sells his cabin to another human, one that might wish harm and cause permanent damage."

Council looked around with worried expressions. "Through my research, I have discovered this human contributes financially to the Wildlife Conservation Society and the Nature Conservancy. He takes care not to harm the forest and goes out of his way to care for the creatures within. We couldn't have hand-picked a human that was more protective of nature to live here."

There was discussion back and forth on the bench.

"And, I have testimonies." Willow announced, "Daisy the black bear, please come to the stand."

She lumbered from the crowd, clacking teeth and grunting. Willow translated for those that didn't speak bear. Daisy said he was the kindest and bravest human she had ever met. He had cleared the forest of traps laid out by hunters and provided an abundance of food. And not just the normal human snacks, but nutritious food like berries, roots, and even fish. He made her life easier by providing safety and nourishment for both her and her young.

Willow recalled how Bray had taken care of those traps. He had accidentally found most of them with his walking staff while hiking. And the supply of fish hadn't been set out on purpose. Bray had been fishing and left the cooler open to go run into the cabin for beer. His catch had been stolen by the time he got back. It was surprising to Willow when he had laughed instead of being angry with the theft.

"Next, I'd like to call representatives from the Steller's Jay clan." Willow waved to the sky and a trio of Jaybirds descended. They chirped praises about the admirable human that had been keeping numerous bowls of seed filled daily.

"And now, I'd like to call Sammy and Dave."

The two Abert's squirrel brothers chattered about the human's nut stock describing in detail the exotic varieties, how it had been the most delicious they had ever tasted. They praised the human for not being stingy, sharing his wealth, setting out bowls several times a day.

With a swish of his bushy tail, Sammy stared at Council for several moments.

He squeaked, "I will be deeply disappointed if the human leaves."

The Council members whispered back and forth, more than likely remembering the month-long strike from years ago that had been led by Sammy and his brother. Many forest creatures had dubbed that period of time the 'Sound of Silence' since no mail had flowed into or out of the forest. When Council had caved to their demands, it had been a huge win for the squirrels in Coconino and had caused an uproar around the globe. More factions of squirrels from other forests now demanded similar working conditions. Willow had been proud of Sammy sticking up for his convictions back then, and was grateful for his support of Bray.

Willow low-fived the little guy before he scurried away.

After all the testimonies were heard, Council continued to debate. Unfortunately, the lower creatures' opinions held little sway. They tended to discriminate against them, unless forced. In Willow's mind, all creatures large and small should have the same equal voice to speak up and be heard. The nine elected Council members were supposed to represent the various factions of the forest. But only one of those seats was assigned to the lower creatures even though their numbers were far greater than all the other factions combined.

By the end of the day, Bray's residence status was still up in the air. It would be a topic of discussion in next month's meeting. In the meantime, his stay was to be strictly monitored. It was considered pro-bationary until Council made their final decision. At least they hadn't outright booted him. Willow considered it a win.

As Donna made one last snide comment about Willow's conflict of interest regarding Bray's residence, she realized nothing had changed since she was sixteen. Council still considered her a child. They would never think she was old enough or wise enough to make decisions for the forest. They would continue to tell her what to do until the day she died. Willow sighed. She could only blame herself. Her Grandmother had taught her that you teach people how to act by your actions. When she was young, she always thought it meant be nice to others, and they'll be nice back. She was kind and patient, honest and loyal. Just like her birth tree, she would bend and twist, accommodating those around her without complaint. But those on Council saw her compassion as weakness. Few understood the concept of integrity. Humans hadn't cornered the market on deception in politics. Council was well versed in lies to get what they wanted. Even the good ones, like Cyrus, had their own agenda. It was rarely for the good of the forest. There were always hidden motives.

As she glanced from face to face, she realized what her Grandmother had been alluding to all those years ago, *my actions dictate how they treat me*. Without putting her foot down and demanding the respect a Guardian should have, she basically gave up her power. She had no idea how to get it back at this point, so many years later. Council had controlled things for half her life. Why would they just give it up now? Willow wondered when they would finally push her too far and she would snap.

Chapter 21

BRAY SAT ON his couch staring at the blank tv. He was still in shock over what he had just learned from Bella. The screen door opened. Willow sprinted across the cabin and launched herself at him. She started kissing him with such enthusiasm, but he refused to kiss her back, no matter how velvety soft her lips were or how right she felt in his arms. He felt utterly betrayed. She had been with another just days ago, and that was only what he knew of. How many other lovers waited for his lusty neighbor to come calling?

"Bray, I missed you so much." She rubbed herself against him. His body responded, but it pissed him off.

"What's the matter?"

He gripped her arms pushing her from his chest. "You don't know?"

She tilted her head. "Know what?"

He groaned. "I know where you've been."

"On my retreat. Like I told you."

"I had a drone follow you."

"You did what?" Willow screeched. She shoved herself away and scrambled behind the couch.

Bray ran fingers through his hair noticing her position. Did she think he would hit her? He might be angry, but he would never physically hurt her.

"Well, I guess I didn't trust you. And it looks like I was right not to."

"What did you see?" Her voice quavered.

"You want me to spell it out? Fine." Bray walked around the couch standing inches from her. She had to crane her head to look into his eyes. "I saw you cheating on me."

She blinked. "That's ridiculous. I did no such thing."

"Really? I have video of you making out with Lucian at one of your nature parties. Do you deny it?"

"No, but you don't understand."

Bray shook his head. "I don't get it. Why go to the trouble of asking to be exclusive if the next thing you do is get drunk and make out with your ex?"

Willow's jaw dropped. "Yes, I got drunk, and yes, we kissed, but it wasn't mutual."

Was it possible? He kicked himself mentally. She was playing games. He had proof. A guilty person wouldn't dive behind the couch when someone had a video of what they'd done.

"Would you have told me about it?"

"Umm."

"So, that's a no."

Willow took a deep breath and ran her fingers along the back of the couch, "Did your drone see anything else?"

Bray studied her movements. Willow rubbed things when she was nervous. There was more she was hiding. He couldn't tolerate dishonesty. He had been so tempted to believe her. Bray growled with frustration. "It ran out of battery charge." He backed away. "But it doesn't matter, by then I was done with the drone, and with you."

"You don't mean that." She whispered.

"Yes, Willow. I do. You cheated and you lied." He gestured to the door of the cabin. "I want you gone."

She stared at him for several seconds. The clock ticked loud in the silence. He didn't move a muscle, just continued to point. Willow turned toward the door shuffling her feet, moving like a zombie. He felt like a bastard, but she was the one who betrayed him, damn it. He shouldn't feel sorry for her. Bray opened the door.

She turned back to him in the open doorway, staring into his eyes. Willow blinked back tears. "I can't believe you think I cheated."

"Why would I trust anything you say?" Bray said through gritted teeth. "There's nothing but lies between us." Bray took a step forward and she took two quick steps back. He slammed the screen door in her face.

She stood there for several moments blinking. He watched her from the one-way glass wondering what was going on in that complex mind of hers. So many expressions flashed across her face. Sorrow, confusion, regret. She ended with determination just before spinning on her heels and stomping off into the woods. As he watched her walk away, his anger bled away leaving guilt in its wake. That frustrated him more than anything. She was in the wrong, not him. So why did he feel like a dick? He sighed and went in search of a bottle of scotch.

He poured a third drink for himself while sitting on his front swing. Bray wondered, not for the first time, if he'd over-reacted to the video. Most of it had been blurry. The only scene clear was of them kissing. Lucian had pressed Willow's body up against a tree, and they had been making out hot and heavy. He clenched the glass recalling the vivid image. *That's my woman.* From the video, Willow looked like an active participant, but could that have just been the camera angle? Was it possible she had been telling the truth or was he just desperate enough to convince himself? He sighed, noticing Bella approach his cabin from the edge of the clearing. She gave a bright smile and sauntered over. Bella had been the one on drone duty. The woman oozed sex appeal. Her breasts were displayed in a low-cut poet blouse of cream cotton. A dark brown leather corset was tied tight around her tiny waist. Tight leather pants accentuated her wide hips. The only unsexy thing she wore was heavy work boots. But they couldn't detract from the rest of her body. Her hips swayed in a mesmerizing rhythm as she walked toward him. Her long dark brown hair blew in the wind, and her wicked kohled eyes shimmered with mischief.

She licked ruby red lips, "I'm hoping you're in the mood to share." She eyed the scotch.

Bray shrugged and grabbed another glass from his tray.

"How do you take it?"

Bella laughed low and sultry. "Give it to me any way you like."

Bray's eyebrows rose as she sat down next to him. He poured her two fingers neat.

"I take it from your expression, the confrontation didn't go well."

He grimaced. "No. But I didn't expect it to. She denied it."

"What a little liar," Bella gasped, "I was there. I saw everything. And you saw it on video."

She took a swig of the scotch, finishing it one long gulp. She licked her lips. "Delicious. I knew you'd have good taste." She leaned forward displaying her ample cleavage and looked up at him from under long thick lashes. Bella held out her glass. When he bent to pour another, she turned around and sprawled out on the bench. After he handed her the drink, she lounged back with her head in his lap. She rested the drink just below her breasts. They looked ready to burst from her top at any moment. Was she hitting on him? One part of him thought this was the perfect way to get over Willow, but his conscience was kicking his ass. She smiled up at him.

"Thank you, Bray. You're such a gentleman. Far too nice for the likes of Willow."

She took a sip. It dribbled down her chin and slid down her cleavage. Like a bastard he followed the trail. Bella had been watching his reaction with interest. He sighed and grabbed a pillow from the chair next to him, placing it under her head. It was a nice gesture to make her comfortable, but he had really done it to put some space between them.

"So, what will you do now?"

Bray took another sip. "I have no idea."

Bella sat up and turned to him, moving the pillow out of the way. "What about that Gail person from town?" She leaned her elbow on the back of the bench. "I can tell you from experience, it's best to get right back on the horse."

His eyebrows rose. "Equestrian reference?"

She shrugged. "If not me and not Gail, then who?

Bray laughed, "Are you trying to play matchmaker?" She smoothed a hand down her corset making his concentration difficult. He took another sip of scotch when she caught him staring at her chest. "Too soon?" She grinned. "You're a nice guy, Bray. Why shouldn't I want to help you?"

He finished off his glass and mumbled, "I'm not that nice."

Bray stopped participating in the conversation. His thoughts turned dark. He grew increasingly moody remembering the hurt look on Willow's face when he slammed the door. Bella left soon after, probably realizing he was in no mood for company. He barely grunted a goodbye before stumbling into the cabin. After making a sandwich to soak up the scotch, Bray forced himself to eat half before going on a long walk. He ended up at a glade where Willow had taken him. He noticed the low stone table in the center where they had a picnic. She had told him it was one of her mother's favorite locations. He sighed knowing that everywhere he went, something was going to remind him of her. Just as he was getting ready to leave, he spied movement on the other side of the clearing.

A young woman, maybe eighteen years old, with rich auburn hair was gathering up plants and placing them into various pockets in her long apron. He had never seen one with quite so many pockets. He counted at least thirty, all filled to the brim. The girl bobbed her head as he approached like she was acknowledging something he'd said. He looked behind him to see if she had nodded to someone else. Nope. No one there. When he turned back, she was gone. Bray went over to the tree she had been kneeling by and found a pile of herb bundles. He peered behind the tree. There was no movement. Where did she go? Bray looked back at the herbs. There were pebbles in front of each bundle. Two by the first pile, three by the middle and one pebble by the last. Next to it was a small fire pit bordered by large rocks holding a tea kettle in the middle. The water was bubbling. He waited a few minutes to see if she would return.

"Hey, lady, you forgot your things!"

Silence.

Bray was intrigued. He decided to take pieces of herbs from each pile matching the quantity of pebbles. Maybe it was a recipe, or maybe it was just the science geek in him finding patterns where none existed. He sprinkled the fresh herbs into the kettle. Glancing around for something to stir, he found a thin branch, stripped the bark clean, and swirled the contents.

Bray jumped when he noticed the girl kneeling beside him. Where had she come from? He hadn't heard her approach. It was as if she had disappeared then reappeared out of thin air. She reached out, palm up, and tilted her head. The girl didn't look angry or surprised, just insistent. He handed over the stick. She took it and continued to stir, occasionally inhaling the concoction. The girl pulled out two small teacups from one of her pockets. She poured the liquid into each and gestured for him to take one. He shrugged, bringing the tea up to inhale the fragrance. His nose scrunched at the pungent odor. The girl hadn't picked up the other cup. He wondered if he was being punk'd. Maybe it was the scotch or the bad day he was having, but he just didn't care. He blew on the tea and gave it a sip. The girl gave him a wide smile. She had long canines, and as they stared at one another, he noticed other details. The young woman had a thin snout with a black-tipped nose and gray furry ears poking outside her ponytail. Why hadn't he noticed them before? That was odd. He looked down at her feet. She had paws, and her backside sprouted a fluffy tail. He eyed the tea. *What the hell was in this stuff?* Must be some hallucinogen. Bray shrugged. This would certainly be a better way to end the day.

Things couldn't possibly get worse. Spending time with the fox girl was at least interesting.

"My name's Bray." He held up his cup in greeting.

The young woman gave a squeaky bark.

Bray blinked. He gave her paw a shake. "Nice to meet you." He mimicked the sound she made.

She smiled a toothy grin.

He took another swig of the tea and lost consciousness.

Later that evening, Bray woke up with cottonmouth. He blinked. His clothes were crumpled up on the floor in his bedroom. He didn't remember leaving them there. Come to think of it, he didn't recall walking home either. Bray stumbled to the bathroom to relieve himself, trying to recollect what happened with the fox girl in the glade. He chuckled back at the memory. Those must have been some crazy herbs to leave him with a dream like that. He went to the kitchen to make coffee and found an apron laying on the kitchen table. There were thirty pockets filled with herbs. He sat down on a kitchen chair and stared at the linen fabric. Had the fox girl been real? Maybe there had been a girl, but had he imagined the strange appearance? That wasn't much better. If he had invited a strange girl back to his place, what had they done? Had he slept with her? A wave of guilt swamped him. Sweat dotted his upper lip. If there was even a chance of getting back with Willow, then sleeping with some random girl wouldn't help. Was the girl even eighteen? *Oh god, what if she were underage?* Bray felt sick. He took a deep breath. Just because he had the apron didn't mean anything happened. She could have just given it to him, right? He ran through the cabin trying to piece together clues. He found two coffee cups in the sink. He might have just invited her in. That didn't mean he did anything with her. He couldn't find anything else out of place. Bray went to the bed, there was no indention on the other pillow. That was a good sign. Although, the covers had been kicked off, which could have happened during sex. His lack of clothes was bothersome. He usually wore boxers to bed, but he had been stoned. He sat on the edge of the bed holding his head in his hands and groaned. Did he just fuck up his chances with Willow?

He heard soft snoring from the other side of the bed and jumped to investigate. The fox girl was curled up in blankets on the floor. There were two things positive about the situation. One, she still had her clothes on and two, she didn't resemble a fox or a girl. The woman had a tanned weathered face with wrinkles. She looked to be in her seventies, or perhaps older. She blinked up at him. Again, the woman showed no surprise even though a naked man was peering down at her.

"You're sporting wood, boy. You oughta cover that." She gestured at his erection.

Bray ran from the room. He was wrong. The day had gotten worse.

By the time he changed into jeans and a t-shirt, the woman was already sitting at the kitchen table drinking coffee. Bray hadn't even seen her get up. He must still be under the effects of whatever herbs he had taken this afternoon.

He sat down, not quite sure how to begin this conversation. "My name's Bray."

"I know." She smiled. "Do you remember my name?"

Bray gave a squeaky bark, that turned into a throat clear. "Uh no. I'm sorry I don't."

The woman shook her head. "You had it right the first time."

Bray gave her a puzzled look. She held out her hand. "You can call me Liska."

He shook it and scratched his head, "I'm a little fuzzy on exactly who you are, and how we got here."

She grinned. "I'm an herbalist. I was out collecting plants and you asked if I would help you do the same. I agreed in exchange for some supplies from town. I don't get to town much at my age."

He nodded excitedly. "Of course." Bray had been fascinated by plants for as long as he could remember. He had read a number of herbal books describing the attributes and uses, but had no guide on what they looked like or where to find them. He had briefly attempted to find a few in the forest with no luck. This was just the thing to get his mind off Willow. "Let me know what you need, and I'll pick it up tomorrow."

Liska wrote a list of the items she needed, then began pulling out items from her pockets. The first was a long stem with several red flowers. She went through the plants one by one, describing their uses and how to identify and where to locate them throughout the forest. The gathering was the hardest part. If Bray was willing to go out with her the next day after he got back from town, she would continue his training. She seemed tickled by his enthusiasm.

"Most of the young have no patience for this sort of thing."

He frowned. "I'm not that young. I'm thirty-five."

"Psshh, You're just a baby." She tilted her head and placed her index finger to his forehead. He felt a spike of power. She rubbed her fingers together with surprise. "Hmm. Interesting."

Bray rubbed his forehead. It was still tingling. "What was that?"

She shrugged and grabbed another plant.

They spent most of the night going over plants. She tested him on identification and properties. Bray seemed to have a knack for this. By morning, the old woman looked exhausted. Bray told her she could stay and take a nap while he went to the store to get her supplies. Liska had paused for a long time like she was listening to something he couldn't hear. She nodded. "Yes, I will do that, Brayden Graham of the Muir."

It wasn't until he was in town at the hardware store that he realized he had never given his last name. How had she known that? He figured it was possible someone from town could have told her. But how had she known the name of the woods he had played in as a child. Muir Woods was by his family's house in California. He had a vague memory of his father taking him there, but his father had died before he turned three. His mother stopped going to the woods a few years after his death. He had been killed while on a research mission in South America. He was a botanist working with a pharmaceutical company. The settlement enabled his mother and him to live quite comfortably.

By the time he got back to the cabin, Bray couldn't wait to go on his scavenger hunt for plants. By the end of the day, Liska was astonished by how much he had accumulated. Bray wondered if his skill for finding plants was genetic. It made him feel a sense of connection to the father he had never really known. Late in the afternoon, he went one more time to the hardware store to purchase a pop-up greenhouse and several storage containers for everything he had collected. That evening, Liska helped him categorize and store the herbs. The next morning, she showed him how to grind the herbs into a fine powder and gave him recipes for simple healing. Bray spent the next week extremely busy hunting for plants and learning new recipes from Liska. He was grateful for the distraction. It meant he spent less time missing Willow and feeling like a chunk of his heart had been ripped from his chest.

Chapter 22

WILLOW WAS FURIOUS at how she left things with Bray. She couldn't believe how she had wimped out, not even defending herself against the accusations. Although, the part about lies had hit a nerve. She hadn't been truthful with him from the very beginning. Their whole relationship was built on deceit. Her original reason for getting to know him had been to find a weakness, set him up for failure, and convince him to move. Once she had gotten to know him, she realized what an incredible person he was. Bray wasn't acting at all like himself. Why would he have resorted to a drone to spy on her? She had given him no reason to worry. Then it hit her. Gail. That little hussy from California. She was the instigator. The woman was anxious to get her greedy little paws all over him. Willow was sure of it. She recalled how they ran into Gail time and again in town, and how she had somehow weaseled her way into lunch. Gail had talked non-stop at the bar and grill. She had slathered him with compliments, bragging on how much he did for the IT industry. Bray had grinned, clearly enjoying the praise. Willow had felt cut out of the conversation. She didn't ooh and aah over all the things he had done, because frankly, she didn't understand. The way Gail had gone on, Bray was a very big deal back home. But out here, he lacked basic survival skills. It was a miracle he made it through most days alive. He had gone through several first aid kits in the short time he'd been here. She wondered if his ego was taking a hit. Perhaps that's why he was feeling insecure and untrusting. All she knew for certain was she needed Gail out of the picture. She would deal with rebuilding trust after she took care of the bigger problem. Step one, get rid of the competition.

Willow had been determined to find Gail this past week., but that slippery little bitch proved elusive. Even with teams of animals posted at roadsides trying to spot her car, they couldn't find where she had gone. Willow concluded the human had to be somewhere in one of the larger towns. With the amount of time Gail spent talking about clothes and shoes, she was probably shopping at one of the higher-end boutiques in Flagstaff or Sedona, or maybe at some fancy resort or spa. Unfortunately, Willow didn't have the resources to track her movements in places like that. It appeared Gail had gone to ground. She was puzzled by the woman's strategy. It didn't make a whole lot of sense. She understood the woman's motivation. Bray was obviously quite a catch in the human world, but why was she playing hard to get? If it were Willow, she'd be reaping the rewards back at his cabin right now. Scouts at Bray's cabin would alert her if she showed. Maybe little Miss Perfect with her sexy stilettos and tight ass was overly confident? Had she assumed that if she triggered doubt, the mistrust would build burying any chance Willow had to get him back?

Fuck that. He's mine, bitch. Oh, Gail, you played a good game, but your tactics are flawed. You never leave a man alone and unsatisfied. Her mother had taught her that much. Even if Ilana had never wanted to keep a male, they always pined for her. So what if she couldn't enchant him magically, she had other resources to tap into. But first, she needed to visit the Sprite clan. If Willow was going to do this, she needed help from the experts. She had just been in too much shock to react appropriately when he had broken up with her. Willow cringed. She could fix this.

Willow placed her hand on the closest pine and traveled to a magically hidden glen. The Sprite's domain was under a log by a small creek. It was a portal rip into a different realm. Usually, you needed an invitation, but she would forgo etiquette. This was an emergency. Willow tensed when she heard movement ahead of her. It was from the portal rift. The scene before her blurred for a moment and Bella emerged carrying a small bundle. The bitch was sporting a grin. What did she get from the Sprites? It could be anything from a mild healing potion to a deadly toxin. All sales needed permission from Council, however, illegal sales were far more common. The Sprites' culture was driven by capitalism, specifically gold. Since their leader was on Council, unmonitored sales were highly prolific. Since Willow was seeking an illegal purchase herself, she could hardly criticize.

After entering the portal, she tracked down the Sprite leader. They discussed what was needed and he grudgingly agreed to meet her late that evening with the test supplies. Fuath complained about the last-minute notice on the busiest night of the year. Willow hadn't realized it was Halloween. She apologized by agreeing to double the gold. That seemed to satisfy him. She had been in a trance this last week without Bray in her life. Even more surprising, she hadn't heard from her sisters during this time. The Ashbrooks always arranged for special scares at the town's hayride. It was a family tradition. Since the Sprites were potion masters, they were in charge of creating poisons and serums that were critical to security. They needed a supply on hand in case humans saw too much. Knowing Red's enthusiasm for Halloween pranks, the batch of forget me serum would be well used this evening. Willow's appointment with Fuath would be late in the evening after all the festivities ended. Fuath agreed to administer the Serce test. It would detect the purity of Bray's heart, if they would be a good match, and would verify with absolute certainty if he was her eternal soulmate.

Willow arrived at her mother's favorite glade, the one with the low stone table at the center that the girls always used for picnics or family gatherings. This time, the table had a large map spread over the surface.

Red looked up. She blew a curl from one eye. "It's about time you got here, sis. Mae was about to send a search party."

Willow grinned at the squadron of squirrels squeaking to Mae. She waved, and with a swish of tails, the squirrels dispersed.

"I'm not the only one late. Where's Ellie?" Willow asked.

"It's almost the full moon." Red shrugged, "Our little Ellie's out party hopping with friends."

"Wow. This is the first year she'll miss Halloween," Willow shook her head, "I guess she's really growing up."

"I think her friends are too rowdy," Mae admonished. "She always comes back scratched and bruised.

"But with a skip in her step." Red wiggled her eyebrows, "Stop trying to cramp her style. Ellie's getting exactly what she needs."

What did that mean? Was Ellie getting serious, or was she just having fun like any normal eighteen-year-old? She felt guilty not paying that much attention to any of her sisters the last few months. Willow wanted to give them space to grow and enjoy their freedom as adults. Dryads were independent by nature, but they still enjoyed socializing in groups. They each had their own birth tree and they didn't live together. It had made watching over them when they were young challenging, to say the least. Luckily, there were charms in place to let her know when one of her sisters would wake or get scared. Willow had tucked Ellie into her birth tree bed at night until she was thirteen. Mae had stopped that fuss at age ten, and Red had been completely independent at age six. They were all so different, in looks and personality.

Red cleared her throat and pointed at the map. "Ok. Let's focus. We don't have much time. Here's the diagram of the hayride path through the woods courtesy of the drama club president at Flagstaff High School."

Mae opened her mouth. Red held up her hand. "I know what you're gonna ask. No. I didn't take the only copy. They had a huge stack. I only snagged one. I know how to be stealthy on occasion."

Mae's eyebrows rose, but she kept her mouth shut. They spent a few minutes going over Red's additions to the map.

A white light burst on the edge of the clearing. The sisters turned as one toward the intruder. Mae already had a weapon in hand. It was some throwing star Willow had never seen before.

"Hope I'm not late." A tall male with caramel skin and long dark hair strolled toward them. He moved with a cat-like grace and studied the sisters carefully. The male was model gorgeous with broad shoulders and lean muscles. He wore only a leather turquoise choker, faded jeans, and a smirk.

"Shoodii." Red yelled and bounded over to him. She gave him one of her infamous bear hugs.

"Stop that." He wheezed pushing her back with a burst of wind that ruffled her hair.

"Oh hell no. You didn't just mess with the curls."

He grinned as she tried to tackle him. Another puff of light and he vanished.

"That slippery mother fucker." Red dusted off her dirty jeans and scanned the clearing.

She sighed. "We don't have time for this. Truce?" Red called out.

Another puff of light and Shoodii appeared sitting by the low stone table staring at the map. "Truce. Where do I set up?"

"You've got graveyard duty."

"Again? Can't we do something original this time?"

"Coyote put in a request." Red gestured to a symbol on the map. "That's his modification right there. But it's your right to refuse. No one's forcing you."

"Fucking hell." Shoodii shook his head. "If it's from Coyote, I don't have a choice. I owe him. But I'm smoking some mushrooms first. Where's Liska?"

"She's probably at her herbal shop in Sedona."

"Ladies." He bowed and disappeared into another puff of white light.

"Who was that?" Willow asked.

"Shoodii? He's a wizard friend from Tempe."

"He's a native?" Mae asked.

"Yep. White Mountain Apache."

"And he's a friend of Coyote?" Willow asked.

Red laughed. "Maybe frenemy is a better word. Ya know, friends sometimes, and enemies at others. Coyote does like to switch sides to keep you guessing."

Willow shook her head. "Coyote loves the pranks you pull at Halloween."

"He said I'm one of his favorites. A true follower of the faith."

Coyote was an ancient animal spirit with a twisted sense of humor. Native American mythology passed down stories of his adventures. Only he wasn't a myth, he was real. Sometimes it seemed his sole purpose in life was to trick humans, but he had no problems conning other spirits too. In fact, any magical creature was fair game. Just like Pixies, he was an equal opportunity trickster. Willow recalled all the mischief her sister would get into when she was young. It had taken her years before she realized that Coyote had taken a particular interest in Red. He had tutored her through the years, and she had grown up as a prankster prodigy. In fact, she was notorious in the Coconino Forest for some of her exploits.

Red pointed to the map going through all the scare locations one by one and how they were being modified for the later hayrides.

"The kids have skeletons and mannequins set up at the moment, but those will be swapped for real werewolves when the time comes. Gnomes will be working the mad scientist's lab. I have actors for the top and bottom half of the victim." She grinned. "And, of course, real witches from Tempe casting illusions. None of that fakey hocus pocus stuff the kids dreamed up. This is the real deal. Shoodii is going to raise the dead in the cemetery."

"Isn't that a little risky?" Mae asked.

"Nah. Shoodii's the best. He'll tuck them all back into their graves before midnight. For him, it'll be a piece of cake."

Red pulled out a long scroll from her back pocket. "Just look how many lower creatures have volunteered to add special effects." Willow glanced at the page. There were quite a few spiders, bats, wolves, and ravens she recognized. This was going to be an amazing turn-out.

"And guess who's promised to play the headless horseman? Cyrus. Can you believe it? Oh yeah, and Olie agreed to play Frankenstein. All in all, the plans are looking pretty good."

"So, how are the Sprites holding up?" Mae asked.

Red chuckled. "You mean Sprite SWAT? They're out practicing now."

Willow groaned. "Do you think their aim is any better this year?"

"If I had to bet, I'd say worse." Red grinned, "But that wouldn't be for lack of trying."

Willow knew exactly what Red meant. The Sprites got paid extra for 'missing' and hitting other magical creatures with forget me serum. Most magical creatures didn't go into town much. Many had features that couldn't be easily camouflaged. This was one of the few opportunities to see humans up close without fear of being hunted. The hayride was like a human zoo on parade. Magical creatures lined the path watching from the shadows as the tractor pulled the humans through the woods. The Sprites would have blow darts laced with forget me serum and would watch for panic from the humans. If one saw too much and became distraught, they would take aim. The darts were both invisible and biodegradable, so humans would never know what hit them. The serum made the recipient clumsy. Their speech would slur and their reaction time would slow. The next day they wouldn't remember a thing. The only side effect would be a killer headache. Since the Sprites made the serum, they got to shoot the darts. Whether or not they targeted a human was at the sole discretion of the elite group of Dart Gunners, or as Red called them, Sprite SWAT. With enough gold, bidders could request a miss, to aim for one of the magical creatures watching the human parade from the sidelines. Several Council members had been targeted in the past.

Red pulled out a secondary sheet of parchment overlaying the first. It had a number of traps along the route.

Willow sighed, "Maybe we should tone down the Halloween pranks this year?"

Red gasped, "Are you trying to squash my fun? On my favorite day of the year? Coyote would have a fit."

Willow looked up at the sky shaking her head. "I'm just saying sometimes the mischief gets out of hand. And you said it yourself. The Sprite's aim isn't always that great."

Red laughed. "I was joking. I've been working with Sprite SWAT. Their blow dart accuracy is perfect. When they want to hit a target, trust me they will. So, they've been a little blow happy in the past. This is war. Casualties should be expected. Plus, they live for this shit. And quite frankly, so do I." She sighed. "Come on sis, I've been working on these plans since last October. Everyone enjoys getting even with the humans. Most of them are already drunk and easy targets." She sniffed, "And we're careful not to target the kids who would probably be thrilled to see real magical creatures. We're only cruel to the nasty adults, especially the ones that are brutal to animals."

Red handed her a list of targets, their name, physical description, and crimes. "I've already investigated everyone on that list personally."

"Are you partial to humans now?" Mae questioned Willow.

"Yeah, I know Bray might be a hot piece of ass, but sis this is D-day for retribution. Halloween is our revenge." Red gave a what gives expression with her hands. "Look at some of the crimes."

Willow scanned the list again. She didn't appreciate her sisters questioning her loyalty, but these humans really were nasty. Her own warrior sense of revenge demanded retribution.

"Ok. I give. Most on this list deserve anything you can throw at them. But you know how discriminating the magical creatures get by the end of the night. As it approaches midnight, no one cares if they are on the list or not. They go crazy. Doing excessive scares with no thought for consequences and the Sprites shoot darts like they're in a machine gun gallery."

Red shrugged, "That's the fun. Even the humans don't seem to care. Most love to be scared. We only go to the extreme on the ones that really deserve it." Red gave an evil grin, "You forget that I've seen you with hunters. Gaia help the ones trying to harm one of your favorites, like say, Clover?"

What did that mean? Had Red spied on her a month ago when Clover had been the target of an attack? Willow admitted she'd been pretty vicious with those hunters. But they had deserved it. Had she been viewing humans differently since dating Bray? Willow had to admit Red made some good points. There were some times when karmic justice needed a helping hand. Those on this list had certainly earned a little payback.

Willow sighed, "You're right."

"Wait," Red choked, "I'm right? Mae, are you hearing this?" She elbowed her younger sister.

"Ow, yes Red. I hear just fine." Mae rubbed her arm.

"I want it on the record that Willow, Ms. Guardian Extraordinaire, admitted she was wrong and I was right."

After they got all the plans in place, Willow decided she could use the hayride as an excuse to visit Bray. She planned to have the Serce test done at his cabin while he slept late in the evening, but that didn't mean she couldn't hang out with him before if things worked out.

She approached his cabin intrigued by the strange clear shed he had built. It had a metal frame with plastic panels. Willow peered in and saw a variety of local plants. He would have needed to travel for miles to gather all of them. She noticed thick mud caked to the quad's tires. Bray had been busy this past week. Maybe too busy to miss her. She smelled his scent and knew he was right behind her. Willow pretended not to notice. Now that she was here, Willow was worried. She didn't want to see anger or disappointment on his face. When had she become so cowardly? She took a deep breath and turned. What she saw was longing. She smiled. He had pined for her after all.

"I like what you've done here." She pointed to a row of potted plants. "You've got quite a collection." She shrugged when he said nothing. It reminded her of their first meeting. She had done all the talking while he had been nearly mute. Was she making him nervous all over again? "I had no idea you were so good with plants." Willow almost bit her tongue. Most humans would consider her a plant, and he certainly was good with her. But she didn't want to lie to him anymore.

Anger flashed in his eyes, "Yeah. I guess I don't suck at *everything*."

Hmm. He was still sensitive. Had she or her sisters made fun of him at some point and he'd overheard?

"Sometimes you suck quite good," Willow murmured in his ear.

She could tell from his hungry eyes that he was remembering tasting her. Bray followed her movements as she delicately ran fingers over the leaves and leaned down to smell the flowering plants. She kept her eye on him while exploring his greenhouse.

"Are you still mad at me?"

His shoulders tightened. "You really didn't kiss Lucian back?"

Had he been thinking about that all week? Willow shook her head. "No. Absolutely not. I *was* drunk, and my reaction time was slower than normal, but I didn't want to kiss him. I put a stop to it almost immediately. I'm surprised your drone didn't capture that image. You would have seen me kneeing him in the balls."

"Really?" His mouth quirked into a smile. "Yeah. I would have liked to see that."

"Look. I know I haven't always been open, and it's obviously caused some trust issues, but I'm willing to try. You know. Force myself to be vulnerable."

"Willow Ashbrook, have you been seeing a therapist?"

She pushed him in the shoulder, "Shut up. I talked to Bobby in town. She's actually quite smart. No fancy head doctor required, thank you."

Bray nodded. The mood had definitely lightened. He held the plastic greenhouse door open, and they made their way to his cabin.

"I've been living in the woods my whole life, but what you may not realize is that it comes with a certain amount of caution. The wilderness can be brutal to those who don't obey its laws. Because of that, trust comes slow. People from town and especially big cities don't think like I do. Things that might seem normal to you are strange and frightening to me. Before you came along, I was scared to drive in a car or truck."

"That's unusual." Bray nodded, "Although not completely surprising. I noticed you grab the dashboard a few times in my truck. That's why I started driving slower. I thought it was my driving style that made you nervous. I had no idea you were afraid of driving in general. Why didn't you tell me?"

She shrugged, "It's embarrassing. Something you think is so normal. I felt like a wimp and didn't want to complain."

He pulled her into his arms. "I don't want you to hold back. I want to know everything about you."

She rubbed her nose to his chest and inhaled his scent. He smelled earthy and warm and it made her boneless. She walked them over to the couch and sat down.

Willow took a deep breath and forced herself to look into Bray's eyes. He was so sincere. She needed to share. Bobby had told her how important this was. "I'm sure you've heard the basics about me from people in town. My mom died when I was sixteen, and my sisters were just toddlers at the time. It was a lot for me to handle on my own. Lucian started coming around more often to help with the girls. Our parents had been friends and so it was just natural that we start dating. It only lasted a few years, then it was over."

"I'm not sure I want to know the answer," Bray swallowed, "But I have to ask, did you two hook up after the breakup?"

Willow frowned, "You mean sex?"

He nodded.

She shrugged, "Maybe a few times, but we haven't had sex in over a decade."

"Wait. I meant after our breakup."

"You mean a week ago?" She shook her head. "No. Of course not."

Bray let out a breath. "You aren't tempted to go back to him?"

"Not in the slightest. When I was young, I thought I was in love, but when I got older, I realized he'd been convenient. He gave comfort when I was going through a tough time. Being teenagers, it was more about raging hormones than finding a mate."

"Mate?"

Willow bit her lip, "You know, a partner for life."

He nodded for her to continue.

"After Lucian and I broke up, we stayed friends. Then a year ago he started acting differently. It was subtle. I didn't notice right away. He would show up at our family parties uninvited. Instead of a quick hug, he would hold on a little longer. It started making me feel uncomfortable, but I ignored it. Then my sisters started noticing and making comments. I confronted him, but Lucian laughed it off saying it was all a misunderstanding."

Willow watched Bray's reaction. He didn't seem angry. His patience amazed her. She sighed, "Then after I met you, his behavior got worse.

"What did he do?" Bray's eyes glared.

"Nothing bad. The kiss was the worst of it." Willow shrugged, "I've been avoiding him. From his reaction at the retreat, he must have been waiting for an opportunity when my defenses were down to try and rekindle things." She gave an evil grin. "That kick to the groin had been building for a while."

Bray snorted.

"In general, I don't like confrontations. I bend to accommodate others, but there comes a point where even I snap. Lucian crossed the line, and he paid for it."

"Good to know." Bray grinned. "I'll have to remember that." He pushed back a lock of her hair and stroked her cheek. "So where does that leave us?"

Willow licked her lips, "Well, since I'm doing such a great job sharing," she smoothed her hands up and down his chest.

Bray's pec muscles tightened.

"Maybe we could start fresh." She bit her lip. "We could have our official first date at the Halloween Hayride?"

"A date on a hayride?"

She grinned. "It's something the kids from town put together every year. I never miss it." She grabbed his hand leading him to the bedroom. "And I can't think of anyone I'd rather share it with than you."

After their bodies stopped thrumming from an afternoon of intense orgasms, they found time to make a vegetarian lunch out on the grill. It seemed their relationship was stronger than ever. She took in the sight of him in denim and flannel and sighed. Willow used to hate the combination worn so regularly by hunters. She hadn't realized how sexy it could be when he filled out those jeans so nicely. And she'd never realized how soft flannel could be. Willow wanted to rub her body all over him, but then they would never get to the hayride and her sisters were counting on her.

They took the quad over to the picnic. Bray bought them tickets for one of the early hayrides. They sat along with several kids from the local grade school. Willow noticed the tractor driver wasn't human. In fact, he was the new Bobcat Shifter, Gary, that had just moved into the area. This time, he was dressed to match the rest of the party, in jeans and a flannel, with a cowboy hat and boots. Mae had told her Gary was trying his hand at farming. He had purchased a few magic spells to help things along until he learned. She recalled their conversation at Festivus and wondered if there was a particular human he was interested in. She nodded as he helped her into the wagon. His blocks were in place. No static shock this time. Bray followed in behind her. The kids on the ride were hilarious. They seemed more interested in the ride and rolling in the hay than in the decorations. Bray was dutifully scared by the paper bats dangling from the trees and the spider webs. The earlier rides were always tamed down for the younger crowd. Full-size skeletons and mannequins stood in for actors that would replace them later in the evening. Bray grabbed punch for both of them, and they made their rounds socializing with the townsfolk. The Halloween picnic always brought the crowds. Red showed up wearing a similar outfit to Bray. She had on skinny jeans and a flannel shirt that was way too tight. The buttons risked popping off at any moment.

Red signaled for Willow. She glanced over at Bray who was in deep conversation about IT with a few of the townsfolk. He would be a while. She walked over to her sister.

"What's up?"

"We're all set for the later hayrides. I just wanted to check to see how you were doing with Bray. I know you've been missing him all week."

She bumped her sister in the shoulder, "You do pay attention."

Red grinned. "Of course, I do. I want all my sisters to be happy."

Willow ruffled her sister's hair with affection.

"Oh no. You didn't. No one messes with the curls."

Red lunged at Willow, but she took off running and dodged through the crowd squealing with laughter.

Red followed and was gaining until a large man turned from the picnic table directly in her path. She plowed into him. Somehow, he managed to remain standing, but the full plate of food he had been holding now decorated his upper torso. Bits of potato salad and baked beans stuck to his flannel shirt in globs. He scowled down at her. She had landed on her butt after bouncing off his body.

Red brushed her curls back from her eyes and groaned when she saw who it was. It was Jake. The lumberjack. The one she had been lusting over for months.

She gave him a bright smile, "Sorry about that, hunkalicious." She jumped to her feet and dusted her jeans. Red ran a hand down the front of his shirt trying to wipe off the mess.

Willow watched in horror. Red was rubbing it into the fabric. She was making it worse. The behemoth of a man stood nearly six and a half feet tall. His jaw ticked and his biceps bulged. Red seemed oblivious to the evil glare he was giving her.

"Maybe a napkin would help." Red reached for one on the table.

He grabbed her wrist. "Stop."

Red squirmed from his grasp. "It's my fault. Let me fix it."

He sighed, "You have some on your shirt as well."

Red looked down. She used the napkin and roughly rubbed the front of her shirt. Two buttons popped. "Well, hell."

"Your shirt's too small," he said through gritted teeth.

"Geez. You don't have to be so angry about it." Red looked up and glared at him, but his eyes were glued to her cleavage.

She grinned. "Oh, I don't know about that. The way you stare, I'd say this shirt fits pretty darn perfect."

His eyes snapped up. He grunted and stalked away.

Willow rushed over to Red. "What was that all about?"

Red shrugged. "Jake doesn't like me, but I'm wearing him down."

Willow glanced at her sister's heaving chest. Her breasts looked ready to burst free from the shirt. "I think your boobs were staring at his face."

Red snorted. "You noticed that too." She shrugged. "Well, at least something caught his eye." She sighed, "Normally he just ignores me." She kicked a small rock with her boot. It flew off into the trees. "I don't understand how he can do that so easily. I mean look at me." She looked down at her body, "I'm freakishly huge." She yanked a chunk of her red curls. "My hair is like a neon beacon. I'm used on human distraction missions because I'm good at them. It might be all I'm good for." Red's shoulders slumped.

Willow had never seen her sister like this. Normally Red was so confident and bold, but in this moment, she was that insecure toddler first learning to swim. Red hadn't floated like her sisters, and early on had been afraid of the water. But Willow had worked with her and gradually she had gotten over her fear. Red was now a powerful swimmer. Some of her best friends were River Nymphs and they competed regularly in swimming races.

Willow nudged her shoulder. "You're not a freak."

Red sniffed. "You have to say that 'cause I'm your sister."

She sighed and stared up into the blue sky with big fluffy clouds. Willow walked over to a stump on the other side of Red. She wrapped an arm around Red's wide shoulders and they stared at the clouds together. They used to do that when Red was little. Red blinked back tears as they stared into the sky.

Willow pointed to a fluffy cloud. "I think that one looks like a bunny with his nose stuck in a hole."

Red nodded and pointed to another. "And that one looks like a crashed pirate ship."

"Wonder why it crashed. Mermaids? No, maybe sirens?" Willow watched her sister for a moment and then around the clearing. A few people stared at them, then looked up into the sky trying to see what was so interesting. *It's a gorgeous day, you idiots.* Most humans didn't appreciate nature. Willow spotted Jake staring at Red, then he turned away in anger. She smiled. He was plenty distracted by her sister. He just didn't want to be. At least, not yet.

"You know, Jake isn't immune to your charms."

"What do you mean?" Red wiped tears from her eyes.

She whispered in her ear. "He gazes at you when you aren't looking."

"Bullshit." Red glanced around trying to find him in the crowd.

He ducked behind a group of people at the picnic table. Willow grinned. He didn't want Red to know he was watching.

"No bullshit, sis. That man is very aware of you."

Red took a deep breath and gave Willow a big bear hug lifting her off the stump and twirling her in a circle. "Thanks, sis. I needed that."

She put her down gently and grinned before stalking back into the trees. Red's large ass in those tight jeans seemed to demand attention. Her red curls bobbed as she walked with purpose. Willow noticed several men and a few women stare in her direction. Jake's eyes followed every swish of her hips. He couldn't seem to help himself. Nice try, Jake, but your days are numbered. Her sister would bag him before long.

After sunset, the Halloween party drew an older crowd. Townsfolk showed up with liquor and they were hitting it hard. Red had been going around the party putting glow-in-the-dark stickers on the backs of several people. Willow had recalled the descriptions and knew she was targeting those from her nasty list. She was an insatiable flirt, with touches here and there, so no one noticed the little stickers. Not to mention, anyone watching would be more focused on her boobs. By ten p.m., Red had disappeared back into the woods. At a quarter to midnight, Bray bought them two more tickets to go on the last hayride for the evening.

Chapter 23

Bray and Willow settled at the back of the wagon. He noticed several people on the ride had glow-in-the-dark stickers.

"What's with the stickers?" He gestured to Willow, "Are we supposed to have those?"

Willow groaned. "No. It just means we're in for a hell of a ride."

She didn't offer more of an explanation. Willow was concentrating on a couple getting frisky under a blanket. Bray thought it looked like a great idea. He took off his jacket and spread it over their laps. He reached under and ran a finger up her inner thigh. She grabbed his wrist.

"What are you doing?" She breathed.

Her eyes were half-lidded just from such a slight touch.

"If you don't know," he murmured in her ear, "then I'm not doing it right."

She gave a nervous laugh. "Behave. We have all night for that." Willow gave him a kiss. It was far too quick.

"I'll hold you to that."

She grinned and held out her hand above the jacket. He wrapped his large hand around hers and they stared off into the darkness. Maybe she just wasn't one for public displays of affection. It didn't make much sense considering her family, but then Willow seemed more reserved than her sisters. He could wait until they were alone. She seemed genuinely excited about the hayride. The adult one must be much better than the kids'. The afternoon's ride had been lame. Lights flashed around the next bend and they heard the sound of a chainsaw roaring to life. The first scene was the scientist's lab. There was a makeshift table filled with glowing beakers and jars. A student in a lab coat raised a fake chainsaw above his head laughing maniacally. At least

Bray thought it was fake. He was really hoping the kids weren't using real power tools. The strobe continued to flash as the victim on the table was cut in half. Each piece moved on its own like it was still animated even after death. Bray stared at the scene with curiosity. "Are there kids in the dummy?"

Willow shrugged. Maybe she couldn't see well in the dark. Bray had excellent night vision. She stared into the trees. He followed her line of sight. "There are people watching us."

"Yeah, must be the kids running this thing."

"Now that I look closer," Bray squinted, "it looks more like animals."

She gave a nervous laugh, "Well, we are in the woods."

The tractor sputtered as it made the next turn. Three women in black gowns and tall pointy hats hunched over a cauldron cackling as they chanted spells. Goosebumps formed on Bray's arms. He usually didn't get spooked this easily, but there was something in the words they were chanting. It rattled his nerves. One of the witches pounded the ground with a staff. Sparks shot from the crystal ball at the top, spraying multi-color fireworks. Everyone oohed and aahed at the display. A gust of wind blew through the trees and swept leaves through the wagon. He noticed Willow frowning at a small black box near the cauldron. The leaves were spiraling into a funnel and sucked back into the box. That was bizarre. He had never seen a Halloween prop like that. It must be something new? Before he could ask her about it, the tractor entered a cemetery. They had driven through it earlier, but the ground was now moving. Instead of just the headstones and spiderwebs, now zombies crawled from the graves. Frayed clothing and black blood stuck to their decayed skin. The makeup was excellent. A lone coyote stood in the center of the chaos staring at them. Bray squinted into the darkness. Maybe it wasn't a coyote after all. A man with a coyote hood sat cross-legged meditating in the middle of the cemetery. That was odd. Was he a part of the scene, or had he just stumbled in by mistake? When they got to the edge of the cemetery there was a line of more zombies, but these looked different. They were shorter than the others and were fighting the other zombies, trying to hold them back.

"Damn it, Shoodii." One yelled as they tackled one of the tall zombies that had broken through the perimeter and had swiped an arm at the wagon.

He stared harder at the group of kids.

"Why are the short zombies fighting the tall zombies? Am I missing something?"

Willow shrugged.

"And what's with the short zombies having pointed ears and tribal tattoos?" Bray gestured. "Don't get me wrong. The rest of the makeup is fantastic. But that's an odd choice to add, don't you think?"

"Uh. I guess?"

Several people were now getting thwacked by branches in front of them. "I don't remember us being this close to the trees last time."

"I think the driver adjusts his course later in the evenings."

Bray looked at the dirt trail. Nothing had changed from what he could tell, but the trees were closer. It had to be different.

He heard a chilling howl, followed by the baying of several more wolves. As they cleared the next bend, he witnessed a Werewolf ripping apart an abandoned jeep. The screech from his long, sharp claws raking down the side of the jeep sent shivers down Bray's spine. He hated that nails-on-a-chalkboard sound. The Werewolf flung hunks of metal across the clearing like they weighed nothing. He turned toward the wagon and gave a low menacing growl that trickled from his lips. His ripped shirt revealed a very hairy chest and arms. Bray scrutinized the student's face. It didn't look like a mask. His face was covered with fur and they had even given him a fake snout that blended in seamlessly. These kids were good, like Hollywood good. It seemed almost too real.

Bray gave a nervous laugh. "Those kids have talent."

The Werewolf's eyes glowed as he watched the wagon roll by. Bray jumped.

"Did you see his eyes? What the fuck? Were those contacts?"

"Sorry. Must have missed it." Willow said. "I was watching the wolves."

Bray squinted behind the fake jeep. There were five wolves sitting on a hill. He had thought it was shadow cutouts, but one turned and stared at him. They were real.

"Isn't that unusual for them to be so close to humans?"

"Maybe."

She seemed evasive every time he asked a question. That didn't bode well for his plans later tonight. He wanted sex, but he needed her certainty. The last thing he wanted was to pressure her into doing something when she wasn't ready. But the week apart from her had been torture. Pushing past her boundaries had worked once before.

The next section they came across showed a dark cave covered in spiderwebs. Bray thought they would turn at the last second like they did last time, but they drove directly into the mouth of the cave coating everyone with webs.

"Eww." Several passengers said at once.

Everyone was trying to swipe the webbing from their hair and clothes.

"I feel spiders in my hair. Get it out. Get it out." A woman at the front of the cart said.

"I think one crawled down my pants." A guy hollered, wiggling in his seat.

"I've got several in my shirt and they're biting!" Another man roared, as he punched himself in the chest.

"Get us out of here." Several people screamed to the driver.

Bray squinted into the darkness but couldn't see anything. No bugs were crawling on him or Willow. He thought it may just be a mental thing with the other passengers. The tractor driver turned off his high beams and switched to a green infrared light that made the cave even spookier.

There were flapping sounds and screeches in the darkness. The tractor sputtered to a stop.

Another woman complained about something tugging at her hair. The screams from the wagon were deafening. Willow chuckled. He took her hand and grinned. She must know the trick the kids were playing. The tractor started back up and they were off. Just as they cleared the cave exit, he saw another student dressed like Frankenstein. He was being chased by several other students with pitchforks. The creature walked on stiffened legs with arms outstretched. The bolts and scar on his forehead looked fantastic, but they had given him hairy legs and a tail.

"What's with all the hair and the tail?" Bray shook his head. "Did they run out of costumes?"

Willow shrugged. "This is the last part." She pointed to the bridge they parked the quad by earlier in the evening. "I asked Gary if he could drop us off here instead of back at the picnic." She made her way up to the front of the wagon and Bray followed. Several of the passengers now looked asleep. From the smell of the alcohol, he figured most had passed out. The wagon stopped abruptly. The momentum sent Bray careening into the hay. Willow laughed and helped him to his feet.

She jumped over the side of the wagon. Bray didn't want to seem less athletic, so he tried to do the same. His shoelace got caught on one of the wooden slats. He awkwardly untangled it and fell ungracefully to the ground.

"Oof."

"You ok back there?" The tractor driver hollered.

"Yeah. We're fine. Thanks for stopping." Bray dusted himself off embarrassed that he was so uncoordinated compared to Willow.

She gave him her hand and a reassuring smile. The wagon started rolling along and they followed behind at a slow pace. Bray watched as the headless horseman chased the wagon across the bridge. He carried a pumpkin head and was riding a horse. Way to sell the ending, kids. Bravo. Bray was anxious to get back to the cabin. From Willow's expression, she looked just as eager.

The kid in costume galloped up behind them.

"Hey, Willow."

Bray turned, and his jaw dropped. The kid wasn't a kid at all. He was a lot older, maybe in his fifties judging by the graying hair at his temples and deep voice. But that's not what had Bray staring. He wasn't on a horse. He was the horse, or rather looked like one of those mythical creatures he had read about in fantasy books. The guy was dressed like a Centaur. But it wasn't a costume. It couldn't be a costume. His heart was pounding.

"Please, Bray. Calm yourself. The others will notice."

She looked around into the darkness with concern.

"Who?"

He heard a thwunk and felt a sharp pain in his neck before his body dropped. Bray heard Willow yell, 'Oh hell' just before he blacked out.

Chapter 24

"ALRIGHT, WHO FIRED the dart?" Willow swung her gaze into the darkness.

The Sprite leader flew over to her. "The human was clearly panicking."

"He was not!" Willow screeched.

Fuath's eyebrow rose, "It's within our security mandate."

Willow wanted to swat that little Sprite across the clearing.

Olie bounded over. "You need help, Willow?"

She blew out a breath and stared at Bray's crumpled body sprawled in the dirt.

"Yeah, Olie." She gestured to Bray, "Can you figure out a way to strap him to the quad so he doesn't fall off?"

"I can do it." Shoodii walked over. He still wore the coyote skin draped over his shoulders.

"Shouldn't you be putting the zombies back?"

"Already done."

With a wave of his hand, Bray's body floated to the quad and was tied to the seat.

She turned to Fuath and scowled. "Will I be seeing you later?" She whispered.

"Of course. This changes nothing."

Willow knew she was stuck. In public, she couldn't discuss the Serce test and Fuath knew it.

Shoodii stood there listening. He was far too curious. Even if they were friends, Red still didn't trust him. The fact he was also friends with Coyote didn't help matters. Wizards were notoriously nosy.

"Are you sticking around to help with cleanup?" Willow asked.

"Fuck no." Shoodii vanished in a puff of light.

She drove the quad back to the cabin cursing the damn blow-happy Sprites. Where were her sisters? They should have seen the whole thing go down. Although it was probably just as well, they would have reamed her for her lack of judgment. When she saw all those glow-in-the-dark stickers, she should have abandoned the hayride altogether. Bray was a casualty. Willow should be grateful Sprite SWAT hadn't shot her as well. She was sure some on Council would pay to see that happen. Luckily, she had made other arrangements with Fuath. Willow had only put down a deposit for services. The final payment would be due when the Serce test was complete.

Bray woke as Willow pulled up to the cabin.

"What's wif the ropes?"

"Ah, you're awake." She smiled. "I didn't want you to fall off."

"Sounds logical."

Willow hopped off and started untying the knots. They were really tight.

"Fucking wizards." She muttered.

Bray watched with amusement. His eyes were unfocused.

"You're so pretty. Ya know that?"

She grinned. "You've told me that before, but thank you."

Willow wiggled the ropes trying to figure out if she was making it better or worse.

"I've got something in my pocket."

"Is this a come-on?" She asked.

"Hmm. Interested?" Bray laughed. "Knife. Front right."

She pulled out the pocket knife and quickly cut him loose.

"And you're quite sexy for a geek."

"Thank you." He climbed off the quad and bowed. Bray immediately lost his balance and crumpled to the dirt.

She sighed and helped him to his feet. They staggered to the front porch.

He was too busy checking his pockets. "Great. Just great." He squinted out into the darkness. "Now we gotta find the rock."

"What are you talking about?"

"You know one of those fake rocks you put the spare key inside." He pointed to his yard. "Look around. It's hidden. I can be sneaky too." He winked.

Willow was confused. "While hiding a spare key might be clever, why would you need it since you always leave it unlocked?"

She turned the knob and opened the front door.

"Woo-hoo. It's magic."

Willow shook her head. Forget me serum affected people just like alcohol. It lowered their inhibitions and gave them a feeling of euphoria. But the most valuable side-effect was creating a black-out period in the person's memory. Even memories prior to the serum being administered were hazy. It was the perfect tool if humans saw too much. It would last anywhere from two to twenty-four hours depending on the person's metabolism, weight, and genetics. There was no way to tell how long it would last with Bray.

Willow got him settled on the sofa. Before long, she heard a flute playing at the front door. Willow opened it and Fuath flew in. "It's a busy night. I hope you appreciate this."

"Of course." She gritted her teeth. "Thank you."

The Sprite leader landed on the coffee table, loosened his belt strap, and slipped off a small pouch. The opening spread wide and he pulled out a huge beaker. It was one of those enchanted bags the witches sold. She knew how expensive they were and wondered just how much gold the Sprite's leader had accumulated over the years. He continued pulling out various jars of liquids and powders, then started mixing. One pink, one green, and another deep purple. With a mix and a dash of powder, the beaker contents turned clear.

Next, he pulled out a long silver needle. He had an evil grin as he flew toward Bray slumped over on the couch. He stabbed his finger and, in a blur, flew to the ceiling.

Bray grabbed his bloody fingertip. "Ow. That butterfly bit me."

"It's not a butterfly."

Willow watched as Fuath floated back down to the table. He dropped the silver needle with the blood into the beaker and swirled the clear liquid. It turned a very pale pink.

"Hmm," Fuath said, "I hadn't expected that. His heart is pure. Really pure." The Sprite leader tilted his head and studied Bray. "Very few magical creatures would test at this level, and never a human."

"So, he's good?" Willow smiled. "What about mate status?"

He sighed. "Not a chance. But if this will stop your obsession..."

Fuath gave her a fresh needle. She poked her finger and handed it back to him. He placed the needle into the same beaker and added a few drops of blue liquid.

The liquid turned a deep amber with silver bubbles.

The Sprite leader's eyeballs nearly popped out of his skull. "Impossible." He pointed to Bray, "Him." He pointed to Willow. "You." He fluttered his wings and swooped around the room. "It's ridiculous. Outrageous."

He pulled out a fresh beaker and repeated the process adding drops of blood from Willow and Bray. Same results. Another beaker of amber liquid with silver bubbles sat on the table.

Fuath fluttered around the room and landed on the kitchen window sill. He stared into the darkness shaking his head. "How can this be? It makes no sense."

Willow stood behind him tapping her foot. "So? What are the results?"

He shook his head. "I can't believe I'm saying this, but he is your eternal soulmate."

Willow twirled around the room giggling. "I knew it." She was so excited. No wonder she felt such a connection to him. Fate had given Bray to her. They were destined to spend their lives together. This changed everything.

Fuath cleared his throat. "This changes nothing. Mating with humans is forbidden. Council will not accept the union."

"What do you mean they won't accept?" Willow shrieked.

The Sprite leader flinched and flattened himself against the glass.

He put up his hands. "Now, Willow. Your role as Guardian is vital to the forest. How can you do your duty if you constantly have to hide what you are from your mate?" He shook his head. "The risk is too great. I'm sorry. Truly sorry."

He gathered up his supplies avoiding eye contact. "Now about the matter of payment..."

Willow walked in a daze to the cookie jar where she had placed the gold necklace for safe keeping. Willow couldn't believe it. She had been so happy just moments ago. Eternal soulmates were rare. How could Council refuse the union? But she knew how prejudiced they were. They hadn't spent enough time with humans to realize Bray was good. The Serce test even said so. What if she defied Council and stayed with

Bray anyway? What would happen? She would probably be labeled a traitor, lose her position, and most likely get kicked out of the forest. Would she ever be able to see her sisters again? And that's only if they were allowed to live. If deemed a high enough security risk, dark Elf assassins would be sent to hunt them down.

She presented the necklace to Fuath. He turned it over in his hand. The charms jingled. He sighed. "I can't take this. It's your mother's. It must stay with the Ashbrook clan." He placed the necklace in her open palm. Willow tilted her head and stared at the Sprites' leader.

"You don't give back gold. It just isn't done."

"I do tonight." He bowed. "A lot of impossible things have happened. Good evening, Guardian." He flew off through a crack in the door.

A Sprite refusing payment? What the hell? The world just went upside down.

Bray blinked looking around the room. "Where'd the butterfly go?"

Willow decided right then and there, they would be together completely. At least for this one night. She wouldn't hold anything back. Willow let her dress slip from her shoulders. She flung her bra across the room. Willow spun her panties on one finger and tossed them to Bray as she sauntered into the bedroom. "Bray, are you coming?"

Chapter 25

Harsh slashes of light cut their way across the bedroom. Bray peeked one eye open and groaned. His head felt like it had been slammed against the wall repeatedly. A warm body snuggled back against his groin. The pounding in his head apparently had no effect on his morning wood. He blew blonde hair from his face. The woman he'd been holding like a drowning man's life preserver turned in his arms. It was Willow. Her hair was in disarray, but she looked like a goddess as she leaned back and stretched. He tried to recall how they ended up in his bed. The last time he saw her, he had been stupid and jealous and had broken up with her without letting her explain. He spent the last week regretting his actions. He was planning to make up the next time he ran into her. Apparently, that had been last night. Based on the clear evidence in his bed, they must have reconciled.

He tried to sit up, but the room spun. He fell back into bed.

"Geez. What happened last night?"

"What do you remember?"

Bray shook his head, but it made the pounding between his temples worse. He couldn't remember a thing. Most of yesterday was a blank. "I take it liquor was involved last night?"

Willow nodded. "Yeah. You had a few shots at the Halloween picnic." She cleared her throat. "You uh, wanted to celebrate." Her voice cracked.

He blinked in the bright light. His eyes popped open when he noticed an open condom wrapper on the bedside table. He reached under his pillow and found another. He raised the foil between his fingertips. "Did we, uh, finally do it?"

Willow gazed past him to the wall avoiding eye contact. "Yeah," she whispered.

Bray licked dry lips. "I hate to ask this," Bray hesitated, "But was it good?"

Willow started crying.

"Fuck." Bray no longer wanted to know the answer. Her reaction said it all. "Well, I was drunk you know." Obviously blackout drunk. That hadn't happened since college. "Come on. Cut me some slack. I swear it will be a thousand times better when I'm sober."

She cried harder. He didn't know what to do. He tried pulling her into a hug, but she refused, backing away.

"I'm sorry. I can't do this anymore." Willow sobbed.

He swallowed. "Do you mean us?"

"Yes." Willow wiped a tear. "I'm breaking up with you."

"Didn't we just get back together?"

"I'm sorry, I have to go." Willow got out of the bed and rummaged through the pile of clothes to find the dark green dress he had bought her. When she put it on, he noticed several large rips in the fabric. Had he been rough with her last night?

"Please Willow, I'm begging you. Tell me why."

She looked him dead in the eyes. "Because we're too different." And with that she left him lying on the bed, head pounding and completely confused.

He thought about everything he knew about her. The differences were what made them work. Bray tried to recall what happened the day before. His head throbbed until he finally passed out from the pain.

He woke hours later hoping the morning had just been a horrible nightmare. He shuffled to the refrigerator for some juice. On his way, he noticed Willow's note. She had surprisingly neat handwriting. It said simply, 'I'm sorry. Willow'. The 'i' in her name had a little heart above it. Was that how she usually signed her name, or was he just desperate enough to take it as a sign of hope? Maybe he was in denial, but he didn't care. He needed her, period. They were good together. He just had to figure out a way to convince her. With his mind made up, he decided to ask around town and get a little help for those that knew her best.

First, he stopped at the Roadhouse Bar and Grill. Most of the townsfolk would stop in for lunch or dinner. There weren't a whole lot of restaurant choices in the area without driving all the way to Flagstaff. He decided to start with the bartender. Max was wearing a plaid sleeveless shirt and jeans. His muscles flexed and his tattoos rippled as he wiped down the bar.

"So, what'll you have, Bray?"

"You remembered my name."

Max shrugged. "There's not that many locals. You're one of us since you moved here and all."

Bray did feel an affinity to this place. This had started out as a vacation cabin, but he felt more at home here than he ever had in San Francisco.

"I'll have a beer. Whatever new microbrew you got."

Max handed him a bottle of Four Peaks Kilt Lifter. Bray took a sip.

"This is pretty good."

"Thought you'd like it." He continued to mop down the bar even though it was completely clean. Maybe he was a clean freak. Bray looked at the guy's scruffy beard, the frayed edges of his shirt, the old ball cap and stained apron he wore. Maybe clean wasn't the right word.

"Is Willow meeting you here?"

"No. Why do you ask?"

"Just saw you two at the Halloween picnic." Max shrugged. "Figured you'd be together."

He sighed. "We uh, broke up."

"No shit." He scratched his chin. "What for?"

It was Bray's turn to shrug. "All she said is we're too different."

"Hmm. My Rosie's way different from me. Don't think we could live together if we were the same."

"Exactly." Bray tapped the bar with his fist. "At least you get it." He rubbed his temples. "Thing is I don't remember a whole lot about yesterday.

"Really? Were you drinkin' at the picnic?"

He sighed. "I guess so. I don't usually drink more than a beer or two even at parties. I can vaguely remember a few things, but most of the day is hazy. I do know I broke up with Willow a week ago. Apparently, we made up yesterday, and when I woke up with a hangover this morning, she broke up with me again."

Max nodded. "I've seen it before. Blackouts. Too much liquor can kill relationships. What was the last thing you remember?"

Bray shook his head. The pounding at his temples drummed a percussion of pain. "I remember waking up thinking of trying to find Willow and apologize for being such an ass, then small snippets of time. It's mostly a blur." He ran fingers through his hair. "It's so frustrating. I have a vague memory of getting some punch at the picnic, then climbing into the wagon for the hayride, then that's it. Blank until this morning."

"Hmm. What were you drinking?"

"I don't remember drinking at all, except for the punch. But my blackout happened before and after." Bray pointed at the man, "And before you ask, I don't drink before noon." *That was a lie.* He recalled the morning after breaking up with Willow. Bray had been drinking heavily the whole day.

Max shrugged. "I don't judge." He scratched his chin. "But if what you say is true, it is strange."

He went back to scrubbing the bar lost in thought while Bray sipped his beer. "Wait a minute. Did you say you broke things off a week ago?"

Bray lowered his head to the bar and started banging it softly. "I was an idiot. It was all a misunderstanding. I thought she was cheating."

Max shook his head. "Willow's a good girl. Not wild like her sister Red."

"What about Red?"

"You've met her, right? She's a wicked flirt. And that's not all she does." Max's eyebrows wiggled. "You wouldn't believe what I've heard. Any man that settles down with that one will have to put her on a leash."

A snort from the huge man sitting next to him at the bar.

"You got something to add, Jake?"

"I saw her at the picnic." The huge man's hands were in fists, knuckles white. "She practically flashed the whole town."

Bray remembered Red from the party at his cabin a few weeks ago. She had worn body paint and nothing else. This guy Jake must not realize they were nudists; Willow and her whole family. Red had been all over his friend Nick, but nothing had come of it, much to his friend's disappointment. Bray hadn't seen much of Willow's sisters since then. They generally avoided town. Finding them would be as difficult as finding Willow.

Bray talked to a few more people at the bar that had seen him at the party. No one remembered him getting drunk. They all seemed to think he and Willow were a couple. Several had witnessed the two of them holding hands and stealing kisses. A few others thanked him for help with their computer issues. He groaned, maybe that's why Willow was pissed. He hadn't been paying her enough attention.

Only one person recalled seeing him and Willow briefly on the hayride. The woman seemed a little embarrassed. She smoothed a dark curly lock behind her ear and introduced herself as Susan. She ordered two beers at the bar and glanced back at an odd-looking man at a corner table.

"Apparently, last night I'd been hitting the spiked punch pretty hard. I passed out in the wagon. The kids couldn't rouse me, so they left me with the guy driving the tractor." She waved to the tall gentleman in suspenders sitting at the table and whispered, "Gary drove the tractor back to his place. He was a perfect gentleman, even put me in his bed and slept on the couch. Wasn't that sweet?"

Bray looked at the guy. He didn't think Gary got many dates, not that the man wasn't good-looking. He was tall and lean, with a dark tan. He had high cheekbones, brown eyes, and long golden-brown hair. He might have looked like a rock musician if it weren't for his outfit and odd mannerisms. The shirt he wore was buttoned up to the chin and had ruffles. His pants were plaid. His gaze kept scanning the bar nervously like he didn't get out much.

"Do you know Willow?"

"Sure. We've been friends for about a year. Are you Bray?"

"Yep." He shook her hand.

"I've been trying to get in touch with her. Do you know where she lives?"

Susan frowned. "Aren't you two dating?"

"Well, yes, and maybe no. I broke up with her. We got back together and now she broke up with me." Bray shrugged. "I guess you could say, it's complicated."

"Hmm." She folded her arms over her chest. "I have no idea where Willow lives. Their family moves around a lot."

Bray's shoulders slumped.

She blew out a breath. "I probably shouldn't be saying anything."

Bray glanced up. He needed some hope right about now.

"Bobby's known Willow and her family for years, she might be able to help you. You'd catch her at the gun range about now."

"Thank you so much."

"Yeah. Well, I'm only doing this because I know how much she likes you. I don't know how you screwed things up, but you better make it up to her."

"I will. I promise. I just have to find her."

The bartender handed Susan two beers. She looked over her shoulder and giggled.

"Romance is in the air. Wish me luck."

Bray nodded. even though he had no idea what for. The guy was obviously smitten. His eyes followed her movement as she sauntered over to the table. He sniffed the bottle and pushed it away and pulled her into his lap. He swatted at her dangling earring. Susan gave a high-pitched laugh.

"Behave." She scolded and reclaimed her seat.

Bray shook his head. He closed out his tab and went to go find Bobby. The Roadhouse had a gun and pawn shop at the back, so he asked the owner if he knew where the closest gun ranges were.

"The closest is High Desert in Flagstaff."

"Do you know if that's where Bobby goes?"

"Sometimes, but she's a regular at Northern Arizona Shooting Range, a little further east. Her late husband used to take her there for date nights. It used to get them amorous, if you know what I mean."

Bray wasn't quite sure if he should laugh or not. The idea that shooting would turn someone on was a foreign concept. So, he just nodded.

"Uh, thanks much."

It was a forty-five-minute drive to the range. He had seen Bobby in town before and had certainly heard plenty about her from Gail. He paid for a day pass and went over to where Bobby was skeet shooting. Her long gray hair was pulled back tight in a ponytail. She wore an army-green t-shirt, tactical camo pants with matching hat and work boots. He suddenly wondered why he thought a gun range would be a good place to talk when they both were wearing ear plugs. She noticed him watching and signaled for him to go further away from the targets.

"So, you're Bray?"

She didn't seem particularly hostile, but she also didn't seem all that receptive.

He held out his hand. "It's nice to meet you, Bobby."

She eyed his hand for a few moments then shook it.

"Susan texted me you'd be coming out here. What do you want?"

"I'm trying to find Willow. Susan thought you might know where she lived."

"Why should I help you?"

"You know I broke up with her a week ago, right?"

Bobby's eyebrows rose. She waved him on.

"We got back together, then she broke up with me this morning."

"What did you do?" Bobby demanded.

Bray put his fingers to his temples massaging. The shooting wasn't helping his headache. "I don't know."

Bobby scrutinized him for several minutes. She tugged him toward the parking lot. "Ok spill. Everything you got. You must have done something but you're too stupid to know what it was."

Others had warned him of Bobby's gruff attitude. Bray gave her the details, even revealing they had sex for the first time, and her reaction this morning.

He rubbed the back of his neck. "Do you know how much experience Willow's had?"

"Relationships with guys?" Bobby asked. "Or do you mean sex?"

He cringed. This was going to be awkward. He swallowed. "Willow's kind of small. And I'm... not. Well, there's the possibility I could have hurt her. Especially if it's been a while. After finding out, I asked if it was good. She sort of broke down into tears."

"Geez-us. You're a fuck-up."

His head dropped. "I know.

She sighed, "She ain't no virgin if that's what you're worried about." Bobby closed her eyes and scrunched her nose. "The last time she dated was maybe ten or so years ago, this fellow called Lucian. She hasn't shown much interest in men since then."

"Him again." Bray's arms straightened, and his hands formed fists.

Bobby watched him cautiously.

She held out her hands counting on her fingers point by point. "Let me get this straight. You broke up with Willow a week ago because you thought she was cheating. You realize now that was stupid, right?"

He nodded.

"You had a hangover this morning but don't recall drinking. You got back together. Went to the Halloween picnic. Had sex. Then she broke up with you this morning."

Bray rubbed the back of his neck. "That about sums it up."

Bobby frowned. "And the only reason she gave is because you are too different from one another, not that the sex was bad?"

"Yeah."

Bray wiped a hand down his face. He had just given that little tidbit to a woman who loved to gossip. If he couldn't get Willow back, his reputation was toast.

She rolled her eyes. "Relax. I'm sure it's not your prowess in bed. If it was that bad, she would have left before morning." She blew out a breath. "That's not what I'd worry about. I can think of only one reason for the blackout; someone spiked your drink, or injected you with something."

Bray's eyes went wide. Susan had suggested the punch had been spiked, which could have just been some rowdy teens, no big deal. But getting injected with something? Could Bobby be right? She was notorious for conspiracy theories, but he had to consider someone might want him out of the picture. Maybe Lucian had been there. Or did Willow have other secret admirers? There was so much he didn't know about her.

"Right now, I don't care about that. I just want to find her, so I can talk to her and figure out what went wrong."

Bobby threw up her hands, "You can't just ignore the warnings. Someone could be out to get you."

He shook his head. "Listen, I'm not concerned about myself. Please, help me. I need her. I'm desperate."

She looked him up and down and shook her head. "You're pathetic, ya know that?"

He nodded.

"I don't know where the girl lives."

Bray's head dropped.

"But, Willow's a creature of habit. She likes routine, just like my late husband Earl." She gave a wistful look back at the targets. "I'm sure she's taken you to some of her favorite places in the forest. More than likely, those locations hold meaning. She'll be back."

"Thank you so much, Bobby." He gave her a hug.

She hugged him back briefly, then shoved him away.

"Just fair warning, boy. If Willow don't wanna be found, she ain't gonna be found. Period. But... you seem pretty nice, so I wish you luck all the same. Now git."

Bray wasn't going to let himself lose hope. His head was starting to feel better. He now had a goal, and there was no one better at reaching those than him.

Chapter 26

WILLOW HAD BEEN purposefully avoiding Bray for the past week. His ability to know where she would be was uncanny. Several times he had almost found her. Willow didn't want to admit how desperately she craved his touch. Maybe deep down she wanted to be caught, but her duty continued to prevent it from happening. She would duck behind a bush or merge with a tree just in time. Willow was exploring areas she and Bray had shared, places that were special to her family but were now linked to memories of him. She hadn't considered the possibility Bray could get back to some of those places on his own. But she should have known better. By the third location, she spotted a pattern. He would show up on his quad with a fierce expression, run through the glen or glade swiftly but thoroughly. Willow's heart would pound as she watched him from the shadows grateful that he was only human and couldn't detect her scent. Although a few times, he would stare in her direction as if he sensed her presence, then he would shake his head and climb on his quad, typing in new coordinates and peel off to another part of the forest. Of course, Bray was using technology. More proof of how humans could thwart their security.

After several days running into each other in various parts of the woods, unbeknownst to Bray, she found him idling up on his quad approaching her home. His clothes were crumpled. His hair was windblown. Beard stubble shadowed his cheeks. Bray's intense eyes had dimmed. He looked exhausted. She couldn't believe he had shown up at her birth tree, a location she had never taken him to. Willow wasn't sure what to do. She could use her own tree as a gateway to travel to almost anywhere in the forest. But travel in this manner opened access for other beings to slip in. Someone with evil intent would have to be waiting for it, and time it just right. The risk was small, but she was too cautious. Willow watched as Bray sat in the shade of her tree. Did he know her kind of tree was unusual in these parts? Weeping Willows were not common in the Coconino Forest, but Dryad trees were unique. They didn't have to be indigenous to the area they were born into. Magical energies sustained them no matter where their birth trees were located. His back rested against her trunk. She breathed in his scent. They were touching for the first time in a week. She heard him sigh and her branches rustled above releasing some tension Willow hadn't realized she's been holding. He put his head to his knees. She watched him. His body shook with emotion. She held her breath as a jackrabbit snuck up beside him. A few birds in her tree started singing a sad melody. He looked up. His eyes were red. His sorrow spilled through her. Bray made her feel. It was like her emotions had been bottled up for years. Getting to know Bray for the past month, the pressure had been building and building. And then on Halloween, the cork had popped spilling all her emotions to the surface in one orgasmic explosion. She had bubbled up with happiness for those precious few moments. Willow knew it had been a lie, but she didn't care. That one magical night with him had remade her. The morning after when she realized he couldn't remember, her world had crumbled. To be so close to happiness, only to have it snatched from her was too much. Willow realized she would never again feel that total connection with another. Eternal soulmates were rare. All her adult life had centered around duty to the forest, to the position she held. It took priority over everything else. But the only thing that really made her happy and fulfilled her in every way was the one thing she could never have. They both felt the heartbreak, but only she recalled that perfect night. She felt the full extent of what they had lost. Willow began sobbing. The clouds rolled in. It was as if the world had closed a curtain muting the sunlight in the clearing she and Bray shared. At least he wouldn't be able to hear the muffled weeping beneath the thick bark.

Bray turned and wrapped his arms around the trunk and rubbed the coarse bark as if trying to soothe. She held her breath as he lightly caressed. She could merge with normal trees and feel very little. They were modes of transportation or places to hide or spy. But this was her birth tree. She. Felt. Everything. A single tear slid down his cheek, rolling off onto the trunk. A willow leaf brushed it away. It was reflex. Her branches folded around him, leaves fluttering in the wind. They held each other. After some time, he gave a deep sigh. He got up and walked away. It took every piece of willpower she possessed not to follow him. It was one of the hardest things she had ever done.

The next morning, Bray found her in her mother's glade. Willow was sprawled out on the low stone table watching the clouds roll by. Willow felt numb. She could still taste the salt from Bray's tear. Willow had absorbed it into her skin.

"Oh, thank god," Bray whispered.

She startled.

"Don't run away." He approached with his hands at his sides as he would a wild animal. Small movements, trying not to scare. His voice low, almost a whisper.

Willow turned her head to watch him approach. Her heart sped at the sight of him. Those dark brown eyes staring into her own. She still hadn't moved from the table. He held out his hand and she reached for it automatically. He placed it over his heart, holding it there.

"Please listen. I know we're different, but that's exactly why we're so good together. I want another chance with you. Willow, come away with me to Flagstaff for a few days. Don't focus on anything else. Just the two of us."

Willow was mesmerized by his pleading eyes. Then it hit her. Sudden realization. She didn't have to deny him or her. Council couldn't control who she spent time with. Even her mother, who they adored, had spent time with humans. Intimately. Mr. Miller was the only one she knew of but there were probably others.

"Ok." She nodded.

That single word seemed to relieve all the tension from his shoulders. He took a deep breath and let it out. "Good."

She could tell he wanted to kiss her, but he seemed reluctant to do anything that might ruin the moment.

"How about you meet me at my cabin in an hour? We'll leave then."

She nodded again not feeling like herself. "One hour. I promise."

Willow arrived at his cabin as he was loading a suitcase into the backseat of his truck. He opened the passenger door and she hopped in.

It felt like a dream to go away with him like this. The first adventure she had experienced in years. She felt herself smile for the first time in a week. He grinned back at her as he closed the door and rushed around to the driver's side. Bray held her hand as they drove into Flagstaff, almost as if he had to reassure himself, she wouldn't slip away. He asked the GPS on his car to find a hippie-loving vegan bakery that served breakfast. She grinned. He was always so accommodating.

"Flagstaff Extreme," Bray said to his car. Willow thought it hilarious to have a conversation with the machine, but a voice would direct them time and again without fail. She shook her head mystified by human magic. The place turned out to be an obstacle course with rope swings and wobbly bridges, and they finished with a zipline. She found it funny how humans needed to challenge themselves in such strange ways. Willow rediscovered just how much fun they had together. It reminded her of how they were when they first met. It felt like a lifetime ago.

Bray checked them into the Hotel Monte Vista in downtown Flagstaff, which was known for being haunted. Willow had an affinity for the ghosts in the hotel, being part spirit herself. She spent less time worrying about the forest and gave herself up to the experience. She felt herself relaxing. In the evening, they went to the bar for karaoke. Bray couldn't carry a tune, but neither could Willow. They had a blast singing on stage to the boos and cheers of the college kids. When they finally made it to their hotel room, she was nervous. The last time they had been intimate, it had been amazing. Of course, he had been shot with forget me serum so she didn't have to worry about him remembering a thing. Now, she had to take precautions.

"I want you. All of you. But I need it dark." Willow pulled down the shades and folded the curtains over the cracks careful to cover any light coming in. "Pitch black."

Bray was staring at her. She wondered if her skin was already flushing green. She yanked off her dress and dove under the covers. "Turn off the lights."

"Honey, men are visual. We need to see if what we're doing is turning on our partner. And after last time, well let's just say I don't want you reduced to tears the morning after."

Willow smirked. He thought she hadn't been satisfied? What a laugh. That wasn't why she cried. She had known it was over between them because she had listened to Fuath. He said Council would never accept their union, and, like always, she had taken the advice without even fighting for what she wanted. She had been devastated because it had been too good and now knew what she was missing. Not that she could share any of that with Bray. Willow refused to think of the future. She wanted to focus on the here and now, to savor every moment with this man while it lasted. Willow deserved this. The forest could just fend for itself for a few days.

"Last time was amazing."

"Then why did you leave?"

"I was confused. It's hard to explain, but regardless we can't have the lights on."

She couldn't allow that. He would see her body change when she came. This whole vacation would be a bust.

"Please. This is a need, not a want. Do you understand?"

Whatever Bray saw in her expression convinced him. He flipped off the light switch. Darkness engulfed the room. Only a single beam of moonlight streamed through a crack in the curtain. That little bit of light she could work with. She gave a sigh of relief.

"Thank you."

She heard his shoes come off, then his shirt and jeans. Willow could see his shadow standing at the side of the bed. Why wasn't he as urgent as she was? She rolled off the side of the bed and grabbed for him. He was already rock hard. She stroked his cock. Bray hissed out a breath.

"Slow down, honey. Lay back in the bed."

His voice was a low rumble. She shivered and followed his instructions. Willow kicked the covers off the bed. She didn't need to hide anymore. Not in the dark where it was safe. He went to the side table fumbling with the condom box and ripped open a packet. He had done the same thing Halloween night. At least the first two times. He walked to the foot of the bed. What was he waiting for?

"Bray?"

She felt the bed dip. He crawled toward her. She parted her thighs. Her heart pounded in her chest. Why was he going so slow? He hovered over her and licked. A quick flick of his tongue at her core.

"Oh, Gaia." She cried out.

Her hips involuntarily bucked, but he had already gripped her ass holding her tight. Her male didn't want to be deprived of her taste. She smiled. It was a possessive gesture and it turned her on like nothing else. She felt a burst of juice gush. Bray groaned and lapped it up. He twirled his tongue the way she loved. He always seemed to know exactly what to do. But tonight, she was urgent.

"Bray. I need you inside."

She tried to pull his head up, but he wasn't giving up his prize. His tongue was relentless. Willow could already feel the pressure building. It was too much. She couldn't wait. She threw her arms over her head and surrendered to a mind-blowing orgasm. If the lights had been on, he would have seen the green glow of her skin. There would have been no way of hiding it. He repositioned on straight arms above her. She felt his cock nudge at her entrance. He wedged himself inside inch by inch.

"Fuck. You're so tight." His voice sounded strained.

"You said the same thing last time." Willow panted.

He finally seated himself in as far as he could go and stilled as if waiting for her to grow accustomed to his size. It was sweet how careful he was not to hurt her, but he had way too much control. Willow was wound so tight. If he didn't move soon, she was going to snap.

"Now Bray." She wiggled her hips.

He seemed to understand what she needed. Bray no longer hesitated. He pulled out and thrust home in one smooth move. Willow's legs wrapped around his waist and she ground herself into him.

"Yes. Oh, Gaia. Yes. More Bray. I need more."

He started pounding. No longer slow. Not anymore. She could feel the tingling in her extremities, the pressure building and building. Sweat-slicked bodies slamming together over and over. Her head thrashed. Her body thrummed. Then sweet release. Nirvana.

"Oh, god." Thrust. "I feel you." Thrust. "Fucking hell. That's good."

He continued pounding and she felt another orgasm building. She screamed out her pleasure burying her face in his chest. Willow bit his pectoral muscle as she rocked her hips.

"Fuck. Willow. Stop biting. Damn. I'm losing control." It was as if something flipped a switch. A low growl trickled from his lips. His thrusts were frantic. Bray yanked her hair back. She had no choice but to release him from her bite. "Tell me I'm yours alone. No one else." He stirred his cock inside her, rubbing her clit in circles.

"I'm yours, Bray. No one but you." She tried to kiss him, but he pinned her wrists. The single ray of moonlight illuminated his features. His expression was fierce, almost crazed. Sweat poured from his body. The words she spoke seemed to satisfy him. He rolled his hips.

"Oh. Yes. Do that again." Willow's eyelashes fluttered.

This was something he hadn't done on Halloween. She blinked up at him. He tried a few other moves, each one better than the last. Where had this man learned all these skills? A quick flash of jealousy. "Tell me you're mine alone."

"Ah hell, Willow. You have me. I'm yours."

She wondered for how long. Willow shook her head and reminded herself not to waste these precious moments.

They hadn't changed positions, but he somehow managed to hit a new spot inside her. A different kind of orgasm built.

"Bray, I'm almost there."

"Yeah?" Another hip roll.

She whispered, "I want you with me." Willow arched her back forcing her nipples to brush against his chest with every thrust.

"Oh god. Fuck yeah." His thrusts lost their rhythm and she knew he was close. She pushed up with her heels, angling her pelvis as he hammered into her. The position tightened her core.

Bray roared incoherent words. The bed banged against the wall. Willow's whole body rocked with each thrust. Her teeth clacked together. And then, he did the one thing guaranteed to drive her wild. He leaned down and bit her neck releasing her wrists. She screamed and scratched his back with her nails as she came harder than ever before.

It took minutes before either could speak. They both lay panting in the darkness waiting for their heart rates to slow. Bray was still buried inside her.

"Did I hurt you?"

She gave a throaty laugh. "I might be a little sore tomorrow. But trust me. It was worth it."

Willow could vaguely see the outline of his smile.

"I meant the bite."

"Oh. Yeah. I fucking loved that."

Bray chuckled, "I could tell."

He pulled out and stumbled to the bathroom to get rid of the condom. In seconds Bray was back, snuggled in behind her. "Will you tell me what else you like?"

She yawned, "Sure." She wiggled her behind into his crotch. His cock was already coming back to life, but she was too tired. "Tomorrow."

"Did I exhaust you after only three orgasms?"

"Mmm. Hmm. I haven't slept well lately."

He wrapped his arms around holding her close. Bray put a leg over her hip. His body cocooned her in warmth. She felt safe and protected.

"I'll give you a reprieve for tonight. Goodnight, sweets."

"Night, Bray." She yawned.

In seconds she fell fast asleep.

Willow woke the next morning with him buried inside her.

"I've been waiting for you to wake."

She blinked up at him. Sunlight was streaming into the room. Willow moaned. He gave a hip roll and she inhaled. Her body was already slick for him. When had that happened?

"How long have you been up?"

He gave her another measured thrust.

"Since you started grinding on me in your sleep."

Willow smiled. "Sorry?"

Bray grinned. "You don't see me complaining, do you?" Another thrust.

She slowly focused on his face. Wait. Willow could see him. That meant he could see her. She started to panic and pushed him off.

"Woah. Okay. Easy."

She rolled off the bed and ran for the bathroom.

Willow stared in the mirror. Her skin was a pale green, hardly noticeable. She had gotten away in time. She took a deep breath, let it out, and concentrated on calming down.

Bray knocked on the door. "Are you ok?"

She unlocked the door. "I'm fine." Willow walked past him.

"I should have woken you first." His head fell. "I just thought after last night." He groaned. "Does this mean no more sex?"

"What?" She screeched. "What do you mean no sex?"

Bray shrugged. "You seemed upset, like I took advantage." He ran a hand through his rumpled hair. "I don't know. Help me, Willow. Tell me how to make this work."

He still wanted sex. She hadn't blown it with him. Willow released a breath. He just needed parameters. She could do that.

"Well, like I said before. No light. This morning, it's too bright."

"So, if it's dark, you're ok?"

She nodded enthusiastically.

"Are you embarrassed by your body? Because I can tell you Willow, you are unbelievably hot. You have nothing to be ashamed of." He scratched his head. "I didn't expect you to have self-esteem issues.

"I don't want you to see me when I'm excited. I know it's a quirk, but this is a deal-breaker for me. Please, Bray."

"I can work with that."

He gave her a kiss, and they took turns in the shower. They spent the day exploring museums and several downtown shops. Bray checked them into another hotel, one that had blackout drapes. She grinned when he showed her how dark the room got. Every day they explored a different part of the city and every evening they explored each other. One night, Willow decided to try something different. She convinced Bray to wear a blindfold while she rode him. Willow could tell he loved how she had taken control. The following evening, they met a couple over dinner at Beaver Street Brewery. They were having a big party over at their place and had invited them. Apparently, they knew all about Bray and his IT world. With no other plans for the evening, they decided to go. She had never gone to a human house party before. Another first, but she could hardly wait. With Bray by her side, she no longer feared this human world. He maneuvered his way through it with ease and made her feel as safe and protected as her favorite pine.

Chapter 27

Bella stared at the lake watching the moonlight dance across the ripples, wondering what creatures lurked beneath the surface. The lake Nymphs would often share fantastical tales about an enormous mythical snake creature that would rise from the depths to snatch unsuspecting prey. She wondered if there was a shred of truth to those stories. More lower creatures were missing lately. Not that she really cared. It was just an observation.

She heard her mother's hoof steps approaching behind her.

"What on earth is that?"

Bella glanced where she was pointing.

"That's the dock Bray built."

Her mother squinted at the structure. "Is it sound to walk on?"

Bella shrugged. "He's not very good with tools."

"Hmm. Typical city human." Donna mumbled.

"You have your latest instructions?"

"Yes, but I don't understand Mother." Bella shook her head. "At first, you wanted me to seduce Lucian, then you changed it to Bray, now you're back to Lucian again?"

"The plan is ever-evolving and complicated my dear. Besides you were never successful with the human."

Thank Gaia. She was relieved he hadn't been interested. Humans made her skin crawl. Manipulating Bray to break up with Willow had been easy. Spread a few breadcrumbs of doubt and give him a snippet of proof and he automatically assumed the worst.

"Well, it turned out not to matter, since you changed your mind."

Donna pursed her lips. "I have contingencies for all possibilities. Since you failed to seduce the human, I decided to use him instead."

Her mother gestured to a stump along the shore. Bella sighed and took a seat. Donna removed the boar bristle from a leather pouch and began brushing Bella's hair. This ritual had started when she was a child. It was meant to be a mother-daughter bonding experience, but felt more critical these days, like Donna was saying with each stroke of the brush that Bella was failing in her duty. Attracting a mate, or more specifically a Satyr, was her job. Silky hair, dark kohled eyes, red pouty lips, and seductive clothing were vital. With the Satyr population being mostly male, you would think the odds would be in her favor, but most were reluctant. Satyr females were notoriously moody and high maintenance. Being Mother Bacchus's daughter meant Bella had a stigma she couldn't shake. The rumors had traveled far and wide that Mother Bacchus had killed her mate in a jealous rage. Whether the rumor was true or not didn't matter. It meant males were reluctant to get serious with Bella fearing she too could snap. One-night stands, no problem. Bella had a string of lovers, but no one wanted to get serious. At twenty-six, Bella was starting to worry she may never find a mate. Her mother warned her that her looks would start fading before long and she needed to snare someone soon. Bella complained that Satyr males preferred Nymphs, recounting the exploits of her brothers. Bella didn't understand why she had to mate with a Satyr anyhow. She enjoyed Demons and Shifters and even a few Centaurs. To other species, Bella was a rare beauty, perhaps wild, but one they thought could be tamed. They couldn't get enough of the curves she flaunted. But her mother wouldn't approve any union save a full-blooded Satyr.

Her mother rubbed a few beads of oil on the bristles and continued to brush. She worked from the ends, getting out every tangle. She would brush for what seemed like hours, continuing until her hair was as smooth as silk. It was usually a relaxing process, meant to calm the nerves.

"You have the potion from Fuath with you?"

"Yes." She pointed to her satchel. "I got it two weeks ago. He was most accommodating, but he did ask questions. He wanted to know what I was using it for."

The brush ripped through her hair violently. It yanked out a few strands. "Ow. Mother, be careful."

"You didn't tell him, did you?" Donna screeched in her ear.

"Mother please." She turned to face her. "I'm not an idiot."

She softened the brush strokes, going back to a soothing rhythm.

"How do you know she's still in Flagstaff?" Bella asked.

"I have sources. Willow and her human are occupied. She's not getting her messages." Donna giggled.

Bella wondered what that meant. Maybe squirrel delivery wasn't possible in the city, or perhaps her mother bribed the filthy little creatures with nuts.

With the ritual complete, her mother placed the brush back in its pouch.

"Let me see your face." Mother Bacchus turned Bella around and squinted, carefully going inch by inch checking for flaws.

Bella had spent hours on her makeup. It should be perfect.

"It's time. I know you've enjoyed the Demon. But we all must make sacrifices for the greater good."

Bella recalled her time spent with Lucian and shivered. His body was like chiseled perfection. The male had so many delicious skills and was so forceful. He was by far the best lover she'd ever had. If only he weren't so devoted to Willow. Such a pity. He would pay for that betrayal.

Donna's grin was pure evil. "Once this mixes with the wine, it will start to break down."

She watched as her mother combined the contents of the potion with the flask of moonwine.

"The longer you wait, the worse it will taste. You must get him to drink this quickly."

"I understand what I must do, Mother. He's at the same bar he always goes to. He won't taste a thing. He's been getting drunk every night since she walked away from him at Festivus."

"Here's the location you must bring him to, but only after he drinks it."

Bella looked at the scribbled symbols on the scrap of parchment. Was it a map?

She opened her mouth to ask, but her mother shushed her before she could begin.

"Just hold the note in your hand. It will let you know once you've arrived."

"How exactly am I supposed to drag the Demon from the bar to wherever the hell this is? He's freakishly huge."

Her mother huffed, "Must I figure out every detail? Just do it. We can be rid of the Ashbrooks once and for all."

"You mean Willow, right? Not her sisters."

Donna shrugged, "They're family. When one falls, they all fall."

She wanted to ask more questions, but her mother was growing irritated. Bella didn't care much for Ellie or Mae, but she liked Red, or at least her attitude. The 'love me motherfuckers or kiss my ass' attitude was one Bella could relate to. Red was the only Ashbrook sister she respected. Now Willow, on the other hand, she could do without. Miss Guardian-ho bag could go straight to hell.

Her mother handed her another pouch.

"You can open this when you've arrived at the location on the map and not a moment before. It will give your final instructions. Do this for me, daughter, and you will get your reward."

Bella's eyes glittered. Her mother knew exactly what she craved. She gave an involuntary squeal of delight.

Her mother smirked and left Bella holding the flask and pouch. She placed everything in her satchel and glanced around the clearing. Hmm. Bray's quad could be useful. She checked the power levels and found the keys. Picking the lock to the cabin was easy. She had been doing that for weeks. Inside, she gathered a few essentials and took off at high speed toward the Watering Hole, the bar where Lucian spent his time brooding over his lost love. Poor Demon. Broken hearts are such a bitch.

Chapter 28

Bray watched as Willow glided through the crowd under multi-colored patio lights. She was such a stunning woman with her long platinum hair blowing in the breeze. While the other women huddled in jackets or wraps, she stood with shoulders back in her sleeveless party dress taking everything in at once. Willow didn't seem to get cold. Her tolerance from living outside all these years must have built up endurance to the elements. Even when she stood motionless, she had such vitality. She was such a contradiction. Sweet and innocent one moment, and bold as you please the next. Willow took such pleasure in each new experience. It humbled him. He had taken so much for granted in his life. He felt himself grinning all the time. The house they were in still had a few Halloween decorations up. Willow stood next to a blacklight. Her skin and hair glowed luminescent. Even her hazel eyes twinkled. Those lashes when she would blink up at him and that sweet sexy smile. She could twist him so easily. And man, that girl could dance, uninhibited gyrations that sent a jolt of heat straight to his groin. She seemed to enthrall everyone around her with those moves, men and women alike. He couldn't believe how lucky he was. Over this week she had finally loosened up. He walked over to the bar and refilled their drinks. She seemed partial to raspberry martinis and Lady Gaga music. He hardly remembered the uptight backwoods hillbilly. She hadn't talked about her sisters in days. He hoped she finally realized that she could have a life outside the woods, one with him. Her sisters were adults and had their own lives. Although to be fair, he didn't understand the family dynamic between siblings since he was an only child. But she seemed insistent on her protective motherly role until this past week. Willow wandered around the pool to talk to a few new friends.

He followed her with the martini.

"I'm not feeling well," Willow said as she sat down on a lawn chair and closed her eyes.

Bray felt her head. "You do feel a little warm."

"I'm just a little dizzy. She took a sip of the martini and smiled. "Thank you so much. This is delicious."

"Let me get you something to eat. The alcohol is probably having its effect on you."

She raised an eyebrow. "I'm not the one that can't hold their liquor."

He laughed. Willow was teasing. She must be recalling his wild behavior when he over-indulged on Halloween. Bray had yet to recall what happened that night but knew he must have done something right. He had gotten her to break the no-sex rule, and yet something so horrible that she had broken things off. Willow still wouldn't give him all the details. As curious as he was, Bray refused to go backward. Their first night in Flagstaff had been a revelation. He just had to work around her quirks. No lights. No problem. Every night they made love and each time got better and better. At times, his curiosity would pique and he would ponder the reasons for her fear. It didn't make sense with her upbringing. How could she be embarrassed by her body? She was a nudist. It didn't make sense. Whenever Bray would think on it too hard, he would grow frustrated. Willow seemed to sense those moments and would distract him with a look or touch. Her libido was off the charts. She would exhaust him physically to the point where he could barely move let alone think. She would cling to him in her sleep with an almost desperation, but it still felt like she was holding herself back.

"Let me get you something to eat just in case. It might help." He sprinted off to find something of substance to absorb all the alcohol she'd been drinking.

When he got back, she was asleep on the lounge chair.

"Willow, honey. I found vegan quiche." He gently shook her arm.

She didn't budge. He tried harder. He looked around at the other guests. No one had noticed she had passed out. There were plenty of people blitzed this late in the evening. He checked her pulse. It seemed to be normal. And she was breathing ok, but then he noticed her arm. There was a bright red splotch on her forearm about the size of his palm. It looked like a rash of some sort. She must be allergic to something she ate. He panicked not knowing her medical history or having any way to reach her family. He picked her up and carried her out the side gate without a word to anyone. Bray couldn't even remember the names of their hosts. He googled the nearest hospital and stepped on the gas. At every red light he checked her breathing. She didn't seem to be having trouble, which he took as a good sign.

Once he got to the hospital, he told the emergency room she was his new wife and he didn't have her medical history. He gave them his black Amex card, and said payment would not be a problem. They got her in right away and did a quick vital check and got them into a curtained cubicle promising the doctor would be in shortly.

"Where am I?" Willow whispered.

"Oh, thank god. I was so worried." His lips found hers for a kiss, but she tensed.

"What's wrong?"

She shook as if having a seizure. He ran for the nurse, coming back with a flustered woman in tow.

"Unhand me, young man."

"She's going into shock." He pointed at Willow. She was still shaking but the tremors had slowed. A sheen of sweat coated her pale skin.

Willow grabbed his arm and pulled him close. "There's so much pain." She whispered.

The nurse examined the wound on her arm and checked the chart. "This isn't a rash from an allergy. It looks like a burn."

"I don't understand. Willow, did you burn yourself on something at the party?"

She shook her head over and over. Willow glanced at the nurse then back to Bray. She was trying to tell him something with her eyes, but he didn't understand. Either she couldn't or wouldn't speak in front of the woman.

He turned to the nurse, "Can you give her something for the pain?"

"No," Willow cried, "I have to stay conscious."

Bray turned back to her, "Let the nurse help you, sweetie."

"You don't understand." She gave a stifled sob.

Bray rubbed her cheek. "It's ok, honey. Explain it to me. Do you know what's wrong?"

She nodded and let out a long breath and looked away. "You won't believe me."

The nurse put some gel on the red mark. It seemed to have grown larger since the party. The red skin stretched from wrist to elbow. It looked raw and bubbled with blisters.

Willow gave a little whimper as the nurse wrapped the soft gauze loosely over the gel.

"I'll just get the doctor to write up a script for ointment and pain meds. There's not a whole lot we can do for second degree burns."

When the nurse left through the curtain, he put his hand under her chin and forced her to look at him. "Trust me."

She avoided eye contact. "There's a fire."

"At the party?"

She shook her head. "Back home. In the woods."

"How do you know this?"

She gestured to her bandaged arm. The red bubbled skin was spreading out past the gauze. "I need your help."

Bray stared at her arm. He didn't know what was going on. Bray was no medical expert, but a burn shouldn't be spreading. Infections spread, not burns. It didn't make sense. Tears filled Willow's eyes. She clutched at her arm. Her body jerked with pain. *Logic could wait.* "What do you need?"

She blew out a breath of relief. "I need to get home. It's close to your cabin." She swallowed. "To my sisters. We need to hurry. Before it's too late." Another full-body seizure and she passed out again.

He checked her pulse. Her breathing was normal. But the red skin continued to spread.

Bray looked outside the curtain. All the doctors and nurses were busy with other patients. He went toward the front desk and saw the head nurse speaking to the rest of the staff.

"There's a fire in the Coconino Forest. It's north of Bellemont off Route 66. The Fire Marshall just called. They are trying to contain it, but we need to prepare for the worst. Pull out the burn kits. All the hospitals and emergency clinics in Flagstaff are calling people in. Let's get busy, you remember the last one."

There were murmurs all around and then the nurses began scrambling for supplies.

He walked back to the curtain in a daze. Maybe Willow wasn't delusional. Maybe she had some sixth sense about the forest. She had an uncanny understanding of nature. He looked down at her limp body. He needed her trust. She wanted his help. He kissed her lips. "I really hope I'm doing the right thing." His logical brain rebelled at the idea of taking a burn victim closer to the head of a fire, but she had looked at him with such trust. She needed him to take a leap of faith. Willow needed to know her sisters were safe regardless of anything else. They were the only family she had. Maybe they knew what was happening to her. The nurse said there wasn't anything they could do for a burn, other than the ointment and some meds. He could get a script from Bellemont after they found her sisters.

Mind made up, he carried her out with barely a glance from the staff. The emergency room was in chaos preparing for fire victims. He got her buckled and on the road in less than a minute. She woke up just as they approached a roadblock.

She sucked in a pained breath and squinted through the front window. "You got me out of there?" She grabbed his hand linking fingers with his.

"I would do anything for you, Willow." He kissed her knuckles, "No matter how crazy."

She gave a sickly smile. "Well, I'm about to ask for a little more crazy. Turn the car into the woods. There's a path to the right in about twenty yards."

"Are you sure?"

"Be my wild knight who asks no questions. Don't think with logic, use your heart. Believe in me like I believe in you." She placed his right hand over her heart and held his gaze.

He looked down at the red bubbled skin on her arm and the gauze, his hand and hers on her left breast. Then he gazed into that soft trusting look in her eyes. That's what finally did it. Her faith in him. Bray had been waiting for that look. He could do nothing but follow her insane demands, even though it defied all reason. He was in love with this irrational outrageous woman. She needed to get to her family. Something was happening he couldn't explain. He left his fears and worries at the roadblock. Bray pulled onto the shoulder, then peeled off into the woods. He thought he saw her smile for a moment as they bounced through the rough terrain. He turned on the high beams, and it was like flipping a switch. He channeled all the hours spent playing off-road video games into avoiding trees and rocks as he followed the bumpy dirt path twisting deeper and deeper into the forest.

Willow sat up a little straighter. "You drive like a maniac." She giggled. "I love it."

She seemed to grow more alert the farther into the forest they got. He slowed down when he saw smoke.

"My sisters." She cried out.

Willow attacked the seatbelt trying to unbuckle herself. Bray slammed on the brakes and helped her unlatch it. She climbed out and screamed like a banshee speaking in a tongue he didn't understand. Was she swearing in another language?

Bray had never seen her like this. She was always so easygoing, like nothing could phase her. He wanted to hold her, comfort her in some way. He desperately wanted to help. Together they could somehow find her sisters. He'd make sure of it.

"Willow, it's ok. Calm down. I'll help." He walked toward her, and suddenly his feet were stuck. Vines snagged his shoes. He didn't remember seeing them moments before, but then his whole focus had been on Willow. He yanked a foot free and took another step. Even more vines encased his foot. It took longer to pull free this time. By the third step, he realized the vines were growing faster than he could yank free. They were climbing up his ankles. He started to panic, struggling to get free. Every move made them grow faster. They reached his knees. It was almost as if the vines were sentient, like they didn't want him to get to Willow. It was such a strange concept, he stopped struggling for a moment. The vines stopped their growth. Even the restriction on his legs loosened. *What the fuck was happening?* He stared at Willow's back. She was slowly scanning the forest, then started to glow. *Green?* Willow chanted strange words over and over in a sing-song voice. All around them the trees started glowing that same eerie green. The trees looked like they were moving closer, but that couldn't be possible. Bray had never been claustrophobic, but somehow the distance between the trees was growing smaller. He felt like they were being surrounded. Tree branches brushed against him. They seemed to be experiencing something straight out of a horror movie. He couldn't move. He couldn't protect her. He was losing his mind.

"Willow, look out. The trees are alive."

She turned toward him, and he saw her once pale smooth skin had turned a crackled greyish-brown. Willow's long pale hair now had bunches of thin green leaves. They whipped around in the stifling wind. She had eyes like an unpainted marionette, no pupils. She stared past him with those unblinking wooden eyes. He couldn't help but shrink back on himself, although the vines prevented him from physically moving. A large tree came toward her and held out a branch. She reached out with her bark-covered arm and touched the tree. Blinding light lit up the forest and Bray shielded his eyes with an arm. He thought for sure the fire had reached them. The heat was so intense, the smoke so thick. He felt like he should be hacking and coughing but somehow, he was still able to breathe. The light faded enough where he could focus and he realized the light had not come from the fire, but from Willow. Her hair of willow branches moved with an invisible wind, whipping back and forth as trees sped through the forest toward them. It looked like the trees were going to crash into them, but they stopped just shy of some hidden barrier. The kaleidoscope of color was mesmerizing as the trees zoomed through the forest reaching out with a limb, a branch, anything for Willow to touch. She pulsed with a pale green light getting brighter and brighter. A blackened willow tree approached slower than the others and she melted into the surface. He could see her face form in the bark, and light filled every inch of the tree, from the base of the trunk to every leaf and branch. Minutes later, the tree's glow subsided. Bray could feel the pulse in his throat pounding. Willow emerged from the tree looking whole and healthy. Her clothes from the party were gone. The red blisters from her arms were healed. The gauze fell gracefully to the forest floor, the only evidence she had been to ER. Even the tree she had emerged from seemed healthy, no longer charred black from the fire. It disappeared, fading off in the distance. He looked around. All the trees were spaced apart again, back where they originally started. Other than the thick smoke, everything looked normal. He looked down at his legs. The vines had stopped growing but still held him firmly in place. He waited several heartbeats. It was bizarre. Had they been standing still the whole time?

Willow stood in another clearing and knocked on an ancient pine. She called out her sister's names one by one. Her voice was eerie and sent shivers down his spine. Slowly her sisters appeared walking from the tree the same way Willow had. Bray knew he was hallucinating, or possibly dreaming. None of this could be real. He must have blacked out. Maybe it was a side effect from smoke inhalation. He watched as the sisters formed a circle and began to sing and dance. Bray didn't recognize the words, but he understood the basic meaning and felt himself swaying back and forth with the rhythm. His voice joined theirs. The sisters were calling for help from Gaia and her elemental creatures to bring the rain. They sang for a long time. Their voices grew hoarse. Even when the smoke got worse, they all continued to sing.

The wind stopped blowing and everything went utterly still as if time halted. The temperature dropped, and the rain began to fall. Light at first, and then a downpour. The sisters hugged and laughed, jumping up and down with excitement. No. Jumping wasn't the right word. Jumping would mean their feet left the ground. Their legs looked like tree limbs anchored in the earth, their feet like roots half in and out of the dirt. He stood frozen in shock watching the scene as if it were a movie. The vines that had held him bound, slid down his legs and flopped around his ankles. So many things didn't make sense. He spoke. No, not spoke. Sang in a language he didn't know. Had the sisters brought the rain? Had he in some way helped? What kind of creatures were they? They were definitely not human. Their skin was green, all different shades, just like their hair. He blinked. Not hair. On top of their heads were branches and leaves. Their faces looked chiseled. His logical mind rebelled against what he was seeing. He closed his eyes. Took a deep breath and opened them. No change. He had to get away. Time. Yes. That's what he needed. Time to process what just happened. Willow looked at him and grinned, but he had no smile for her. Another creature stood before him. Not the one he had fallen in love with. She was a stranger. Bray felt completely numb as he walked to his truck and climbed in. He turned the vehicle around, backing up slowly. He stopped and looked over his shoulder for one more glimpse. He wanted to grab Willow, make her change back. Force her into the truck so they could get away from here as fast as they could. Get away. His mind screamed. She seemed to understand what he was asking with his eyes. She shook her head. Sluggishly he pulled back onto the path, directing it back to his cabin. He looked at his cell phone for guidance. His homing chip still worked. That single piece of technology was the only thing that made sense this whole damn day.

Chapter 29

"DID YOU SEE his expression?" Willow cried, "He's not coming back."

"There, there, sister." Mae patted her shoulder, "You knew he wasn't from our world. Did you really think he could accept you for what you are?"

"Yes." She sniffed. "He's my eternal soulmate."

"Woah," Ellie said, "That's deep. How can you be certain?"

"I can't enchant him. At first, I thought I had lost my mojo, but it wasn't that. I can't use my powers on him. He's the only one. I spoke to Abraham about it. He's the one that suggested it as a possibility."

"No shit," Red said. "Well, if Abe says it's possible, then it's a sure thing." She noticed Willow's shocked expression. "What? I'm not as dense as everyone thinks. I can read between the tree rings."

Willow hugged Red. "I was in denial at first, trying to come up with any other possibility. When I finally did believe, you were all up in arms about him being a threat. I didn't think you would believe me. I should have told you all sooner."

"We should have realized by the way you acted around him." Ellie shook her head.

"I'm so sorry, Willow." Mae hugged her arms around herself looking away. She moved from the others. "I stirred up so much animosity against him." She blinked back tears. "I never would have called for Council to vote him out if I had known."

"Come here, Mae." Willow took a step forward, and Mae ran to her.

Words spilled together in between sobs. "Sorry, so sorry. Never would have. You must hate me." Mae clutched her close.

It was so wonderful to have the truth out, even if her heart was heavy. Bray's reaction had been everything she had feared. Ellie and

Red joined the hug and the sisters all held each other as the rain continued to fall. Willow allowed herself to cry, something she rarely did. They stood as a family, holding each other, sharing their emotions. Comforting each other with love and acceptance. Together. Four Dryads sisters bound to the earth. Linked to the forest and one another. Heavy magic flowed through their veins, cleansing their souls, wiping clean years of regret. The tears finally ebbed with the rain. It turned from a drizzle to a soft mist. Willow took a shallow breath, then another; each one a little deeper. This little pocket of forest had cocooned the sisters, protecting them while they worked their magic. A popping sound went off in her head, like a champagne bottle being uncorked. The fire was extinguished. They all took a deep breath and sighed in unison. They fell into a fit of giggles. It was something they used to do long ago. She felt in sync with her sisters once again. She hadn't felt this connected to them since they were all kids playing hide and seek. That had been the day their mother had died. In fact, she hadn't been back to that pocket realm in sixteen years.

"So, when are you going to get your man?" Red asked. "I can hog-tie him if you like?" She grinned. "This cowboy I met once showed me a few tricks."

Mae shook her head.

"What?" Red elbowed her sister. "Although, I bet you've got some hidden skills yourself. Maybe some way to persuade him without violence?" She wiggled her eyebrows.

Mae hit Red's shoulder. "Stop making things weird. I don't want to hear about her sex life or yours for that matter."

"Sorry, Mae. Didn't mean to shock your virgin sensibilities." Red snickered.

"What are you going to do?" Ellie asked.

Willow sighed. "Well, the monthly Council meeting is in a few days. I'm not sure how happy everyone will be after the fire. I should have been here, but instead, I was off with my boyfriend, getting some. Not really doing my job, now was I?"

"Council can suck it," Red exclaimed.

Willow grinned. "You've always had a way with words."

"They can't kick him out after they know he's your eternal soulmate," Mae stated confidently. "Plus, we brought the rain. Could you feel the energy? We haven't all united like that in years."

Willow patted her sister's shoulder. "I wish I had your confidence. I'm not sure what Council will decide. I shouldn't tell you this but I illegally recruited Fuath for a purity and soulmate test on Halloween. He knows the truth but already told me that Bray being human trumps being an eternal soulmate. Humans are forbidden. Period."

"That little motherfucker." Red punched a fist to her palm.

"If not Fuath, what about Abraham? He'll let Council know, right?" Ellie asked.

Willow rolled her eyes. "You should know better. He said he would think on it."

The sisters all groaned.

"That sounds like his typical bullshit," Red said. "I think he does it just to fuck with us."

Mae gasped. "Why do you always sound like a trucker?"

"My language skills are an art form." Red shrugged, "And don't knock truckers 'til you try 'em."

"Come on, girls, let's get some rest." Willow gestured for the girls to follow. "I'm beat after calling the rain. We'll figure everything out in the morning."

She said goodbye to her sisters and stumbled to her birth tree with a yawn. Willow whispered a prayer to Gaia thanking her for her help with the fire and asking for assistance with Bray. For him to somehow be able to accept her as she was. For them to be together as true eternal soulmates with no secrets between them. She stretched her branches and let the wind blow through her leaves, lulling her into a dream world full of possibilities for the future.

Crunch, crunch crunch. It sounded like footfalls in the leaves right outside her tree. Willow groaned. She needed more sleep. She merged with the bark, blinking at the intruder. It was Bella and she was pacing back and forth. How did she even know where Willow lived? A Dryad only revealed the location of her birth tree to those she trusted implicitly. Bella was not on that list; in fact, she was as far from it as possible. Willow looked up into the dark sky. Not even a hint of dawn. Bella was not a morning person. What could have gotten her up and out of bed so early?

"What's up, BB?"

She bowed low. "Guardian, I have a request from Council. There are many in need of your services. I have a list of areas that need healing."

Willow sighed. She knew this had been coming. The fire was one thing, but the damage was where the real work began. She had wanted to visit Bray first thing, but that would have to wait. Duty called.

The scroll from Council was unbelievably long and the healing was exhausting. Willow was still recovering from the fire damage done to her birth tree. But there were so many others that needed her help. Willow couldn't refuse. She worked the whole day, then collapsed into her tree needing a few hours of sleep before confronting Bray. When she awoke, Willow rushed to his cabin anxious to talk to him. The lights were out and the front door was locked. That was unusual. She knocked on the door but there was no answer. She peeked into the windows but all the curtains were drawn. Well, if he thought that would keep her out, he didn't know her at all. She climbed to the roof of the house and merged with the Rainbow Eucalyptus, traveling down the trunk and exiting into the living room. It left her whole body tingling. It was similar to how her hand felt after joining with Abraham. Willow knew this tree was "the heart of the forest" and required protection, but she didn't have much history beyond that. She now wondered if this tree could have been an old TreeAnt that had died. She briefly thought about asking Abraham, but how would she phrase the question without insulting him? She'd think about it later. Willow focused back on her task and went through the house searching for Bray. Everything was silent. He wasn't in the living room, bedroom, bathroom, or kitchen. She was getting ready to leave when she noticed a folded slip of paper sticking out of the bowl of nuts on the kitchen table. It was filled with her favorites. Willow snatched the paper and smoothed it flat on the table. She collapsed into a chair and read.

Willow,

I don't know how to feel about any of this. We come from such different backgrounds. I mean, I knew you were different, but geez, not that different. I love being with you, but I have to wonder with so many secrets between us, can we really make this work? Now I understand why you hesitated before our trip to Flagstaff, but our trust issues haven't gone away. I have to know you are in it to win it. No more lies between us. Am I still an outsider to your world or have you finally learned to trust me? Can you accept me for who I am? It's so frustrating not being able to reach you. I can't stay here any longer. I'm heading back home for a while. I have to take care of a few things. I'll be thinking of you.

Take care,

Bray

She clutched the note to her chest. What did it mean? Willow needed to discuss this with her sisters. She walked out the front door and for some reason locked it behind her. His strange human customs were wearing off on her. She let out a half-hearted laugh. Red. She would go see her first. Out of all her sisters, Red seemed to understand humans best.

She found her sister in the woods overlooking the Pilot gas station. "So, what are you doing?"

Red jumped like she'd been caught. "Um. Nothing."

Willow pursed her lips. "Are you looking for that big guy? What's his name? Jake?"

Her face heated. "Yeah, I want to bang him. What's it to you?"

Willow shrugged. "Bang away, sis."

She knew it was Red's normal defense mechanism to react with anger when embarrassed. Willow scanned the gas station parking lot. Bray's truck wasn't there. She wondered if he was on the road to Flagstaff, or already on a plane back to San Francisco.

"I'm sorry." Red bumped her shoulder, "I'm in a snarky mood today."

"Yeah. I get that. Me too." Willow handed Red the crumpled note.

She read it and laughed. "In it to win it. Gaia, he's lame."

"I wasn't quite sure what that meant," Willow admitted.

"Don't worry. It's a good sign. It basically means he wants to be your eternal soulmate. You have to convince Council that Bray is safe, so they don't zap him with forget me serum, then spill your guts. Tell Bray Every. Fucking. Thing. No holding back. Truth is his deal-breaker."

Willow grinned. "You always did tell it like it is. No fluff. You've been that way since you were a little girl."

Red looked longingly at a pickup as it pulled up to the tanks. The driver got out to pump gas. It wasn't Jake. She sighed and turned back to Willow. "Yeah, I know. I was born without a filter. Most people don't appreciate my blunt insight. They say I'm just a foulmouthed bitch."

"Who said such a thing?" Willow demanded, "You're an Ashbrook warrior, and the Guardian's sister. No one should disrespect you!"

Red chuckled. "Thanks for trying to defend me. But I don't need your scrawny ass fighting my battles." She looked back toward the tanks as another truck pulled up. "Why don't you go talk to Abe? See if he can give you some advice on how to handle Council. If he's not willing to stick up for you, maybe he can give you some eloquent shit to say."

It was a brilliant idea. Willow thanked her sister and went to go find him. Surprisingly, Abraham was up. Her sister Mae was visiting.

"I'm surprised to see you here," Willow said to Mae.

She shrugged. "It's the least I could do to try and smooth things over with Council now that I know Bray's your eternal."

"Prospective eternal soulmate," Abraham stated. "It has not been confirmed."

Mae glared at him. "When have your suggestions ever been wrong?"

Abraham paused for a long while. "Hmm. I see your point. I am very wise."

Willow laughed. That was the one thing about TreeAnts, they didn't have a shred of humility. Although to be fair, if she lived to be their age, she would probably be just as arrogant. But Willow knew without a doubt Bray was her eternal. The Serce test had been done by the Sprite's leader himself; twice. Because the request was outside normal procedure and not authorized by Council, the results could not be shared. Fuath and now her sisters were the only ones who knew the truth. Since the test was illegal, she had vowed not to tell a soul it had been done. Willow knew she couldn't break her word, especially to a Council member.

"Most wise and venerable Abraham, if we agree Bray is her eternal, what is needed for Council to allow him to stay in the forest with full knowledge of our world?"

Abraham's branches went back and his leaves stood straight. He seemed to love the praise. Willow listened to their conversation without saying a word. Mae didn't seem remotely aggravated by the long pauses in between questions and answers. Her sister had turned into quite the diplomat. Willow realized she had been treating her sisters like little girls instead of grown women. She had accepted the mother role for so long, it felt odd trying to let that go. But if she wanted a life with Bray, she needed to see her sisters differently. Mae's questions were quite perceptive. She seemed to understand what needed to be said to Council in order to sway the verdict their way. She also had a knack for asking questions in a way to allow Abraham to make suggestions rather than committing to one side or the other. She even got him to agree to speak on her behalf in front of Council. She did it all by praising his sage guidance time and again. Willow had to give Mae props. She couldn't have done better if she tried. Willow gave her sister a big hug, and they left Abraham snoring peacefully.

It was the day of the Council meeting and Willow needed to get a few supplies at the town store. She trekked her way through the woods wearing a blue dress Bray seemed to favor. She missed him terribly. Bobby spotted her walking and waved her over to the Roadhouse for some lunch. Willow reluctantly went. She didn't feel like company today. They placed their orders and sat at a table away from the bar.

"How are you doing?" Bobby asked.

Willow shrugged. "Ok. I guess."

"I see." Bobby nodded knowingly.

Willow shook her head. She knew Bobby. The woman was practically bursting to share the latest gossip. The hesitation only meant one thing. It wouldn't be good.

"Come on. Out with it."

"Well, um. I happened to notice Bray left town."

"Yeah, a few days ago. He left me a note."

Bobby took a sip of iced tea. "Hmm. A note. He didn't tell you in person?"

"Nope."

"Did he mention he was leaving with anyone else, like maybe Gail?"

Willow's jaw dropped. "No. He. Did. Not."

"It might not mean anything." She patted Willow's hand. "Gail hopped into his truck at the hotel. She had just checked out and was heading to the airport in Flagstaff."

"Bray mentioned he was heading home in the letter. Maybe he offered her a ride?" Willow cringed at the phrasing. Her thoughts went haywire thinking of all kinds of rides he could be giving her.

"Are you two having trouble?"

Willow shrugged. "I'm not really sure. We might have broken up."

"You don't know?" Bobby rolled her eyes. "Why are men so unclear about their feelings?"

"Do you think Gail is digging her claws into him?" Willow asked.

Bobby chuckled. "I doubt Gail would damage her manicure. She's slick, that one, but I don't think Bray is swayed. He's still sweet on you."

"But they have so much in common. They live in the same town. Go to the same parties, know the same people. He wants someone who understands him." Willow's voice quavered.

"Now, you don't really believe all that nonsense, do you? You're an exotic beauty and as down to earth as they come. Who wouldn't want you?"

Willow smiled. "That's nice of you to say, but Bray isn't like most men."

"So, are you planning to go after him?"

Willow choked on a bite of salad. "What?"

"Well, it's not like the old days, where you have to wait for a man to come to you." She nudged her shoulder, "Where's your warrior spirit? If you want him, fight for him. Go get him and bring him back."

Willow thought about traveling all the way to San Francisco by herself and shivered. Flagstaff was scary enough, and Bray had been with her the whole time. Although in her youth, she had dreamed of traveling to exotic locations all over the world. It had filled her with excitement, not fear. After she was crowned Guardian, travel became impossible. Council would never allow something like that. But Bobby was right. Somewhere along the trail, she had lost her Warrior spirit. If she had really wanted to pursue traveling, she should have fought for it, just like she should fight for Bray.

"I've never been to San Francisco," Willow whispered.

"Could be an adventure," Bobby suggested.

Willow decided to give it some serious thought. She was immensely grateful for the information and the distraction from her worries. But her heart felt heavy when she walked back into the forest. She had forgotten all about stopping at the store. All Willow wanted to do was get to Bray. She scaled his roof and merged into the Heart tree. Willow walked to his bedroom and crawled under the covers. His scent still clung to the sheets. She hugged his pillow and fell asleep dreaming of him.

At sunset, Willow stood in the sacred clearing as Council arrived and took their seats. Her nap at Bray's hadn't made her feel any better. She was nervous, but as prepared as she could be for the meeting. Willow had rehearsed exactly what to say. Her main worry now had more to do with what Bobby had shared with her at lunchtime. This month's Council session was being modified due to the fire. They were forgoing the traditional grievance line, which Willow was immensely grateful for. She had worried about the complaints she would hear and the guilt she would feel over the property destruction. Miraculously, no creature had died in the fire, but a lot were now homeless. Ellie had organized a makeshift table and had been making suggestions on several animals sharing homes until new ones could be located. Her sisters never ceased to amaze. She was so proud of them. Mae and Red stood on either side of her as she approached the Council bench.

Mae cleared her throat. "May we begin with a few words of wisdom from our most venerable Abraham."

Abraham's leaves rustled and he seemed to stand a little taller. Everyone turned to him as he spoke. He gave thanks to the sisters who were given their due for bringing the rains to put out the fire. He recommended a committee to investigate what started the fire for prevention in the future and he ended with the bombshell about Bray being Willow's eternal soulmate. That got Council whispering.

"Willow step forth." The Sprite leader began. "You should be aware of the laws for the Guardian. As protector, you will not leave the forest for any reason. Is that still your understanding?"

Willow shifted her stance. "Yes. I'm aware of the rules."

"Yet you continue to break them by going into town."

"It's important research." Willow bristled, "We have to know what's going on outside our borders for security reasons."

"You could have delegated the responsibility to someone else."

That stopped Willow. She could have. But it had always been her desire to seek out new places and meet new people. "I already have a relationship with the townsfolk, and I have the best ways of getting information from them."

"You use sex to get information from humans?" Terra asked.

Willow gave her a dirty look. "No."

"I heard otherwise." Mother B replied.

Willow watched as the two Council members whispered to one another. When had Mother B and Terra become close?

The Sprite resumed. "You are called upon to answer for your absence on the night of the fire. What say you?"

"I admit, I followed my eternal soulmate to Flagstaff for a few days. I had no idea such a tragedy would happen while I was gone. Would anyone else refuse the request of an eternal?"

That seemed to hit a nerve for a lot of the forest creatures. Willow and her sisters had strategized over what she would say, and they all agreed to use the soulmate card as much as possible. It was a rare thing to find, and most everyone in the forest respected that as a special kind of magic that could not be questioned.

Terra turned to Donna. "I thought you said she was back with her ex."

"Who knows who she's screwing at the moment? The Ashbrook Dryads are fickle, just like their mother." She sneered.

"Do you mean Lucian?" Willow asked.

Fuath nodded. "We've heard rumors you convinced him to start the fire."

"What?" Willow was outraged. "Why would I do something like that? It would take a monster to start a fire here. The drought hit us hard this summer. And my birth tree was damaged in the fire. You think I wanted to die?"

Council shifted uncomfortably in their seats. Most would not meet her gaze.

"And, as the wise Abraham stated, my sisters and I brought the rains. We coaxed the spirits to help as soon as we could. Even though the destruction was extensive, we helped save lives."

"Maybe that was your plan. To look like a hero." Donna's lip curled. "You didn't count on us learning the truth."

"You're delusional." Willow threw up her hands.

"Nothing more to add for your statement?" Fuath asked.

"No. That's everything."

The Council members all gathered together behind the bench to discuss the matter in whispers.

After a few minutes, Fuath stood at the head of the table and fluttered his wings, hovering in place as he projected his voice to the crowd. "Because of the allegiance with Lucian and the implications of colluding to start the fire—Because of Willow's continued disregard for the laws of her position, her negligence of duty, and total disregard for the lives in the forest, and especially for her distraction with the human, we have made the decision to have Willow removed from office." He turned to her. "You, Willow Ashbrook, are no longer Guardian. You protect the forest no more."

There were gasps from the crowd. She felt like she had been punched in the chest and stumbled back a few steps.

Fuath nodded and one of his soldiers flew over to her. She recognized him as one of the members of Sprite SWAT. She couldn't recall his name.

The male fluttered over. His wings beat an uneven rhythm, a sure sign of hesitation. He rubbed his neck and looked back at his leader. He flew to Willow's ear and whispered. "Sorry about this, but I don't have a choice. My leader has ordered me to confiscate your crown."

Willow blinked. Her limbs went numb. How could this be happening? She had never heard of a Guardian being removed from office. Willow detached the wreath she had worn for sixteen years. The bay laurel leaves had stayed fresh and perfect with Dryad magic. She handed it to the Sprite.

The Sprite soldier mouthed 'thank you,' and bowed his head. Seconds later, he dropped it in front of Fuath. It made a soft crunch as the crown, now dry and brittle, hit the Council bench.

She looked at her sisters. Red looked ready to kill. Mae's jaw hung open in shock. Ellie just offered a hug. Willow wasn't sure what to feel. She knew she was in shock. She imagined a lot of scenarios on what would happen in front of Council, but never this. Surprisingly, she wasn't angry. Willow was resigned and oddly a bit relieved. She had given half her life to protect the forest. Willow had originally seen it as a burden when she was sixteen. Early on, she hadn't felt worthy of the position. She realized now that she had never grown out of that feeling. Now Council was forsaking her. Failing at her job was something she had worried about for sixteen years. Willow had made a huge mistake, but she had also made up for it, or at least thought she had. And what was that bit about Lucian? Could those rumors be true? Could he have started the fire? And why would they assume she was working with her ex? The whole thing was ridiculous. She had just announced her eternal was a human. Council's information must be a mistake, not that it seemed to matter at the moment. Luckily, there had been no loss of life, otherwise, the penalty could have been death. Not just dismissal from office. She should be grateful.

"Who's the replacement?" Red asked. "Come on. Out with it."

The Sprite's leader looked nervously between the other Council members and cleared his throat. "Council has elected Faustino Bacchus as the new Guardian."

There was a mix of emotions from the crowd, a few cheers and whistles, but mostly groans. The whistles came from a group of Nymphs. The loudest was Maggie.

Red glared at the Sprite. "You're fucking with us, right?"

His wings twitched, and he floated down a few inches, then seemed to regain his composure. "I would do no such thing."

Willow watched the expressions of the Council members and realized the sisters had made a vital mistake in their strategy. Faustino smiled and waved to the crowd and winked at a few members on Council. With a wide grin and cocky stance, the Satyr could be exceptionally charming when he wanted to be. They had not counted on Council having a replacement waiting in the wings. Always in the past, Council was indecisive and moved slowly making decisions. They were reacting on pure emotion, and apparently were being fed information from someone who had everything to gain from her being removed. She didn't see Faustino as being the instigator. He had never seemed that ambitious. Bella had been the one dating Lucian, but he hadn't seemed all that taken with her. There was no way she could have convinced him to do something so drastic. He would have been punished by his own people for using fire powers to cause such senseless damage. And the rumor mill about Willow and Lucian. It was preposterous. The only one who had anything to gain was Mother Bacchus. She smiled at her son and turned to Willow. Her smile was smug. MB's eyes twinkled with such hatred. Fuath cleared his throat. It drew her gaze to him. His smile slipped and he was staring at Donna with a look of concern. She blinked and her expression blanked. When she met Willow's gaze again it was devoid of all emotion.

Several Goblin guards held Red back from approaching the bench. Red stomped her feet. Her body shook, clearly vibrating with anger. She stared at each Council member one by one. "An Ashbrook Dryad has been a protector of this forest since it was founded." She faced the TreeAnts. "Tell 'em Abe."

Abraham scowled at the shortening of his name. "She speaks the truth. It is tradition."

"So, why don't you tell Council this is nuts?"

Abraham rustled his leaves. "The TreeAnts do not take sides."

"Fuck sides," Red said. "It's your obligation as the oldest among us to guide these imbeciles." She gestured to Council.

Ellie whispered to Red. "Ease up. I don't think you're helping."

The Council members were clearly getting upset. All of them straightened their backs and glared at her. They did not take kindly to criticism.

The Sprite leader called order. "That's enough. The Ashbrook sister's help is no longer required."

"Excuse me?" Red looked ready to blow a blood vessel. "Are you dismissing us?"

His wings flapped nervously. "Uh." He looked around at the other Council members. "Yes?"

"Have you lost your ever-fucking mind?" Red screeched.

Ellie tried to hush Red.

"I won't be silenced." Red's voice boomed in the clearing. "This is fucking insane." She looked at Mae who had paled. "Sorry, Mae. I know how much you like Faustino, but he's not a protector. He's a fucked up wannabe." Red huffed. "You pretend all you want. Believe all the lies. But mark my words, you will regret this decision. You'll be begging the Ashbrook sisters to come save your ass. We won't forget this moment." She shook off the hold of the Goblin guards and signaled for her sisters. "Come on. We're leaving."

Willow and Mae both bowed to Council and the TreeAnts before leaving. Ellie shoved her homeless initiative scrolls into Faustino's chest, and Red flicked off everyone in the vicinity.

Bella's smug smile was the last thing Willow noticed before she departed the sacred circle.

Willow convinced her sisters to go to Bray's since his cabin was empty.

"He should have locked it up," was Willow's excuse for raiding his liquor cabinet.

"Exactly." Ellie grinned.

Red opened up the third bottle of scotch. She had mentioned several times how much she wanted to beat up Council. "Come on. Most of them are old. It'll be a piece of cake."

There was a loud pounding on the door. Mae went to the window.

"You won't believe who it is."

Willow rushed to the front door. "Bray! He's back." She swung the door wide and got hit with a whiff of Eau de Moonwine. She scrunched up her nose from the smell. It was Faustino with a laurel wreath hanging off one horn. From his off-balance gait as he stumbled through the doorway, he had been hitting it hard at his coronation celebration.

He held up his hands when Red rushed him with a haymaker. He caught her fist before it made contact, surprising all the sisters. Even drunk off his ass, his reflexes were fast.

"Look, I don't want any trouble. I swear I didn't ask for it. My mom nominated me. You know Mother Bacchus once she gets an idea in her head. There's no stopping her."

Willow supposed he was right. Donna Bacchus always had it in for her. She remembered back to her coronation when Council had debated Faustino as Guardian the first time. He had gotten two of the nine votes even back then. Had his mother just been biding her time, waiting all these years for her to screw up? It certainly looked that way.

"Council said they were looking for someone who was popular with the masses." He gave them his patented lop-sided grin, the one that made females swoon. "Most of the forest loves me."

Willow snorted, "Maybe the female half."

His grin faltered realizing his charm was lost on the Ashbrook sisters. Even Mae glared at him. He cleared his throat. "Well, in any case, I'm sorry you were the scapegoat for the fire. Most realize it wasn't your fault. Even if you were here, how could you have known where it started and been able to stop it?"

Willow looked at her sisters. They understood the connection Dryads felt with the trees, and the Guardian ties were stronger still. Even miles away from the fire, she had felt something was off. Now that she thought about it, Willow was surprised she hadn't felt more. Passing out from the pain when her tree was damaged delayed her response time further. Faustino obviously didn't sense the forest the way she did. In fact, he seemed to understand very little about what the Guardian role entailed. But she guessed that's exactly what Council wanted, a figurehead. They didn't want to give up power. They would run things in the background like they always did. It wasn't much different from how things had been with her. Council had it covered. They could delegate her duties to someone else. The forest was no longer her problem. An enormous weight lifted off her shoulders. She took a deep breath and plopped back down in a kitchen chair. "You know what? I don't give a fuck."

Red high-fived her sister. "Damn straight."

Ellie poured another round.

Mae patted Faustino's shoulder. "Well, thanks for letting us know."

"I talked to Council after you left." Faustino said. "Convinced them the Ashbrook sisters could stay in the forest as long as you don't make trouble."

Willow laughed. "That was a possibility? How absurd! Kick us out? We've lived here our whole lives. The Ashbrooks have been here from the beginning."

"Well, I took it that way." Red said through gritted teeth, "That's why I was so mad."

Ellie rubbed Red's back in circles. "Calm your temper, Red. They just wanted us to leave the meeting. Everyone could tell you were itching for a fight."

Mae nodded. "That's the last thing Council wants. No confrontations. Just peace. They do like to keep up appearances." Her gaze fell on Faustino.

Willow studied him for a few moments. He loved to entertain and have fun, but he lacked real direction. Council didn't want someone political who had an agenda. They wanted someone who wouldn't ask questions, a pretty face to distract from the fire. Faustino was perfect. He couldn't care less what happened in the forest as long as he had a good time.

"You can go now." Mae held the door open for him.

Faustino frowned. He stared at Mae like he had never seen her before.

She tapped her foot. "Thank you." Her words were clipped.

"No prob—," Faustino said.

He was cut off by the door slamming in his face.

"Damn, Mae." Red snickered.

Willow watched in awe as Mae took her seat. Her infatuation with Faustino hadn't clouded her view of the truth. She had taken her sisters for granted. Despite feeling deserted by Council and the citizens of the forest, her sisters were still loyal. The words from Susan from several weeks ago floated back to her. Family was everything. She held up her shot and clinked glasses with her sisters. They all downed their scotch and grinned at one another. Despite a hell of a day, Willow felt pretty damn lucky.

Chapter 30

WILLOW WOKE UP the next morning hungover but filled with zero pressure. It was so unusual for her and such a welcome relief. She didn't have to do the various tasks she normally did; checking different parts of the forest to make sure they were safe and protected. It was someone else's job. Council had voted her out. It still stung, but she had other things to do. She would devote her entire focus on Bray. Finding him and bringing him back was now her mission. Her biggest problem was she had no clue how to get to San Francisco or where to look once she got there. She needed help. Willow woke Red up by pounding on her tree. Her sister was a very heavy sleeper. She peeked her face from the bark blinking.

"Wud up?" Red's voice came out gravelly. Her eyes blinked open. "Is there another fire?"

"Nope, I just need your help."

Red looked up at the sky. It was barely daylight. She groaned. "It's fucking early." She put a toe out of the tree and wiggled it, then another toe. Very slowly she emerged. Her hair looked like a ratty bird's nest. It was usually wild in the mornings, but this was ridiculous.

Willow giggled. "You have bark head."

Red blinked. It took her a few moments before the insult registered. She gave her the finger.

"Do you know where Ellie is?" Willow asked.

Red yawned. "She's probably out picking flowers or playing with bunnies. You know Ellie."

"What about Mae?"

"Last night she mentioned going to see Abe early this morning. Something about meeting up with us later. Why wake me at the ass crack of dawn?"

"Bray is out there in San Francisco with that clingy little human, Gail. Every minute I waste here she could be sinking her claws into him."

"I don't think I've ever seen you jealous." Red laughed. "Lucian never got you riled."

Willow shrugged. "I have no idea why. I mean Lucian does have that yummy bod, and he's loads of fun to be around. But we grew up together. I guess in the back of my head he always felt more like a cousin than a lover. Does that make sense?"

"Yeah, I get it. Faustino's youngest brother, Olie, is close to my age. As much as we hang out together, I could never see him like that. He's asked me to go troll hunting with him." Red laughed, "I think it was his idea of courting me." She snorted. "Like I would fight alongside a Bacchus brother. He couldn't handle a beaver battle."

"You have no idea how true that is," Willow laughed, "Olie's gay."

"Fuck off."

Willow shook her head. "I swear. He wasn't trying to hit on you. Olie trains with the Goblin army."

"Huh. I had no idea. Well, that puts a whole new spin on things. He might actually be cool."

Willow knew what she meant, most of the Bacchus brothers were lovers not fighters. It was something Faustino repeated numerous times. Apparently, Olie was the exception in a lot of ways.

Willow's gaze kept going back to her sister's crazy hair. "So, how about you meet me at the cabin once you're ready?"

Red chuckled, "My hair must look really bad this morning the way you keep staring at it. I'll manage this," she rubbed her hair, making the curly rat nest even worse and getting a big grin from Willow, "and I'll meet up with you in a little while."

Later that afternoon at the cabin, Willow showed Red the drawer where Bray kept his paperwork. They piled the papers on the kitchen table pulling out things that looked important. Mae and Ellie joined them later that evening.

Red found a memo on company letterhead that identified Bray's work address and a few bills forwarded to the P.O. box from an address they assumed was his condo. This confirmed what Red had already researched on the computer. Willow was impressed by how much intel her sister could gather, and so quickly. But what astonished Willow the most was Red's incredible knowledge of human technology.

"How did you learn all of this?"

She shrugged. "When you hang around humans and 'borrow' their equipment," she used air quotes, "you pick up a few things."

"So, by borrow, you mean steal, right?" Ellie asked.

Red grinned.

"Let's see," Mae demanded.

Red pointed to the duffel on the floor. Mae passed her the bag.

"Where is the borrow-ee?" Willow asked.

She stared up at the ceiling, "Uh, Camp Navajo."

Willow groaned, "You stole from a military base."

Red shook her head, "Again sister, *borrowed*, and it's the only laptop we've got that has satellite internet. This beauty," she pulled out the chunky hunk of metal, "is how we'll map your route."

As much as Willow wanted to tell her sister to take it back, she needed all the help she could get. "Alright, as long as you return it after my trip."

Red gave her a grin. "Uh-huh. Sure, sis."

Mae rolled her eyes.

On the computer, Red marked the starting point A where they were now and point B where Bray's condo was. Willow was deeply disappointed when she saw the distance. It was over ten days of walking. Red kept pointing to the little airplane icon, but Willow shook her head. She didn't have an I.D. or money to buy a ticket, plus she was scared to fly and told her sisters as much.

"There are ways around such things, you just need the means."

"I'm afraid to ask," Willow said.

"Do we think Abraham might have contacts in other forests along the route?"

Mae cleared her throat. "Actually, I've met most of the Guardians on this route.

"How?" Willow sputtered.

Mae sighed. "I guess it's time I finally tell you. I've been commuting back and forth between forests for years now."

"What?" Red asked.

Ellie smiled. "That sounds fun."

"When did this start?"

"The first time was an accident. I was thirteen. Luckily, I ran into the Guardian of the Roosevelt National Forest. She helped me get back home. But it was scary."

Willow frowned, "Why didn't you tell me?"

"The Guardian took me to Abraham. He said it made sense the gift developed at such an early age. He said I listened to the trees more than all my sisters combined. Since I was able to commune better, it allowed me to visualize the links between trees. Abraham advised me to keep the secret." Mae shrugged and turned to Willow, "He told me you were feeling inadequate as Guardian, and it might make you more insecure." She turned to Red, "He said you were too competitive and it may stir up problems if you tried to do the same." She turned to Ellie, "And you, he said you couldn't keep a secret."

Ellie blew out a breath. "Well, he obviously doesn't know me as well as he thinks. I can definitely keep a secret. In fact, I've been keeping a big one." She crossed her arms. "While Mae has contacts in several forests, so do I."

"You can travel between forests as well?" Red asked.

"Well, no. I mean yes."

"Which is it?"

"Yes, I can get to other forests, but I don't go via tree. I travel by truck."

"Ellie's been hitchin'. Nice." Red went to high-five her little sis.

She high-fived back. "Not exactly. You know I'm friends with most of the Shifters? But I'm really close with the local Werewolf pack." She gave a shy grin, "And I'm friends with several other packs in the west. They have socials once a month." She shrugged, "And, well, they owe me favors."

"How'd you get these favors?" Red wiggled her eyebrows.

She ignored her sister. "Anyhow, if you want, I can get you rides part of the way. Most pack members have trucks. And several of them transport supplies. I've memorized most of the routes."

Willow raised her eyebrows. There was so much she didn't know about her sisters.

Mae supplied the list of contacts she had assembled over the years in addition to strategic details regarding portals and who to trust and not trust to help. When there were large gaps between forests with no portal connection, Ellie suggested the Werewolf transportation service. Red mapped the entire route and listed bus and train schedules once she got to San Francisco and handed her a credit card to use for Muni and BART tickets to get her around town. The friend she borrowed it from asked her to be gentle with it. Red's advice was to do as much monetary damage as possible. With the plan in place, she was ready to go. Willow just needed to pack a few clothes and shoes, so she didn't look out of place when she got to the big city. Red handed her a real human backpack, a camouflage one with pockets galore. It was filled with gadgets and vegetarian MREs for her trip. Red explained MREs were packets of food. Some of the snacks were edible if Willow was desperate, but she didn't really recommend them. The pack was a gift from one of her military friends. Willow was so excited. Just a few months ago, she would have only dreamed of such an adventure. And here all she had to do was to destroy her career and lose the love of her life.

Chpater 31

Wɪᴛʜ ᴛʜᴇ ᴘᴀᴄᴋ strapped to her back, Willow waited along US 180 for the Werewolf transport under the designated deer crossing sign. Someone had stamped a wolf symbol on the back bottom corner. It would have been a seven-hour hike from Coconino to Kaibab, but Ellie convinced Willow it was a more efficient use of time to get a ride. And since Kaibab didn't have a portal, she would have to travel several more hours until she got to the Grand Canyon National Park where they did have one. Luck would have it that the local Werewolf clan was doing a supply run to the Grand Canyon portal the day she planned to leave. Ellie had called in a favor.

Willow giggled when the truck pulled up. It was an old ten-foot Uhaul. The au in the name was scratched out and ow was put in its place. *Uhowl.* How fitting. She climbed into the passenger seat.

"You Willow?"

She looked at the long stretch of road. "You see anyone else out here trying to hitch?"

He grinned and held out his fist. "Name's Hunter. Good to finally meet one of Ellie's sisters. She's a real sweetie."

Willow bumped his fist in greeting. Ellie had mentioned a few habits she might find odd. Fist bumping was one of them. Willow had to practice several times before Ellie told her she was doing it right. Apparently, there was a certain amount of fist thrust to bump impact that was appropriate. Anything harder would indicate aggression. Anything softer would indicate weakness.

He pulled back onto the road carefully checking for traffic, which there was zero at this time of morning. She watched him more than the road trying to figure out if this was the Werewolf Ellie was hung up on. She knew once a month she went away with friends to parts unknown.

"

His hair was dark brown with golden highlights. It was shoulder length with a little wave to it. The beard shadow gave him a rugged look, and he had a dimple when he smiled. He was pretty cute for a Werewolf. Was this the one that made Ellie dance like she was floating on air whenever she came back from those monthly retreats?

"Hope you don't mind, but I have to pick up a souvenir at Bedrock City for my niece. She's got this thing for Bam-Bam."

Willow blinked at him. "I may have understood half of what you just said."

Hunter tilted his head, "You don't get out much do you?"

She shrugged. "Not at all."

"Hot damn. A Flintstone newbie. We'll do the tour."

Hunter was an energetic tour guide explaining all the details of the architectural wonder inspired by the 1960s cartoon. He showed her the homes and buildings of the Bedrock citizens describing in detail the characters and a few stories that made her laugh. Hunter took her picture in some of the cars and she took a picture of him in front of the dinosaur. They stopped for breakfast at Fred's diner and at the gift shop for his niece. Before he helped her back into the truck, he took a long whiff of her hair.

"Why'd you do that?"

He shrugged. "Just checking."

Willow frowned. Ellie had mentioned this other odd Werewolf behavior. She said if one of them sniffed her hair or neck, to just roll with it and not ask any questions. It was totally normal. They did it to her all the time.

It didn't take him long to drive to the Grand Canyon National Park and drop her off at the portal. Hunter picked up a few packages from the portal technician and waved goodbye. "Tell Ellie I'll see her next month. It was really nice meeting you, Willow."

"Same to you, Hunter. Take care." She waved back.

Willow turned to the portal technician. The troll had yellow wrinkly skin and black greasy hair. His beady black eyes squinted at her. He had seemed pleasant enough with Hunter, but the troll turned icy as soon as he left. Willow took a deep breath and immediately regretted it. The troll not only looked unappealing, he smelled foul. She coughed and wheezed before she could get out, "I'd like passage to Mohave National Preserve, if you please."

The troll frowned. More wrinkles covered his already crinkled face, turning him uglier than she thought possible.

"Do you have the toll?"

She smiled sweetly and handed him a gold coin.

He took the coin, put it in a pouch, and clicked a few buttons on a tree stump she hadn't noticed. Willow tilted her head for a better view. The troll growled over his shoulder, "No peeking."

Willow flinched, startled by the reprimand, "Sorry. I didn't mean to pry."

"Is this your first time in a portal?"

She nodded. "Yes. How did you know?"

The troll shook his head. "Why me?" He dug around the tree stump and moved a couple of rocks. He dusted off a scroll and began reciting a list of rules. Willow tried to memorize everything he said, but the list was long and he read too quickly. She focused on one section and missed the rest of what was said. Based on his attitude, Willow was afraid to ask him to repeat it.

"Do you agree to all the terms and conditions?"

"Uh, what if I say no?"

He shrugged, "Then no portal ride, and no refunds."

She smiled. "Then yes. I agree."

He pushed one last button on the stump.

"Mohave National Preserve awaits." He gestured to the portal.

A swirl of white light appeared between two pines.

Willow tentatively put her foot into the light and watched it disappear. She looked back at the troll. "Am I doing this right?"

He shook his head and walked up behind her. The troll bared his teeth in what she assumed was a grin and gave her a hard shove.

Willow landed face-first in gravel. She pushed to her feet and dusted herself off.

"Well, that was uncalled for."

There was no portal operator on this side. She seemed to have landed in a lifeless wasteland. Although Willow knew that wasn't true. There were sections of the Coconino Forest that had the same desert landscape. It was actually teeming with life, but she didn't particularly care for the environment or the creatures. They tended to be moody. She guessed the attitude stemmed from the excessive heat and drought. Gaia knew she would be miserable in that sort of environment. She enjoyed her spot by the lake, the shade from the large pines and the feel of the brisk winds further to the north in her forest. Willow shook her head. It wasn't her forest anymore. She sighed and spun in a circle. Ah, the cliffs with the holes Mae had mentioned. This was where she was to meet her contact. Mae had set up a meet and greet with the Guardian. Willow was to travel through Rings Trail, and somewhere along the path she would meet up with Bri, a Bighorn Sheep Shifter. As she walked along the path, Willow thought of how Mae had traveled to another forest at thirteen. And the fact she had been traveling between forests for the past six years. She had already amassed a network of contacts. Abraham had been right. She would have felt insecure if Mae had told her at that age what she had accomplished. Even at her age now, Willow felt like she was missing out on so much. Mae had assured Willow that she would help teach her the connection as well, but she had to spend time communing with the trees. Of course, Mae had been meditating with trees since she was two years old. Willow didn't think she possessed the same patience as her sister. But she had to admit, it would have been extremely useful now to be able to transport herself directly to a tree close to San Francisco.

Half an hour into her hike, Willow noticed she was no longer alone. Shadows moved above her on the cliffs.

"Bri, is that you?"

Silence. She let out a series of bleats introducing herself as sister to Mae, friend to Mohave. Willow heard hooves clack across the cliffs, but she couldn't determine the direction. The echoes made it sound like it came from everywhere at once. She continued to walk further down the trail. A Bighorn sheep came into view. It watched her from a ledge. He was a large male with huge horns. She bleated another greeting. No response. He continued to stare. Willow shrugged and walked past him. So much for the friendly welcome. The clickety-clack of his hooves continued to follow her. Willow finally bleated, "It's ok. I mean no harm. I seek your Guardian. I am one as well."

He shook his head. Could he tell that last part was a lie? Around the next bend of the trail, she found a woman sunning herself on a flat stone table. She had golden skin and wore a tiny sheepskin bikini. She was all curves, and the scant fabric left little to the imagination. Short horns sprouted from her curly auburn hair. The woman propped herself up on her elbows. She gave Willow a huge grin.

"I see you've met Big D."

Willow looked over her shoulder. The Bighorn was still watching her cautiously.

"He seems quite protective. Is he your mate?"

The woman gave a quavering bleat. It sounded like a laugh. She hadn't spent much time with the Bighorns in her forest. It was a realization that left her feeling guilty. She had been a Guardian for sixteen years, and she hadn't gotten to know such a large population of her forest.

The Bighorn male stomped his feet in agitation.

"Oh, Big D. I didn't mean anything by that. You know matehood is not in the cards."

The male bowed his head and backed away. He held her gaze for a moment, then turned and climbed the cliffside with strong agile leaps. Willow admired the graceful movement of the large Bighorn as it made its way further up the cliff and disappeared into the craggy rock.

The woman sighed. "Big D is so sensitive." She climbed to her feet. "Greetings, Willow Ashbrook, Guardian of Coconino, sister of Mae, friend of Mohave."

Willow bowed her head. "Greetings to you, Bri Bighorn, Guardian of Mohave and friend to my sister Mae." She cleared her throat. "I would like to return the favor and grant you status as friend of Coconino, but I uh," Willow shuffled her feet, "I sort of got kicked out of office."

Bri's puzzled look turned to a smile, "Ah, you joke like your sister Red."

Willow shook her head. "It's no joke. They've replaced me with a Satyr named Faustino."

Bri's mouth pinched and her brows furrowed in thought. "I'm sorry. I don't understand. Who kicked you out?"

"Council of course."

She shook her head. "Nope. Still don't get it."

"Listen, it's embarrassing. I was out of the forest spending time with my eternal soulmate. There was a fire. I wasn't there to protect my people. Council voted me out. It's done."

Bri's eyes bulged. "Wow. Coconino is strange. That's not how we do things here. Council can give suggestions and help with disputes when I'm not available, but the Guardian rule is absolute. Being voted out of office just isn't an option." She snorted, "Frankly, I find the idea absurd. It sounds like you need a new Council. Vote. Them. Out. Not the other way around. How did Coconino's politics get so twisted?" She gestured for Willow to follow her down the path.

Willow was stunned by the revelation. She had no idea her forest was so different from others. Of course, never having been in another forest, she had nothing to compare it to. Yet another flaw in her leadership. She had neglected communing with the trees, and avoided sections of her realm she found unpleasant. Willow realized the only thing she had been good at was believing Council had everyone's best interests in mind, while she remained oblivious. Luckily, she didn't have to remain clueless any longer. Her eyes had been forced open by the circumstances.

Bri must have felt the silence had gone on too long. "So, tell me about your eternal. Mae mentioned him in the message she sent."

Willow grinned, "He's wonderful. Bray makes me feel alive. It's unlike anything I've ever felt. We have this connection," she sighed, "Only he left for California before we could work things out. He's seen things, and he's having a tough time working it all out."

Bri frowned, "Mae mentioned he's human, right?"

She nodded.

"And he got away with knowledge of the magical world?" Her eyebrows rose, "You let him escape without dosing him with something to make him forget?"

Willow sighed, "I didn't know he was going to leave. I was cleaning up damage from the fire. He left abruptly. I thought he just needed time."

Bri scratched her chin, "But you don't think he's a security risk?"

She shook her head. "He won't say anything. People would think he's nuts. I just need to explain everything. If we can come to some kind of understanding, I think we can work through our differences."

Bri's head dropped and she shook her head, "Geez. I thought I had issues. Finding a mate that is so different. That'd be hell on earth."

Willow desperately wanted to change the subject. She didn't want doubts. She needed hope that Bray would reconcile once she found him, otherwise this whole trip would be a waste.

"What sort of issues do you have?"

"Well, for one thing, there's Big D."

"Go on."

"He's the largest male, well, at least in sheep form." She grinned, "In human form, he is sexy as sin and hung like you wouldn't believe, but he's short." She sighed, "Not that I mind. But he's got a complex about it, which causes a whole bunch of issues. He's not my eternal soulmate, or at least I don't think he is. He doesn't stay in human form long enough for me to know. And he refuses to mate any other female but me. He's possessive, fearful of outsiders, and aggressive to any male who gets close."

"I know how that goes. He sounds a little like my ex, Lucian. He's this big Fire Demon I dated years ago. It never evolved beyond friendship, but even with that I still planned to take him as my mate until Council refused."

Bri shook her head, "I don't understand how you'd tolerate that."

Willow shrugged, "I came into office when I was young. My mother hadn't taken the Guardian job very seriously. She was a free-loving flirt who loved to party. Politics were handled by Council. She was far too busy having fun."

"Well, I also came into office young. I was crowned at thirteen, but my father taught me to be fierce and decisive and to lead with power. In our culture, only the strongest survive. Females don't typically hold office in Mohave, but I was an only child, and my father didn't raise a quitter. Any Council member who didn't share my vision of the future was removed by force." She abruptly stopped walking and her eyes flashed with anger. Willow turned to her, but Bri was focused on the rock as if staring into a scene from the past, reliving some sort of visceral memory of that time. Willow felt a pulse of power like a hot stifling wind flow from Bri. It was almost too much emotion. She tried to take a deep breath but couldn't. Willow pushed her own cool, calming energy. Bri inhaled a deep breath and suddenly the heat was gone, as if she sucked all the hot anger back into herself.

"Sorry about that. I don't usually show so much emotion, especially to someone I've just met. Anyhow, through the years I've assembled my own Council of strong warrior females that share my vision."

Willow had to admit she was impressed with Bri's warrior spirit and her passion for her role. But she did have some major anger issues.

They started walking the path again at a slow leisurely pace. "So, with Big D always lurking in the shadows, does that cramp your love life?"

Bri snorted, "What love life?"

Willow frowned. "Do you celebrate Festivus?"

She shook her head, "There are no fun-lovin' Satyrs or Centaurs out in Mohave. We don't have those decadent celebrations that Coconino puts on. Mae has filled me in on some of the details." Bri grinned, "It's wicked what you all do out there."

Willow smiled. "Maybe a little. But we don't have to fight to survive like you do here. Still, you need to have some fun between all the fighting. Doesn't life require balance?"

Bri remained silent for several moments as their feet crunched on the gravel pathway. Willow wondered if she had offended her guide.

"You seem grounded, like your sister Mae, but perhaps much wiser in the way of males. I'd like to ask you a question, but we can't do it here. There are too many ears listening." She pointed to the canyons. "It echoes across the lands. Conversations are never private along Rings trail."

Bri bleated a phrase Willow didn't understand. Big D poked his head out from high above and nodded.

"I've asked for privacy." She gestured to a stone wall and put her hand in one of the crevices and felt around. Something clicked, and a panel slid open to reveal a dark cavern path. It took Willow's eyes a few moments to adjust to the dim light. They walked in silence for several minutes. "This leads to a lava tube. It's a sight to behold this time of day. But before we get there, tell me about the Shifters from your forest. How do they, you know, do it?"

Willow was puzzled. "Do you mean sex?"

Bri nodded.

"Well, they do it like everyone else."

"I mean, do they change forms? Are they in animal or human form?" She cleared her throat, "Mae mentioned you were a bit of a voyeur. I figured you might have some experience, um witnessing, you know, a lot."

Willow watched the flicker of uncertainty in the Mohave Guardian's eyes. She wondered if Bri was a virgin like her sister Mae. They looked to be close to the same age. It wouldn't be unheard of and could very well be where her anger was coming from. But she wasn't sure if she should ask such a blunt question.

"I've witnessed Shifters in human form and half animal-half human form going at it hot and heavy. Festivus is by no means tame. And even our minor celebrations tend to bring out the hedonistic side of even our most reserved citizens. Our Satyrs' supply of moonwine can loosen the inhibitions of the most battle-raged warrior."

"What about as straight animals?"

Willow tilted her head, "Why would they do that? Most Shifters in pure animal form would perform sex strictly for reproduction. The act would be perfunctory. The pleasure almost nil."

Bri's face turned red. Perhaps Willow had been too blunt, or there was more to these questions than pure conjecture.

"Do you have Nymphs out here?"

Bri was lost in thought. "Nymphs, here?" She scoffed. "Why would they want to come out here?"

"You might try to spice things up." Willow shrugged. "Throw a party. Perhaps we could set up an ambassador program, help shake things up. I believe the type of male you seek may show up to something like that."

"Hmm. I will think further on this. Perhaps banning parties was not the wisest decision. Thank you for your advice."

Bri rotated a jagged rock on the wall and a panel next to it slid open. It revealed another path, but this section was brightly lit. Willow had to shield her eyes as her vision adjusted. It was a short cave with holes in the ceiling. She took a deep breath not realizing how damp and musty the cave had been until now. The sunlight was warm and welcoming. She watched as Bri walked directly under one of the holes into a stream of light. It was glorious. Bri's body glowed. To Willow, she looked like an angel that had been touched by the gods. Willow stepped beneath another hole and soaked up the sunshine. They grinned at each other. Magic swirled around them and power pulsed from the cave walls.

They spent the afternoon together chatting about their citizens and all the antics of the lower creatures while they walked across the preserve. She was introduced to several Council members who were careful to bow to Bri and ask if they could do her a service. The lower creatures would also stop by and offer help in any way they could. Bri held the exact same position that Willow had for half as long, but she had never been given this much respect. Not even close. Willow wondered what would have happened if she had taken a more aggressive stance early on. Would they have treated her with respect? Or would she have been removed from office that much sooner?

When they finally stopped at the edge of Mohave, Willow gave her a hug. "I'm so glad I met you and hope to see you again."

Bri grinned. "Say hi to Mae for me. I expect a visit from her soon. She enjoys training with the Bighorn."

Willow shook her head. The further she traveled, the more she realized how little she knew about her sisters.

Chapter 32

SHE STOOD WAITING next to another sign with a wolf stamp along Highway 15. The sun was just starting to set. Willow wondered if it would be dark before the transport showed up. A few minutes later, a Uhowl truck pulled off onto the shoulder. This truck was larger than the last. She shuffled along the rocks and debris to the passenger door and stared through the open window. The driver looked enormous behind the wheel with wide shoulders and thick bulging biceps. He made no move to open the door. She sighed.

"You on your way to Sequoia?"

"Yeah." The man gave her a thorough inspection while he chewed his gum.

She shifted her stance under the scrutiny. "Mind if I hitch a ride?"

He shrugged and looked straight ahead.

Was he looking for traffic or watching for a threat? She glanced at the road ahead. A few cars had passed, but no one seemed to be watching their interaction. Vivid streaks of orange and yellow blazed across the desert sky. Willow opened the door and hoisted herself into the cab. The Werewolf leaned his long torso over and buckled her seatbelt. He was even larger and more intimidating up close, especially all stretched out in her personal space. She pressed back into the seat, but his body was just there, big and imposing. Maybe she should have gotten references or at least descriptions before agreeing to this transport service. He didn't make any threatening moves, just stayed way too close and gave a long inhale at her neck.

"Can I help you?" She asked.

"Nope. No good."

"Excuse me?"

"You smell like Ellie, pine and butterscotch, but you're not her."

"You mean my sister?"

"No."

Willow was confused by this conversation. He didn't offer any more explanations, just checked his mirrors. "Are we waiting on someone?"

"Nope."

She sighed and stared straight ahead with her arms crossed. Ellie said the Werewolf transport was a little odd and not to ask too many questions. And they were driving her for free after all. They sat in silence for a few minutes watching the light fade from the sky. A scrape of metal from the back had Willow turn in her seat with wide eyes. She hadn't heard anyone pull up behind them. The driver just sat there checking the road ahead. The only sound in the truck was the snapping of his gum as he chewed. There was a clunk and a rattle like the door had opened and a ramp had slid out. The truck shook from side to side. Someone was either loading or unloading something in the back. Another rattle and clunk, then two knocks, pause, and another two knocks. The driver grinned. He put out a fist to Willow. "Name's Dylan. What should I call you, little bit?"

She rolled her eyes at the nickname and bumped his fist. "Willow."

"Your first ride was with Hunter, right?"

She nodded, "Yes."

"Did Hunter make you take the oath?"

"Uh, oath?"

Dylan sighed, "That figures. He's young and only does the level one run. In the glove box, there's paper and pin." He flipped on the lights to the truck.

Willow opened the compartment. There was a single sheet of paper. The document said she would not reveal anything that happened during transit, otherwise, it would violate code 23, whatever that meant.

"I know I'm not supposed to ask questions, but if you want me to sign this, what happens if code 23 is broken?"

"Death," Dylan said deadpan.

Willow gave a nervous laugh, "No, really?"

He stared at her. She gulped. The silence stretched until she couldn't take it anymore. "Don't you think death as punishment is a little harsh if someone accidentally mentions something minor?"

Dylan groaned. "This is exactly why civilians aren't allowed during transport. You're all a pain in the ass." He grabbed a black velvet pouch from the glove box. "Here's the pin. It's simple. Read the rules. Sign in blood. Follow the rules. This is a level three run. It's higher risk. No civilians allowed normally, but Ellie put in a request. She has a place of honor in our pack, and she's put up with a helluva lot."

Willow grinned, "You really like Ellie?"

Dylan smiled wide. "What's not to like? She's loving and kind, and she helps everyone in need. Any male would be lucky to have her," he muttered, "except maybe the one she's stuck with."

"Does he not treat her well?'

He shook his head. "I shouldn't have said anything. Let them work it out. It's best not to get involved."

Willow shook her head, "But I'm her older sister. If he's no good for her, I need to know."

He shrugged, "I doubt she can talk about it. We have a lot of oaths. Anything deemed a security risk can't be shared."

Dylan sighed. "Listen up, I agreed to this as a favor to Ellie. We all owe her, and we pay our debts when they're called in. But if you can't agree to keep silent about this trip, then you're a security risk plain and simple. Do you understand?"

Willow nodded. "Ok. I won't say a thing. You have my word." She pulled the long silver pin out of the velvet pouch. The Werewolves had old customs. Most modern Shifters had verbal oaths and treaties that were signed in pen if they were more complex or multi-generational. Very little was signed in blood anymore. She took the silver needle, pricked her finger, and signed her name at the bottom. Willow handed him the document.

"Nope, that copy is for you to keep if you need the transport service again. See the address at the bottom." She noticed that the text had blurred except for her signature and an address with a squirrel code. "You keep the document. We keep the pin. Place it back in the pouch."

"What will you do with my blood?"

He shrugged his shoulders. "It'll be stored. Kept safe. Any transport driver will verify you by your scent. It's one more layer of security to know that we're picking up the correct passenger."

Willow didn't like the idea of a whole clan of werewolves having access to her blood. She wasn't sure how much she could trust them. Blood could be used in dark magic. Not only had she willingly given it, but her youngest sister had done the same. "How do you know my sister Ellie?"

Dylan shook his head, "I won't discuss clan business. Just know that she is very well-known and highly respected among several Werewolf packs. Enough questions." He pulled onto the road glancing everywhere at once.

The four-hour drive was grueling. Dylan didn't say much. The silence ticked by as they made several more stops along the way. He would pull off the freeway and turn off the lights with no explanation. She bit her tongue to keep from asking questions. At each stop, Dylan's body thrummed with tension as he checked the mirrors and their surroundings. After each set of knocks, when whatever had been added or removed from the truck, he seemed to relax a little more. After the last stop in Kernville, he cracked his neck and let out a long sigh. He pushed a button on the dash and "Body Like a Back Road" blasted from the speakers. Dylan grinned and he continued driving on Sierra Way into the forest. It made her breathe a sigh of relief to be back among the trees. They both sang. She had a terrible singing voice, but what she lacked in talent she made up for with enthusiasm. She belted it out like she didn't care.

"You're alright." He nudged her shoulder and Willow bounced against the door. He didn't seem to know his own strength. She was reminded of her sister Red.

They followed the road for another fifteen miles singing tunes from his CD. The scents and sights of the forest were amazing. Even though it was still five days from the full moon, there was enough light to see the Kern river. Bits of it could be seen from the road as it peeked and then hid like a mischievous child. Willow was anxious to get out and stretch her legs. This forest made her want to run. The trees were enormous, dwarfing her pines back home. Dylan stopped at a sign called Road's End.

"That sounds ominous."

He shrugged. "It's just a name, and the road still continues for a little bit, but this is where I leave you. Ellie said you would meet up with someone else here." He checked his pockets. "Hmm. I may have forgotten the slip of paper. Oh well. Just follow the river north. When you get to a road that crosses the river, head right. That's Sherman Pass. It will take you to Sherman Peak. That's where you're headed, right?"

"Yes. Thanks again for driving me." She climbed out of the passenger door.

"Say hi to Ellie for me." He waved. "Oh, and ask her to wear something red at next month's shindig. It's Jordan's favorite color."

So that was the name of her wolf? She really wanted to ask more about Jordan and exactly what they did every month, but Ellie had made her promise not to pry. Willow nodded. "Sure thing. Will do, Dylan."

He turned the truck around and headed south where they had just come from. Willow followed the river for a few miles and was tempted to wash up after the dusty walk through Mohave. The truck drive hadn't been much better. Dylan had kept the windows down. Not that she minded the fresh air, but since they had traveled through the desert, she was coated in dust and grime. She yawned. Maybe she was more tired from the trip than she realized and decided to bed down for the evening. She found a comfortable pine and drifted off to sleep.

Willow woke the next morning anxious to continue her journey. Not far from the tree she slept in, the river opened wide. The water looked calm and deep enough for a quick bath. Her body was still coated in dust. She picked up a lock of hair and scrunched her nose at the smell of gas fumes. It was a wonder she could have slept with the smell. Willow undressed and put her pack in a rock cubby pulling out her natural shampoo. She couldn't call power like she could in her own forest, but she did have enough power to camouflage it. Willow didn't want to risk anything inside getting damaged. She still had a long way to go.

While washing her hair, she heard a loud neighing sound from the shore. She plunged her head underwater and watched from under the surface. She saw the flank of a large golden horse with a long white tail in the undergrowth. She surfaced. It was just a wild horse coming to drink from the river. Willow ignored the animal and finished her bathing. She shook out her hair as she exited the water and went in search of her pack. She bent to grab it.

A throat cleared behind her.

"Gods almighty. Are you Willow?"

She looked over her shoulder. The golden horse was now attached to a very attractive male torso. This must be her contact. She had forgotten that the Guardian of Sequoia Forest was a Centaur. She suddenly couldn't remember his name.

Willow's eyebrows rose as she took in every inch of this magnificent male. She hadn't fully appreciated him at first glance. Her jaw dropped as she stared at his very large distended cock. She shivered. He was hung. Well, like a horse. Not that she hadn't seen Centaurs. Her own forest had plenty, but she had never seen one quite so beautiful or quite so well endowed.

"You're on a journey to find your mate?"

She blinked at him, then nodded. Oh yeah. She mentally slapped herself for salivating over this stranger. What was wrong with her?

"Yes. His name is Bray."

"Mae sent me a message her sister would be traveling through, but she told me nothing of your beauty."

Willow blushed a deep green. She loved the compliment but didn't want to encourage flirting even though she may have already done just that by her stare.

"Maybe, I'll just put something on before we begin." She pulled out the first thing she could find. It was a short silk and lace dress in gold. It was something Bray had bought. She thought he had called it by some exotic name. Ah yes, lingerie. She wiggled into the dress. It fell to mid-thigh with a slit on one side that made moving around much easier than some of the everyday dresses he had bought her. Stretchy lace molded over her breasts. Willow remembered the shopkeeper showing her how to adjust the straps. She tightened them until everything was secure. The last thing she wanted was for something to pop out unexpectedly. She gave a quick shake to test it. Everything held. The Centaur groaned and she turned toward him with a frown.

"Being more clothed was preferable, right?"

He shook his head. "Not gonna help."

"While I appreciate your interest, even if it weren't for my eternal," she gestured at his cock, "I'm not sure we'd be anatomically correct for one another."

He gave a hearty laugh, full-bodied and rich. "I don't know about that. But I won't take advantage. Your sister warned me of your mission." He held out his hand for her pack. "My name is Pax. I'm Guardian to Sequoia and you are an honored guest. Once he got the pack settled onto his shoulders, he reached for her and set her gracefully on his back.

"I've never ridden a Centaur before. Where do I grab you?"

He muttered a curse under his breath. "Hold on to your pack. Let me know if you have any trouble."

Pax didn't give her much of a chance to get settled. He took off in a gallop traveling away from the river and up into the mountains. After a few hours, they stopped to rest. She shared a handful of berries packed for the trip. Even though he didn't appear all that excited, he was polite and commented on the unique flavoring, with a sweet, tangy after-bite. She was a connoisseur of berries the way others were with wine. She appreciated the apt description. He was far more enthusiastic when she pulled out the moonwine from Red's borrowed flask. They shared a few swigs before setting off again. Pax was pleasant and had a calm, even demeanor. It was so unlike the Centaurs from back home that tended to rage and fight. Most of them reminded her of her ex-lover Lucian. She figured Fire Demons and Centaurs just shared the same aggressive traits for high tempers, but getting to know Pax, she realized she might have stereotyped his species. She had lumped all Centaurs into a certain category, which was completely unfair. This one had proven to be protective and kind and very open-minded. He gave careful thought to everything he said. Pax shared the story of how the forest had chosen him to be Guardian. His brother had been chosen Guardian of the forest to the North at the same time. Both his uncle and father died together in the same battle leaving both Guardian positions open. They were on their way to meet his brother. Their forests shared boundaries. She asked questions about forest Council and how politics were handled. Willow found that here too the Guardian led. Council did not step in like they did back in Coconino making decisions for the Guardian. He seemed confused when she asked him if Council would choose a mate for him since he seemed to be looking.

As they journeyed, they took a few shortcuts through mountain walls. They were short portal jumps moving them to different parts of the forest. It was similar to how Willow traveled from pine to pine in her forest, but they wouldn't lose supplies or clothing in transit. Gnomes would greet Pax bowing low to the ground. Each would hand him a token, usually a large gemstone that glittered in the sun. He would turn them over this way and that, inspecting and giving them the proper praise before handing them back refusing payment, even if they made a special request. He was a kind and gentle leader and very well respected.

Pax came across two trolls yelling at each other. He laid his hands on their heads and asked them to say kind words to each other for the rest of the day. Surprisingly, they walked off as if in a trance holding hands. Willow wondered what sort of powers Pax possessed to get trolls, creatures notorious for arguing, to stop fighting. She didn't sense him using magic. It wasn't a typical Centaur talent. She assumed it must be tied to the forest. He told her he wanted to show her the Giant Forest even though it would be busy in the middle of the day. Pax assured her the illusion spell would make it look like they were both riding horseback.

"I want you to see the view first. Moro Rock is just up these steps. For obvious reasons, I can't join you, so I'll wait down here."

Willow grinned and made her way up the stone steps. The view of the mountain was amazing, but as she scanned the range of trees, she suddenly felt ill. Instead of green, so many of the trees had turned orange. It wasn't the normal turning of leaves in the fall. This was death. So much of it, she started hyperventilating. She let her spirit float on the winds reaching out to the forest below. Before long, she lumbered down the steps. Pax was waiting patiently at the bottom. He smiled until he saw her tear-tracked face

"What happened? Didn't you like the view?"

She shook her head slowly. "How many?"

"The trees?" Pax neighed. "I'm so stupid. I didn't think. The drought hit us hard a few years back, then the bark beetles came and ravaged more of them. Sierra was hit worse than us."

Willow nodded. "Coconino as well, but nothing like this. And you said Sierra is worse?"

He nodded.

"I'm really sorry." Pax picked her up and pulled her into a tight embrace. It was awkward at first since it left her feet dangling in the air. She briefly wondered what it would look like to humans walking past. He had one hand on her ass and the other on her back, but it wasn't sexual. It was all about comfort. She snuggled into his muscled chest and sighed. He was so warm and soothing. Pax readjusted his arms and cradled her. She curled her body closer. He shared his deep calming energy with her, rubbing his cheek over the top of her head as she cried softly. Pax continued to hold her until her body relaxed and her tears stilled. She took a deep breath.

"I'm ok now."

Pax tilted up her chin and looked her over. He must have been satisfied because he helped her onto his back.

"We're off to the Giant Forest next. Many years ago, a human overheard one of the magical creatures talking about the Forest Giants in the area, and doing what humans do best, they misunderstood, assuming they were talking about the trees."

Willow chuckled.

"Many Forest Giants live in the area, but they usually don't come out until after dark. The forest magic can only do so much."

"I know what you mean. We're lucky in that regard as well. Only a few Giants come down for Festivus, but when they do, it's always a tax on the magical concealment spells."

Exploring the "Giant Forest" with Pax was delightful, especially the very old and humongous General Sherman Tree. The conversation with the tree was hilarious. It turned out to be a TreeAnt who was constantly annoyed by the human's incessant need to call her General Sherman. Her name was Eleanor and had been for over 2,000 years. As was typical with TreeAnts, at the end of their conversation, she merged her hand beneath the bark and they shared energy. The power exchange left her entire body tingling and them both a little tipsy. Before settling in for a long nap, Eleanor wished Willow luck rekindling the connection with her eternal.

Pax smiled when Willow returned from her chat with the TreeAnt. "So, this stop was worthwhile?"

She grinned. "Yes. Thank you. I felt foolish for my overreaction at Moro Rock. But you did well. It was a great idea and the perfect place to visit."

He puffed up his chest clearly enjoying the praise. "It's not far from here, just a couple of jumps through the mountains and we'll meet up with my brother."

He set off at a gallop, and Willow had to hang onto the pack as they bounded across streams and down rocky trails. It was a vigorous ride with the wind blowing her hair. She felt the vitality of the forest as they rode, merging into mountains, galloping through valleys. The clean crisp air filled her lungs and she felt the connection to the forest, not as a Guardian, but as something else she couldn't quite identify. The interaction with the TreeAnt had changed something deep within her.

"We're here." Pax panted. His chest heaved with the exertion from the run. He gestured to the waterfall just ahead. "Grizzly Falls."

She missed the last part of their trip contemplating how she had been altered. Willow watched as the soft white mist swirled through the trees. She inhaled the refreshing, moist air and sighed. He helped her down and handed her the pack. She strapped it to her shoulders. It had been a relief to be free of the heavy weight while they traveled in the mountains, but now the bulky pack seemed reassuring, a reminder of her mission. There were so many wonders to behold and so many things to distract from her goal. If she had traveled like this years ago, Willow would have enjoyed spending more time exploring. Pax told her to get a closer look at the falls while he searched for his brother. Water was always precious but falls held a special rejuvenating magic that echoed their power through the forest. Willow felt it pulse through her limbs as she walked up the rocky path. The sound from the water pounding the rocks was deafening. It drowned out the rest of the world while she beheld the beauty in front of her. She longed to climb into the water and rinse off but didn't risk setting down her pack. Willow got close enough where the water misted over her skin. Even that left her skin stimulated with pinpricks of energy.

She went back to where she left Pax wondering if he found his brother. He had. The two stood side by side in the shadow of the trees, and she blinked slowly. They took a few steps closer and into the sunlight, and it was almost too much to take in at once. Chase was just as devastatingly handsome as his brother. In fact, they were identical twins, something both Pax and Mae had failed to mention. She couldn't seem to look away from their beauty. They both had golden bodies and long, straight white-blonde hair on their heads and tails. They had strong chins with roman noses and hazel eyes. She sighed.

"Brother, her hair is almost the same shade as ours. Are you breeding with her?"

"What?" Willow sputtered.

Pax whispered a few words to his brother.

"No fucking way?" Chase yelled.

Pax shrugged and turned to Willow. "You're in good hands. My brother will ensure your safety through Kings Canyon. Mae is an honored guest and so are you." He bowed and trotted off back toward his forest.

Chase stalked around Willow thoroughly scrutinizing her. She wondered if this was typical of the Centaurs in this region. Willow glanced down at herself. The heavy pack pulled her shoulders back, her chest thrust forward. The mist from the spray of the waterfall made her gold silk gown cling to her breasts and hips. Her nipples were tight little points from the chill. She shivered. Chase wiped a hand over his mouth and stared at her breasts. This brother was quite different. Pax had been reserved and respectful. This one with his wild eyes seemed to be having wicked thoughts. A few months ago, she might have considered taking him up on all those things his eyes were offering. She stared at his stiff cock. Well, maybe not. This one might be even bigger than his brother.

"Your brother let me ride him. Will you offer the same?"

Chase's jaw dropped. He stared hard.

Did she word that incorrectly? Sometimes things didn't translate well in the common language. She hadn't spent enough time with Centaurs in her own forest.

She cleared her throat. "I meant no offense."

He gave a crooked grin, "Just give me a minute. I'm working through the visual of you *riding* my brother."

Willow rolled her eyes. Now she got it.

"I believe I'll let you *ride* me too."

He helped her climb onto his back but didn't offer to take her pack. "Where do I grab you?"

"Fuck me, female. Do you have to keep pushing? I'm not a paragon of virtue like my brother."

Willow frowned. "I don't understand. I'm asking where I hold on so I don't fall off. I'm not used to riding Centaurs."

Chase sighed and muttered a few curses. "Grip with your thighs. If you feel unsteady, wrap your arms around my chest."

He took off at a slow trot. She leaned forward and watched the scenery go by. It was incredibly beautiful countryside, mostly mountains and rivers interspersed with towering sequoias. Just like his brother, he would reach sections of mountain and they would pass through portal jumps further to the north. Chase enjoyed showing her the wonders of his forest just like his brother had. They were both proud of their forests. Although this one spent more time flirting and making outrageous comments along the way. He reminded her more and more of her sister Red.

"I know you have an eternal. I could never compete. But I want to leave you something." His eyes twinkled, "Something special to remember me by." He gave a devilish grin. "Do you trust me?"

"Uh." Willow wondered what that mischievous gleam in his eyes meant.

He glanced back over his shoulder, "Just hang on for the *ride of your life.*"

He grabbed her hips positioning her higher up on his back and his graceful trot turned into a canter, then a full-out gallop over the rough terrain. She hadn't noticed before, but his back between his shoulder blades was ridged just right. Her new position placed her perfectly. She couldn't help but undulate on his back. He gripped her hips rubbing her over that one sweet spot, back and forth as he ran. By the time they reached their destination Willow was out of breath, nerve ends tingling, eyes rolling in the back of her head. She had somehow managed not to come from that thrilling hip-thrusting ride. Chase helped her down from his back. She stood on wobbly legs trying to relearn how to breathe. Her pussy was throbbing, but she hadn't wanted to be disloyal to Bray. Even though using Chase's extraordinary back seemed like such a good idea, as soon as she visualized Bray, it kept her from going over that last delicious edge, keeping her on the verge, just shy of orgasm.

"I'm shocked." He shook his head, "The Nymphs from my forest usually bathe my withers in cream." He puffed out his chest with pride. "They say I'm ridged for their pleasure."

Cocky Centaur. Willow took in a big shaky breath. "It was actually quite hard."

"No. This is hard." Chase pointed to his shaft.

Willow giggled. "It looks like you could club someone with that."

He threw his head back laughing, a full-body shake. "I like your humor."

"Well, it wasn't easy to resist your charms." She waved to his cock and then the ridge on his back."

He raised a brow, "No last hoorah?"

Willow shook her head, "I'm truly taken. Even my body won't let me betray my mate."

"Fair enough." Chase bowed, "It was a pleasure to meet you Willow, Guardian of Coconino."

"It was wonderful to meet you as well, Chase, Guardian of Kings Canyon, but I'm afraid I no longer hold that title. Council kicked me out of office."

He scratched his chin and frowned. "Guardianship is a position for life. Council doesn't wield that kind of power."

"Things are different in Coconino." Willow shrugged, "But it doesn't matter. Right now, I'm focusing on bringing back my mate."

"A worthy mission." He nodded, "I hope you'll think fondly of me and send others my way." Chase gave a cheeky grin, "I do love making new friends."

"I'll just bet you do." Willow chuckled. "Has Mae ever mentioned our sister Red?"

He shook his head. "No. But I've only met Mae a few times. She spends most of her time at the Centaur warrior camp training for battle. She's obsessed with weapons and combat strategies."

Willow couldn't believe it. Mae was training for war and apparently had been for years. While all Ashbrook Dryads had warrior training when they were young, Willow saw no need to provide extended training. Coconino had been at peace for twenty-three years. The last thing she wanted was to waste time focusing on a threat that didn't exist. Still, she was disappointed that Mae hadn't confided in her. Mae apparently wanted more training but had been afraid to ask. Instead, she had gone to strangers. It left Willow feeling hollow inside, like she had failed her sister.

"So, tell me about her."

Willow blinked. What had they been talking about? Oh, yeah. Red.

She gave him a sly grin, "How to describe my sister Red? Hmm. Well, she's got curly red hair, green eyes, about six feet tall, and all kinds of curves. She's got a wicked sense of humor, and I believe her jokes could make even you blush."

He cleared his throat, "I like 'em big and bold." Chase's hooves pawed at the ground, "When can I meet her?"

"Don't worry, when I get back, I'll tell her all about you. She'll be sure to visit soon."

They walked a short distance until they came to a lake.

"This is the south end of Forest Lake. We're inside the borders of John Muir Wilderness, not to be confused with Muir Woods further to the west. This section of the forest doesn't have a Guardian. It's neutral ground and all magical creatures are welcome. The Guardians surrounding the area will all come together in a crisis to protect the lands named after the famous naturalist and writer."

Willow had heard of him. It was rare to find someone widely revered by both magical creatures and humans alike. John was one of very few humans who could see past the magical illusions to their true nature. He promised not to share that knowledge and had vowed to do everything he could to preserve the forests. That made Willow recall Bray's reaction to the magical world. He too could see through the illusions, but would he keep the secrets of the forest? Willow hoped he just needed time away to get his thoughts in order before coming back. But what would happen if she couldn't convince him? What if he chose his precious technology over their mated connection? He might reveal what he saw to other humans, and Gaia help them if that happened.

Chapter 33

Chase pointed to a small cave where she was to meet her next contact, Dee Dee the black bear. She would take her to Mono Hot Springs in Sierra National Forest where she would meet another Guardian who could grant access to the Muir Woods portal. The black bear had two cubs and reminded her of Bailey from back home. They grunted back and forth talking about the differences in their forests as they walked. Dee Dee's cubs were absolutely adorable. They made little cooing sounds as they scampered about trying to pounce on Willow's painted toenails. They kept thinking they were bugs moving among the twigs. She giggled when they licked her toes. Willow continued to scold them, but they kept forgetting. Either that or they just had too much fun pouncing. The mother seemed delighted that the cubs were preoccupied and she had someone to help watch for predators while she hunted. Willow helped roll over logs to uncover grubs and she picked berries from bushes so the cubs wouldn't get thorns in their paws. The mother came back with fish, and the black bears feasted while Willow happily munched on various seeds and berries she had collected. The journey went by quickly. Soon they were at the hot springs. Willow was a little disappointed. She would genuinely miss the black bear family. Dee Dee clacked her teeth warning Willow of the humans surrounding the hot springs. The resort was close by. Dee Dee suddenly bowed low to the ground and started backing her cubs from the clearing. Willow turned to see a stunningly beautiful female Elf appear from the shadows and smile.

"Welcome Willow, Guardian of Coconino." She nodded, "I am Thea, Guardian of Sierra."

"Greetings Thea. I thank you for your hospitality. The black bear family who escorted me was excellent company."

Willow waved and grunted her goodbye to Dee Dee. One of her cubs seemed reluctant to leave, the one Willow had secretly called Heidi. Dee Dee hadn't given the cubs names yet. But the female cub liked to hide in trees or bushes as they traveled through the forest. Willow would call out questions asking the male cub where his sister Heidi was knowing full well where she was hidden. It had been a fun game, but the extra attention and the berries had created an attachment.

"Heidi, go to your mother," Willow said in a bear grunt.

Dee Dee tilted her head.

Willow shook hers. "Sorry. I started calling the female cub Heidi."

She hoped she wasn't overstepping. Willow would often name the young of Coconino lower creatures when they were born. The parents never seemed to mind, and Willow enjoyed meeting and getting to know each newborn as they grew. It gave her a sense of connection to each new generation of forest creatures.

Dee Dee nodded grunting a reply, "It is a good name. One I will keep. Thank you, Willow, Guardian friend." The black bear family disappeared into the trees.

She turned back to Thea and grinned. The Guardian was tall and lean with cocoa skin and long dark brown hair with platinum streaks. Willow had seen hair similar on women from town who spent all day at the beauty salon. But, of course, she knew on Thea it was all-natural. Mae had told her a little of Thea's history. Her mother had been a wood Elf and the Guardian of Sierra Forest. They had gone to war with the Drow, the dark Elves that lived inside Mount Whitney. Thea's mother had been captured. Mae hadn't gotten all the details, only that Thea grew up without her Drow father. Her mother had raised her and after she had passed, Thea took up her mother's role as Guardian. Her hair and skin showed the beautiful blend of her mixed heritage.

"Up ahead we have a spot that is hidden from humans. This way." She walked a short distance and in between two large pines.

Willow followed and felt the magic seep into her bones as they passed the barrier. There was a small clearing with a large stone tub. Steam floated from the hot springs. She gestured to the water.

"I bet you would enjoy a nice soak after your long journey."

Willow dropped her pack and swished off her gown in one motion. She stuck her toe in to test the temperature and jumped into the water with a splash. Willow came to the surface moaning in bliss. The hot water was already melting the knots in her sore muscles. The Eleven Guardian chuckled and started unlacing her boots.

"Thank you, Thea. This is heaven."

She tossed her boots on the ground.

"I've never met someone quite so eager to bathe. Does Coconino have hot springs?"

Willow stretched her limbs in the water. "Oh yeah. I often visit Verde Hot Springs. And I've been missing this."

She blinked up at the warrior fascinated by the intricate lacings tying the pieces of armor together in layers. "I had no idea you had on quite so many clothes or weapons."

The pile of Thea's belongings was huge next to the rock tub. Willow watched as Thea walked into the tub with long graceful steps. She had a warrior's body, toned with muscle. All that muscle had been hidden beneath leather.

"How goes your travels?"

She grinned. Willow felt an instant affinity for Thea. She was another female warrior and they had both been raised by single mothers who had also been Guardians.

"Well, it all started out pretty ordinary. Just a walk from Coconino until I came to the freeway. Then I, uh, hitched a ride to Grand Canyon."

"Is it easy to, what did you call it, hitch?"

Willow shrugged. She knew she couldn't reveal anything about the Werewolf transport. "It's not too hard. Humans are easy to manipulate."

Thea nodded.

"When I got to the Grand Canyon portal, I met a really rude troll."

Thea snorted, "Aren't they all?"

"Well, it was my first time through a long-range portal, and I guess I wasn't moving fast enough, so he shoved me through. I landed face-first in Mohave gravel."

Thea laughed. Loud. "Sorry. Just the image. Continue."

Willow grinned. She could appreciate the humor now. At the time, not so much.

"Anyhow, I met Bri, the Guardian of Mohave, and she showed me the wonders of her land. Have you met her?"

"No, but I don't get out much. The only other Guardians I know are in forests connected to mine."

Willow nodded. "I was the same way. I'd never met any until this trip. Bri is a Bighorn Shifter. She's young, close to Mae's age, innocent in some ways, but she has a fierce warrior spirit. I found out that Mae has been training with the Bighorn Shifters for years."

"That doesn't surprise me. She's been training with the Wood Elves as well."

Willow shook her head. "I can't believe how little I know of my sisters. In every forest I've visited, Mae has trained with the local warriors learning strategy and weapons." She laughed. "Is there a battle coming I don't know about?"

Thea frowned, "There is always a battle brewing. Don't you know my history?"

"Only a little. I was curious about your family. Do you ever visit your father?"

Thea's fist hit the rock ledge leaving a deep crack. "The Drow who imprisoned and raped my mother? Why would I see that male?"

Willow startled at the rage burning in Thea's eyes, "I meant no disrespect. Mae didn't share *those* details."

Thea took a deep breath. "I should have realized you would ask questions about family. It makes sense with your quest to find your mate. Your mind would naturally turn to those topics. I appreciate Mae's respect for my privacy. I share my history with very few." Thea rolled her neck, "So how about your family? Did you grow up with both parents?"

"My mother until I was sixteen, but my father was more absent than not. I have some good memories of him before I was six. After that, he started going on missions. My mother was furious. She would take a new lover each time he went away. They would fight when he returned. Over the years he showed up less and less. After my Grandmother died and my mother became Guardian, she would host lavish parties. The levels of debauchery I believe are still legendary."

Thea gave a throaty laugh, "I've heard stories."

Willow grinned. "Well, my mom had so many lovers at one point, she couldn't keep track. Those were the years of my sisters' births. She had no idea who the fathers were and didn't care. My father had shown up every year to see my mother pregnant yet again. After the third year in a row, I believe the proof of infidelity was too much. He believed they were fated eternal soulmates, but Ilana insisted that Dryads weren't meant to have eternals. I always wondered if life would have been different if my father hadn't left on secret missions all the time. If he had been around more, would she have strayed? He seemed to be the only male she ever really loved. The last memory I have of my father was of him storming off in a rage. He never said goodbye. A few months later, we learned of his death."

Thea touched Willow's hand. "I'm sorry to bring up such a painful memory."

"It's not. He wasn't a good father. I barely knew him at all. He hardly noticed I existed. When he visited, he spent most of his time yelling at my mother in between bouts of make-up sex. It was such an unhealthy love-hate relationship. But it could have been worse, my sisters didn't even have that much. They don't even know their fathers' names let alone anything about them."

Thea's eyes darkened and her voice grew cold as ice. "My mother gave me my father's name and description, so I would know who to kill onsite." Thea bared her teeth and slid a finger across her neck.

She swallowed. "Uh, yeah. I see where you're coming from."

Willow had always thought she had daddy-daughter issues, but Thea had her beat hands down. She had never once contemplated patricide.

"After my father died, my mother forbade military training for a short while. At the time, I thought it was so she could spend more time celebrating, but I wonder if it was her way of mourning my father's death."

"That whole concept doesn't make sense. I can't imagine a life with no training drills, even for a short time." Thea's brow furrowed.

There was a lull in the conversation while Willow thought more about her mother and father. The talk was stirring up a lot of old feelings. It was a wonder with her upbringing she had any desire at all to commit to a relationship.

"So," Thea hesitated, "now that you've found your mate, are you going to want young right away?"

Willow grinned, "Maybe. I'm hoping. If my mate is willing."

"Mae mentioned that Coconino has been at peace for many years. It sounds like a nice place to raise a family. You must have a lot of control of your forest."

Willow laughed. "I have zero control. Especially now. Council kicked me out of office."

Thea tilted her head. "You lost me."

She shrugged. "Someone took over for me. That's why I'm searching for my eternal."

"Ah, a temp. Very good. I get it now."

Willow sighed. Thea didn't get it, not really. But she was sick of trying to explain. Every forest she had visited, the relationship between Guardian and Council was different. She already felt bad enough as it was. Having to re-hash how she was fired from a permanent position left her feeling like a failure all over again.

After a few minutes of silence, Thea slapped the water.

Willow looked up in time to get a face full.

Thea gave her a wicked grin, "So, tell me the rest of your story. You haven't told me what you thought of the Centaur twins?"

Willow grinned. "Well, after Mohave, I got another hitch to Sequoia and met the incredibly hot Guardian Pax who took me on a tour of Sequoia. He took me to Moro Rock so I could see the spectacular view."

"No. He didn't?" Thea rolled her eyes, "Why do males never think?"

She shrugged. "Anyhow, I started sobbing, completely embarrassed myself. I had no idea how bad the drought was here."

Thea nodded, "And Sierra got the worst of it. I'm glad you won't be visiting that part of my forest. It's a pine graveyard. I warned your sister not to go, but Mae insisted. She said the experience has haunted her ever since."

"You can't unsee stuff like that." Willow shivered, "But after Moro Rock, the rest of the tour was fun. We visited the Giant Forest and I met the famous General Sherman tree, aka Eleanor. It was a hoot finding out the TreeAnt was female. Then we met Chase at Grizzly Falls. I hadn't known they were twins until that moment. Both of them together, standing next to one another. Wow." She fanned her face, "It was almost too much eye candy to take in all at once. And both the Centaur brothers gave me a ride through their forests, but Chase's," she blushed a deep green, "was a bit more vigorous."

Thea gave a throaty laugh, "Vigorous. Yes, I bet. He does that for all the newbies traveling through." She shrugged. "I think he does it more because he's hoping they'll give him a go." Thea's gaze glazed over.

"So, did you give it a go?"

Thea grinned. "I might have been neighborly."

"Pax?"

Thea nodded.

"And Chase?"

"Oh. Yes."

Willow laughed. "You've got guts. I mean I like them big, and Pax is definitely that, but Chase is scary big."

She shrugged. "With no female Centaurs, I feel bad for the brothers. Their choices are limited."

"Really?"

Thea's lips twitched. "Trust me. The twins have no shortage of admirers, but a non-Centaur mate would be nearly impossible. Only heavy magic and a really devoted mate with a high tolerance for pain could even attempt such a thing. Plus the danger to the Mother and the child would be great.

"I wish I knew why so few female Centaurs have been born in the last few generations. It hit Coconino as well. We only have a handful of females. But we're lucky. Most other forests don't have any. Our youngest, Diana, will reach mating age next year. She is protected by old magic to keep her safe, but I worry for her. She is so shy and hates the idea of an arranged marriage. Her father is ecstatic by the list of proposals. I feel like I should step in and say something."

Thea shrugged. "It's a hard call. Most Centaur families are old-fashioned. Their culture is steeped in tradition."

"Exactly. But as a female warrior, I should empower other women, not idly stand by as her father sells her off to the highest bidder."

"Preach." Thea nodded.

Willow mulled over what to do when she got back to Coconino. Her status as former Guardian left her with little-to-no authority. Would Cyrus even listen? It was a family matter after all, but regardless, she felt compelled to speak her mind. At this point, what else could she lose?

Thea stretched, "Are you ready to get out?"

Willow yawned, "Actually, do you have any pines I could rest in for the night?"

"I have the perfect place."

They both stepped out. Thea snapped her fingers and several hawks flew down to sit on a low tree branch. She snapped again and they flapped their wings fast causing a small wind to blow dry her body and hair. Willow watched in fascination. She had never thought to ask birds from her own forest to do such a thing. After Thea re-dressed, she reached into a pouch and gave each hawk a dead mouse in thanks.

Thea signaled for Willow to follow. She led her to the far end of the glade and pointed to the pine she would sleep in for the evening.

"I'll be back in the morning to escort you to the portal."

Willow nodded. She placed her pack in the cubby provided and felt herself melt into the pine. It was an old one, around 400 years. The tree was filled with such joy with the binding. It was slow at first moving its roots to massage her tired feet. She responded by heating her palms and massaging the inner stem, pulsing it with energy. The tree shivered with delight and the branches shook scattering leaves across the forest floor. If the tree could have spoken, it would have sighed. Willow spoke quietly murmuring soothing words calming the tree. She faded off feeling protected and at peace.

The next morning after making her apologies to the tree for having to leave so soon, Willow dressed quickly and met up with Thea. They walked to another hidden pathway leading from the hot springs, one she hadn't noticed last night. Of course, there was another troll at the portal control, but this one treated her with respect. Willow felt a little less uncertain than she had last time, but she didn't think it was her confidence, it was the intimidating glare from Thea that kept the troll on its toes.

"I hope you visit again soon, Willow, Guardian of Coconino."

She shook her head. "You keep trying to give me a title I no longer hold."

Thea shrugged. "I call it like I see it."

Willow gave her a hug. "It was good meeting you. And as thanks for your hospitality, I'd like to return the favor. Perhaps you could come visit Coconino sometime."

"A trip? Me? But I've never left the forest." Thea grinned. "You know, I think I'd like that. Thank you."

Willow smiled and walked through the portal when the troll nodded. This time when she landed, her feet hit solid ground. She blinked up at a huge troll, nearly six feet tall. Since most trolls averaged four feet in height, it was highly unusual. His skin was also an olive green instead of the normal sallow yellow and his long black hair was braided into a single plait. Even his beard was braided. His eyes were lavender instead of the normal red. And this one seemed much cleaner than the average troll. Willow glanced at his sharp claws. They looked recently manicured. His leather breeches and tunic were immaculate. How odd. Trolls were notoriously rude, smelly, and dirty little creatures. He read off information from the portal screen with a thick Scottish accent. The vines reformed and he grunted an approval.

"What be yer reason fer coming ta Muir Woods?"

The troll held a short sword to her neck. When had he drawn his weapon? Damn, he was fast. She had been concentrating on the portal screen wondering what sort of information was being transmitted. Well, he at least had one troll attribute. Rude.

"I seek my eternal soulmate who lives in the city. Might you be so kind as to direct me to San Francisco?"

He shook his head. "Why would someone like ye be seeking city folk?"

Willow sighed. She hadn't expected an interrogation. This creature hadn't been vetted by her sister. It was never wise to give a stranger information about someone you cared about. They could use it later to their advantage. He didn't lower his sword. It looked like he would be demanding an answer. She gave as brief a description as possible explaining how she met Bray Graham and how she needed to find him at any cost. She bit her tongue recalling their nature and greed for gold. If she wasn't careful, all the coin she had left would be spent at this single stop. He nodded and lowered his sword.

"Verra well. Ye can head east." He pointed over his right shoulder, "Keep walking fer a few miles and there be a bus station. It goes to the city."

She let out a breath and scurried away before he decided to keep her at sword-point. Willow turned around. She had almost forgotten to give him coin for his information. It was a grave insult. She pulled the coin from her backpack and handed it to him.

He eyed the coin like it was an insect and sneered at her. Willow looked at the coin. It was solid; a good piece of gold. Isn't this what they craved beyond reason? This creature was so unlike any troll she had met.

"I wish to pay and thank you for your assistance."

He frowned. "Bring Bray's mother tae dinner and we'll call it even." The troll gave an evil grin baring sharp pointy teeth.

She gulped loudly. How could she have been so stupid? Why couldn't she have just left well enough alone? Willow couldn't offer Bray's mother as a sacrifice. How was that conversation going to go? Hi, Bray. I traveled all the way here, but oops, I might have promised your mother to a troll as dinner. So sorry. My bad. Hope you weren't too fond of her.

Maybe they could go another route back home. All they had to do was avoid the portal. Easy, right? What could happen if she failed to deliver? Did trolls have debt collectors? Would they hunt her down and exact payment? He didn't look like he would be letting her leave without an answer. Maybe she could negotiate with him later.

"Alive?" She asked.

He made some kind of choked sound.

"O' course."

"I'll see what I can do."

He nodded and pointed a gnarled finger to a path leading east.

Willow blew out a breath and hurried in that direction. She was grateful he hadn't pressed further. She hadn't exactly promised.

The portal vanished when she stepped onto the dirt trail. Willow felt a pulse of power when she walked between the trees. Portals always had magical protections keeping those little pockets hidden from unsuspecting humans. The path winded through tall coast redwoods and she was reminded of her sister Red. This patch of ancient forest had been purchased by William Kent long ago. He named it in honor of his friend John Muir and had given the land to the federal government as a way to protect it for future generations. President Roosevelt had proclaimed it a national monument. Humans were strange. She guessed it didn't really matter what they called it as long as they took care of the land. This handful of humans saw the beauty of nature and fought to keep it safe. More of these nature warriors were needed. The magical community could only do so much. Willow hoped with all her heart that Bray would be one of them, sharing her passion and defending the forest by her side.

As she strolled down the trail, Willow noticed a plaque embedded in stone bearing Willam Kent's name. Not only had he saved this land, he also founded 'Save the Redwoods League' over a century ago. Red kept a picture of him in her birth tree, a pin-up of the man she worshipped like a hero. Red had been deeply embarrassed when Willow had found her with it. She didn't know what the big deal was, but Red had gone on and on about privacy. It was the year she started planting traps around her birth tree. *Ah, the teenage years.*

As Willow walked through the trees, she reached out and touched a few and heard them sigh like the wind softly whistling through the leaves. This forest didn't have a Guardian and they hadn't been visited by a Dryad in a very long time. They wanted her to stay and talk, but Willow let them know she was on a mission to find her eternal soulmate.

"The young never have time for us."

"Can you rub my roots?"

"My bark is brittle."

"Fred's blocking my sun."

"I can't remember my name."

Willow was inundated with questions and requests.

"I will ask my sister to come visit when I get back home. She's a redwood Dryad."

All the trees in the area shivered with excitement. They began talking back and forth with one another already planning for the arrival, their voices growing louder and louder. It sounded like cicadas in the summer, a buzzing in the ears she couldn't get away from. Willow began tuning them out like she did back home. Now she remembered why she listened to the trees so rarely. Their chatter was incessant, the constant questions exhausting. She started looking forward to the city.

When Willow got to the bus stop, she pulled out Red's notes on what to do. They were precise color-coded instructions depending on the day and time she got to the city. Red suggested if it was on a weekday, that she should try the office first. If Willow arrived on the weekend, she was to try his condo or one of the clubs he frequented. She turned on the "borrowed" phone. Red told her not to waste battery life until she got close to the city. The phone said it was Tuesday at nine a.m. Willow pressed the button that said 'office.' Red had programmed all the routes into the phone along with all the potential addresses where he might be. The phone mapped out the route showing her the bus numbers and where to switch lines. She must look like a tourist with the strange looks everyone was giving her. Willow shrugged. She didn't care. She would sometimes get odd expressions when she visited town back home as well. The map and directions were surprisingly simple, but she could tell by the sheer number of people and traffic she would have been lost a hundred times over if not for the very careful instructions of her sister. She owed Red a very big debt indeed.

Chapter 34

THE LAST BUS dropped Willow a block away from Bray's office. She followed the map from her phone app. When it said she had arrived, she zipped it back into the pack. She blinked up at the large metal building. It seemed cold and menacing. There had been fewer and fewer trees the further she had traveled into the city. Everywhere she stepped had thick concrete, preventing her normal connection to the earth. Her body felt a bit like a phantom limb. She could vaguely sense things, but nothing felt real. Several people stared at her as they ascended the steps. None of them seemed nervous to go inside. She was a warrior. Nothing frightened her. It's not like the building would eat her. She laughed at that ridiculous thought and followed a group inside. The odd rotating door stopped in mid-turn. She peered through the glass. The people in front of her had made it through. What sort of trap had she stumbled across? She pushed against the glass. It wouldn't budge. Maybe it had a security field like the circle of trees back home. Did that mean she couldn't cross unless she was human? Would they keep her locked in this glass cage forever? *Deep breath*. No reason to panic. Someone would notice her soon. Oh, Gaia. What if there wasn't enough air? Could she suffocate in this trap before someone came to collect her? No sun. No water. She was trapped away from the earth. Her breaths came faster. The walls started closing in on her. She pounded on the glass and screamed.

"Ma'am. It's ok. Your backpack is just stuck."

She turned. There was a young man behind her in another glass triangle. *A fellow prisoner?* He pointed to one of the straps on her backpack that had come loose. It was caught in the door frame.

"Lean back against the glass and give the strap a good yank."

She nodded and followed his instructions.

The mechanism released and the door started moving again. She gave an involuntary squeal of delight. She was inside the building. What an overwhelming relief. She embraced the young man as he exited the spinning glass.

"Oh, thank you so much." She kissed his cheek. Steam fogged up his thick glasses.

"I-it was nothing ma'am." He stammered. He removed his glasses and polished them on his black and white plaid shirt. When he put them back on, his eyes went wide. "Wow."

He cleared his throat. "I, uh. I'm late for a meeting." He stumbled a few feet and placed a card on a tall metal block. A lever raised and it allowed him deeper into the building.

Huh? Another level of security. Willow glanced around the lobby and her eyes widened at the huge open space. There were large tv monitors spread out on one wall in a mosaic pattern across a four-story atrium. Random pictures flashed across showing all sorts of images, most of which confused her. People milled about on couches conversing with one another, or huddled over laptops in deep concentration. More people walked past her scanning cards into the waist-high metal blocks. The gate opened after each person showed their card to a tiny flashing screen. It reminded her of the troll's portal monitor, except it wasn't covered in vines and the being guarding the portal didn't look as threatening. A plump woman in a purple suit and pink glasses frowned at her from behind a large desk. Willow threw her shoulders back and marched over. Confidence. That's what was needed.

"I'm here to see Brayden Graham."

The woman studied her thoroughly and frowned.

Willow shifted her stance and smiled.

"I see." The woman glanced at her computer screen. "Is he expecting you?"

"Well, um." Willow shrugged. "No. I guess not."

"I'm sorry but you'll need to make an appointment."

Willow eyed the machines to her left. It looked easy enough to hop over. If there was a chase, she didn't think the woman behind the desk posed much of a threat. But she had no clue where to look for Bray. This building was enormous. How long would it take the woman to call in reinforcements? How long did that leave Willow to find Bray? She needed a better strategy. While working out a plan, she spotted someone she recognized. Liam was sitting at a small café just beyond the scanners. She jumped up and down waving wildly.

"Liam! It's Willow."

He turned. His jaw dropped. Several people had given her similar stares. She looked down at herself. Well, damn. She had forgotten to put on one of the city dresses before the bus ride. Willow was still wearing the gold gown she had traveled in for the past few days. It had been at the top of the pack. She shrugged. Well, it was too late now.

"It's ok, Erika. Willow is with me. Can you get her a visitor's badge?"

The receptionist handed him a badge with a snicker. Willow clipped it to the strap of her silk gown. It looked a little worse for the wear with grass and dirt stains. A few days of travel had taken its toll. Her sandals may have even looked worse than the dress. She wiggled her mud-caked toes and sighed wondering what her face and hair looked like. Judging by Liam's expression, they probably matched the rest of her. Willow smoothed a hand through her hair. It got stuck halfway through. Her hair was a tangled disaster. A finger snagged on a twig and she pulled it free. She eyed the pristine tile floor and stuck it back in her hair. She grinned at Liam.

He walked her to the elevator shaking his head.

"Bray didn't mention you were coming to visit."

"Well, it's sort of a surprise. I had no idea when I'd get here. It's been quite a journey."

"Looks like it." He gestured for her to get into the elevator and pressed the top floor.

Willow didn't like elevators. Bray had shown her a few in Flagstaff. Small boxes with no escape route made her nervous. This elevator had glass walls so she didn't feel quite so claustrophobic. She pressed her face and hands to the glass as she watched the people in the lobby get smaller and smaller as they ascended. She gulped loudly. Maybe the glass walls were worse than the solid ones.

"So, does Bella ask about me?"

"What?" Willow faced Liam glad for the distraction. "Bella? I don't really hang out with her much, so I wouldn't know."

Liam cocked his head. "That's strange."

"What do you mean?"

"Well, Bella asked all sorts of questions about Bray, what he did for a living, what his personality was like. I figured you were close and she was vetting him. I know girls do stuff like that. They interrogate a boyfriend for their friends to make sure the guy's ok."

"Hmm. That's interesting." She wondered what Bella was up to. Her involvement never meant anything good. She was way too much like her mother.

The door opened and Willow gratefully stepped out following Liam down a long hallway.

"Bray is in a meeting right now, but you can wait out here." He gestured to a sofa outside a frosted glass room. Liam glanced at his watch. "He should be finishing up soon."

She set her pack on the sofa and paced. What would she tell him? Would he be excited to see her? Or upset by the interruption? This was his workplace, and she didn't know the customs. Already she had received numerous stares. No, she told herself. It wouldn't matter to Bray. He never seemed to mind when she made mistakes with human customs. He would understand. She couldn't wait to see him again. The excitement built until she could barely stand it. More stares. She sighed and sat down. What was taking so long? Each second seemed to pass like an eternity. Maybe she should have set an appointment? The lady at the front desk seemed to think so. Liam had wondered if Bray knew of the visit. Is that what humans did? Did they need warning ahead of time? Willow had no clue how these corporations worked. Would he get in trouble with the boss? She had never asked him about his work and hated feeling like she was doing everything wrong. Maybe this was a mistake coming here. What if he turned her away? This entire trip had been building up to this moment. He could crush her hopes so easily. Finally, the door opened to a peal of laughter. A husky feminine voice mentioned something about nailing down a date and getting a photographer. Gail appeared in the doorway. She looked gorgeous in some fancy gold and black tweed suit. And those awful shoes. Shiny gold and black to match her suit. Big, sharp weapons on her feet. With one arm draped over Bray's shoulders, she pulled him into a hug. Her breasts pressed against his chest and something snapped.

Gail. That bitch. She reacted without thought. It was instinct driven by pure adrenaline. She launched herself at Gail with a shriek.

Willow got in a few punches and kicks before Liam got between them. He got clocked in the face for his efforts.

Bray helped Gail to her feet and turned to Willow with fury.

"What the fuck?" His muscles were bunched, fists clenched, breathing heavy. In other circumstances, she would be turned on, but his anger was directed at her. His expression transformed into confusion. His eyes roamed her body, from her dirty toes to the top of her tangled tresses. "Willow, is that you?"

She blew out a breath knowing she didn't look her best. She should have changed, or at least tried to clean up. Willow's eyes flashed back to Gail. She shifted from one foot to the other waiting for another chance to strike. "Yes. It's me." The words came out as a hiss.

Two beefy security guards jogged over. Gail held her cheek and stretched her jaw. She glared at Willow. Liam seemed reluctant to release his grip from Willow's arm. Like the pathetic human could have prevented her from attacking.

The guards seemed uncertain how to proceed. They glanced at Bray.

Bray looked between Willow and Gail and sighed, "Liam, can you take care of this?" He took Gail by the arm and led her away.

Willow's jaw dropped. This wasn't happening. He was leaving? Bray had rushed to Gail's side. As if he were with her. Was she too late? Had Gail swayed him to her side now that he was back home? Willow stopped struggling against Liam's grip. She plopped down on the sofa next to her pack. Willow had traveled all this way for nothing. She vaguely heard Liam explaining to the guards that it was all a misunderstanding and Willow was no threat. The voices faded out as she thought about her long journey here and her building expectations of how Bray would react. Bray hadn't been excited to see her at all. He had been shocked and then turned away. She felt tears threatening. She had to get out of here. She was embarrassed enough as it was. Why prolong the whole thing further? Willow glanced around wildly, looking for an escape. A door that said exit was next to the bathroom. Liam sat next to her on the couch and awkwardly patted her knee.

"I'm not quite sure what came over you, but you should stay here, at least until you've calmed down."

She sniffed and wiped a tear. "I am calm. I, uh, need to clean up."

He handed her a tissue from a box sitting on a low table and gestured to the bathroom door.

She dabbed at her eyes. It was all so humiliating. What a waste. She had traveled all this way, and he had already fallen in love with another. Damn fickle humans.

Nick walked over. He towered over the guards and gave one of them a whack on the shoulder. "Good job, guys. Danger averted." He gave Willow a wink and turned back to the guards.

At least his friends were still nice to her. The four men conversed in low voices. It was now or never. She walked to the bathroom. With a quick glance to make sure no one was looking, she veered into the stairwell. It led to a side door. No security. Nice. She was grateful she didn't have to pass by that woman at the front desk. She inhaled the fresh air and followed the sidewalk. Willow felt numb as she walked over to a group of people standing at a bus stop. A minute later, a bus pulled up and she climbed aboard in a daze. She handed the driver a ticket she had bought earlier. He handed it back and motioned for her to take a seat. The piece of paper must still have some magic left. She had no idea where she was going. All she wanted was to get as far away as possible before she completely broke down. All the events of the last few weeks came flooding back to her. Scenery flashed by her window but she hardly noticed. A little girl across the aisle smiled at Willow. She was holding her mother's hand and bouncing on the bench. The little girl had been chatting with anyone who would listen.

"We're going to see giant redwoods."

Willow nodded numbly.

"Have you ever been to Muir Woods?" The little girl asked.

"Yes, I have. As a matter of fact, I was just there."

"Was it dreamy, like out of a fairy tale?"

Willow's mouth quirked. The kid was cute. No doubt about it. She was reminded of her sisters when they were young. Willow sighed realizing there was no reason to stay in California. Might as well make her way back home. It would be good to see her sisters again. She missed them. They could drink the rest of Bray's stash of expensive liquor. He was back at work, and now with Gail. The skank. He didn't appear to be coming back. Her original goal from months ago was complete. She had rid the forest of the human. Maybe she could try to get her old job back if she begged? The thought made her ill. Begging Council? Forget it. Hardly worth it. Bunch of ungrateful hot air bags. She would find something different. Something better. There were plenty of other jobs. She could be an entrepreneur. Maybe work to get Coconino their own permanent long-distance portal. It was ridiculous they didn't have such a thing already. It sure would have made the trip home a lot easier.

Willow turned to the girl's mother. "I'm traveling back to Muir Woods but I'm from out of town. Do you think you can help me take the correct transfers? I had a map coming out this way, but I don't have one going back."

Her mother scrutinized Willow from head to toe just the way Bray did. She still hadn't cleaned up. She sighed.

"Were you mugged?"

Willow blinked. She wasn't familiar with that term, but she nodded anyway.

The woman seemed satisfied and agreed to let her tag along with them. The little girl was thrilled to have a captive audience. Through all the chatter, she found out the little girl was Victoria Miller, great granddaughter to Jim Miller, the very same one that built the cabin in her woods. It was proof there was still a speck of hope for humans. At least the love of nature was being passed down for future generations.

After what seemed like hours, their final bus pulled to a stop Willow recognized.

"This is us." The mother said as she gathered their snacks and supplies.

They had barely climbed from the bus, when the girl launched herself at Willow and gave her a bear hug.

The little squirt reminded her of Red as a girl.

"Owf." Willow grunted. "Thanks so much for getting me here."

"Aren't you waiting for the shuttle? There should be one every thirty minutes."

"Nah, I like to walk. And I've got someone waiting for me up ahead."

"Ok. But be sure to pull up your ticket on your cell first. You lose service at the park."

Willow frowned. What was she talking about? She had never purchased a ticket. A ticket to get into the woods? Why on earth would humans do such a thing?

She turned back. "Where exactly do they check the tickets again?"

The mother frowned. "At the front gate of course."

She would avoid that area. No problem.

"Sure thing," Willow nodded. "I'll do that now." She waved. "Bye, Victoria. Bye, Mrs. Miller. Take care."

Willow walked off down the road and chuckled to herself. A gate for the forest. What a hoot. Those humans.

As she approached the portal, Willow tried to figure out the best way back. She didn't have Ellie's Werewolf contacts, so it would mean long walks between portals or hitchhiking. Her emotions started boiling to the surface. The little girl Victoria had been a great distraction on the bus ride, but everything flooded back as she entered the pocket realm with the portal. She had traveled so far for no reason. Bray had fallen for another. She had been too late. But not only that, he was the cause of everything; her downfall, her loss of job, her breaking heart. Her human had changed her view on the world and there was no going back. The depression slammed into her hard. She couldn't breathe.

The Troll watched her, anxiously looking over her shoulder.

"Did ye bring Juliet Graham?"

Oh crap. She had forgotten all about Bray's mother. Her ticket home had just gotten way more complicated.

Chapter 35

"WELL?" THE TROLL asked.

Willow stood there with her mouth hanging open for too long. "Sorry. I sort of forgot."

He shook his head. "No payment, no portal."

"Listen," Willow pleaded, "I'm sure we can work something out. I still have some gold." She pulled out coins from her pack. "Can't you take this instead?"

He turned his back and played with the panel. The power from a minute ago vanished with a pop. Willow couldn't even detect the magic anymore. The troll turned and slumped on a stump. His arms crossed as he glared at her. Willow had no idea where to go. Her only option was the portal. She had stupidly flung that phone thingy in the lake on the walk back. The beeping noise had been driving her nuts. She had lost her patience. It was foolish and rash, she realized now. The phone had a source of knowledge and she had chucked it. Red was going to kill her. Well, if she ever got home. She considered her options. She could try to fight the troll in battle, make him turn on the portal and send her somewhere by force. Willow had the advantage of looking small and weak, but she was a warrior and had skills, although they were a little rusty. And the troll was tall and muscled. Not like the normal anemic-looking ones with stringy hair and smelly clothes. This one was tidy and neat and probably worked out by the looks of him.

She sighed. Even if she did manage to take him, who was to say he wouldn't just send her somewhere for spite, possibly somewhere in the opposite direction of where she wanted to go. Willow didn't have a clue on how these portals worked. She added that to an ever-growing list of all the things she didn't know, but needed to learn.

"I saw Bray, but his mother wasn't with him." She cleared her throat. "And I have no way of contacting the woman. I've never met her."

"That be the reason? Ye nae have her address?"

Willow nodded. "Yes. Of course. No address. No directions. Sorry, but it can't be done. You'll simply have to come up with another payment."

The troll grinned and his canines gleamed in the sunshine. His smile was creepy and made Willow shiver despite the warm sun on her shoulders.

"Well, why didn't ye say so in the first place?"

"Listen. I need to get out of here. I traveled for days to get here from the Coconino Forest. I finally get here and my eternal soulmate is banging some fancy human in high heels. I just want to get back home, drink moonwine until I pass out, and rethink my whole life." Willow's eyes misted. "If not, you are going to have one weepy Dryad on your hands, heading into a world of depression. If you want that, by all means, wait me out."

His eyes softened and he offered her a seat on the log next to him.

Willow took a deep breath and sat down.

"Moonwine?"

Willow plopped down her bag and pulled out the flask. She handed it to the troll. He sniffed the contents and grinned.

He took a healthy swig.

"Me name's Oscar." He nodded and handed the flask back.

"I'm Willow." She took a swig of the moonwine and stared up into the sky. She could only see a small piece of it from their clearing.

"Why don't ye tell me what happened? Sometimes ye feel better talking about it."

She sniffed. "Ok."

Willow spilled every detail in between bouts of tears. The troll didn't seem to be put off by her weeping. He would wait patiently for her to finish and hand her back the flask. They talked for hours, or rather she talked and he listened.

"And that's everything." Willow slurred. "My life is fucked." She hiccuped. "Sorry, I sound like my sister Red."

He shrugged. "Not a bother, lassie."

This Oscar had a stash of his own liquor and they sampled a few throughout the evening. In fact, he had a whole bar camouflaged by magic.

"How about ye get some rest? There's a pine over there ye can bed down in for the night."

She grinned. "Thank you, Oscar. You're the best." Willow stumbled to the blurry tree line and merged with one of the many pines to choose from. She wasn't sure if this was the tree he had pointed to, but it didn't matter. She needed to pass out.

The sound of drilling woke her at dawn.

"Aaagghh. My head." Willow peeked out from the tree and stared at a family of Acorn Woodpeckers delightfully shoving nuts into various holes in the tree she was sleeping in. She unstuck her body from the tree and rolled onto the ground still gripping her throbbing skull. She blinked around the forest. Most of the trees in the area were decorated in holes. She hadn't noticed it last night when getting tanked. Each tree had a large extended family. One standing guard and others swooping in with their stash and packing it in wherever they could. No wonder her back was sore. She had been laying against acorns all night.

She glanced over at a small fire. Oscar was busy making breakfast. "I tried to warn you last night."

He pointed to the tree in the middle. It was larger than the rest and had no woodpeckers or holes in it. It looked so warm and comfy. Willow desperately wanted to crawl over to it and get a few more hours of sleep, but she needed to figure things out. She was embarrassed by how much she had complained last night. The alcohol had loosened her tongue, and Oscar had been easy to talk to. He held no judgement because he didn't really know her.

Willow wrinkled her nose at the smell of rabbit. He rotated the poor dead animal on a spit above the fire. He pointed down at the lake. "I'll have breakfast ready soon if you want to go wash up."

She stumbled down the hill trying to figure out a way to politely refuse breakfast. There was no way she was going to eat meat. It didn't matter how mortified she was by her behavior.

When she got back, she eyed a small cloth over a piece of bark. He whipped off the cloth.

"Yer feast, me lady."

It was a salad with nuts and some raspberry sauce that looked delicious.

"Thank you, Oscar. This was very thoughtful."

He nodded and took his plate, another sheet of dried bark and sat on his stump.

"Ye need to eat them nuts first." He pointed at the trees. "They steal 'em fast if ye ain't lookin." He shrugged. "Well, even if ye are lookin' they may try."

Willow eyed the birds. He was right. They looked to be plotting something already. She quickly scarfed down her food.

"Thanks again for breakfast." Willow reached out for his plate. "You cooked. I clean. It's only fair."

When she got back from washing the plates in the lake Oscar was dancing on his toes. He was practically vibrating with energy.

"I've come up with a plan, my wee lassie."

"Yeah, what's that?"

"I got hold of Juliet's address. And the directions ye be needin."

He handed her a slip of paper.

"Wait. Juliet? You've already named your food?"

He blinked. "What are ye talking about? Juliet's not food. Ye think I wanted to eat her?"

"Well yeah. That's why it was so awkward. I was going to meet Bray, try to rekindle our romance, and then offer his mother up for a sacrifice. I wasn't looking forward to that conversation."

Oscar made some strange grunting noise that turned into a wheeze, and Willow realized it was his way of laughing.

"Oh my." He wiped a tear from his eye. "I haven't laughed that hard in years. Ye are a treat to have around."

She was glad to amuse.

"So, if you don't want to eat her, that must mean you know Bray's mom."

"Aye, and I ken Bray's father as well. We were quite close until his father died and I think it was too hard for Juliet to come round after that."

"I didn't know about his dad. We didn't talk much about his family. He mentioned his mother, but it was usually around some complaint about the woman."

"I can see that. She's a bit o' a whirlwind. And quite stubborn, but then again so is Bray. They butt heads. But she usually wins. Actually, I should rephrase that. She always wins." He chuckled. "Fair warning, lassie. Don't get into a fight with Mrs. Graham. It's futile. Accept defeat from the beginning."

Willow grew intrigued. Now, she couldn't wait to meet the woman. What kind of childhood did Bray have, to be raised by such a strong female figure? Perhaps she shouldn't give up quite so easy. She now had an in she hadn't counted on.

She looked at the slip of paper again. "This isn't far away. Why have you never gone to see her?"

"What? Visit a human town?" Oscar choked. "Nae. That be improper." He shrugged. "And nae allowed."

"Do you mean while you're working?"

He sniggered. "That be always."

"What?" Willow's jaw dropped. "You don't get breaks? You can't leave ever?"

"Aye. That 'bout sums it up. The Troll king forbids us to leave our posts."

"Wow, and I thought my job was bad."

He shrugged. "It's always been this way. No use arguing 'bout it."

Willow had once felt that way about her job. And if she could help, she would. And one thing that would cheer this guy up would be seeing an old friend from long ago.

"Alright. I'll bring Juliet to the woods. But you have to give me details about her."

Willow put on one of the dresses Bray had bought for her, even adding some fancy sandals that hurt her feet. She arrived at Juliet's house clean and presentable and hoping to make a good impression.

She rang the doorbell and it was such a beautiful melody she closed her eyes and began to dance on the porch.

"Yes?"

Willow blinked. A woman in a burgundy suit with pink trim stood in the doorway. Her dark hair was piled on her head in an intricate pattern. A double strand of pink pearls rested on her neck. She looked like a tall porcelain doll. Her makeup was perfect. She reminded her of Gail, only slightly older and more sophisticated. Willow glanced at the woman's feet. More pointy shoes with colors to match her clothes. What was it with human women and their shoes?

She cleared her throat. "Hello, I'm Willow. You're Juliet Graham, right? Bray's mother?"

"Yes, but Bray doesn't live here. He hasn't for years."

"I'm not here to see him. Oscar from Muir Woods sent me. He wanted to invite you to tea."

Her eyebrows rose and she tilted her head. Juliet studied her for several moments.

Willow shifted her stance. The woman's stare was unnerving.

"That is quite interesting. Please come in."

She ushered her through a huge foyer and down the hallway. The clipped sound as the woman's heels hit the tile echoed off the flooring and walls making the house seem ominous. They walked into a lavish living room filled with very expensive-looking furniture. Tan tiles covered the floor. The walls were cream, and the furniture white. The room looked stark and lifeless, with the exception of a few splashes of color. A red pillow thrown here and there. A vivid black and red abstract painting hung on the wall. A strange sculpture in black sat on an end table, and a large black grand piano sprawled to the side of a huge black and white fireplace. Willow was afraid to sit on the white couch for fear she would leave dirt marks. She spun around before she sat checking her backside and legs before sinking into the cushions.

Mrs. Graham grinned.

"What did you say your name was, my dear?"

"Willow."

"And you're a friend of my son's?"

She nodded.

"Where did you meet?"

"He moved into my woods."

"The little cabin, up near Bellemont?"

"Yep. That's the one."

"You don't say. Hmm." She tapped a finger to her lips. "If you know Oscar, does that mean my son has met him as well?"

"I doubt it."

"Perhaps you should tell me what this is all about. Oscar would not have sent you to come get me for tea. He would have used one of the squirrel messengers."

Willow's jaw dropped. "So, you're part of the community?"

She sighed. "Of course. Let's stop playing games, shall we? What flavor are you?"

"Flavor?"

"What magic do you possess?"

"Oh. I'm a Dryad. What about you?"

"Now we're getting somewhere."

Willow couldn't believe that Bray's mom was somehow tied to the magical community. She was in shock. Everything was starting to make sense. Their relationship. The connection she felt for him.

"Have you enchanted my son?"

"It's the other way around if you ask me," Willow mumbled. "He saw a few magical things that couldn't be explained and he sort of freaked out. I came here to bring him back."

She blinked. "Let me get this straight. You left the forest, your birth tree in Arizona, to travel to California for my son?"

"That's about it." Willow nodded. "Oh, and I also left my position as Guardian of the forest, so there won't be any worry of human prejudice to contend with."

"Fascinating."

Juliet rang a bell and a man in a white smock, white pants, and funny little hat came running from an adjoining room.

"Yes, ma'am. What would you like?"

"Oh, would you be a dear and make us some of those lovely cucumber sandwiches and bring us some tea."

"Of course."

Nice. Mrs. Graham had servants. What would it be like to live in her world? She thought back to when she had first met Bray, she assumed he had a cushy life. Just his handling of power tools made her question the exotic land he lived in. Apparently, he had grown up having others do things for him. No wonder he lacked basic survival skills. It made perfect sense.

At some point during lunch, the tea switched to wine. Several hours and wine bottles later, Willow had disclosed most of her encounters with Bray. She even told her about all the tricks they had played on him at first, and the Serce test that proved Bray was her eternal soulmate, and how Council refused to acknowledge the union. Juliet was just as up in arms about her mistreatment. Bray's mom was easy to confide in. Plus, she had the best selection of wine. Willow perused her wine cellar and fell in love. She lovingly stroked bottle after bottle, before selecting the next one from the rack.

They moved from the living room to the sunroom. The room was filled with wicker furniture and colorful pillows and plants. Loads and loads of plants. It connected with a greenhouse that contained species from all over the world. Bray's father had collected them and Juliet had lovingly cared for them after he had died.

"I can see why Bray is so enchanted by you."

"You have it all wrong. I tried to enchant him, but my Dryad powers failed. It was quite embarrassing."

"The correspondence with my son over the last few months had been suspiciously vague. I knew something was up. I made up a fake illness to bring him home last week. Now everything makes sense."

"But what about Gail from his office? He's smitten with that sexy little skank. She's got her claws in him. I know it." Willow made little claw gestures in the air.

Juliet laughed. "Don't worry about Gail. Trust me," She patted her hand. "He won't get away from you. I have a plan."

"Why would you do this for me? You hardly know me." Willow asked. She didn't want to be mistrustful, but it seemed too good to be true.

"Because, Willow, I like you, and I'm a good judge of character. You are perfect for my son."

Juliet rubbed her hands together. "Oh, this is going to be great fun. There is so much to do. You'll stay here."

She didn't make it a question.

"I'll need your size. Hmm. Stand up. I've got an eye for this sort of thing."

Juliet was just like Bray. It seemed to be all about the clothes. Since clothes were optional in her society, she had to defer to Bray's mother.

"I've already got dresses." Willow unzipped her bag to show her.

"Those are very nice, but I have something different in mind." She smiled. "You have such lovely curves, and we need to highlight those eyes. I'll have appointments set up for everything by the weekend.

"So, what's the plan?"

"To play hard to get, of course."

"I don't get it." Willow frowned.

"Exactly. And neither will Bray. That's why it will work. It's perfect."

Willow shrugged. She would take Juliet's word. She didn't have anything to lose, and she didn't want to travel all the way back home. Not yet. Not without giving it at least one more try. She sighed. At least Mrs. Graham seemed confident her plan would succeed and Willow definitely needed the boost. A maid came and took her to a bathing chamber with a huge tub filled with bubbles. As she soaked, she smiled thinking of the expression Bray would have when he realized where she was staying. That alone made it worth it.

Chapter 36

BRAY PULLED INTO his mother's driveway and debated turning around and heading to his condo. All he wanted to do was crawl under the covers and stay there for a week. He knew it was Thanksgiving and she would be expecting him, but his heart just wasn't in it. He had lost the one woman that mattered. Bray hired a P.I. who was working with local transit to see if someone recognized her and could point them in the right direction. Bray himself had explored several parks hoping to find her in one, but it was no use. She had arrived out of nowhere and disappeared the same. He shuffled up the steps and rang the doorbell. His mother answered with a flourish. She wore a silver ball gown.

"Son. It's so good to see you."

She looked at his clothing and frowned. He wore jeans and a long-sleeve shirt. It was cotton and comfortable.

"I see you didn't get the email about the dress code."

Bray tilted his head. What was his mother up to? She normally did a casual Thanksgiving and a more formal Christmas.

"Sorry, mom. I've been distracted. I haven't gone through my emails in a few days."

She smiled. "No matter. The tux in your closet should still fit. You can just pop up and get dressed."

She left him to greet her other guests.

He trudged up to his old room and looked in the mirror. A couple days of beard stubble made him look more rugged, reminding himself of the cabin and *her*. The one he couldn't stop thinking of. His mother would probably complain, and say he wasn't presentable for her guests. But he didn't care. He'd don the tux and dress shoes, but that was it. Since this was a formal affair, that meant his mother would have invited her social circle as well as family. It meant they would be in the large dining room and ballroom and his evening would be excruciatingly long.

He followed the delicate notes of the piano in between the sound of clinking glasses and polite laughter. He shook hands and gave hugs as familiar faces greeted him.

"Don't you look all spiffy in your tux," said his favorite Aunt Ophelia.

"Thanks, Aunt O. When did mom switch this to formal? Please don't tell me this is one of her plans to set me up."

She winced and he knew he was screwed. There was no place to escape.

"I only overheard a snippet of conversation before your mother noticed me. It may be nothing." She patted him on the back and went in search of her favorite hors d'oeuvres.

Bray went to the bar. He would need scotch to get through the evening. He bypassed the bartender Tristan, found the bottle he wanted, and poured himself a double.

"That bad?"

He shrugged. "My mother."

"What do you mean? Juliet's the best." Tristan said.

"You have to say that. You work for her."

"Her intentions are always good."

"Yeah, but she's not trying to marry you off."

"Ouch. Yeah, I wouldn't like that one bit. I like my bachelor ways."

Bray chuckled. He knew Tristan's reputation with the ladies. He had worked on his mother's staff for a few years. She knew he was a scoundrel, but she enjoyed his flirting and seemed to encourage the drama.

"You have a date set up for later?"

"Date?" He chuckled.

Bray knew Tristan didn't really do dates. He did hookups.

Tristan stared out at the guests and got that intent look on his face. He was on the prowl. This should be entertaining.

"So, who's the conquest?"

"That one in the tight red dress."

Bray followed his line of sight to a gorgeous blonde. She wore a strapless satin ruched gown that hugged her ample curves. There was something about her that looked familiar, although he couldn't quite place from where. Then she turned and he about fell over. It was Willow. The woman he had scoured the city for. The one he had left back in Bellemont but had no way to reach. The one who punched Gail yesterday. He had been replaying the fiasco at the office in his head over and over, wishing he had done things differently. Bray had stupidly tried to smooth things over with Gail first instead of focusing on Willow. He should have known better. Willow had been skittish from the beginning.

Tristan whistled low. "Check out her ass."

Bray's jaw ticked. He wanted to flatten Tristan.

A growl slipped out and Tristan stared at him.

"Sorry, Tristan, but this one's mine." His voice was gruff and mean. "She's the one I met at my cabin in Arizona."

"Wait. You mean to tell me that hot little number is the nudist?"

Of course, that's what he'd remember from the conversation.

"Yes."

"Lucky bastard." He muttered. "I thought you said she was earthy?"

"She is."

"I guess I expected something different. She looks polished and sophisticated."

That was an apt description. Bray had never seen her with her hair up, and never with makeup. She looked like one of the high society women his mom wanted him to date.

Their eyes met and held for a moment before she glanced away. Willow glided further into the room away from him. What the hell? He followed. Not a chance he'd let her slip away again.

He heard Tristan chuckling behind him.

His mother blocked his path.

"Not now, mom." He glanced over her shoulder trying to keep tabs on where Willow went.

She was talking to some Hollywood actor who was on a charity board with his mother. Willow laughed at some joke.

"Honey, will you announce my new charity assistant for the Muir Woods project."

"What?"

She shook her head. "You never pay any attention to my charities. Fine. I'll do it myself."

"Excuse me." She announced. "Everyone, I'd like you to meet my new assistant. Please make the rounds and introduce yourself to Miss Willow Ashbrook. She'll be handling the donations. Your funds won't just help educate underprivileged children about the importance of sustainability, it will inspire and transform the next generation, giving them a love of nature that will last a lifetime. At this time of year, we realize how much we have to be thankful for, and just what we take for granted. I hope you'll dig deep and donate to this very worthy cause."

Willow waved and was instantly overwhelmed by guests wanting to socialize and donate.

Bray tried to talk to her, but it was no use. Each time he made eye contact, she would turn and strike up a conversation with someone else. She was obviously still mad at how he had left things. He couldn't blame her. Bray wondered how she met his mother and exactly when she had been hired. From what he knew, she'd only been in town a few days.

He messaged his P.I. to let him know Willow had been found.

She's at your mom's?

Yep, he texted back. *Can you stake out the house? I want to know where she goes when she leaves. She's been dodging me all night.*

No problem, I'll be there in 10. His P.I. messaged back.

Bray walked over to the bar and put his empty glass out to Tristan.

"No luck with your nudist?"

"Don't call her that."

He shrugged and poured Bray a scotch. "I call it like I see it."

"Yeah. Well, you won't be seeing anything. So, wipe that look off your face."

He put a hand to his chest. "You think I'd poach? I know the score. You called dibs."

Bray knew he was being testy, but he'd been that way since the beginning with her. Territorial.

The evening didn't improve. For dinner, she was seated at the opposite end of the table. He watched her every move. She had to be aware he was staring, but he couldn't tear his gaze away. Had Willow told his mom they knew each other? Or about her life in the woods? She certainly wouldn't have shared what she was. He wasn't even sure himself. But he knew she wasn't human.

Of course, that didn't stop him from wanting her.

At the end of dinner, Bray went to look for her and ran into Aunt O.

"I see you're quite taken with Juliet's new assistant. I couldn't help but notice over dinner."

He nodded. "Yeah. You could say that."

"Didn't you say mom was trying to matchmake?"

"I might have been wrong about that." Aunt O shrugged. "Seems she's more interested in business tonight. Of course, it hardly matters. She wouldn't have been able to tear your eyes off that girl long enough to introduce you to anyone else."

He grinned.

"A little obvious don't you think?" She smirked. "That's not like you."

No. It wasn't. In fact, he'd never been like himself around Willow. Or at least the version of himself he pretended to be in public. Maybe that's why he loved being with her so much. When he was in the woods, there was no investment board to impress, no customers to schmooze. He could fail spectacularly and there was no one to judge. He had expected Willow to make fun of his attempts in the wilderness, but she was the least judgmental person he'd ever met. It was freeing to have that level of acceptance. No one had ever done that for him, not even his mother. And he had left Willow when things got strange. She had accepted him with all his faults and he hadn't done the same. No wonder she wouldn't talk to him. He'd been a fool. Bray said goodbye to his mom and aunts and headed back to his condo. Willow had already left, slipping out when no one was looking. He felt confident they could now track her since she was working for his mom.

Bray texted his P.I. the next morning.
What's she doing?
There was a lengthy pause. A few minutes passed before he replied.
I lost her for a moment but found her again. She's sneaky.
Bray exhaled. He hadn't realized he had been holding his breath.
Where is she?
Macy's.
That couldn't be right. Bray thought of the few times he took her shopping. She hated it. Plus, it was Black Friday. That would have been her worst nightmare.
Are you sure it's Willow?
He didn't want to doubt the guy but it didn't make sense.
His P.I. sent him a pic with Willow and what looked like another woman wrestling.
Yes. She just fought a gal for the last Coach purse. She won.

What the fuck. Willow didn't even own a purse. Why would she even need one in the woods?

She just presented it to your mother.

Of course, his mother was involved.

Keep following and let me know when they stop for lunch.

Bray received a message hours later with the name of a restaurant.

"Hello, mother." Bray kissed her cheek.

"What a surprise. Will you be joining us?"

Bray watched as Willow ducked behind one of his aunts. She still didn't want to talk to him. He knew she needed reassurance, but they also needed privacy for this sort of conversation.

"That's alright. I just wanted to check on you all. See how you're doing."

"Isn't that thoughtful," Aunt O said.

"Where are you heading when you're done?"

"Your mom's house." Aunt O offered.

His mother's head whipped around and there was some exchange he couldn't see.

She cleared her throat, "Or we could take in a show? It depends on how we all feel."

"Ah. Well, have fun."

That was interesting. Aunt O was being evasive. That could only mean one thing. She was colluding with his mother.

Where is she now? Bray texted his P.I. that evening.

Another long pause.

They were all at your mother's then I lost her again.

Unbelievable. His P.I. was the best.

I put up temporary cameras all over your mom's house. Inside and out. She must be leaving out an exit I'm not covering.

Don't worry. Mom will keep her close. If you keep tabs on her, we'll find her again.

On Saturday, Bray received another text. *You were right. Your mom and Willow just walked into Pleasant Valley Spa.*

One more place he would never have associated with Willow.

Later that evening, he received another message.

They're at a charity event in a jazz bar. I'll text you the address.

Bray debated about going. It was a small venue, not able to hold more than eighty people. It would be difficult to remain unnoticed. In the end, he couldn't help himself. He watched her from the bar. She was everything he remembered. She seemed to captivate the other guests. His mother had chosen her assistant well. It seemed donations were flowing in for the charity. Willow wore another designer gown, this one in black taffeta, an off-the-shoulder number that had Bray salivating. Where had she gotten the money for the dress? Where was she staying?

They lost her again when she left. Bray's P.I. was again embarrassed.

I don't understand how she can sneak past me.

I've got her again. Sunday brunch with your mother at the country club.

Bray showed up and discreetly watched from a distance.

A half-hour later his favorite Aunt stopped by his chair in the lounge and popped his newspaper with the flick of her finger.

"Stop being all nonchalant. We all know you're here."

He should have known. Peeking over a newspaper was so cliché.

"Give it up. You never spend time at the club or your mother's charity events, and suddenly, we see you everywhere"

Aunt O followed his stare. He had the perfect view of Willow in the dining room.

"The girl?"

He swallowed. "Yeah."

"Why don't you talk to her if you're interested? I've never seen you act shy around a woman before. Not since you were little."

"I screwed up, Aunt O. And she's important."

She stared at him for several moments, then seemed to come to some decision and opened her purse. She unfolded a fancy invitation and handed it to him. "Get yourself together. For god's sake shave. You look a mess. We'll be at another charity ball tonight. I'll make sure you two have some alone time."

He looked down at the invite and groaned. Just what he needed. The Hamond mansion. Gail would surely be there at her parent's big charity gala. Did his mother know that Willow had slugged the woman just days ago? Probably not, or she never would have hired her. Somehow, he'd manage to keep the two women separated and rekindle things with Willow. He'd get Aunt O's help and everything would work out. What could possibly go wrong?

Chapter 37

Bray's mother had a seamstress finishing the last-minute touches to an emerald green gown that Willow was to wear this evening. She was trying to balance in the uncomfortable spiky shoes. They were torture on her feet. She couldn't believe what human females endured to seduce males. The plucking and waxing alone was ridiculous. She could understand the makeup, at least that was something she could identify with. Often, a warrior would paint themselves before battle. She didn't really equate a mate to a battle, but she would go along with the human custom. She wanted to draw the line with the spiky shoes. She saw no use at all for appearing taller and unbalanced. At first, it seemed like a challenge, perhaps a dare from one female to another to see if they could carry out duties with a handicap. But this dare seemed to be the norm. The women in flat practical shoes were somehow seen as less attractive. She had puzzled over it for hours and finally gave up. Willow would never understand some human customs.

After another bath, with oils and perfumes that made her nose twitch, she walked to Juliet's suite in her robe. The hairdresser was ready for her. He swished and swirled and twirled her hair into elaborate curls, sweeping them into a complicated up-do that made Willow's eyes cross. He placed an emerald and diamond tiara on her head and she had to admit it looked fabulous. The seamstress hurried in.

"It's ready, Mrs. Graham." The woman exclaimed, "It's my best work ever."

"Oh, Willow, try it on. I can't wait to see it."

Willow was excited too. She knew Bray was coming to the gala. Just getting to see him even from a distance was soothing. Aunt O stopped by earlier, filling them both in on the details. She hadn't liked ignoring Bray the past few days. It went against everything in her being. Willow didn't know how these human games were played, so she took the woman's word for it. If this is what it took to get a male in the human world, she would play along. Apparently, this charity event was going to be huge. It was sponsored by the Hamonds. The family apparently had loads of money. Willow recognized the name, but couldn't place from where, which meant the family was probably from the magical world like the Grahams.

She stepped into the dress and the seamstress zipped her up. It was a form-fitting green lace gown with slits up the side. Taffeta fabric swooped from her hips to pool about her body in layers. The bodice was a sheer nude with strategic lace roses covering her essentials. There was only one full-length sleeve of lace, with the other bare, which she thought might have been a mistake. The seamstress assured her this was couture, whatever that meant. Willow spun in a circle and Juliet let out a gasp.

"Oh my. You are so beautiful, my dear. Bray won't know what hit him."

Willow frowned. These human phrases continued to confuse. Hit him? She didn't want to hurt him. Just make him want her as badly as she wanted him. Oh well, Mrs. Graham seemed to know what she was doing. She smiled and it was impossible not to smile back.

"I've had so much fun these past few days. I've always wanted a daughter. But a daughter-in-law, well, that'll work too."

"In law?"

She nodded.

It was another term she needed to look up.

They pulled up to an enormous building called a 'mansion' in one of the fanciest cars she had ever seen. It had tinted windows and seats running all along the interior walls. The car even had a bar, which Willow was immensely grateful for. Both Juliet and her clinked chilled glasses of aged whiskey.

"To victory."

Bray's mother exited first and looked around before she signaled for Willow.

"Now." Juliet commanded.

The chauffeur appeared and offered his hand. She awkwardly climbed from the car, grateful for the help.

"Thank you."

Bray's mother held out her arm to escort her inside. They had agreed on this after much debate. Juliet had watched her walk in the new heels and sighed dramatically. She thought Willow would make more of an impact arriving solo, but Willow had insisted she needed help on the steps. Aunt O had come up with blueprints of the house and garden to strategize the best place to stage and present. The two talked for hours about setting and mood, lighting and music. She would enter the house, make one full turn around the ballroom, then head to the gardens. Aunt O would secure a gazebo in the shadows where she would direct Bray at the appropriate moment. It all seemed a little over the top to go through a battle plan of the evening's events. But Bray's mother seemed certain, and there was little dissuading her when she set her mind to something.

"Don't forget to lift your skirt at the steps."

Willow nodded.

"Chin high, my dear. Remember you're a goddess."

Just inside the doorway, Juliet released her to talk to an old friend. Willow bolstered her nerve. She just had to swim through the sea of humans once around this enormous room, then she could exit to the safety of the gardens. She could do this. Of course, she noticed Bray right away. His reaction was priceless. He was taking a sip of champagne and sucked in a deep breath at the same time. An older gentleman tapped him on the back as Bray coughed and wheezed.

"Excuse me." Willow sauntered past. She couldn't help the slight smile that formed on her lips.

After her round where she was stopped numerous times to discuss the charity and where to make the donations, she slid out into the gardens and breathed a sigh of relief. She was going to take off those dreadful heels as soon as no one was looking. Willow delicately touched rose petals and ran her fingers through the leaves of the sculpted shrubs. Aunt O was waving to her. She made her way further along the path.

"Did I go slow enough?" Willow asked.

Aunt O looked over her shoulder. She grinned.

"Perfect. Just perfect. He's heading this way. I feel a little bad deceiving Bray like this, but it's for his own good. Sometimes men need a little shove now and again. I see something real special when he looks at you, Willow. You're the one."

With that, Aunt O left her alone in the gazebo. She turned to watch as Bray walked along the path. He spoke briefly to his Aunt and continued closer, never taking his gaze from her. Willow felt like she was being stalked and it gave her a thrill. She hadn't noticed what he was wearing before, but now in the moonlight with that wild, smoky gaze, he looked dangerous. She didn't think he could look better than he did in worn jeans and a flannel, but him clean-shaven in a black tux sent shivers down her spine.

"Are you planning to ignore me again?" He leaned against the entry of the gazebo.

Willow turned toward the bench at the back. She could sense him following deeper into the shadows. She sat and pulled off her shoes. He was there in a heartbeat, kneeling at her feet.

He started massaging her feet without a word.

She groaned, long and throaty. If anyone had overheard, they would have thought something else was going on in the gazebo. It made her smile. It would be good for these uptight humans. It might add a little spice to their very dull lives.

"Bray?" A female voice called from the path.

What the hell? Someone had overheard. Willow straightened her skirt.

It was Gail. What was she doing here?

She stopped when she saw Willow.

"You." Her voice lowered to a growl. "What are you doing at my parent's house?"

That's where she remembered Hamond from.

"I'm here with Juliet Graham helping with the fundraiser."

"You're the new assistant?"

"Yes."

Bray watched as the women circled each other.

"The makeup can't hide it."

"What?"

Willow knew she was being mean and petty, but she just couldn't help it.

"The bruise."

Gail attacked. She got in a few punches and kicks before Bray pulled her off. Willow was impressed. The woman hadn't offered much of a challenge back at his office, but she had some strength behind her jabs.

Willow felt liquid on her lip. A little blood, or rather sap was leaking from her split lip. She grabbed hold of a vine and healed herself. Others were rushing over to witness the commotion.

"What's going on?" Juliet asked.

"She assaulted me!" Gail screamed.

Willow cocked out a hip and stared at the woman.

"At his office." Gail corrected. "But she baited me here." She turned to Bray. "Tell them."

He groaned, looking up into the sky. "It was all a big misunderstanding." He explained to Willow. "Gail was setting up an interview for her father's magazine. Nothing is going on between us."

Willow gulped. Could that all be true? Had she misread the signs? Maybe she had jumped to that conclusion rather quickly.

"And it was so not worth the trouble." Gail rubbed her cheek, smearing the makeup from her bruise. A larger crowd had formed around them.

"Daddy, I want her gone."

"Fine by me." Willow held out her hand to Bray. With a grin he took it.

"Not a word, mother." He glared at Juliet. "No more games." He turned to Aunt O.

Mrs. Graham looked offended with a hand to her chest, but Willow knew better. It was all an act. Juliet winked at her.

She grinned ear to ear. It worked. Although maybe not quite as they planned. She was leaving hand in hand with Bray. She left her pointy shoes and that devil woman Gail back at the party.

"Where are we going?" Willow asked as she jogged to keep up with him.

"My place."

His words were so gruff, they filled her with anticipation.

Bray's impatience with the valet was adorable. His mother's chauffeur approached him cautiously.

"A note from your mother, Mr. Graham."

Bray held out his hand. "She always has to have the last word."

He looked at the note and snorted. Bray shoved it in his pocket.

Willow wondered what that was about.

"No more interruptions." Bray locked the condo door and walked them back to his bedroom. She grinned recalling how they had raced to the elevator. Her claustrophobia had barely registered over the lust. Bray looked ready to tear the dress from her body, but she knew his mother had spent a fortune on it.

"Bray, quick the zipper's in back. It's hidden." She turned around.

He managed to find it and she wiggled out of the dress. It pooled beneath her on the floor.

"No underwear or bra." He breathed.

"Not with that outfit."

"I can't wait." Bray shoved her knees to the bed.

She watched over one shoulder as he yanked his pants to his knees and slid on a condom. He was inside her in one smooth thrust.

She made incoherent grunts as he pounded her into the bed. It was fast and brutal and oh so perfect. Gaia, she had missed him. This was exactly what she needed. Before long, they were both coming hard, screaming with pleasure.

He separated for a few moments to throw out the condom and finish undressing. That was fine by her. She couldn't move. Her face was still planted in the pillows, knees apart, and ass in the air. Her body thrummed with happiness. Bray carried her limp form to the top of the bed settling them both under the covers. With her head on his chest, he smoothed a palm over her cheek as they snuggled together basking in the afterglow.

"I'm so sorry, Willow. I don't know what came over me. I felt like an animal."

She thwacked him on the chest. "It was perfect. You're ruining the moment. Don't you dare screw this up."

"My mother said the same thing."

"What?" She sputtered.

"I mean about not screwing things up. That's what she said in the note. I tend to overanalyze my relationships. My mother knows this about me. She must really like you."

"Um. That's nice, but do you mind not discussing your mother right now?"

"You're one to talk. You've been her assistant for days. How did you land that job?"

"It's kind of a funny story, but I should probably start at the beginning."

He smoothed a hand through her hair and kissed her head. "Go on."

She let out a deep breath and turned to him.

His eyes held no anger, no judgment, just expectancy.

"I'm a Dryad, and a Guardian—or rather was a Guardian of the Coconino Forest. There are more magical creatures in the forest than you can imagine. You've met quite a few already. On Halloween, you saw through the illusions. We have protection methods in place to keep us hidden. One of those was used on you."

"How?"

She bit her lip. "You were shot with a dart. It was laced with something to make you forget. It lowers your inhibitions and gives you short-term amnesia."

"So, I wasn't black-out drunk?

"No."

"You know it killed me knowing I couldn't remember our first night together."

"I know, and I'm sorry I couldn't tell you."

"What happened that night?"

"So much. That was when I asked the Sprite leader to give you the Serce test."

"The what test?"

She smoothed a hand over his chest rubbing in circles. "It's used to test your soul. The basic one tests soul purity and the advanced tests for eternal soulmates. It's a rare magical connection, the deepest one can feel for another. Our bodies, minds, and souls are united into an unbreakable bond."

He held her chin. "And what did you find out?"

She grinned. "Your soul is pure, and yes. We are eternals. The test was done, and the results were the same. Twice."

"Then why did you leave the next day?"

Willow frowned. "The Sprite leader, Fuath, said it didn't matter. Council wouldn't accept a human as my mate. You're forbidden."

"And now?"

She shrugged. "Council kicked me out. So, I'm free."

"Are you oversimplifying?"

"Maybe. But I can't concentrate anymore. Your erection is digging into my hip and I need you again."

Bray rolled her underneath him and kissed her. He slid his cock over her mons and she rocked her hips and gasped.

"Anything else I should know?"

Willow groaned. "I blush green, not red. It's why I always had to hide when we had sex."

"That's why you wouldn't allow sex at first? Or why you couldn't allow yourself to come?"

"Yes. I was concerned you'd see my skin and panic. But we don't have to worry anymore. You can do anything you want to me. Oh, Bray, I'm yours."

His eyes gleamed. "Anything?"

He took her lips in a fierce kiss. Licking and biting. She wrapped her legs around his waist as he ground against her. His cock met her folds and pressed in, just the tip. Their wide eyes met and he cursed. "Well, maybe not anything."

Willow wanted to wipe that look of regret from his face. He started pulling away. She used her strength to pull him back forcing his cock inside her.

"No lies between us. I said what I meant. Anything. I want nothing between us. Damn it." She growled.

"Are you sure?"

Willow didn't waste words. She flipped him onto his back and rode him hard.

His eyes devoured her every move. He really was visual. His eyes were wild, darting from her bouncing breasts to her hips, to her thighs to where they connected. He pinched a nipple with one hand and rubbed her clit with the other. She threw her head back and moaned. The sensation pulled at her core.

"Fuck. I feel you tightening. You're going to make me come so hard."

Bray put his feet flat on the bed and pounded into her, gripping her hips. She whipped her head back and forth crying out his name over and over. The intensity was almost frightening. It kept building. He lost his rhythm for a moment, and then his speed was almost blinding. He yelled out his climax and it released hers in an explosion that sent her spiraling over the edge. Her body collapsed like a rag doll. Their pants sounded loud in the quiet room. They lay unmoving, relearning how to breathe.

With a hoarse voice, she mumbled, "That was—" She paused. Her mind had blanked. Willow couldn't think of the word for it.

"Yeah," Bray muttered.

Exactly. There were no words to describe.

The next few weeks flew by as Bray took her to all his favorite hangouts. She had already met his closest friends in the woods, but he had so many acquaintances and business associates as well. By the end, she felt like she had met half the city. She loved all the parks he took her to, especially Golden Gate Park. The Winchester Mystery House was bizarre, and the sounds from the Wave Organ were hilarious. They met friends at underground bars, went dancing in clubs, and played laser tag and video games in arcades. The first time she experienced the ocean she was blown away by the waves. It seemed like they had explored a lifetime of experiences in those few short weeks.

"Willow honey. Time to get up."

"Again?" She yawned. The man was insatiable. She glanced out the window. It was still dark. Dawn was still hours away.

He chuckled. "No sex. I have something special planned and we have to get on the road."

"No sex?"

"Don't tempt me. Throw on some clothes, and I'll pack snacks for the road."

She stretched and found a dress that was less wrinkled than the rest. Willow found Bray in the kitchen looking through the cabinets. He was bent over and Willow wanted to grab his ass and pull him back to the bedroom, but his body vibrated with excitement. Whatever he wanted to show her was important. She sighed and went in search of the bathroom. After brushing her teeth and splashing some water on her face, she called herself ready and joined him at the front door.

Willow drifted off on the drive.

"Wake up, sleepyhead. We're here."

It was moments before dawn. The fog was thick as she looked out the front window. Just ahead of them was a row of Monterey Cypress trees forming an arch over the road. He parked and held out his hand. As the sun touched the treetops, they walked hand in hand underneath the twisted limbs intertwining above them. She touched the trunk of one tree and felt the harmony resonate through her. She knew by the look of surprise on Bray's face, he felt it as well. Willow hadn't realized she had been missing the connection to the trees until that moment. She had been away too long from her forest, and felt a powerful need to go back. She wondered how best to pose the question to Bray. The trees swayed back and forth, dancing to the surge of power. Her Dryad magic flowed through Bray like a conduit, but as it cycled, she realized it wasn't just her power and the trees. Bray had added to the mix. Her eyes flew open with surprise. She had never felt such a steady stream from a human. It was one more level of proof they were perfect together. They shared their energy and the trees shared their joy. She wasn't quite sure how long they stood reconnecting to the earth, but by the time they were done, the fog had lifted and the sun shone brightly in a cloudless sky.

"I've more to share with you, my love."

He escorted her back to the car and they traveled back where they had come from. She had missed so much scenery on the drive in. The view was gorgeous. Tall rocky cliffs against a backdrop of the turbulent ocean. Bray gave her a tour of the lighthouse, a place she found immensely fascinating. It had such a rich history. After learning about how many ships had met their doom against the rocks, she lost her desire to sail. Bray had offered to take her out on the ocean, but she forcefully declined. They walked down the steps to an overhang to watch the elephant seals settle into a cove just below. Willow thought it would be fun to go visit, but they realized too late that the males were busy battling with one another for territory. Bray's attempt to replicate the trumpeting sound met with hilarious results. Another bull chased him off thinking he was trying to hit on his harem of females.

"Maybe next time, we bring an interpreter." Willow laughed.

He had a picnic lunch planned on a private beach. It had been prepared by a catering company and set up for their arrival. It, of course, had all of Willow's favorites. They explored the inner trails of Point Reyes National Seashore finding natural treasures and reconnecting to the land.

At sunset, he took her to yet another beach.

"I have something to ask you." Bray swallowed, going down on one knee.

Willow's head tilted. "I'm not wearing heels. I don't need a foot rub."

"Please let me do this right."

She pursed her lips and gestured for him to continue. It must be another human custom.

"Willow, you are my world."

Aww. Her heart pounded. He was making another romantic gesture. This day had been filled with them.

"I want you to be mine in all ways. Will you marry me?"

He pulled out a ring from a tiny velvet box. Bray slid it on her finger and she melted. It was a gold band of tiny vines intertwined with emerald leaves.

"Say yes."

Willow nodded. She knelt, joining him on his knees.

"You are everything to me as well. I can't wait to take you as mine in front of my family. I think a May ceremony would be perfect. We could hold it on Beltane in the Coconino Forest. I have the perfect place."

Bray rubbed the back of his neck. "Well, my mom may want it a bit sooner."

Chapter 38

B RAY STARED AT his radiant bride as she adjusted the seatbelt. She fussed with her satin gown in frustration. He smiled. Willow wasn't used to such a fancy dress, even with all the practice and parties, it wasn't really her. Not that she had much of a choice. His mom had insisted on taking Willow shopping at an upscale shop for wedding couture. She had protested the need, but his mother was a force of nature. He grinned recalling Willow's bewildered expression. She had no idea how to tell his mother no. *Yeah, I've been having that same trouble for years.*

Even though Willow was planning an official pagan binding ceremony in the spring, his mom wanted them married before they left. Somehow his mother had acquired a birth certificate and driver's license for Willow, so she could legally wed her son. It didn't make a whole lot of sense since the I.D.s were fake, but it made his mother happy. The wedding had been a simple courthouse ceremony in San Francisco.

Just before the wedding, his mother had shocked him with a revelation about his father. He was a Druid. While his official job title was a botanist for a pharmaceutical company, he had also worked with the magical community healing forests all over the world. He had been killed in South America during a business trip and the company had paid a fortune as a settlement. She alluded to mysterious circumstances surrounding his father's death, but she refused to give details. Soon after his dad died, she severed her ties to the magical community. With a tear to the eye, his mother admitted his father would have loved seeing the two of them together. A Druid and Dryad were a perfect match. Willow invited his mother to the pagan hand-fasting ceremony on Beltane and his mother accepted. She was excited to immerse herself in the magical world once again.

Willow clenched his hand hard. "Is it always this loud?" She yelled.

Bray nodded as they roared down the runway.

Her eyes went wide when the plane lifted into the air. She seemed to calm once they leveled off.

Bray turned to look at his new wife. "Ok. Spill."

She took a deep breath and faced him. "You must understand, I may have deceived you in the past, but there was a good reason. Your cabin was built around a very special tree. There are at least three in every magical forest. One represents the mind, another the body, and the third the heart. Each must survive and thrive to keep the forest healthy."

"The Rainbow Eucalyptus growing inside the cabin?"

"It's the heart. Knowing who your father was, it makes sense why you were so drawn to it in the first place."

"Why all the deception?"

She sighed. "Humans aren't usually good to nature. It was too great a risk for you to stay. At first, we had no idea what you'd be like. For all we knew, you might cut it down. We couldn't let that happen. It needed protection at any cost. So, we might have, you know," she rolled her wrist, "caused a little mischief. Made the cabin a little less appealing."

He thought about all his mishaps when he first moved in.

"The ladder?" Bray asked, "That was you?"

"Yep, and the broken dock." Willow said, "And the vines blocking the road. We had hoped you'd get lost. Oh, and the bear and the mosquitos and all the garbage."

Bray's eyes went wide. "You arranged all that to get rid of me?"

Willow shrugged. "Yeah, and that was just the first day you moved in. We did tons more after that."

"It seemed the wilderness hated me in the beginning. No matter what I did." Bray's eyes glittered. "I have so much ammunition to hold over my sexy new wife. So much she needs to atone for."

Willow pouted, "But that was before I got to know you and fell in love." She fluttered her eyelashes and gave him a tender kiss on the cheek.

"Are you going to use that in every fight?"

She grinned. "Probably. So, best plan on losing. It'll be easier that way."

"Never." Bray said and started tickling her.

She swatted his hands. "Not fair."

Willow pointed at the flight attendant. "Look, our drinks are here. You need to behave. I watched that safety video before we took off."

"So, tell me what my mother gave you after the service that made you flush such a dark shade of green?"

"Hmm?" Willow munched on a few nuts. "Didn't she tell you?"

Bray shook his head. "She told me to mind my own business because I would find out soon enough." He put his hand on her knee making small circles, going up her inner thigh. She held her breath. "What are you doing?"

"Getting my sexy wife to spill her secrets."

"Fine." She giggled. "I promised to tell you everything." Willow pulled out a catalog from her carry-on. "Your mother enrolled me in this club. I get something new every month. I'm wearing the first one."

Bray flipped through a few pages and his mouth went dry. His mother had enrolled his new wife in a lingerie-of-the-month club. Geezus. That's one way to fast track the grandkids. He turned page after page. Each new picture revealed less fabric. He imagined Willow in those little scraps of lace and silk and had to adjust himself. And she was wearing one of these outfits right now. Fuck. He debated on asking her which one. The flight attendant must have noticed Bray's predicament when changing out fresh drinks. She handed him a blanket with a wink. Willow had already told the woman they had just gotten married. Bray explained that her wedding gown had been a dead giveaway. The flight to Flagstaff was sexual torture, anticipating everything they would do back at the cabin. Willow curled into his side, trying for secret touches under the blanket. It kept him primed. He distracted her with snacks and questions. Before they landed Bray discovered that her skin flushed green when flustered as well as when she was aroused. Willow had been so concerned early on that he would discover that completely inhuman trait. That's why she always wanted it dark. She whispered that her best orgasm had been in Flagstaff when he allowed her to blindfold him. That had been the first time Willow hadn't worried he would see something odd. He had found that act incredibly kinky and loved the experience as well. Bray got her to promise a repeat. The plane ride continued to drag on, the drive out to the cabin even longer.

They stood on the front porch as Bray tried to explain the custom where a groom carried his bride over the threshold.

She stared at him, "But my legs work. Human customs are just weird."

She grudgingly agreed after he kissed her senseless. He carried her into their cabin and realized it felt like home. Bray grinned knowing how to win fights in the future. She couldn't resist his kisses. Willow told him that his lips tasted like the sweetest berry she had ever tasted.

He set her down in his bedroom and went to work on all those buttons. Bray wanted to rip the dress from her body, but they had waited through the plane and car ride. He could be patient for a few minutes more. After unbuttoning the last one with trembling fingers, her wedding gown slid down her hips and pooled on the floor at her feet. She stood before him surrounded in satin. The tiny white lace panties covering that lush backside had him stiffening harder than he thought possible. When she turned to face him, he got the full impact of those beautiful breasts, perfectly displayed in a white satin and lace push-up bra. They seemed barely contained, ready to spill out at any moment. Her stiffened nipples made his mouth water. Bray couldn't wait anymore. His lips wrapped around one tight point. He gave a tug with teeth licking the fabric and watched the green flush of her skin. Bray smiled realizing how much he would grow to love the color green. He licked the other nipple and heard her panting. She rocked her hips in time with the flicks of his tongue. They had waited long enough. Four hours on a plane and an hour drive. Foreplay was over. His wife was strung tight. It would be a quick release this first time together. But he promised himself he would last the whole night. He never wanted her to regret making this commitment to him.

"Strip for me, love."

Willow looked up from blonde lashes, cheeks flushed, body shaking with excitement. She roamed her hands over her breasts cuddling herself before she undid the front clasp. He stared as he quickly undressed, throwing his clothes in a pile. She hadn't even removed her panties yet. He grabbed her around the waist pulling her with him to the bed. Willow laughed at his impatience. Bray captured her lips and she moaned against them, rubbing her body along his length. He stopped her movements, barely controlling himself. He kissed down her body ripping off the lace panties amazed by his profound need to possess this woman.

"This is mine." He gave her a fierce look as he palmed her mons. "I won't share." She nodded and her legs fell apart in surrender.

He feasted like he was starving. She tasted like honey. His honey.

"You are so sweet." He said in between licks. She cried out, already coming. He kept the relentless flicks of his tongue. Sucking on her little clit until she screamed with pleasure. Her skin flushed a deep green and her hazel eyes flickered with bursts of color.

She was still spasming from the orgasm when his shaft met her opening. The bulbous head pulsed at her folds. They gazed into each other's eyes for a heartbeat. He wanted to tell her how much she meant to him, but he was at a loss for words. He thrust home in one plunge and something clicked. Bray spoke ancient words in a language he didn't know, but seemed to understand the meaning. It was a vow of devotion and love to his eternal soulmate. She seemed to recognize the language. Her lips parted, and she gazed at him with wonder. Bray tried to hold still, allowing her to adjust to his size, but his wife couldn't wait. She rocked her hips.

"Please, Bray." She panted.

He smiled. "Impatient, my love?"

Bray began with slow measured pumps and watched with amazement as her eyes changed. Twin orbs swirled with a rainbow of blue, green, and brown. It was mesmerizing. She gazed up at him like he was her entire world. He could grow addicted to those looks. *Connection.* One he had waited for his entire life. They held each other's gaze coming together harder than ever. The cabin seemed to shake but he didn't stop pounding into her. He threw back his head and roared his climax. She cried out burying her nails into his back, scratching his arms. Her pussy was milking every last drop of his seed, demanding it. They lay panting afterward, unable to speak. On shaking arms, he rolled over keeping himself buried deep within her. Willow lay sprawled across his chest, giving kisses to his torso, lavishing praise on her husband. He couldn't believe how happy he was. This was what his life had been missing for so long.

His dick twitched inside her and she laughed. The vibrations made him laugh as well. He pulled out and hugged her close, giving kisses to her forehead, her nose, and cheek.

She leaned up on her elbows. "Can we do that again?"

Bray laughed at her enthusiasm. Didn't he promise himself on the plane he would go all night? "Yeah, but I think I'll need a few minutes."

Willow crawled down his torso and licked his shaft. It was still sensitive, but he couldn't move. He watched in bewilderment as she ministered to his cock, lovingly rubbing her lips back and forth. It didn't take him long to recover. His sexy wife jumped off the bed and grabbed something from the floor. It was the satin sash from her dress.

As she wrapped it over his eyes, she whispered in his ear, "Didn't I promise you a repeat?"

Willow seemed to want control this round. He was more than willing to accommodate. She rode him hard, bringing him to the edge several times before allowing them both to come. By morning, Bray had fulfilled his promise. He had lasted until sunrise and they had both collapsed into a deep sleep. By afternoon, they woke to a loud pounding at the front door.

It was one of the Bacchus brothers, the enormous bald one. Bray was surprised by his appearance. It wasn't necessarily that the male wore no jeans or shirt today. His bottom half was hairy. Really hairy, like thick fur hairy. He looked down at his feet. His eyebrows rose. Not feet. Hooves.

"Willow, we have company," Bray yelled.

Willow came bounding from the bedroom wearing nothing but concern.

"Clothes, woman."

She gave a 'pft' hand gesture and escorted their guest to the living room.

"Olie, what's happening?"

Bray wrapped his arms around her from behind, covering her breasts with his hands. He didn't like this feeling of jealousy. The only reason Olie got to stay was he didn't outright ogle her bare body. He tried to convince his brain this was normal; she was a nudist after all. If she walked around like this all the time, no one would think it was a big deal. Bray's possessive instinct didn't seem to care. He sat down on the couch pulling Willow next to him and covered her with a throw.

Chapter 39

WILLOW FOUND IT adorable that Bray was concerned Olie might be after her. She was completely safe from that happening. He was the only Bacchus brother that was gay. Most in the magical community were omnisexual, but some preferred a gender. Olie had decided long ago that females just didn't do it for him. Bray had a better chance of being hit on than she did. Her husband rushed to throw on a pair of loose shorts before answering the door. It did nothing to hide his erection.

"So, what's so important?" Willow asked.

No response. Olie was staring at Bray's junk. Willow snapped her fingers. He shrugged and gave her a wink.

"Your boyfriend's packin'."

Normally she would feel jealous, but after last night she felt secure that Bray would never stray even if he too was omnisexual. His vow in an ancient Druidic language had surprised her. It was done as part of a claiming ritual that few used anymore. She wanted to ask him later how he had learned the language. She climbed into Bray's lap, covering them both with the blanket. She wiggled in his lap earning a grunt.

"Stop that." He whispered. His eyes were still locked on Olie's hooves.

"I take it he can see through the illusion."

Willow shrugged. "Yeah. It doesn't seem to work on him anymore."

Olie nodded. "Good. That makes things easier. How much does he know?"

He's got the general lay of the land, just not all the specifics." She sighed, "I wasn't sure how much I could tell him before..."

Bray turned so they faced Olie together. "We are one. There are no more secrets between us." He gave her a fierce kiss, with a little tongue action. She groaned, melting into his embrace. She wanted to kick Olie out and make love to her sexy husband again and again, but Bray pulled back from the kiss too soon. She stifled a moan. Willow licked her lips to get more of his taste while blinking up at him.

Bray's eyes glittered as he stared at her, but he spoke to their guest. "Tell us, Olie. You are here for a reason."

He grinned. "Right to business then. I'll give you the latest from Council."

Bray tucked her back against his chest. He listened without questions for the remainder of the conversation. Olie and Willow discussed political matters of the forest. Bray held her securely in his arms, occasionally tightening his grip when he heard something disturbing. Willow was able to concentrate on Olie since Bray wouldn't let her turn to see his expression. She wondered what he thought of everything that was revealed.

Apparently, Faustino Bacchus's parties had exceeded even his normal levels of debauchery while she had been gone. Olie winced when retelling all the things that had happened. He seemed genuinely embarrassed.

"It's not just the parties, which were bad enough. The forest has rebelled. It's been absolute chaos since you've left. Disturbances with the trees. Unnatural behaviors by the animals. It's raised red flags with the humans. They've sent out teams to investigate. Sprite SWAT has been working around the clock knocking out humans left and right. Red has been working with her military contacts and witch friends from Tempe. The latest story in the media is that there is some sort of chemical that is causing issues and the government is working on the cleanup. It's keeping humans clear from the area for the moment. But that's not all. The squirrels are on strike. No mail is getting through. Suffice to say, Council wants you back as Guardian." He rubbed the back of his neck, "My brother's behavior," he sighed. "Let's just say I'm deeply ashamed. More magical beings are coming forth sharing stories. He's been deemed a security risk."

"What about your mother?"

Olie shrugged. "There are more rumors about her. Nothing concrete about her involvement. But the other Council members are pressuring her. She won't fight you."

This was better than she could have hoped. She felt a little vindicated by their desperation. But did she really want the headache? A month ago, she would have jumped at the chance, but her confidence had grown since then. She saw how other Guardian's ruled their forests. Interactions with their subjects went beyond respect. Guardians were treated with reverence. Willow refused to go back being Council's puppet. She also wanted Bray's opinion. She linked fingers with him and spared a glance over her shoulder. He was right. They were a bonded team. She wouldn't make a decision this important without him.

After Olie left, they made their traditional breakfast. Willow got the tea ready in silence as Bray got out the scones purchased from an airport shop the night before. He still hadn't said anything when they sat down at the kitchen table. When he took a big bite of his scone, she couldn't take it anymore.

"So, what do you think?"

Bray swallowed and wiped a napkin over his mouth and took a sip of tea. "I think we have a lot to discuss. You have way more secrets than I could have imagined."

Willow reached for her cup of tea with shaking hands. The first day of marriage and she was already in trouble.

He reached a hand to steady hers. She looked into his deep brown eyes; they were filled with compassion. Bray leaned forward to brush his thumb over her lower lip. She wanted to climb into his lap.

"I'm so sorry for not telling you. There's just so much." Her voice quavered, "I haven't had time yet."

"Hush," Bray whispered. "We'll get through this." He grinned. "I'm not going anywhere."

The relief was overwhelming. She let out a breath and leaned back into the chair. She nibbled on her scone and sipped her tea. They ate in companionable silence.

Willow smiled at him and let it show how much she appreciated his patience. She leaned forward holding out her hand. He entwined their fingers and she told him more about her job as Guardian describing how she had first been elected when she was sixteen and how Council treated her. He listened, rubbing his thumb in circles on her palm when her body tensed. She talked for an hour. It was a brief overview, but it covered the basics. It seemed to get easier the more she shared.

"Traveling to San Francisco was a real eye-opener. I saw how Guardians in other forests are treated and how they lead. What do you think I should do?"

"Council needs to give you the respect this role deserves. If they aren't willing to do that, you should walk away."

She nodded. It was a bold move, and she wasn't sure how Council would respond.

Later in the afternoon, Olie stopped by to let her know Council would convene at sunset.

Willow wanted to talk to her sisters before then. She reluctantly left Bray to seek them out telling him she would meet him back at the cabin after the meeting to let him know how it went. He left her staggering on wobbly legs after a devastating kiss. She waved at him from the edge of the trees and sprinted off into the forest. Willow felt more of a connection to the forest since she'd been back. It felt like it missed her. Her feet padded along dirt paths as she ran. Tree limbs moved out of her way as she raced to her mother's favorite glade. Her sisters were gathered around the table. She grinned. Olie must have told them.

"Thank Gaia you're back," Red exclaimed. "You have no idea what I've had to do."

"Olie mentioned a little."

"The forest was in downright chaos. Didn't you get your text messages?"

Willow frowned.

"On the phone."

"Oh. That phone thingy kept making these beeping noises. I ended up throwing it in a lake. I think it was defective."

Red groaned. "I was sending you messages to see how things were going."

"Congratulations on finding Bray and bringing him back by the way," Ellie said.

She gave her sisters hugs one by one.

"I'm surprised you could be away so long from your birth tree," Mae said. "I've never been able to manage long trips. I usually grow weak and get sick."

"You know, it made me curious as well. But after a while, I didn't think about it."

Red blew out a breath. "Yeah. That's not typical. You owe me big time. Your tree was reinforced with heavy doses of magic to keep every-thing kosher. I wanted to give you all the time you needed with your eternal to work things out."

"How did you do it?" Willow asked.

"Not me. My witch friends from Tempe." Red ruffled her curls. "Lucky for you, I have them on retainer for emergencies. And lucky for me, they suck at cards. I've won most of what I owed them back."

"Thank you, sis. I don't know what I would have done if I didn't have that extra time. I may have lost him forever."

"So, tell us what happened in the human world?" Mae asked.

Willow relayed all the things that had happened in the last month, her travels, her time in San Francisco, ending with the wedding.

Mae seemed confused by the idea of a ceremony in a big city courthouse.

"So, you're married?"

Willow grinned. "Actually, twice already."

Red shoved her shoulder. "Shut up. You've had two weddings and we weren't invited?" She crossed her arms. "That's it. I had a surprise for you, but forget it. I'm not giving it now."

"Come on. The human courthouse wedding was for his mom, and the other," she blushed a deep green, "it was more of a pledge in the throes. I'd hardly have you witness that."

"What do you mean by pledge?" Mae asked.

She grinned. "Bray is half Druid." Willow explained, "He pledged his love and commitment to me in a Druidic binding while we made love. Don't worry. I still want the traditional pagan hand-fasting, so of course, you're all invited to that in the spring."

Ellie hugged her. "Congratulations, O'ma. I don't think I've ever seen you so happy."

Willow held her arms out as she spun in a circle. "It's incredible. I feel lighter than air, but so grounded." As she spoke the words, her toes formed roots and wiggled in the dirt. It stopped her in mid-spin and she let out a peal of laughter. Vines sprouted from her scalp forming a laurel wreath. Willow's body shimmered back and forth between skin and bark, a Dryad's way of shivering.

Red shook her head. "I've never seen this much emotion from you. Ever."

Mae pointed to Willow's head. "Your crown's back."

Willow touched her temple and felt the wreath. She grinned. Maybe Council had already voted her back into office. It hardly mattered now. The office wasn't this giant scary dead weight hanging around her neck. She had already decided. She could never go back to the way things were. Willow had underestimated her sister's strengths, just as Council had underestimated her.

"I have to apologize. To all of you. I have been in a pseudo-mother role for so long, that I didn't realize you had all grown up. I've been self-absorbed and depressed. I didn't even realize it. I've been going through the motions in a kind of trance. Everything's going to change."

She turned to Red, "Your knowledge on all the technology once I got to San Francisco was invaluable. I never would have found Bray so quickly without you. I would have been lost in that huge city for days or weeks."

Willow knelt by the stone table finding the hole she had sent her sister's gifts this afternoon. Sammy had shown up earlier at the cabin to let Willow know the squirrel strike was over, now that she was back. He agreed to deliver the items personally. He even hugged Bray's leg which was completely out of character for the gruff little guy. Willow pulled out a crystal snow globe with the Golden Gate Bridge and handed it to Red.

Red shook the globe and watched the flakes of snow float around the scene. "Aww. It's a tiny human bridge in a snow storm."

"It reminded me of you because YOU are the bridge. My bridge to the human world. I have completely underestimated you for far too long."

Red cradled the gift to her chest and wiped a tear from her eye. "Come here, you." Red embraced her sister in a giant bear hug that left Willow wheezing with laughter.

"Thanks, sis," Red croaked. "Fine. You earned your surprise, but I'll give it to you later."

"And for you, Ellie," Willow reached again into the hole and dusted off a small stuffed wolf. "Because of your ties to the Werewolves, they were able to get me past obstacles I never would have overcome."

She grinned and snuggled her cheek to the stuffed animal. "It's so soft. I love it, O'ma."

Willow turned to Mae, "And now you, dear sister. I can't believe how blind I've been. I had no idea you had been traveling between forests for years. I'm overwhelmed by the sheer number of contacts that not only know you but who trust you." Willow sighed, "You. Inspire. Me."

She reached into the hole and pulled out a small wooden box and handed it to her sister.

Mae opened it and gasped. Sparkles of light illuminated her face. Magic flowed up her fingertips and two gold strands of leaves wrapped around her forearms forming metal bracers.

She stared at them with wonder. "How did you know?"

Willow shrugged. "I made a few inquiries, found out what you might like."

She knew that Mae wanted to be a true warrior more than anything. Battle bracers laced with protective magic were the perfect gift. Willow could already tell, she was proud. Mae touched the gold with reverence. She threw back her head and giggled.

"Our forest is weak. I realize that now. Seeing other forests and meeting other Guardians has opened my eyes. We are warriors, but I haven't been acting like one. That changes now. We need to build our defenses and increase training."

"Fucking finally!" Mae exclaimed.

Red and Ellie stared at their sister in shock. Willow grinned.

Red shook her head, "Everyone's acting way too weird for me. Mae is swearing. Willow is giving compliments. Next thing you know, Ellie will stop braiding flowers in her hair and I'll lose at cards. The whole world is upside-down and ass-backward. Let's talk about something normal. When is this shin-dig with Council?"

Willow got them seated around the table and passed out refreshments. Sammy had stored those as well as the gifts, minus a few choice nuts for his delivery fee, of course. She went over her concerns and together they came up with a list of demands before officially reaccepting the job. Her sisters told her all about the problems in the forest this past month, promising she had nothing to worry about. Council would give in to any demands at this point.

Red grinned evilly, "I told Council they would regret their decision. Willow, you should make them beg for it." She rubbed her hands together. "Especially that Mother-fucking Bacchus Bitch. Make her grovel."

The ever-diplomatic Mae struck the table with her fist. "The Bacchus family must pay with blood."

Red's jaw dropped. "When did you turn so bloodthirsty?"

Mae shrugged. "I've been that way for a while. I'm just usually quiet about it. Council has been pushing Willow around for years, especially Mother Bacchus." She turned to Willow, "You are negotiating from a position of power. Never forget that. You are the Guardian. Teach them how you wish to be treated. Don't ever allow them to take advantage again. You're an Ashbrook warrior." Mae sat up straight. "Like all of us."

Willow, Red, and Ellie shared a glance. Mae had really come into her own this past month. Where had all this confidence come from? Good for her.

She nodded. "Mae, you're right. I'm no one's pushover anymore. And neither, it seems, are you." Willow inclined her head giving Mae her due.

Mae nodded back with a fierce grin.

All four of the Ashbrook sisters entered the sacred circle of trees and stood before Council in full war regalia. Mae had suggested this as a show of power and solidarity of the Ashbrook clan. They formed a unified front before the bench. Willow stood with her chin held high, glaring in defiance directly at Donna. Mother Bacchus scowled back at her but after a quick glance at the rest of Council, she bowed her head in respect. Willow's eyes went wide. She made eye contact with her sisters. Red had a huge grin, Ellie had a look of surprise, and Mae shrugged her shoulders and gestured for Willow to speak.

"I have answered your summons to Council. Speak your piece."

The powerful Centaur leader's voice quavered, "Ah, yes. Thank you for coming. I hope your trip went well?"

Willow glared at him.

"Ah right, straight to business then." He took a deep breath. "Willow, we want you back."

"Why?" She stretched out the word.

The Sprite leader's wings snapped open. He fluttered above the bench. "What kind of question is that?"

Red rolled her eyes. "She wants to know why you give a shit?"

Mae dropped her head. Willow thought her sister might be counting.

"I'd like to know why you want me back when a month ago you removed me from office. Don't you think I deserve a reason for this change of heart?"

He bristled, "I would think you'd be grateful."

"Should I? Grateful for the accusation that I betrayed my own people? Grateful you had removed me from a position I've held half my life? On the other hand, maybe I should thank you instead, for unburdening me from such an unappreciated job. Perhaps I should let you fend for yourselves."

"That's not what I meant."

She waved him to silence. "If you want me back, there's going to be some changes. One of my contingencies for reaccepting the role as Guardian is a formal declaration of Bray as my eternal soulmate. There will be no more discussions on this matter. He is mine. This is, as the humans say, a deal-breaker."

There was movement behind her. A gasp from the Council bench made Willow turn. Bray appeared from the shadows. Willow's jaw dropped. How had he gotten into the circle of trees? Was his half-Druid blood enough to make it into the clearing? Apparently. But how would he have known of the location? Abraham approached the bench nudging Bray closer to Willow. *Ah, the ancient TreeAnt.* She hadn't seen that coming. Abraham leaned in to whisper something to the Elven leader. While Council whispered amongst themselves, Bray slid in close.

"I like that outfit you're wearing. The leather is hot."

Willow looked down. She had never considered her battle dress sexy, but by the way Bray devoured her with his eyes, it must be.

She reached a hand out to him. His smile was glorious. Had he thought for a moment she was embarrassed? Half-Druid, whole human, it didn't matter to her. She loved him with all her heart. Their fingers entwined. Vines climbed up between them wrapping around their hands binding them together. She felt whole for the first time in her life.

"He is my eternal soulmate." Willow's voice rang out strong and clear. With chin lifted, she addressed Council, "Our fates are inter-twined." She held up their hands. "He goes where I go."

Donna sputtered, "But he's human."

Abraham's deep gravelly voice boomed in the clearing, "You are mis-taken, Donna Bacchus of the Coconino Satyrs. He is only half-human. His other half is Druid. The combination is rare. His heart is pure and he is Willow's eternal. The forest has spoken. Do you not see the binding?"

Willow grinned at her sisters. They took a step back allowing Bray to remain at her side. It was a great sign of respect. They were acknowl-edging the union and his place in the forest. So many impossible things were happening at once. Abraham, the impartial observer, was taking a stand. He was not only backing her, he was also backing Bray.

Donna frowned at the glowing vines that bound their hands together.

Abraham shook his branches and spread them wide. "The forest chose Willow Ashbrook for Guardian sixteen years ago. That has never changed. The crowning of Faustino Bacchus was a farce. Did no one question why the forest was in such chaos when she left? Look. She wears the crown of the Guardian even though Council has not voted to restore her status. She brought her eternal back, and the forest acknowledges the union. What I find funny is that Council believes they have a choice in the matter," He chuckled, turning to Willow bowing his branches in a show of respect, "And even more humorous is that Willow still believes she needs to wait for their decision."

Willow's soul over-flowed with happiness. She released that last bit of uncertainty and reached out to the forest, reconnecting herself more completely. Her toes tunneled into the earth breaking the red stone dais with a loud crack. Everything became crystal clear. She had been the puppet for Council for years, but the power had always been hers. She had just lacked the confidence to lead.

"Well, now that's out of the way." Willow smirked, "Any new business to discuss while I'm here?"

Chapter 40

Bray raised his free hand. He cleared his throat. When Willow's toes had tunneled into the earth, he felt like his body had been a live wire. Energy flowed through his veins from her hand into him. He wondered what it would feel like to take off his socks and shoes. Would he feel the flow of energy from the earth as well? He was so new to all of this. That ancient tree being had asked him to come support his new wife. He brought him here for a reason. Bray was familiar with board meetings. If these magical beings had steam-rolled her in the past, he wouldn't allow that to happen anymore. Not on his watch. He may not know all the intricacies of how this Council worked, but he knew things were going well, and now was the time to negotiate for a few job perks.

"Willow will need vacation time."

Donna sputtered, "What?"

"Rok, Rok," said Roz. Surprisingly, Bray knew it to be the raven's version of laughing.

Willow had described the nine members of Council to him, their physical descriptions and personalities. The only one he had met before was Liska, the Shifters' leader. She had mentored him, teaching him about plants and herbal medicines. She nodded to him. One of the nine, was on his side. How could he sway the rest?

The Pixie leader whispered something to the Elven leader. Bray watched the interaction as they talked amongst themselves. They didn't realize how much they were giving away.

He cleared his throat. "Do you have an H.R. department?"

The Gnome's leader blinked slow, "H.R.?"

Red yelled, "Human Resources."

Donna rolled her eyes. "Of course, it is." She sneered. "What did you expect from a human?"

Bray glanced around at the confused faces. He sighed. "I see. No H.R. So, do you have backups for when a Guardian takes a leave of absence?"

"Why would a Guardian need to leave the job?" The Sprite leader spat, "That sounds like negligence of duty."

Willow pleaded with her eyes and shook her head. She wanted changes, but she had mentioned wanting to ease them into things. He knew that was a mistake. If they had taken advantage in the past, they would continue to do the same.

"I got this, honey." He addressed Council. "Maternity leave."

"It's a little early to be discussing this don't you think?" Willow whispered, "I know your mother's hoping, but it could be years before we have kids."

Bray grinned, "You don't know?"

Willow blinked up at him with a bewildered expression.

He whispered in her ear, "You're pregnant."

"I'm what?" Willow shrieked. She looked around the clearing. Everyone was watching the two of them.

Abraham snickered, "Willow, my dear. You are still not listening to the trees. The young is two months along."

"That means," Willow's legs seemed to give out. Bray caught her from behind. "That means our first time," She gazed at him from over her shoulder. He rubbed his cheek to hers.

"Apparently, my love."

Bray thought she was waiting to surprise him after the first trimester, but she hadn't known. He felt horrible for shocking her like this and in front of everyone. He sighed. Sometimes he really needed to learn to shut the fuck up.

"You're happy, aren't you?"

She turned in his arms. Her eyes sparkled with swirling colors; her skin flushed green. "I couldn't be more ecstatic." Willow gave him a scorching kiss.

It made the forest creatures hoot and howl and stomp their hooves.

Willow faced Council with determination, "Well now. I think the birth of a future Guardian warrants a little time off."

Abraham cleared his throat, "If I may offer a suggestion."

The clearing grew silent. Bray noticed a pattern. Whenever the TreeAnt spoke, everyone quieted. He wondered how rare it was for this creature to speak to get such a reaction every time.

"Maple Ashbrook would be a good substitute."

Willow nodded. "Yes, she would be perfect."

Liska's voice rang out, "All those in favor."

Everyone from Council tapped the bench. Willow's eyebrows rose. A unanimous vote must be unusual.

Willow smiled at Mae who had a wide grin. "So, any other new business?"

The Satyr leader, the one Willow called Mother Bacchus, massaged the back of her neck and avoided eye contact. What was she so nervous about?

Red nudged Willow's shoulder. "Here's your surprise, sis."

A Goblin guard escorted Bella to the stand. She scowled at Willow.

The Elven leader cleared her throat, "Welcome, Bray. I'm Terra, the local Elven leader." She nodded to both Willow and Bray, but spoke to the crowd, "Bella Bacchus of the Coconino Satyrs is brought before Council court to answer for her crimes. We have information that she was involved in the forest fire."

"That's bullshit and you all know it." Bella screamed, "Why would I start something like that?" She pulled at the rope. The Goblin jerked it forward and Bella lost her balance falling to her knees. She growled at the guard.

Bray wondered how well he knew this woman. Bella had been so helpful in the past, giving him advice, and spending so much time with him. She had made him feel welcome when he'd been lonely. Had it all been an act? If so, she'd been really good at it. She had seemed to understand him so well, sympathizing with how he must be feeling being away from everything familiar. He considered her a friend. But now her disguise was melting away before his eyes. Bella had hooves just like her brother, and extremely hairy legs under her flouncy short skirt. When the Goblin yanked the rope again, her skirt flew up revealing a tail. Bray's eyebrows rose. But it wasn't the physical attributes that were the most disturbing, it was her behavior. She was rude and brash, and downright mean. He wondered how she could have manipulated him into trusting her. He never thought of himself as naïve. He thought back to his interactions with Willow in the beginning. Bella had been the one to plant the seed of doubt about Willow. She had taken the drone with her to the party. Bella had brought the video back to him. That was what caused their initial breakup. Had she plotted against them this entire time? What wasn't this woman capable of?

They heard the forest creatures' testimonies, anyone who had seen Bella before and after the fire. Several animals had witnessed her talking to Lucian right after he had set the fire. She saved her own skin and hadn't warned a soul. Later, after the fire had been put out by the Ashbrook sisters, other animals overheard a conversation between Bella and Willow. Bella had given Willow a scroll sent from Council outlining sections of the forest that needed healing. This caused a heated discussion between Council members. No one had given such an order. Bella was caught in a lie. Bray realized that's why Willow hadn't come over that first day after the fire. He thought Willow would've stopped by to discuss what happened. They could have talked things through. He knew he had left things badly. The day after, he had to fly home. His mother had sent an urgent message. He wasn't sure if any of this information would be useful. He whispered to Willow the different things Bella had done while they were dating.

She gasped, "And not only that, she repeatedly tried to sabotage the relationship with my eternal." Willow glared at her, "That's so uncool, BB."

Bella stuck her tongue out.

The Centaur leader stood. "These are all serious crimes. Knowing who started the fire and not coming forth. Not warning anyone about the fire. Lying to the Guardian about a message from Council. Trying to sabotage an eternal union. You should know how sacred an eternal is. Bella, state your defense."

The Goblin loosened her hands from the rope and she rubbed her wrists. "First, all you have is hearsay from the lower creatures. There's no proof." She sneered. "Even from the testimony, Lucian started the fire, period. It was all her ex's fault." She pointed at Willow, "Not mine."

Donna cleared her throat. "It seems from the evidence that Lucian is clearly to blame for starting the fire. Several witnesses saw him get angry and ignite the first tree. It doesn't matter that Bella didn't spread the news. The alarm and buddy system that Willow implemented worked just fine."

Liska looked down at some notes written on the parchment in front of her, "Luckily, there were no casualties from the fire. It's true. The system was efficient and saved lives. No thanks to Bella."

She smirked. Her smug expression nettled Bray. From the looks of things, Bella thought she would get off scot-free. Is that how it worked around here?

He cleared his throat, "Even though she may not have broken any specific laws, surely the nature of her attitude alone warrants some reprimand."

Bella's eyes about popped from her head.

"We don't want to encourage this kind of behavior." He continued, "If you see something, say something. It's everyone's responsibility."

Willow grinned. "I think Bray's got the right idea. I know we haven't punished for things like this in the past, but we should start now. I believe community service would be the perfect reminder to BB on how she should help others before herself."

A low growl trickled from Bella's throat. Her eyes glittered, directing so much hatred at Willow. Council discussed various types of community service. Most agreed she wouldn't be very good at helping relocate animals that hadn't yet found homes. Some of Council cringed when the idea was suggested.

"You can't be serious?" Liska hissed. "We don't want to inflict more harm on those poor homeless souls. Really. Haven't they been through enough?"

Roz gave another hearty squawking laugh. Bray took that as agreement.

In the end, they assigned a length of service and where she should report for her community service. Bella would spend the next several months giving blood for healing ceremonies. She would work with the TreeAnts to help restore the land damaged by the fire.

"I can't believe how I'm being treated." She grumbled. Bella glanced at her mother.

Whatever Mother Bacchus shared with her in that piercing gaze made Bella's lips purse together tightly, silencing her complaints. She was taken away by the Goblins.

"Before we get to Lucian's crime, we have one other matter to take care of." Fuath flew to the opposite side of the bench and nodded to Rabuwa, the Goblin leader.

She made a high-pitched sound that was a cross between a yodel and a screech. It sounded like a warrior's cry before battle. Most of Council clenched their ears. Suddenly, four Goblin warriors had Donna surrounded. They held her at sword-point.

Bray wondered where they had come from. It was as if they had materialized from thin air.

"What's the meaning of this?" Donna squinted at Willow.

Willow and her sisters looked between one another in confusion. Bray was equally puzzled, but then again, he was still trying to wrap his head around the whole magical community in general.

Donna turned her fiery expression to the Council members on either side of the bench. She stopped at Fuath and her eyes glittered with such hatred. She mouthed the words, *You. Will. Pay.*

His wings stutter-flapped, and he moved closer to the Centaur leader.

"Donna Bacchus of the Coconino Satyrs." His voice carried in the clearing as his wings fluttered nervously. "Your crime is treason. We have proof you tried to overthrow the Guardian."

She rolled her eyes. "Political ambition is not proof, you morons."

The gray stone creature turned and faced the accused.

"That's Goron, the Gnomes' leader," Willow whispered.

"Regardless of your motivation, Donna, your actions were reckless." He said with a deep gravelly voice. "You convinced us to take measures." He stared with cold eyes. "The results, I think we can all agree, were catastrophic."

Several Council members nodded.

Roz the raven ruffled her feathers and squawked. "The lower creatures felt it the worst, like a part of our body was missing when Willow left. You said you had everything under control. You were wrong."

Donna shrugged. "How could I have known?"

Tori, the cute little Pixie in pink flapped her wings and flew in front of Donna. "Please understand, Mother B, we voted." She said in a high pitched syrupy sweet voice. "*You* are to blame. It isn't personal."

Something passed between them. Donna launched herself forward trying to snatch the Pixie with her claws. She easily dodged the attack and giggled.

The Goblin guards fell upon her as she screeched and bucked.

They locked Donna in chains and pulled her to her feet.

Bray wasn't sure if anyone else caught that, but it was clear to him, Tori had just indicated that the rest of Council had thrown Donna under the bus, so to speak. The forest creatures were angry and they needed someone to blame. She was their scapegoat. How ironic she was a Satyr.

"You will all pay for what you've done to me. I will not forget this. You can't destroy my family. We built this Council. It was nothing before the Bacchus clan came along."

"Donna, please," the Centaur leader pleaded. "Pay your debt. Serve your time. You are sentenced to one year in the Frost Giant's prison. It will be over before you know it."

She momentarily stopped struggling, "I must get a message to my replacement. Who's it to be?"

Liska the Fox Shifter smiled, "Bo Bacchus will do nicely." Her eyes changed colors, gold, to brown, then black, back to gold again.

"Not him. He won't do what needs to be done. You've doomed us all."

"Aren't you overreacting?" Terra asked.

"No. You don't understand." She yanked at the chains. "None of you do. If we don't give them what was promised, they will come and destroy us."

"Who will?" Terra asked.

Donna shook her head moaning, bucking her body. It was as if she was possessed.

"Take her away." Rabuwa commanded.

"Nooooo!" Donna screamed as the Goblins dragged her off into the tree line.

Fuath flew back to his place on the bench as Donna's voice faded.

"What was that all about?" Bray asked.

"Oh nothing," Willow said, "That's just Mother B's usual theatrics when she doesn't get her way."

The remaining eight Council members didn't seem the least bit concerned about Donna's outburst. They were already in a heated discussion of Lucian's punishment. If no one else was worried, he wouldn't waste his time either. He knew now that Bella was a liar, it would make sense that her mother would be as well.

"Torture is on the table?" Fuath asked.

"Definitely." Terra agreed.

"Execution?" Tori's eyes glittered.

Liska shook her head. "Sorry, but there was no loss of life. Better luck next time, Tori."

She sighed dramatically.

Bray had started out thinking good riddance to Lucian when he was accused, but now he reluctantly felt sorry for the guy. Torture? Execution? What kind of world was this?

"How can they decide Lucian's fate when he's not here to defend himself?" Bray asked. "He can't even tell his side of the story."

"Normally, they would, but in this case, they have too many witnesses confirming he started it. And as you saw before, Council is all about saving face. They need someone to take the fall. Donna's little one-year stint won't satisfy them. Hundreds of wildlife creatures have to relocate."

"I still don't know. Crucifying the guy before he can defend himself just seems wrong." Bray shrugged. "I mean, from what I know of the guy, he's kind of a pompous dick, but something just feels off about this whole thing. Wasn't the guy in love with you? Why would he try to burn down your tree?"

Willow's cute little mouth scrunched. It made him want to kiss her, but this wasn't the time for that. "You're right. It doesn't make sense, but this is how Council works. Sometimes it's not fair."

Bray's eyebrows rose. "Aren't you the Guardian?"

Her lips parted, and her eyes widened. "You're right."

Cyrus cleared his throat. "Council has voted. By scorching the earth, Lucian has prevented the growth on sacred land for many years. The punishment is ten years in jail. Since he lives on the fringe of the forest up in the mountains, he is under Goron's jurisdiction."

"The Frost Giant's jail is just punishment for a Fire Demon." Goron rasped.

"I'd like to add something." Willow interrupted. "If future evidence is presented, we can reopen the case."

Council looked at one another in confusion. One by one they mumbled their consent. Clearly, this wasn't something they were used to.

The Goblin leader stood introducing herself as Rabuwa. She looked like she wore more armor than her body could hold. Rabuwa had a stout frame of three-and-a-half feet. She was packed with muscle and covered with tribal tattoos.

She bowed to them both and turned to Willow, "Since he is your ex, and you are Guardian, it is your right to bring him in. But it would be my privilege to send my top squadron in your stead."

Willow sighed, "I appreciate that. But like you said, it's my duty. I won't shirk my responsibilities just because it's uncomfortable. But I would be grateful for your assistance."

"I'll come as well," Bray said.

Willow's jaw dropped. Council whispered. He wondered why. How difficult could it be?

"I will send someone for his measurements right away. We'll have his armor ready for battle in three days." Rabuwa bowed and took her seat behind the bench.

Yep, Bray had over-committed this time. Fuck. Armor? Battle? He thought they would just go with the Goblin police and watch from the sidelines while Lucian was taken into custody. How much trouble could a jealous Fire Demon give them?

Three days later, Bray shook his head in the mirror. He felt ridiculous. The studded leather tunic was heavy and stiff. He wore it over black jeans. He refused the borrowed leather pants. No way. Bray imagined some dude going commando in the worn leathers and had forcefully declined. He shifted the long sword in the thick belt and sighed. Why would they have given him a weapon? Intel came back with Lucian's last known whereabouts. He was on the outskirts of the Kaibab Forest, not hiding well if he didn't want to be caught. It was normally a seven-hour walk, but the Goblin's leader had a portal medallion. She took her squadron in groups and got them assembled. Willow and Bray were the last ones to transport.

"My spies verified that he's inside The Watering Hole. Rabuwa pointed to the ramshackle shed hidden at the edge of the trees.

Willow nodded. "I'm going in alone."

"No." The Goblin leader protested. "It's not safe. You need backup."

"Bray will be by my side." She grabbed his arm.

He raised a brow. Willow knew he had zero fighting skills, but obviously, Rabuwa did not. The Goblin leader gave a terse nod.

The sign on the door said, 'Protections in place. NHA.'

Willow explained that meant No humans Allowed. Surprisingly, Bray could enter. He was still trying to wrap his head around the fact that he was only part human.

Once he walked in, Bray's attire no longer felt awkward. Most of the patrons wore similar fashion, dressed in leathers and a few even had metal armor. Several people, or rather beings, had swords or daggers sheathed at their hips. A few had back quivers with arrows jutting up to one side. *Just how dangerous was this new world?* Bray added martial arts training to his mental checklist of items he needed to learn in a hurry.

Glancing around the bar, over half the creatures he recognized. At various tables sat Demons, Goblins, Satyrs, and Nymphs. Pixies fluttered from table to table bringing food and drink. No one looked remotely human. Each time he met a magical creature over the past few months, a little more of the mental filter chipped away. After entering the sacred circle a few days ago, whatever illusion remained had shattered. It was surprising how well he was handling it. Of course, his mother had taught him to be tolerant of those that were different. Whenever he noticed some physical difference or odd behavior of someone as a child, she would comment on the beauty and uniqueness of everyone. She had obviously witnessed her share of strange and wondrous creatures when she was married to his dad. It was either that or all those diversity trainings at work were finally sinking in.

Willow spotted Lucian at the bar and nodded in his direction. Bray followed her line of sight. He wasn't surprised to find her overly muscular ex hunched over a drink, but he was surprised by the dark red skin and horns. The TreeAnt Abraham had shared details on how the protection spell worked. It acted like a filter modifying the appearances of its citizens to something humans could accept. Those wards wavered at the edges of the forest and were nonexistent outside the border. Bray recalled Lucian's appearance the last time they met. His physical shape was still the same, but instead of having a dark bronze tan, his skin looked like the color of a pomegranate. His hair was still the same dark shade of auburn with blonde frosted tips, but now there were deep mahogany horns sprouting from his temples. They were only about four inches and curved slightly along his hairline, but it wasn't something he would have missed.

"Watch his horns," Willow whispered. "If they grow, it shows aggression. He won't attack me. I can't say the same for you. Stay slightly behind me at all times."

"Are his horns a threat? They don't look all that big or sharp."

Willow shook her head. "Trust me. He's a grower, not a shower."

"Honey, that means something entirely different to humans."

"What do you mean?"

"Nothing. Go on."

"His horns can extend at least a foot, and the tips get deadly sharp and emit a stunning toxin."

"And you used to date him?"

Willow shrugged and started making her way through the bar. Bray followed a few steps behind. His hand rested on the sword hilt at his side, trying to recall sword fighting scenes from movies. Channeling his inner 'Highlander' he did his best to look menacing.

Willow tapped Lucian's shoulder. He turned and gave a long sigh. "I knew you'd come."

Lucian's red eyes flicked to Bray and frowned. Bray wondered if that was his natural eye color or if they were just bloodshot from drinking. He focused on his horns. No change in size.

"I need to take you in. Do you come willingly?" Willow asked.

"You two really eternal soulmates?"

She nodded.

"If I had known, I never would have come between you."

"You didn't."

"Way to bury the stake." He put a hand to his heart like he had taken a blow.

He stood up slowly and threw a few coins on the bar. Willow gestured for him to go first. She followed him out the front door with Bray bringing up the rear. He was shocked it had been that easy. Or was this a ruse for a chance to escape?

Once they were in the shadow of trees, she gripped Lucian's arm and spun him around.

"What happened?" Willow demanded. "I need to know the truth. Did you really start the fire?"

Lucian took a deep breath and nodded. "Bella and I met up at the lake close to Bray's cabin. She shared a new moonwine recipe from her flask and we went for a walk. We decided to stop seeing each other. No big deal. It had been heading that direction anyway. Then things got fuzzy." He pounded his forehead with an open palm. "I have vague images of anger and jealousy. I felt a spark from my fingertips. Then everything went blank. I passed out. You have to believe me. If I had been conscious, I would have contained the fire. You know that, right?" Lucian seemed so sincere.

"Do you think you were drugged?"

"I don't know." He shook his head. "It's possible."

"Well, I believe you didn't do it deliberately, especially so close to my tree."

Lucian hung his head, "I woke up covered in flames. The whole thing was embarrassing. A Fire Demon almost burning to death. Bella risked herself to drag me to safety."

Willow looked at Bray and frowned. That didn't sound like Bella at all. He might have believed it in the past but he had seen her in front of Council. She only cared about herself. That meant she needed him alive.

Lucian sighed. "Once I regained mobility, it was too late. The fire had grown too large. I wanted to help in some way, call in a few Fire Demon magic users. But Bella told me to leave. She knows the laws since her mother's on Council. Starting a fire is an act punishable by death. My life was forfeit. Bella swore she would make up some story about a camper starting the fire and she would warn everyone as long as I left the forest immediately. I was to stay hidden until she contacted me."

Bray and Willow shared a glance. Bella hadn't warned anyone. She had ratted Lucian out at the first opportunity to save her own skin. What other things had she lied about? Bray noticed Rabuwa's red eyes glow from the shadows. She must have overheard the entire conversation.

"You didn't hide very well."

"No. Not at all." Lucian gave a rough laugh devoid of humor, "The guilt has been eating me alive. I wanted to be caught."

"I'm really sorry, Willow." Lucian shook his head. "Take me in." He held out his hands.

"You're really turning yourself over, knowing what awaits you?" Bray asked.

Lucian stood tall, chin jutting. The epitome of pride. "I'm a Fire Demon. We have honor above all things. I accept my fate. I've settled my debts. My duties as leader have been passed to another. I await my punishment."

Willow nodded. The Goblins came forward locking chains around his wrists and ankles.

"We'll take it from here." Rabuwa bowed, "There is no reason either of you need to journey to the Frost Giants."

Lucian flinched. He shook his head and gave a derisive laugh. "How fitting. Our worst enemies. My execution will gladden their hearts." He took a deep breath. "So be it. I'm ready.

Rabuwa appeared impressed. She shared a look with Willow. Without words they seemed to agree on something. Willow gestured for the Goblin leader to speak.

"The fire caused no loss of life." Rabuwa stated.

The relief on Lucian's face was palpable.

"Your sentence is ten years in the Frost Giant's prison. Because you have shown remorse for your actions, you will be treated with respect." She gave him a slight bow.

"Not death?"

"Nope." Willow embraced him. "Good luck, Lucian."

He gave a half-hearted smile.

She backed away and reached for Bray's hand. The Goblin leader gave instructions to her squadron and they began to march north through the woods.

Rabuwa turned to Willow. "I'm not needed for the rest of the journey. I can portal you both back." She stared north through the trees like she could still see her Goblins leading their prisoner. "This case is not as cut and dry as Council believes. I have more questions than answers. Unfortunately, this changes nothing for the prisoner. If something further is discovered, Council can reevaluate. That was wise of you to add that stipulation during sentencing."

Rabuwa held out her hands. Willow and Bray linked hands forming a circle. The three portaled back to the Coconino Forest. While the world spun, Bray wondered how quickly he could adjust to this new world. Technology changed at a rapid pace, and he had always prided himself on keeping up with those changes. But this was so different. There was so much to learn. Bray would have to start from scratch and leave all his preconceived notions in the dust. Human rules didn't apply here. Looking back all those months ago, he remembered what he had wanted above all else. A challenge. Apparently, he had gotten exactly what he wished, and way more than he bargained for. He stared at his beautiful new wife and she grinned back at him. When the swirls of color subsided and the trees came into focus, a wave of peace flowed over him. Connection. To this forest. To the woman at his side and to their unborn child. Life was pretty darn sweet.

Epilogue

THE DAY HAD arrived. All the final preparations had been made for Bray and Willow's mating ceremony. It was the first of May. The traditional Beltane festival was being combined with their union. The vows would be exchanged at sunset. The Pixies had been working on the sacred circle for weeks. Willow still hadn't seen it yet. It was supposed to be a surprise. Ellie had designed everything in between traveling with her Werewolf buddies.

Bray's mother would be arriving by portal early afternoon and would be bringing her troll friend Oscar. They were deep into discussions about setting up a permanent portal between Muir Woods and Coconino Forest. The witches from Phoenix were working with the powers that be to figure out logistics for permanent stability. Temporary portals could be set up in a few days, but permanent portals required a lot more setup time and magic. Mrs. Graham used her business savvy and finances to convince the witches and trolls to work together for this incredibly profitable business venture. She had a knack for convincing those to her point of view. It was impossible to tell the woman no because that word wasn't in her vocabulary. With the idea of a granddaughter just months from being born, the woman's power of persuasion had doubled. She was an unstoppable force of nature. At times, Willow wondered if his mother was fully human. Mrs. Graham would often distract her when she asked too many personal questions about her past.

A few guests had started arriving last night and were camping out in various parts of the woods, just outside the circle. The Sprites were in a good mood. They were set up as sentry guards watching for any humans that may wander upon the scene. They always enjoyed it when they had full reign to shoot humans.

Willow invited several friends she had met on her trip to California. They had helped on her travel to find Bray. It seemed fitting they should be here to celebrate. The journey had been enlightening in so many ways. Understanding how other forests operated brought clarity to how different Coconino was, and how many changes needed to be made. It was a slow-going process dealing with Council, but with Bray by her side, they were making huge strides on reform.

Beltane was usually a wild affair filled with moonwine and all kinds of debauchery. Red had been more than interested in the Centaur Brothers from Sequoia and Kings Canyon. The twins were quite popular with the females. As a matter of fact, quite a few Nymphs had already given it a go with Chase. The older female Centaurs were reluctant, but the youngest had her eyes on Pax. She was smitten.

"Have you ridden Chase?"

"Nope." Red said, "Been too busy helping with the ceremony."

"Trust me. Before he leaves, you have to ride him bareback."

They watched a few Nymphs talking with Chase get shoved out of the way. Maggie wiggled and bounced her way closer to him. She had gone with traditional Beltane attire, au naturel with the exception of strategically placed body paint. Hypnotic spiral designs decorated her boobs, like she needed help flaunting her body. Chase's eyes were riveted to her chest. She whispered something in his ear and he nodded. She climbed on his back and Chase took off at a gallop.

"Maggie's interested. No thanks. Don't do sloppy seconds."

Willow shrugged. "Well, in that case, can I ask a favor? The Bighorn Sheep Shifters are not used to parties. Can you help loosen them up a bit? I'd love to be able to pay back the Guardian of Mohave for all her kindness."

"So, you want me to get her drunk?"

Willow sighed, "I think she may need a bit more than that. Bri might be a virgin."

"What? At Beltane?" Red screeched, "That's sacrilege." Red put a hand on her hips, "So basically, you want me to get Bri liquored AND laid. I can do that."

"There's something else you should know. In the Mohave Bighorn Shifter culture, they only have sex in animal form."

Red's mouth twisted. "Really. Why? There's way more pleasure in human form."

Willow shrugged. "Not sure. Maybe it's a cultural thing?"

"Don't worry, sis. I'll sex-educate them. Beltane will not be lame on my watch." She held up a flask of moonwine, "I make a solemn promise. Your mating Festivus will go down in history as *the* wildest, most debauched party of all time."

They both took swigs from the bottle and grinned at each other.

"Oh, and don't embarrass Bray."

"Yeaahh." Red gave an evil grin. "Sure thing, sis."

Willow shook her head knowing that Bray was in for it. Well, he had to learn how to deal with her sisters sooner or later. Surprisingly, instead of worrying, she looked forward to all the craziness. Willow would take things as they came. Bray was usually pretty easygoing. She didn't need to worry he would take things the wrong way. After all, he had displayed so much patience time and again when he was getting used to the wilderness. And her eternal had a wicked sense of humor. Even though he grumbled, she knew he loved Red's antics.

"Well, I better run. Ellie is braiding flowers in my hair before the ceremony." Willow cupped her swollen belly. "I need something to distract from this."

"Oh, shut up. You're gorgeous even with your massive baby bump."

She ducked when Willow took a swing. "What? It's a compliment."

It was time. She adjusted the wreath of gardenias in her hair and smoothed her gown. It had been designed by Bray's mother. She had worked with the spiders on it for months. Several adjustments had been done in the last few weeks as her baby bump had grown larger. The gown was gorgeous and sparkly, which she loved. The full-length gown of cream webbing, with gold threads throughout had tiny crystals meticulously sewn in patterns of willow leaves. Willow took a deep breath surprised by her nervousness. She was already married to Bray in the human world, and he had bound her to him as a Druid without even knowing what he was doing. But the handfasting ceremony was a pagan tradition she had dreamed of as a little girl. In her teens, she had imagined Lucian standing beside her. For once, she was grateful that Council had rejected him as her life mate. If they had joined, she would have felt obligated to move to the mountains to rule the Fire Demons by his side, giving up her job as Guardian. It would have been the biggest mistake of her life. Funny how Council's prejudice had made them get something right all those years ago. Lucian and she had remained friends for years only because they hadn't been forced together as mates. Lucian hadn't realized how unhappy they would have been together. When he had been coerced to start the fire, he had been confused. His temper always ran hot, and Bella could bring out the worst in most creatures. She had a gift. Willow hoped he was doing as well as could be expected in the Frost Giant's prison. More evidence had come forth in the past few months regarding Mother Bacchus's role in the treason. It wasn't enough to extend her jail sentence, but the revelations did allow Willow to reduce Lucian's stay from ten to two years. Hopefully by that time, Bray will have worked out his jealousy issues. Their daughter would be a little over a year by then. She could just see the little one climbing all over Uncle Lucian like her own personal jungle gym tree. The idea made her heart lift remembering times they played as children.

The music started and it pulled her from her reverie. Willow smiled. It was one of her mother's favorite songs. Ellie remembered. Tears filled her eyes as she walked down the pathway. She thought that Ilana would have loved Bray and this union would have filled her with delight. Willow regretted that her sisters had so little time with their mother before she passed. She had died when they were so young, but some little piece must have stayed with them. The fringe of vines pulled back and she gasped at the sight. The sky was lit with the final rays of sunshine casting a gold glow over the clearing. Spiderwebs draped from the trees. They looked to be intertwined with gold thread. Everything sparkled. Willow realized the music was coming from all around. Frogs, crickets, and birds were at the edge of the trees being directed by of all things the Gnome leader, Goron. Satyrs played flutes and Pixies played harps in a symphony of such beauty. As the sunlight faded, Willow noticed all the lanterns come to life. They were filled with lightning bugs as they danced and hummed with the music. They were in synchrony with the sounds. Everyone must have been practicing for months. And she had never known. What a glorious surprise. The unity of the moment was breathtaking. Her eyes followed the circle where all the guests stood waiting. Each wore a wreath of willow leaves and lily of the valley. Her focus then went to Bray in the center. He stood just in front of the Council member Liska, the Fox Shifter. She had been teaching Bray about herbs. He was getting so good; she had taken him on as an apprentice at her shop in Sedona. Liska had been given the honor of binding their hands and speaking the words of the ancients.

Bray pulled down on the front of his tunic. She knew that gesture well and smiled. He was getting aroused and was embarrassed about it. Like it mattered to anyone in this crowd. Bray could have been completely naked for all she cared. In fact, she'd prefer that. But he was still part human and incredibly modest. He refused to come to Festivus in the buff. He didn't like to flaunt although Willow had told him repeatedly just how much she appreciated his body. And he felt the same. Willow was delighted that even six months pregnant she could still turn him on.

The same gold thread and crystals that ran through her own gown ran through his cream muslin pants and matching tunic. There were intricate designs shaped in willow leaves around his collar and the ankle trim on his slacks. He had complained about the outfit saying it looked like glitter, but his mother had designed it, so the argument was over before it began. She raised her eyebrows and put her hands on her hips. The stare lasted for twelve seconds before he caved. Willow wondered if she could get lessons from his mother. This silent negotiation tactic could prove useful.

He stood waiting for her in front of the Council bench. The red stone dais that had cracked in the winter had been removed and made into tables in the meadow. Willow stared at Bray's bare feet. She had always found them incredibly sexy. She shared that with him once and it had sent him into a fit of laughter. It hadn't been a joke. Most males in the magical community had hooves. Bare human feet were exotic. His wrists and ankles had been inked. Rabuwa had done the honors. She wasn't sure Bray understood the significance. It showed great respect. They were symbols of protection, but more importantly, they represented his rank as a warrior. He hadn't raised a sword or fought in a battle yet. Thank goodness no one had tested him. Willow had tried in vain to teach him how to use the sword, but he was horribly awkward. Although to be fair, it probably had more to do with his sparring partner. He was afraid of hurting his pregnant wife. She walked toward him and reached out her hands. When their hands clasped a great current of energy flowed from her into him and down in the earth. A connection of power cycling in a perfect circle. They both hadn't been back to this spot since Winter when the forest had united the pair in front of all. Both their eyes widened and they grinned at each other. Liska wrapped a vine around their hands calling upon Gaia to bind this couple and grant them her protection and love. As they spoke the words they had prepared for one another she felt their souls unite, intrinsically tied, bound for eternity in this life and beyond. It was everything she could have hoped for. Reality had blown away her childhood fantasies. Her heart and her eternal's beat in synchrony with the music still softly playing in the background. She stared into Bray's eyes and had no idea if Liska had finished the binding ceremony. Nothing existed but her and Bray. He looked equally as gone, his eyelids heavy.

Liska cleared her throat. "Are you two even paying attention? I said you can kiss now."

Bray gave her a lop-sided smile and pulled Willow into his chest and molested her mouth with tongue and teeth leaving her dizzy. Whoops and whistles from the clearing had them both laughing. They held up their bound hands and the cheers got louder.

"I feel like I won the greatest prize in the world." Bray grinned.

Willow cocked out a hip. "You have."

Red watched Willow and Bray dancing. The dude seriously had two left feet. It was hilarious. Her big sis either didn't notice or didn't care. They were so fucking in love. It made her long for her own happily ever after. A tear rolled down her cheek. What's this? Oh hell no. She was getting weepy. Fuck that. Focus on something else. Anything. She spied the Bighorn Sheep Shifters. Her lips curled with an evil grin. Well, she had promised.

Most of the Shifters were in half-human form except for one massive male with huge horns. After intros, it didn't take her long to convince Big D to join one of her infamous poker games. Newbies were so easy. Simple. He bet. She won. Now he had to shift to half-human form. Red was shocked that one of the largest Bighorn Sheep Shifters from the clan became one of the shortest in his half-human form. Big D stood fully naked and embarrassed.

"I don't like this form. I'm sensitive about my height."

"You're preaching to the choir, Big D. Trust me I've got height issues too. It's not easy being this tall and female. It would be one thing if I was built more like Ellie, tall and thin. But no, I'm built like a truck."

Red looked him over. "Let me give you the low down," she slapped his cock, "You're not short where it counts."

He gasped and put a hand over his privates.

"I don't see what the problem is. You've got high cheekbones, a strong chin, those sexy curved horns, and that long mane of hair. Your body has sleek muscles and the hair on your chest was made for females to hang onto while they ride that glorious cock."

Big D stood there with his mouth open. Red did that to a lot of people.

"So, how's your cunnilingus skills?"

He sputtered, "Wha?"

Red grabbed him by the shoulders, "Don't worry about a thing. I got you covered. You've unknowingly recruited a Sex Ed Expert. I'm a teacher, ya know. I've got a forged diploma and everything." She walked him over to the banquet table. "Step one, supplies. We need your favorite treat. Hmm, maybe a desert sage salad and a lot of moon-wine for your Guardian."

Big D turned and watched Bri take a swig of moonwine from a goblet at the bar. The wine dribbled down her chin and she laughed at something the bartender said. He bared his teeth. His hands formed fists as he marched to the bar. Red stopped him before he got far.

"Hey now, Big D, remember you got this. Bri is digging you in this form, not that Satyr bartender." She handed him a wooden bowl filled with desert sage. "Get Bri somewhere comfortable, sprinkle this between her thighs, and feast." She smiled. "Trust me. And remember, no turning back to sheep form for the whole trip. That was the bet. I'll be watching you."

"Love is in the air tonight. Can you smell it?" Red inhaled a deep breath.

Ellie snorted, "That's moonwine you smell. Everyone reeks like they've bathed in it."

"Yeah," Mae sniffed, "The Bacchus brothers at their best, well, at least most of them."

Willow rubbed her shoulder. "I'm sorry Faustino left. I had sort of hoped he'd be your date."

Mae shook her head, "I'm nearly the last one he wants to see right now."

"He's such a big baby. So what? He got kicked out by Council. Big deal. He was a horrible Guardian. Red shrugged. "I told him to lose the Satyr pants and go join the Pixies since he had such epic party skills."

"You didn't." Willow groaned. That would have been a huge insult. No wonder he left in such a rush. Especially if he thought everyone felt that way.

Red shook her head. "The guy couldn't take a joke. He needed to get outta here anyhow. Faust was depressing as fuck. You didn't need his sour puss around here dampening everyone's spirits."

"Well, he checked on me after my ungracious ousting by Council. It would have been nice to return the favor." Willow murmured.

"Oh, please." Mae exclaimed, "Even I could tell he was gloating and covering his ass. He knew we were together. He probably feared us plotting his downfall."

"Yeah. Like an assassination in his sleep." Red bit a nail. "I might have started that rumor."

"Have the Bacchus brothers heard from him? It's been months since he left."

"Olie is the only one getting messages via squirrel, but he won't comment." Mae gritted her teeth. "I haven't gotten him to talk. Yet."

Red grinned. "Look at you and your bad self, Mae. Swearing. Threatening. You're turning into quite the badass. Being backup to big sis is good for you."

Mae blushed. "They should have asked you, Red. You're the next oldest. I feel guilty they passed you over."

"You think I give a fuck?" Red waved it off. "I got better things to do."

"And by things you mean that male you've been salivating over." Ellie grinned.

"I have not."

Ellie laughed. "I've seen actual drool."

"Well, he does look tasty." Red shrugged, "But I meant I haven't done him. He's been dodging me. It's frustrating as hell."

"So does that mean humans are no longer taboo?" Mae asked.

Willow shrugged. "Council has their opinion, but I trust you guys. If you found a human and bonded, and felt they could be trusted, why not? It was horrible when I fell for Bray and we couldn't be together. I refuse to put anyone else in the same position. And if things go sideways, we can always send in Sprite SWAT."

"You're serious? If I want a human. For real?" Red's eyes were wide and hopeful.

Willow grinned. "Yes. I'd back you. One hundred percent."

"Me too," Ellie nodded. "We have to support one another."

"I agree. The Ashbrook sisters must unify. Together we can accomplish anything." Mae pulled them all together for a group hug.

Ivy sprouted around them, cocooning them in, drowning out the sounds of the celebration. They laughed as they held each other. Willow had never felt happier. She could hear the thrumming in the earth and the whispers from the trees. The forest held so much joy, she felt like she would burst from it. The unborn babe gave a kick. The sisters all felt the movement and laughed harder.

"She's a feisty one," Red said. "I like her already."

"A true warrior." Mae grinned. "I have no doubt."

Ellie laid her palm on Willow's belly. "Nope. She's going to be a sweet little thing that hugs animals."

"I wonder if mother is watching us now." Willow sighed.

They all looked up into the sky.

She placed a hand on her belly. "Another generation of Ashbrook Dryads, to build back what we've lost in the war. She will be the perfect blend of human and nature, a balanced union without prejudice. She will be brilliant and beautiful and filled with all the magical energy of the forest. She will bridge the gap and unite our worlds."

"But will she be able to cheat at poker?" Red asked.

The sisters laughed at Red's serious expression.

"She's got Ashbrook blood," Willow grinned. "There will be nothing she can't do."

Author's Note

My writing comes from an almost child-like innocence of the world. I'm still awed by the beauty all around us. Most people are too busy blowing past parks and forests at top speeds in their carbon monoxide choking SUVs. They miss the connection to the earth as they scurry about trying to take over the corporate world. I'm not saying that we should all go live in the trees and compost our own waste while we wait for the inevitable destruction of the natural world. I'm just saying we should stop for a moment and contemplate our actions before we destroy what's around us. A moment of time, a wish, a prayer, and perhaps more of us will begin to see the connection we all share. We are witnesses and magic is everywhere. It's within our grasp. We have but to reach out with fingertips and touch it. My hope is to bring this small piece of wisdom to others. Share a little speck of light and let it shine through the mist of the vacuous eyes of the automatons as they work their way through life behind blinking screens. It's not too late. Throw open the door. Curl your toes in the dirt. Let the sunshine seep into your soul. Eco Warriors Unite!

About the Author

A.M. Ladd writes fantasy romance with powerful female Eco Warriors. While she has spent decades working for technology companies in large cities, the forest is where she feels most at home. Her eccentric dog enjoys exploring new scents and dragging her doggy mom into the wilderness whenever possible. She believes you can never have enough bacon, chocolate is a food group, and pizza can be a religious experience.